Death in
Little Venice

Leo McNeir

Death in
Little Venice

Leo McNeir

enigma
publishing

enigma publishing
a division of *specialist* publishing services
Wicken, Milton Keynes, MK19 6BY
www.enigma-publishing.com

First published 2001
© Leo McNeir 2001

The moral rights of the author have been asserted.

Death in Little Venice is a work of pure fiction. None of the incidents described in this book ever took place. The characters who take part in the action are all fabrications, and any resemblance to real people, living or dead, is entirely coincidental. Some familiar household names are used solely to help create an authentic background to the story. The same is true of placenames. Saddest of all is the fact that there are no long-stay car parking spaces in Little Venice.

A CIP record for this book is available from the British Library.

ISBN 0 9524052 7 X

Printed in Great Britain by Bell & Bain Ltd., Glasgow

Dedication

For Caroline and Owen

Prologue

She had all London to herself. At least that was how it seemed. The towpath was deserted. The darkness of the December evening surrounded her, relieved only by the lights from the blocks of flats some distance away outside the park. At the front end of the boat, the headlamp did no more than reflect off the surface, warning other boats of her approach. There were no other boats.

The engine clattered under her feet, a reassuring solid thumping from the diesel. Good old *Sally Ann,* Marnie thought, staring into the frosty air as they slipped slowly through the water of the Regent's Canal, heading towards Little Venice. She pulled her collar up to keep out the chill and steadied the tiller to hold the narrowboat in mid-channel.

This section ran through London Zoo and in daylight she had often seen African kudus looking down at her from their compound, and exotic birds in the aviaries, their food plundered by sparrows that slipped in and out through the mesh. Now it was so dark she could scarcely see the boundary fencing.

On one such evening in 1874 a boat carrying munitions had exploded along this stretch of canal, killing the three-man crew and a boy passing on the towpath and destroying Macclesfield Road bridge, subsequently rebuilt and ever after called the 'blow-up bridge'. Marnie could see its sturdy steel columns in the beam of the lamp. She took care to steer *Sally Ann* between the bank and the flotsam in the water, straining her eyes to make sure it was just another plastic bag floating on the surface and nothing more substantial that might damage the hull. She slowed down to ease past, watching carefully to make sure it did not slide under the stern and foul the propeller.

Her cheeks suddenly tingled as she realised that the shape in the water was not a plastic bag. She pushed the heavy lever into reverse gear and revved the engine to bring the boat to a stop, while she lunged forward to grab the torch from its hook by the control panel. The shape in the water was a body, face down, barely visible on the dark surface.

Moaning to herself, Marnie guided the boat into the bank, trying to work out how she was going to pull the person clear, knowing all the while that there was no hope. She held the stern mooring rope firmly and jumped ashore, kneeling at the edge of the path to reach the lifeless form in the black water.

"Oh God, not again," she muttered, "not again."

Part 01

Tuesday 6 December

"You've done *what*? You've had it *all* cut off? I don't *believe* it!"

"Well, not *all* exactly ..." Marnie reached for the mirror on the desk, putting the pen in her mouth to give herself a free hand. "I didn't mean *literally* all ... just, well, *most* of it ..."

"*And* you've started smoking again!" Beth sounded irate. Marnie exaggerated the mumble caused by the pen protruding from the corner of her mouth. She often did this to wind her sister up.

"What do you mean *smoking*? You know I gave it up years ago ..." There was a hint of Bogart in the voice.

"I'm sure you just do that to wind me up."

"As if I would ..."

"Marnie, no sooner have we begun to get you better, no sooner is my back turned, than you start doing crazy things. Has the air up there gone to your head?"

"I'm not *up there*," said Marnie. She ran her glance over the large open-plan office at Everett Parker Associates. It had been her place of work for nine years as head of interior design. "I'm in London. I thought I'd look in on the old firm, say hallo."

"Well, perhaps while you're here you can say hallo to that rotting pile of junk that's been cluttering up my garage for the last few years."

"Do you mean ... my *classic* sports car ..." The tone was mock-indignant. "... my 1936 MG TA?"

"I mean that thing under the dust sheet I have to squeeze past every time I want to get to the lawn mower. You said you'd take it away and put it in one of your many barns once you moved to the country."

Marnie's conscience gave her a twinge. "Okay, fair enough, but I'm not sure I can get over to you this trip. It's a flying visit ... I've come down to see Ralph ... we're going to a sort of Christmas party."

"*Christmas party?* It's a bit early, isn't it? Christmas is three weeks away."

"Well, it's more like a *pre*-Christmas party. Actually, it's a reception ... in the House of Commons. It's for arts organisations, writers, actors, musicians. There'll be some famous people there. I couldn't go with my hair the way it was, so I decided to get an appointment with Joanne."

"And *she* said you should have it all cut off?"

"That's what I've been trying to *tell* you ... She said it had been hacked about so much at the hospital when they were stitching my head wounds, the only logical thing to do was ... well, start again from scratch."

"That makes it sound as if you had head lice!"

"Ha ... ha," said Marnie slowly.

"But you had such *nice* hair, Marnie, thick and wavy. It always disappointed me that I didn't have hair like yours, considering we're sisters. I took after Dad in the hair department."

"Dad's bald," Marnie pointed out objectively.

"I meant *before* he went bald," said Beth. "Anyway, you seem to have decided to follow his lead now."

Marnie ran a hand over her newly cropped hair. The initial shock was wearing off and she had seen how expertly Joanne had cut it, taking care to conceal the areas where the medics had chopped it when Marnie had almost been murdered that previous summer. She had left it to see what would happen, and at first it had been hidden by dressings, but it was obviously not going to sort itself out and firm measures were needed. She wondered what Ralph would think when they met at the Commons that evening.

"It's not bad, really," said Marnie. "Joanne is very good ... and underneath it's still the same hair. It'll be all right when it grows out, I expect."

"But is now the best time to have it done?" said Beth. "Mid-December's hardly the ideal season to have your hair cut off. I would've thought you could've waited till the weather got a bit warmer, that's all."

"Just because I live in the country, it doesn't mean I have to follow the life pattern of the sheep!"

"You know what I mean, Marnie. It's the dead of winter. You don't want to catch your death, do you?"

Marnie shuddered, even though the office was warm. "No. I don't want to catch my death. Once is enough ..."

She was putting the phone down when Faye Summers crossed the office carrying two cups of coffee.

"*Real* cups on *real* saucers!" said Marnie, starting to get up from Faye's chair that had once been her own. The movement caused her some discomfort and Faye signalled her to stay where she was.

"You know how we like to treat our visitors, Marnie. It's great to see you. I *love* that hairstyle. You're giving me ideas ... perhaps I should get my hair straightened." She patted her tight dark curls, the heritage of her West Indian father. Marnie smiled at her over the top of the coffee cup.

"Mm, this is good. I'm glad to see you haven't gone totally downhill since I left."

When Marnie had moved away to set up her own business in the early summer of that year, Philip, the principal partner in the firm, had offered Faye the job of senior interior design associate. It was a bold move and it had proved successful. Faye, at twenty-four, was almost ten years younger than Marnie, but the same age Marnie had been when she had joined the firm in that position.

"Your imprint is all over the company, Marnie." Faye perched on the corner of her desk. "In fact, we still get clients asking for you by name. Some of them remember me as your assistant and agree to put up with me as second best."

"You were never second best."

"Well, third best then." Faye laughed a deep, rich chuckle.

"It's about time you changed the decor around here, put your own stamp on the place." Marnie rose carefully to her feet and walked over towards the window. It was mid-afternoon and already a gloom was descending over London. "Not much seems to have changed ... same colour scheme ... same faces ... new receptionist ... probably the same litter on the canal." She looked up and down to see if any boats were passing, but all was still in the pale winter light reflecting off the surface. Faye came up to stand beside her. She spoke quietly.

"Marnie, I haven't said anything to you about … you know … what happened … It must still be a painful experience. Don't think I've forgotten, *we've* forgotten … Everyone here talks about you … in a nice way, I mean … we were all terribly upset …"

Marnie put her hand on Faye's arm. "Of course," she said. "I know that. I remembered as soon as I came into the room. Naturally, living in the country prepared me for that experience."

"What experience?" Faye was puzzled.

"When you cross a field of sheep, *they* all tend to look at you like that and stop chewing for a few moments." She smiled.

"Then they baa," said Faye, "close their mouths and get back to their drawing boards."

"Exactly."

"Seriously, though, Marnie, I wanted to give you a big hug, but I was scared I might hurt you. When you came in, there was something about you that told me you were still suffering."

"Actually, it's not too bad now. I tend to stiffen up if I sit in the same position for too long, but the headaches have gone and they tell me I'll have no permanent damage … well not physical at any rate."

As they stood talking by the window, a boat slid quietly past, lights shining from portholes. They watched it go, Marnie raising a hand to the steerer from force of habit. He noticed her and nodded back.

"It's funny," said Faye. "Since you went off for your summer sabbatical last year, I've started looking at the boats that go by. Once I used to think they were all the same, but they all look different now. I expect you recognise the styles and know all about them."

"It's not difficult when you spend time on the waterways," said Marnie. "That was a sixty foot trad built by Black Country Narrowboats about 1989 … three cylinder Lister engine."

Faye was astonished. "You can tell all that just by seeing it go past the window? That's amazing!"

"Not really. It belongs to Roger Broadbent, my solicitor. The boat's called *Rumpole* … moored in Little Venice about six boats from *Sally Ann's* old mooring."

Faye laughed. "I'd thump you but you might break! Are you still using the boat … it's your sister's, isn't it?"

"Yes and no. I've still got her and I'm still living on her while the building works are in progress at Glebe Farm. But she isn't my sister's boat any more. She's mine. I've bought her … well, in principle I've bought her. There hasn't yet been any actual passing of money between bank accounts, but that's only for a technical reason … All my money's tied up in buildings at the moment, so Beth's agreed to be patient."

"That's nice of her," said Faye.

"Well, perhaps *agreed* is a slight exaggeration …."

"Marnie, sometimes you're impossible! I'm sure you'd get away with …" The words faded on Faye's lips and her smile vanished.

"I'm sure you're right," said Marnie. "Come on, let me finish that coffee. Then I really must be off. I want to look in on Little Venice before I go to the House. I want to call in on a few more old friends so that next time they see me they might actually recognise me … unlike Roger."

• • • • •

The taxi emerged into Parliament Square from St James's Park and waited for a gap to pull across the flow of traffic. The driver leaned back to speak over his shoulder.

"Do I pull into Carriage Gate, miss, or do you want the main entrance?"

Marnie stretched forward. "St Stephen's entrance, I think it is."

"Okay." He accelerated out and crossed to the far lane where the lights obligingly turned to green, giving him a clear run turning right along the front of the Houses of Parliament. Marnie looked up at Big Ben. Nearly seven. Good. The cab came to a halt at the point where the road widened opposite the flying buttresses at the eastern end of Westminster Abbey.

"Good evening, madam." The policeman stood foursquare in front of Marnie as she walked up the steps to St Stephen's tower.

"Good evening. I'm expected by Michael Blissett MP."

"Through security and straight on to Central Lobby."

Marnie had to wait a few moments while a small queue of people put their bags on a conveyor and walked under the scanning arch. It was just like airport security apart from the setting. Looking round, Marnie took in her surroundings and saw a broad flight of stone steps descending into a vast dimly-lit hall, the size of a small cathedral under a huge hammer-beam ceiling structure: the original Westminster Hall, almost a thousand years old. When it was her turn to advance, a policewoman held out a black plastic tray.

"Any keys, metal objects, credit cards?"

Marnie put her shoulder bag on the conveyor belt. "It's all in there." At the other side of the arch she saw her bag pass under the X-rays on two screens, one in colour, the other black and white. The policeman at the desk looked up at her.

"Is that a mobile phone?" He pointed at a shape on the X-ray.

"Yes, it is."

"Can you make sure it's switched off, please, and don't use it while you're in the building."

"Right." She took her bag, reaching in to switch off the mobile, and continued up the steps, along the concourse flanked by vast paintings of scenes from British history and on to Central Lobby. Across the crowded space she caught sight of Ralph in conversation with a tall man with grizzled grey hair. Ralph waved, shook hands with the man and made his way through the crowd.

As he leaned forward and kissed her, she took off her hat. He drew back smiling, suddenly saw her hair and his eyes widened in surprise. "Good heavens! Who is this stranger I'm accosting in a public place?"

"I should've warned you, but you didn't give me much time. I hope it's not too big a shock."

Ralph studied her for some seconds. "It's really … glamorous. Marnie, you look like a film star, or a model."

Marnie shook her head and her reply was pure Eliza Doolittle. "And you was finkin' I was just a poor flower gel what dropped 'er haitches. I'm a good gel, I am." Ralph hugged her gently.

"Come on, let's announce ourselves and get out of this crowd." He guided her across to a tall desk where a man in white tie and tails stood beside a policeman.

"Good evening, sir, madam." His tone was formal and pompous and Marnie wondered if he was consciously playing a role like an actor. It was hard to imagine him in jeans pushing a trolley round Tesco's.

"Ralph Lombard and Marnie Walker for Michael Blissett." The steward consulted a directory and pressed the buttons on the phone.

"Mr Blissett's visitors are in reception. Mr Lombard and a lady." There was a pause while he listened. "Thank you." He turned to Ralph. "His PA will be down to collect you." Ralph thanked him and led Marnie towards one of the four lofty arches leading out of the grandeur of Central Lobby. The 'lobby' was spacious and as tall as a church nave, decorated in the Victorian Gothick style, with mosaics of the four patron saints of Britain and Ireland looking down on the mass of visitors waiting to be met by their hosts. Apart from the entrance through which Marnie had arrived, there were three other arches, one each leading towards the chambers of the Commons and the Lords, the other leading into the body of the building. They stopped at a sign that said 'private'. Opposite where they stood, Marnie saw that part of one wall consisted of a post office, with a small queue of people waiting to be served. It looked strangely domestic in the extravagant setting and made her think of the village shop and sub-post office at home in her adopted village, Knightly St John in Northamptonshire.

"Linda will be coming this way," said Ralph . "Have you been here before?"

"No, never."

"What are your impressions so far?"

"Well, as a designer, I've always thought Gothick was quite fun ... when it's well done like this. The trouble is, some of its imitators have made it too heavy. I prefer a lighter touch."

Ralph raised a hand and briefly stroked the side of her hair. "I see what you mean. Why did you have it cut?"

"Well ... you saw how it was. It wasn't going to get any better. I don't think I had any choice. Do you mind?"

Ralph looked at her carefully, studied the clear complexion, the clean features in the intelligent face, the brown eyes. It was like seeing her for the first time. He could see how carefully and expertly the hairdresser had shaped the hair to the contours of Marnie's head. "I think you look wonderful."

"Thank you, Ralph. I'm sure I don't, but it's reassuring to know you don't think it's a complete disaster."

"The only problem ..." Ralph began, "... is what Anne with an 'e' will think of you copying her style. The only difference I can see is that she's fair and you're dark."

"And I'm twice her age," said Marnie.

Their conversation was disturbed by the bustling arrival of Linda, Michael Blissett's PA, a stocky woman in her forties who gave the impression of battling her way through a whirlwind, with a folder under one arm and a security pass hung round her neck on a chain. She exuded good-natured willingness to take on any challenge and overpower it by force of will-power, all of this laced with a heavy dose of long-suffering world-weariness. Clearing a path through the throng, she maintained a steady flow of comments on the amount of work she had to complete before the

Christmas recess, the unreasonableness of constituents wanting their problems solved in time for them to enjoy the festivities, and the iniquities of the Whip's Office, throwing in a blast at the Serjeant at Arms for good measure. Reaching the lift, she managed to side-step a group of MPs, including a junior minister from the Foreign Office, and usher her guests in, deftly hitting the button and leaving the MPs stranded to contemplate the 'Members Only' sign as the doors closed.

Marnie found the best course was simply to smile and nod at appropriate intervals, confident that Linda had scarcely even noticed her ... *and the accommodation in this place is ridiculous, something's got to be done, well, you know how it is, Ralph* ... Ralph muttered encouraging comments under his breath and was obviously no stranger to Linda's style. It occurred to Marnie that they must be about the same age, mid-forties. They certainly had little outwardly in common. Ralph, tall and elegant in a long navy blue coat over a dark suit, had kept himself in good shape. His brown hair, flecked with grey at the temples, contrasted with Linda's mousy wisps that struggled against all odds to hang on to some sort of style.

They exited the lift and turned right past a security desk like a Victorian box pew set in between two columns. One of the policemen on duty nodded at Linda who raised a hand while wafting by, continuing her commentary all the while ... *and you wouldn't believe what the Home Office wrote to two of our constituents ... it's not as if they'd just arrived ... I mean, they were thrown out by Idi Amin ... their kids were born here* ... She led Ralph and Marnie along an ornate panelled corridor, thickly carpeted, with committee room doors on one side, each surmounted by a title written in ornate gilt letters with coloured edging ... *well, all we can do is go and see the minister, but it all takes time to organise, and guess who that falls on* ...

Marnie was fascinated to be there. Like most people she was used to seeing the Houses of Parliament on television, in films, on adverts, even on sauce bottles in the supermarket, but to be inside, actually walking the real corridors of power, struck her as a privileged experience. Linda stopped the banter as they reached the end of the corridor and she pushed open a door, went up a short flight of steps, crossed a lobby, mounted more steps and pushed open another glazed door. They followed in her wake past a photocopier and into another corridor, a complete contrast with the first. This had plain primrose walls with plain white doors at intervals every few paces. Ralph let Marnie go in front of him and she glanced back at two men standing by the copying machine. One of them raised his pipe and smiled at Ralph.

"Tony Benn?" Marnie whispered over her shoulder. Ralph nodded. "Photocopying?" she mouthed.

"It happens."

Marnie noticed that some of the doors bore a sign: *This door to be kept locked at all times.* She pointed at one of them. Ralph whispered, "Security. Some MPs are dealing with very sensitive subjects and don't want anyone entering their rooms when they aren't around. You'll see Michael has a sign like that. He was on a committee dealing with the Iraq super-gun affair."

"This is our rabbit hutch along here," said Linda. "We're luckier than some ... at least we *have* an office. Some MPs have a desk in a corridor downstairs." *Corridors of power*, Marnie thought.

She could picture already the office that awaited them and prepared herself for piles of papers and files tilting at crazy angles on every flat surface, books stacked at random and the overspill from the waste basket cascading onto the floor. The reality was a pleasant surprise as Linda backed through a door and held it open for the visitors. The office was just big enough for two people, each with their own desk and paraphernalia. There were two filing cabinets, two low armchairs, a tall glass-fronted bookcase and shelves high up on the walls. What pleased Marnie most was the atmosphere. It came from the lighting: two desk lamps, each with a green glass shade and two modern reading lamps. Above the desk on the opposite wall was a tall wide window looking out over a rooftop towards Westminster Abbey, its stained glass windows bright in the clear dark winter air. The office felt cosy, but with a sense of purpose.

Seated at the desk below the window, with his back to them, was Michael Blissett MP, speaking quietly into the phone. A veteran backbencher, sometime minister in the Wilson and Callaghan governments, he was a familiar figure to many, with a thick crop of grey hair and a beard to match. Now he was an elder statesman in the party, no longer destined for high office if it were returned to power, but respected for his honest and frank views and liked by MPs on both sides of the House. Once a left-wing firebrand, he had settled into the role of conscience of the party and keeper of its values.

Linda took their coats and hung them up, gesturing towards the armchairs. Ralph remained standing and smiled at Marnie. Their host was obviously bringing his conversation to a close.

"Well, those are my views," he was saying. "As long as you quote me accurately I don't mind you using that in the programme ... No, I don't see how I can fit in an interview, not today, no ... too much going on ... All right Barry, good, good, glad I could help ... See you." Putting down the receiver, he immediately stood up, turned and held out a hand. "Nice to see you, Ralph."

"Hallo, Mike. It's good to see you. May I introduce Marnie, Marnie Walker." He turned to Marnie. "Michael Blissett, an old friend from way back."

"I don't like to think how far back!" exclaimed the MP. Marnie shook hands as Michael Blissett looked her in the eyes with a broad smile. She had the slightly uncomfortable feeling of being in the presence of a man whose professional skills included greeting people and winning them over.

"Will you want coffee before going down?" said Linda.

"Yes! Let's have some coffee. You'd like coffee, wouldn't you Marnie – is it all right if I call you Marnie? What about you, Ralph?" The voice was gruff but kindly, with a northern warmth to it.

"Fine, if we have time."

Linda picked up a tray and pulled open the door. "I'll wash these while the kettle boils. Love that hairstyle, Marnie. The loo's down the corridor on the right." The statements were made in one breath without a pause and the sequence threw Marnie momentarily.

"Oh ... er, yes, thank you."

"Before you go Linda," said Michael. "What did you do with that betting slip?"

"Under the lamp on your desk." She disappeared and the room became calm.

"Sit yourselves down. Make yourselves at home." Marnie was still thinking about the betting slip and wondered if the reports of MPs leading dubious lives were true after all. Michael reached over and handed Marnie a slip of buff-coloured paper. "Message for you ... from someone called 'Anne with an "e"'. She said that would do, so that's what I wrote." Marnie took the note. "My handwriting's not very legible at the best of times. She said would you ring her when you get a moment. It's quite urgent, apparently. Quite a live wire, that one, I'd say."

"A *live wire*?" said Marnie cautiously. "She gave you that impression?"

"Well, I asked her if she had any other message for you and she said to tell you not to fall over the speaker's chair during the party!"

"That's Anne with an 'e'," said Marnie with a sigh. "Actually, where *is* the party going to be?"

"In the Jubilee Room," said Michael. "It's an annexe off Westminster Hall."

Marnie reached in the bag for her mobile but suddenly remembered the restriction. "Okay ... I'll call her later."

"No, no, ring her from here," said Michael. "It's quite all right if it's urgent. Do you want to talk to her in private?"

"Not at all. It'll only take a minute."

"Use Linda's phone, then. Press nine for a line."

While Marnie rang her office, Michael and Ralph chatted quietly. She had been right. Anne needed to confirm a date with their major client, Willards' Brewery in Leicester. Marnie wrote it in her note-book and added two more items before hanging up.

"Thanks very much, Mr Blissett."

"Michael ... and it's a pleasure. I hope everything's fine." At that moment the door swung open and Linda returned with a tray of crockery. Michael looked pointedly at Marnie's note-book. "I see you have your list of jobs to do like I get mine. She must be a younger version of Linda, your Anne with an 'e'."

"Much younger," said Marnie. Linda stiffened as she put the tray down. "Anne is only sixteen ... working with me for a while before going to college." She smiled amiably at Linda.

"Why is she Anne with an 'e'?" said Michael.

"When I met her last year I was travelling on my boat, *Sally Ann*, and she told me her name was also *Anne*, but spelt differently. Somehow it's stuck ever since."

"Well, she keeps you in line, like Linda does me."

"Never fails."

"Right, well, let's have that coffee." He began pouring from the pot. "Have you been to the Commons before, Marnie?"

"First visit. It's interesting to walk down the corridors of power that we hear about."

"Oh, there's no power here," said Michael with a twinkle in his eye. "Is there, Ralph? Ralph's books remind us of that all the time."

"Michael will tell you," said Ralph, "that an MP, apart from those who are ministers, has no real power, except a certain nuisance value to the government of the day ... especially if it's his own party in power."

"Oh, yes," said Michael. "That's quite true. When I was a minister in the

15

sixties and seventies the most difficult problems always came from our side."

"Not from the opposition?" said Marnie.

"Oh, they can be a pain in the bum as well, but that's business, nothing personal."

"I suppose the Tories will be at the Christmas party," said Marnie mischievously.

"Of course. It's a cross-party party, so to say. You'll be surprised who'll be there tonight, just you wait and see. You don't take sugar, do you Ralph?"

• • • • •

"It's called *rubbernecking*," said Ralph quietly, handing Marnie a spritzer. There was already a good turnout and groups of people were arriving by the minute, hanging coats up in the vestibule and walking over to the table set out with drinks, manned by staff from the MPs' offices. As soon as they had entered the room, Michael had been collared by a member of the shadow cabinet and the two had stood to one side for a few moments, heads close together, locked in intense conversation.

"What is?" said Marnie.

"What you're trying hard not to do ... staring round to see how many well-known people you can see."

"Was it that obvious? I was trying to be discreet. It's not easy when there are so many famous faces."

"Haven't you noticed people looking at *you*, trying to place you, too?" said Ralph.

"Not really. No reason why they should. I'm not famous."

"You don't need to be famous for people to be looking at *you* ... specially men, specially MPs."

"Are MPs any different from everybody else?" said Marnie, sipping the spritzer.

"I think they are," said Ralph.

"How different?"

Ralph looked round the room, as if searching for inspiration or evidence. "It's the kind of life they lead."

"I take it you don't think the power goes to their head," said Marnie, "if you don't think MPs have any *real* power."

"Maybe not, but power is part of it. Many of them are far from home, often living alone in a small flat, treated like VIPs ..."

"They *are* VIPs," Marnie interrupted, "compared with most people."

"Yes ... and many expect to be treated like it."

"I thought you knew a lot of them as friends. You make it sound as if you didn't like them."

"That wouldn't be true," said Ralph. "I've known some of them for years and years ... on all sides of the House. I'm just trying to explain how it is for them. A lot of them are *prima donnas*. People boost their egos, flatter them. Despite that, sometimes they feel insecure because of all the pressure. They work late nights, there are temptations ... It's understandable."

While they stood talking, the room was filling and people squeezed past them, many nodding at Ralph and glancing appraisingly at Marnie. The level of sound was rising and from one corner came the raucous laugh of an MP who was often on television and radio. Looking round, Marnie discovered she was standing next to a group comprising the Heritage Secretary, the Director of the Royal Opera and the Head of Channel 4 Television, the latter narrating a story that had the other two smiling.

"I could get used to this," said Marnie.

"You could even meet some potential clients," said Ralph.

"Well, actually ..." Before she could finish the sentence, Michael Blissett joined them.

"Sorry about that. Jack's been trying to talk to me all day. I didn't mean to abandon you as soon as we arrived. It's always like that here, Marnie. Always someone wanting to have a quiet word."

"Everyone has problems to sort out," said Marnie agreeably.

"Yes ... most of ours are because we've been in opposition too long. Ralph could give you a two-hour lecture about that."

"At least," said Ralph.

"That's quite a burden," said Marnie. "Being in opposition all that time, I mean."

"Of course, but it's just as bad for the Tories," said Michael. Marnie raised an eye-brow. He went on. "Their problems are because they've been in government too long."

"I can manage three hours on that," said Ralph. "On a good day."

Marnie had become aware that all the time they were standing in conversation, Michael was discreetly watching the movements of the other guests, glancing away briefly every few seconds. Suddenly, he reached over and took Marnie by the arm.

"Do you know Peter Menchip?"

"I've seen him on *Newsnight*, I think. Wasn't he an environmental campaigner?"

"That's right," said Michael. "Still is. And he'd like to meet you."

"*Me?* What for?"

"Something to do with canals. He's a member of our Waterways Policy Group. Would you like to say hallo?"

"If you think so," said Marnie.

They picked their way through the crush, trying not to spill drinks down future ministers and leading figures in the arts world. Marnie thought this must be the first time the high point of an evening was just crossing a crowded room, but then it was not every day you rubbed shoulders, literally, with the Great and the Good, people you only normally saw on television, and it was not every day that the Leader of the Opposition, tipped to be the next Prime Minister, moved over with a friendly smile to let you squeeze past. She turned to make a comment to Ralph, only to find that the Leader of the Opposition was talking quietly into Ralph's ear, one hand on his shoulder. Ralph smiled and made his reply before the two men nodded and Ralph continued on his way. When he caught up with Marnie, she muttered, "It's like walking through *Who's Who*."

"Then be careful who you tread on," he replied, steering her round the Deputy Prime Minister. "Are you enjoying this?"

"It's probably naff to admit it, but I'm quite thrilled."

"I think you might like the next part even more," said Ralph. Marnie gave him a quizzical look and he indicated with a nod the group of people they were approaching. There were three of them, all laughing together and, as they turned at Michael Blissett's approach, Marnie recognised Peter Menchip MP, long time campaigner for the planet, and his guests. They were two of the most famous faces in the land, Priscilla Barnes and Anthony James, each in their different fields established as leading actors on stage, television and radio. Michael once again took hold of Marnie's arm and introduced her and Ralph. For one second, Marnie had the awful feeling that Michael had made a mistake, that it was someone else that the MP had wanted to meet and that they would stand in embarrassed silence, desperate to find something relevant to say. But as they shook hands, she was drawn immediately into the conversation.

"Marnie," said Peter Menchip, "good to meet you. Is it okay if I call you Marnie? I expect you already know Priscilla and Anthony."

"Pleasure to meet you," she said. The group made welcoming sounds.

"You hadn't met before?" said the MP.

"We don't normally mix in the same circles, I think," said Marnie, wondering if he had in fact made a mistake.

"Oh, but you *do*. You have a great deal in common."

Seeing her bewilderment, Anthony James leaned forward. "I think he's referring to our mutual interest in narrowboats."

"Ah," said Marnie. "Right. Yes. I see." She had no idea the two actors had such an interest and only dimly remembered that they were married to each other.

"That's it," said Peter. "I'm on the Waterways Policy Group, so that gives us all an interest in common. I've been wanting to meet you ever since I saw you on television."

"That ought to be *my* line," said Marnie. She had only once been on television, the previous year when she had officially opened a new gallery at the National Canal Museum. The gallery housed a special collection of the lost drawings and papers of the great canal engineer William Jessop, documents that had been bequeathed to Marnie and that she had offered to the museum for permanent exhibition. It had been the end of a mystery lasting two hundred years and for a short time Marnie had been a national celebrity.

"That was very generous of you, Marnie," said Priscilla Barnes. "We knew the old man who left the drawings to you ... Old Peter. He often came past our mooring. I think he had friends near us."

"Where do you keep your boat?" said Marnie. "Are you in Little Venice, too?"

"No. We have a mooring in Islington, not far from the tunnel. It's not as pretty as Little Venice, but it's more private."

"I didn't realise you even had a narrowboat," said Marnie. "It doesn't seem ... well, glamorous enough for actors, especially famous ones."

Suddenly, Peter Menchip broke in. "Sorry, but there's someone I *must* talk to who's just come in. Will you excuse me? Marnie, I wanted to ask you something. We're setting up a focus group on waterways issues. Would you be interested in joining us?"

"Well, I'm not the most knowledgeable person ..."

"Maybe not, but you've done more for the waterways than most people ever do. Will you think about it?"

"Okay. Thanks for the invitation."

"I'll be in touch with more details when we get it started. Where can I contact you?" Marnie reached into her shoulder-bag and handed him a business card. "Great. Thanks. I look forward to seeing you again." He set off through the crowd.

"My turn now, I think," said Michael Blissett. "No peace for the wicked. Gordon's arrived and I promised him a reply about something. I'll catch up with you later." He took his leave and vanished.

"I don't know how they do it," said Priscilla. "They seem to have an extra set of antennae that detects movement that other people can't see."

"They're born with it," said Anthony.

"I thought they had it fitted by Central Office," said Ralph.

Priscilla looked at her watch. "Nearly time for me to go, I'm afraid. I'm on in the Strand this evening."

"Won't you be late?" said Marnie. "I always imagined actors having to be hours early to get made up and dressed before the curtain rose."

"It's only five minutes away by taxi and I'm not on till the second act. Modern dress, too, so no crinolines to worry about." She laughed. "Perhaps we'll see you in Little Venice, Marnie."

"Actually, I moved to the country this year. We're up in Northamptonshire on the Grand Union at Knightly."

"Very pretty spot," said Anthony. "We know it well."

"Don't you ever bring your boat down to London, then?" said Priscilla. "Pity you aren't here for the carol singing. I always think that's the nicest of all the events in Little Venice."

"It does sound very tempting," said Marnie. "I've heard it's a lovely occasion, but I've never been."

"If you can make it, give us a call," said Anthony. "You can come on our boat, *Thespia*, if you can't bring your own." They exchanged cards.

• • • • •

Ralph opened the cab door for Marnie and called in to the driver. "Can you take us first to Euston and then go on to Paddington, please." He climbed in beside her. The taxi rumbled over the cobbles in New Palace Yard, through Carriage Gate and turned left into Parliament Square, accelerating away towards Lambeth Bridge.

"Well, that was fun," said Marnie. "I know it's ridiculous but I feel like a child who's been taken to the pantomime."

Ralph moved closer on the seat and they clasped hands. "That was a rather special occasion," he said. "It's not usually like that."

"You know who'd really like to see it all, don't you?" said Marnie.

"Anne with an 'e'?"

"She'd love it. She's so curious about everything."

"Well, I can ask Linda if she could arrange a visit, perhaps even get tickets for Prime Minister's Questions. She'd like that."

"Tickets?" said Marnie. "I know it's quite a performance, but I didn't realise they had a box office!" Ralph chuckled beside her in the darkness as the cab moved into the outside lane on Lambeth Bridge to take the Northbound tunnel. "It's a strange feeling, but it somehow makes me feel part of everything to think I've just been standing next to Cabinet Ministers and someone I've been talking to is just over there getting ready to go on in a West End play."

"It makes a change from the routine of the office, living on a canal boat and working in the middle of a building site," said Ralph. For a moment Marnie felt slightly put down. Ralph went on. "Well, it also makes a difference from sitting in a study analysing economic statistics on the computer. My life isn't all about mixing with the high and mighty."

"It's nice to have a bit of glamour to brighten things up, then," said Marnie.

"That's what I thought when I saw you this evening!" Ralph laughed and Marnie smoothed her close-cut hair with her free hand. "That new style certainly suits you. You had lots of admirers at the reception. I expect you noticed."

"No, I didn't, actually. And there's no need to boost my confidence, Ralph. Though I must say I feel rather strange. I haven't had short hair since I was about a year old."

"I wasn't being polite. Really." The cab pulled up at traffic lights and on both sides of the street Christmas illuminations shone down on them, making a party atmosphere in the back of the taxi.

Marnie squeezed Ralph's hand. "It was a nice start to the festive season. Thanks for inviting me. Now I can feel Christmas is coming."

"Talking of which ..." said Ralph.

"Yes, please. I'd love to."

"You're sure?"

"Absolutely. The only reason I didn't accept your invitation at first was because I wasn't sure how I'd be feeling. But now, I know I'm on the mend."

"I'll order the tinsel at once," said Ralph.

"And is it still all right if Anne comes over for a day, as you suggested?"

"Of course. In that case I'll get a tree. We'll have to do the job properly." Marnie laughed. "What's the matter?" said Ralph.

"I had this sudden vision of you dressed up as Father Christmas!"

"Perhaps I'll burst into song. How about a quick chorus of 'I'm Dreaming of a White Christmas'?"

"Actually, that would be nice ... no, not you bursting into song. A white Christmas, I mean. Your cottage, crisp bright days, deep snow, a log fire in the inglenook ... Perfect."

"We can live in hope," said Ralph. "Just you being there will make it perfect for me."

"Thank you, kind sir." The cab rounded the square by Euston station and made for the underground taxi rank.

"And do you think you'll get down to Little Venice for the carols with your new theatrical friends?"

"Don't know. It'd be fun, but I'm not sure what else I'll have to do just now. It was good to be invited, though. They seemed really pleasant, even though they are famous." They came to a halt near the escalator leading up to the main station. "What ever can they see in someone like me?" They kissed briefly as Marnie got out of the cab.

"I could write a book on that subject," said Ralph, "or at least a major feature for the *New Statesman*!"

Part 02

Wednesday 7 December

Anne with an 'e' came into the office towelling her hair. It was fine and blonde, very short in an urchin cut, almost sculpted to her head. Marnie was at her desk already involved in a detailed conversation on the phone. With the onset of winter they had opted to take their daily showers first thing in the morning, using the bathroom installed at the back of the small barn they had converted into their office.

Anne loved their routine. Up before seven on *Sally Ann*, which was now heated by timer-controlled electric radiators, they had breakfast in the saloon and walked through the spinney from *Sally*'s mooring on the canal. The only sound to break the silence during their short walk was the cracking of brittle twigs under their feet as they made their way through the frosty darkness. While Marnie had the first shower, Anne would give the office what she called a 'good sorting out', emptying the waste-paper baskets, filling the copier with paper, checking the fax roll and generally tidying up. They had organised their workplace to make it snug for the winter, with an electric storage heater, and there was a catflap for Dolly so that she could take refuge in the warm at any time. Anne wandered back to the bathroom, gave her hair a sixty-second blast with the dryer and returned ready to face the new day.

Marnie was still on the phone dealing with some kind of problem. This was nothing new, as they were surrounded by the buildings of Glebe Farm in the process of renovation. One of the cottages was already completed and had been occupied by its tenants, Jill and Alex Burton, a newly-married couple, since September. Any day now the final touches would be put to the second cottage and Marnie and Anne would be able to move in. Outside it was still dark at eight o'clock and Anne wondered who could be on the phone so early.

"So what about an alternative supplier?" Marnie said into the phone. She frowned as she listened to the answer. Anne sat at her desk, trying to work out who it could be.

"Have you tried … you know, that place in Birmingham?" said Marnie. "I thought they were huge and had everything …" She listened again and sighed. "Well, I suppose that's all you can do right now. When can you get back to me? … Right … Yes, I know you're doing your best. Okay. Talk to you later. 'Bye now." She put down the receiver and consulted the diary, muttering something under her breath.

"We've got a problem," said Anne.

Marnie nodded without looking up, biting her lip. She swivelled her chair and looked at the year planner on the wall. "If we can't get them now, we're stuck till after Christmas." She turned back to face Anne. "What are you smiling at?"

"It's your new hairstyle. I can't get over it … it makes you look so different. Anyway, what can't we get? What's the problem?"

Marnie ran her hand over her hair. "The radiators for cottages two and three."

"They were ordered *weeks* ago," said Anne.

"Yes, well, it's a right mess-up. Tony says they were sent out last week to a big contract at Lutterworth or somewhere up there. They were running ahead of schedule so the supplier let them have ours. When we said we wanted them for this week, it was too late to get any more from the factory before they closed down for Christmas."

"Can't we go to another supplier?" said Anne. "We did for some of the timber."

"That's what Tony's trying now. The best bit is that they've got the radstats and can let us have them. It's only the actual radiators that are missing."

"Very comforting," said Anne. "We can move into number two and huddle round the thermostats to keep warm! It's going to make a mess of Christmas."

"Yes ... Good job we haven't got someone waiting to move in." Marnie stood up and walked over to the window, looking out across the courtyard towards the main farmhouse and the cottages. They formed an L on the other side of the cobbled yard. In the occupied cottage there were lights showing, but the rest of the buildings were in darkness.

Anne came to stand beside her. "It's nice to see curtains up at the windows. I wonder if they'll have a Christmas tree with lights. Marnie, why don't we get one in a tub and stand it outside with white lights on? It'd look nice."

"Sure. Why not? There's a garden centre on the main road. They've probably been selling them since October."

"I'll put it on my list," said Anne.

Marnie smiled. The world would not be the same without Anne's lists directing their lives. "Good idea. Let's get on, then."

"Anything I can do about the radiators, Marnie?"

"Not really. The factory will've closed its order books now. No chance before Christmas unless another wholesaler's got some in stock."

"Does that mean all work on two and three has to stop now?"

"That's just what I was wondering," said Marnie. She sat down and looked at her planner. "There's just some paperwork to do for the Willards contract ... and the next job is the restaurant on the Grand Union at Braunston. I'll give the manager a ring, but I can't imagine them wanting us there in the run-up to Christmas."

Anne applied herself to the monthly accounts while Marnie tackled the restaurant manager. It was a short conversation.

"What did he say?"

"At first he laughed! Then he gave me a quick run-down on their bookings, their staff problems, the leaking water pipe under the car park ... I got the picture."

"Well, we don't have to worry about cash-flow," said Anne. "I banked that cheque from Willards the other day. Good old Willards."

"Mm ... we're well ahead of ourselves," Marnie muttered. "That's largely thanks to you keeping everything running smoothly." She studied her filofax and tried to decipher the hieroglyphics, notes she had scribbled hastily during phone calls, at traffic lights, in meetings ..."I think we can have a break."

"Okay, I'll put the kettle on," said Anne jumping to her feet. "We might as well enjoy it while we can." She reached the sink at the back of the office.

"I meant something longer than a coffee break," Marnie called out to Anne's back. "We could take a few days off … have a breather … take life a bit easier for a change." Anne was standing at the sink. "Not the best time of the year for a holiday, perhaps, but we don't seem to have much choice … Anne? Are you all right?" Anne had not moved but stood with her head tilted forward. Marnie got up and quickly crossed the office. "Anne? What is it?" The girl took in a deep breath. Marnie put an arm round her shoulder.

"Not sure …" Anne's voice was a croak. She swallowed. "I think I must've got up too fast … I feel a bit dizzy … silly …" Marnie guided her gently to her chair.

"Just take it easy. I think this is called 'vertigo' or something like that." Marnie left her for a moment and returned with a cup of water. "Have a sip of this."

"Thanks … that's better." Anne managed a faint smile. "Don't tell me I look pale … I'm always this colour."

"I know." Marnie ran a hand affectionately over Anne's fine light hair, even shorter than her own. "Just sit quietly for a minute. Have you been feeling unwell?"

"No. I'll be okay. I'm feeling better already … honest."

"Do you feel sick?"

"No."

"Do you think I ought to push your head between your knees?"

"I think that's banned by the Geneva Convention. I'm an unarmed civilian."

Marnie laughed. "Don't tell me … you did a project on it at school."

"I got an 'A' for the coursework."

"I might've guessed. Are you okay for a minute while I put the kettle on?"

"Of course I am. Marnie? What did you mean about a break?"

Marnie paused while the water gushed into the kettle. "Well, there's nothing urgent to be done here. All the Willards projects are up-to-date. Mrs Frightfully-Frightfully is away in Barbados for the next few weeks, so we can't start on the Hall. We can't complete two and three until the heating's finished. I was wondering …"

"The list of lock closures is in the British Waterways file," said Anne.

"The list … Are you a mind reader or what?"

"I think it said there'd be a period before Christmas with no maintenance work on that section, so we could go down to Little Venice on *Sally* if you wanted."

"Would you like to?"

"Absolutely! A winter cruise. It'd be fun."

"And you're –"

"Yes. I'm feeling fine."

"Then we'll give Tony a chance to check the wholesalers, and if nothing comes up we'll take *Sally* and head down to London. You could just look up the closures list for after Christmas, so we can get back. We'd look right idiots if we got trapped and had nowhere to live up here …"

• • • • •

George Stubbs had just got back into the Range Rover when he saw Marnie's car draw up outside the village shop about twenty metres from where he had parked. Stocky, late fifties, bullnecked and with a balding head under his tweed cap, he was a leading figure in the community, as his forebears had been for generations. He thought it was typical of Marnie these days to use the car for the short trip up from Glebe Farm and he was convinced it was not just because of the winter weather. She was still not fully recovered from the injuries she had incurred when she was almost the victim of murder in the summer. He waited before switching on the engine, to watch her. Marnie and Anne got out and went into the shop, Marnie walking carefully, with less fluidity of movement than in the past. *Damaged goods,* thought George. *How sad to see her now.* He wondered if she would ever be quite the same again and shook his head. *Lovely lady*, he thought.

He turned the key in the ignition and drove home. He had promised to help his wife with her preserves and was looking forward to a Scotch and soda to fortify him for the task.

• • • • •

As the two customers came into the shop, Molly Appleton looked round from stacking the shelves with baked beans, did a double take and almost dropped a tin on her foot.

"Well I *never*," she said. "I didn't *know* you for a moment, Marnie." Marnie smiled and shrugged. "Richard … just take a look at this." Molly's husband was counting sheets of stamps in the glass booth that was the village sub-post office. He craned his neck to see, grinned and nodded with approval. "Well," said Molly. "I thought you must be Anne's sister!"

"Thanks, Molly … it's a slander on Anne, but it was nice to be told that." Marnie quickly explained about the need for a new hairstyle, while Anne produced their shopping list and began to fill a basket, systematically moving along the shelves.

"Having visitors?" said Molly.

"No," said Anne. "We're setting off on a cruise."

"In this weather?"

"Actually, it's not bad as long as you dress properly," said Marnie. "The forecast is cold and dry."

"But won't you freeze on the boat?"

"*Sally Ann*'s got central heating," said Anne. "She's lovely and cosy."

"And we'll be dressed for skiing," Marnie added. "I'm not sure purists would find that acceptable, but it's the best way to travel at this time of year."

"So you're stocking up for the journey," said Molly.

"Have you any more ground coffee?" Anne's voice came from the far end of the shop. "We'll need two tins."

"I've got some Original Blend in the stock room. Anything else while I'm out there?"

"You don't seem to have any eggs. We'll be needing a dozen."

"Ah, no. I've ordered more from George Stubbs. He was in here just now on his way home. Can you wait till tomorrow?"

"We're not going till the day after," said Marnie. "That'll be fine."

"But I've got a huge list of things to do tomorrow," said Anne. "I'd rather get all the shopping done today rather than leave it till the last minute."

"He said he had plenty," said Molly. "I'm sure he'll be able to let you have some if you want to call round. You know where to go."

Marnie glanced at her watch. "I've got one or two phone calls to make."

"Don't worry," said Anne. "We can load everything into the boot and you can get back while I go and fetch the eggs."

"We can go in the car," said Marnie.

"Not if you want to be home in the foreseeable future. You know how Mr Stubbs likes to chat to you, Marnie." Anne raised a seductive eyebrow. At least it was as seductive as a thin, waif-like sixteen-year-old could manage. "Anyway, I wouldn't mind a bit of fresh air."

Marnie looked at Anne. She was right. You could not tell if she was pale or not, especially in this season. A brisk walk back to Glebe Farm would bring some colour to her cheeks.

• • • • •

Anne always enjoyed walking through the village. The cottage gardens along the high street were sleeping now, only the odd clump of Brussels sprouts and winter cabbage protruding from the cold dark soil. She took deep breaths and felt the warmth in the condensation on her cheeks as she exhaled.

At the other end of the street, at right angles to the road, stood the Old Farm House, owned by the Stubbs family for generations. It had stood there for nearly three centuries, a fine building in spacious grounds with stables and outbuildings all in the same honey-coloured stone. Anne turned into its drive and walked past the dormant herbaceous border, trimmed back for the winter, past the heavy oak front door of the main house and along the stone pathway that lead to a cluster of outbuildings.

Through a drawing room window she caught a glimpse of light coming through from the kitchen and turned round the corner to approach from the rear in true country fashion. There was Mrs Stubbs busy with pans steaming on the dark blue Aga, stirring one with a wooden spoon. Anne thought of all the Christmas preparations that had gone on in that place over the years, all those turkeys and hams, all the baking and boiling. She was looking forward to the time when she and Marnie would have their kitchen ready in the main house at Glebe Farm and hoped they would be able to have an Aga, too. Mrs Stubbs looked up and smiled. She ran the back of a hand across her forehead as she came to the door. Her cheeks were pink.

"Sorry to trouble you, Mrs Stubbs. I've come for some eggs."

"No trouble, Anne." She had a voice that was instantly recognisable as upper class. "You've come at just the right time. Mr Stubbs is round the back at the moment." She lowered her voice and smiled again conspiratorially, woman to woman. "I've given him a job to do … keep him occupied and out of the way so I can get on." Anne had always felt welcome in the village, probably because of her reserved manner with strangers. But since the summer, when she had been instrumental in resolving the mystery of the church tower and its two murders and had narrowly prevented a third at risk to her own life, she knew she was universally regarded with real affection.

"Round the back," she repeated.

"Yes. You'll find him in the butchery."

"Thank you." Under her padded jacket, Anne the vegetarian shuddered as she made her way along the path. She knew that Mr Stubbs kept his free-range eggs in the small stone barn with its scrubbed workbenches, the building that for long had been the village butcher's. He still used it for storing meat and cutting it into joints, but at least it was no longer used for slaughtering. The only remnant of those days was the tin plaque nailed over the door, bearing a skull and cross-bones, placed there by Mr Stubbs himself as a boy in the 1940s. Despite the cold fresh air, she still felt slightly dizzy and could well do without a visit to the butchery.

Standing under the plaque, Anne banged twice on the heavy door with her fist. No sound came from inside, and she waited patiently. Snuggling inside her jacket, she looked round at the garden, at the clumps of heather giving winter colour, the borders of evergreen shrubs and the neat flower beds dug over to wait for the first shoots of spring. Behind her, Anne heard the door ease open and turned to greet Mr Stubbs. Her eyes were drawn to his hands, to the short-bladed knife he was holding and the stains on his hands and arms, the deep red stains reaching up beyond his wrists. He smiled in recognition.

"Anne, my dear, what can I ..."

Without warning, the girl crumpled in a heap on the ground before he could move to catch her.

• • • • •

Marnie made a note on the pad. "Yes, of course it's convenient. I can pick you up from the pool of Little Venice at three and we can go on to Camden Lock together. No problem." She flicked on the desk lamp. It was nearly four o'clock and dusk was descending quickly. In the background she was aware of a car pulling up outside the office barn and guessed it was Alan, the postman, with a late delivery. "Fine, that's agreed then ... I'm looking forward to it. See you on the eighteenth ... Okay. 'Bye now." She entered the date and time in the filofax. It seemed strange to write in such famous names, somehow unreal. She got up to meet her visitor and was surprised to find George Stubbs coming to the door.

"Hallo, George. That's a strange coincidence. Anne's gone to see you at home."

"Marnie, good afternoon. Actually, she's in the car." He looked worried.

"What's happened? Is she all right?" They went outside. Anne was just swinging her legs down from the high bodywork of the Range Rover. Seeing Marnie, she smiled ruefully. George went to help her down.

"Passed out at my place," he said. "On the doorstep, so to speak. Didn't say a word, did you, my dear? Gave me quite a shock, I can tell you."

"I am sorry, Mr Stubbs." She held his arm and Marnie was surprised that she allowed herself to be assisted into the office.

"I don't usually have that effect on the ladies ... at least not any more!" He guffawed so strongly that Anne had to hold on to avoid overbalancing. She sat down and undid her jacket. "You'll have to take it easy, young lady. Don't you think she looks rather pale, Marnie?"

"Oh, she's always ..." Anne glared at her. "Well, yes, actually, she does look pale. It was very good of you to bring her home, George."

"Least I could do, my dear. Hope she's not going down with anything nasty."

"Don't worry, I'll take good care of her."

"Oh, I was forgetting! Just a moment." He scuttled out.

"What happened?" said Marnie. "Are you really feeling bad?"

"I'll tell you afterwards," said Anne, nodding at the door. Seconds later, George Stubbs came in carrying two packs of eggs. Marnie reached for her bag, but George held up his hand.

"No, no. These are a get-well present from me. Help build up your strength." They thanked him warmly and he set off with more admonitions to take care.

"What was all that about?" said Marnie, standing in the doorway to wave him off. Anne sighed.

"It was *so* embarrassing, Marnie. You wouldn't believe it."

"Try me."

"Well ... I went for the eggs and had to go round to the butchery barn to collect them from Mr Stubbs. His wife said she had him doing a job to keep him from being on top of her in the kitchen."

Marnie pulled a face. "Now there's a sobering thought ..."

"You know what I mean ... Anyway, when he came to the door he was holding this knife and his hands and arms were covered in blood ... at least I thought it was blood. Usually I'm okay when I go round there, but this time it was such a shock, I just ... well ... keeled over. One minute I was waiting for him to come to the door, next thing he was picking me up from the ground. There was this sweet kind of smell and I realised he'd been doing something with ... beetroot." Her voice trailed away.

"*Beetroot!*" Marnie laughed. "You passed out because of beetroot?"

"Honestly, Marnie, it looked just like blood. I must've imagined all sorts of things going on in there." She giggled.

Marnie became serious. "You're sure that's all it was, really?"

"Of course. I feel fine now ... just a total idiot."

"What about that performance when you came in holding onto George's arm? You looked like Little Nell!"

"Well, I felt I had to see it through. I didn't want him to think I was a complete wimp."

"You know what he's like. He'll be phoning up for progress reports next ... he'll set up an account with Interflora. It's a good job we're setting off the day after tomorrow ... that is if you're up to it."

"Of course I am. Marnie, I'm absolutely fine."

• • • • •

That night they were reading in bed, Marnie in the sleeping cabin, Anne on her camp bed in the saloon. *Sally Ann* was warm and snug.

"Anne?" Marnie called out.

"You're not going to ask me if I'm all right, are you?"

"No. I meant to tell you ... I've made all the arrangements for the Little Venice carol singing. I did some phoning while you were getting the eggs."

"Good. That's great."

"Also, Ralph rang up."

"Oh yes?"

"He reminded me he'd like you to come over to Murton for a day at Christmas."

"Super! When?"

"He thought the twenty-seventh, so you'll have Christmas Day and Boxing Day with your family."

"That'll be smashing. I'm dying to see his cottage."

"You'll love it. It's beautiful." They settled back to their reading. After a while, Anne closed her book and switched off the lamp.

"G'night, Marnie."

"Good night. Sleep well."

"Marnie?"

"Mm?"

"You haven't asked me how I'm feeling."

"How are you feeling?"

"Don't ask."

Part 03

Thursday 8 December

Marnie was putting the phone down as Anne returned to the office barn, walked briskly over to her desk and crossed through another item on her checklist. Her usual energy had returned. Outside, it was now daylight, just after nine o'clock.

"How cold is it out there?"

"Not bad," said Anne. "Above freezing and no wind. Okay if you keep moving. I saw Jill and Alex on my way out. Told them we'd be away from tomorrow. They said they'll be happy to feed Dolly and we should come over for a drink when we get back before Christmas. I'd better put that in the diary."

"That's nice. Did they say anything about the radiator in the bathroom?"

"Oh, yes. It just needed bleeding, like you said. Alex said it's fine now and he knows what to do in future."

"Any other problems?"

"I asked them if things were all right and Jill said they were *blissful*." She chuckled. "I've put the last lot of our clothes on *Sally*. Anything else you need to do?"

Marnie looked at her own list. "I'd be clear already if you didn't keep adding things. Anyway, we're nearly there."

"Did you remember to ring Frank Day and warn him we wouldn't be moving into number two as planned? They were due to bring the furniture from storage next Tuesday."

Marnie hesitated. "All under control."

"Good. Shall I go and connect up the new gas bottle on *Sally Ann* before we have coffee? I want to polish the mushrooms too ... get *Sally* looking her best for the trip."

"Good idea."

Marnie waited a few moments after Anne left before looking up the phone number of Days of Yore, furniture removers. Yore was a village a few miles up the road towards Northampton. Luckily there was no one in the office, and she just left a quick message on the answerphone, because Anne was back seconds later.

"We've got visitors, Marnie. There's a car coming down the track. I don't recognise it. A white Escort." She stood at the window, craning to see who was coming. "It's a man ... oldish ... white hair. I think I've seen him in the village. Oh, I know! It's the temporary vicar."

"Mr Fowey," said Marnie. "He came to see me in hospital."

The old man got out of his car and stood beside a cement mixer among the farm buildings. Most of the complex was a construction site, with heaps of stone, scaffolding and stacks of materials dotted about. It was orderly and business-like, but gave no clue as to where the office was located. Anne stepped outside and waved. The vicar began making his way cautiously over the cobbled yard. Now over seventy, he had been brought out of retirement to look after the parish of Knightly St John while a new vicar was being chosen. The Bishop and the Rural Dean wanted the village to have a period of calm before a new permanent incumbent arrived, following the death of the previous vicar, Toni Petrie last summer, only a month after she had arrived. Jim Fowey was a safe pair of hands.

Marnie stood up to welcome him. "Come in Mr Fowey. Nice to see you. Can we offer you a cup of coffee?"

"Oh thank you. That would be nice. I hope I'm not intruding. I should have phoned first, but I won't be long. Molly in the shop said you were going away on your boat for a while and I wanted to see you before you left." He accepted a seat while Anne put the kettle on.

"That's fine," said Marnie. "We're not busy at the moment. What can we do for you? Is the porch okay?" She had been involved in works on the church, the building project that had first brought her into contact with Toni.

"As far as I know. It seems all right. I just wanted to have a word about the new vicar."

"Has one been appointed?"

"Not exactly, but I think it's clear that the village is likely to have another *woman* vicar and I'm telling everyone who ought to know, so that there are no surprises this time."

"Well that's thoughtful of you, Mr Fowey. Do you think there'll be any problem with that?"

"Frankly, I don't think so. I believe Toni's death had a very profound impact on the village and I've tried to settle things down here. As for the replacement being a woman, the fact is, at the moment the majority of new candidates for ordination are women. We have several women curates and any one of them would be first class."

"It's kind of you to take the trouble to come and see me like this," said Marnie. "But I'm sure you know that I'm ... not a churchgoer ..."

"Of course. But you were a good friend of Toni's ..." He turned his head towards Anne, who was pouring coffee. "You were *both* good friends of Toni's and I wanted you to know the situation. I didn't think of trying to persuade you to come to church. That's entirely a matter of personal conviction. I respect your views. But you both played an important part in what happened here in the summer. Without you, goodness knows how things would have turned out."

Anne set cups down in front of the vicar and Marnie and went back to fetch sugar and cream. Marnie was glad to focus attention on the coffee. She still found thoughts of the events surrounding Toni's death and her own near-fatal injuries painful. The vicar went on.

"There was one other thing I wanted to say. The fact that you don't attend services doesn't mean that we in the church do not regard you as a good friend ... both of you. We all prayed for your recovery, Marnie, while you were in hospital, and for Anne after the terrifying ordeal she suffered. I wonder if you're both aware in how much respect and affection you're held in this community."

Marnie and Anne exchanged glances. Neither of them was prepared for this kind of interview. The old vicar drank his coffee.

"I ... really don't know what ..." Marnie began.

"There's nothing you need to say," said the vicar. "And I didn't wish to embarrass you. This coffee is *extremely* good. What a pity you're not regular churchgoers. I could come and see you more often to talk about parish matters."

• • • • •

"You won't believe this, Marnie." It was mid-afternoon and Anne sat back in her chair.
  "I'm not easily shocked. Try me."
  "I've completed everything on my list."
  "I don't believe it!"
  "Told you."
  "We'd better go before you start writing another one. Actually, I've only got one or two bits and pieces to do and I'll have done all my jobs. We can look forward to a few days of peace and quiet." The phone rang.
  "Ralph, hi!"
Anne left Marnie to her call while she took the two brass air vents – the mushrooms – back to the boat. They were thoroughly polished and shone brilliantly, and she carried them in separate bags so as not to scratch them. The spinney was silent apart from the crisp leaves crackling underfoot and she could see *Sally Ann* and *Thyrsis,* Ralph's boat, through the tree-trunks now that there was no undergrowth to block the view. Dolly, their sturdy black cat, was hopping along behind her, probably on the off-chance of food. As they drew nearer, *Sally Ann* looked good, her paintwork washed and shining, the windows cleaned, a tub planted with fresh herbs on the roof. On board, Anne gave Dolly a saucer of milk and made a final tour of inspection. The clothes were in their respective lockers; the galley store cupboards were filled to capacity; there was a mixed case of wine in the "cellar" under the workbench. Anne knelt down to check the pilot light under the gas fridge and Dolly butted her head in friendly fashion.

• • • • •

"What's the matter?" Marnie studied Anne as she came back to the office barn.
  "Nothing."
  "Anne, we've lived and worked together for months. I know you well enough to tell when something's not right."
  "I'm fine."
  "You were gone a long time."
  "I wanted to check *Sally* again. You know what I'm like."
  "She's only a forty-five foot narrowboat, not the QE2. There isn't that much to check."
  Anne sighed. "It's nothing."
  "Do you want to lie down … have a hot-water bottle?"
  "No. Really. I'm all right. How was Ralph?"
  Marnie frowned, knowing that she was being deflected. "He's okay. We've sorted out our plans for Christmas and New Year. I've phoned my parents and told them I'll be going to see them for a week at the beginning of January. While I'm in Spain, Ralph's going to Japan for a high-level seminar in Tokyo. He's giving a paper on the impending crisis in the Far East tiger economies, or something like that."

"I didn't know there was one."

"Ralph thinks it's going to happen and he's going to explain why."

"That should make him popular. Will he be away for a week, like you?"

"A day or two longer," said Marnie. "He wants to call in on someone in America on the way back."

Anne began tidying the papers on her desk, slipping them into folders. "Ralph's such a nice person, isn't he? It's funny … to the people who know him as an economics professor, he's a real VIP, but to us, he's … well, he's Ralph, though you always know he's somehow special. The way he gives his opinion on things … very *considered*. He never says anything stupid like most people. I've never known anyone like that before. And he has a really exciting life … I mean, *dropping in on someone in America*. I bet it's someone important. Who is it … the President?" She laughed.

Marnie said nothing, but raised an eyebrow in reply.

"Blimey!" said Anne.

• • • • •

Friday 9 December

"Friday the ninth of December, 1994." Anne was sitting at the table in the saloon on *Sally Ann*.

"All day," said Marnie, making her bed. "What are you doing?"

"Starting the log for our trip. Do you realise this is my first actual *journey* on *Sally*? I've only 'tootled' before. This is the real thing and I want to do it properly."

It was eight o'clock and outside it was still dark. Anne had checked everything for departure half an hour ago. Ropes were in place ready for locking. The headlamp was in working order. Outdoor clothes, ski jackets, gloves and fur hats, were laid out on chairs in the saloon. Boots were standing to attention beside them. She even had the kettle filled with water in preparation for their first cup of coffee on the move. For the nth time, Anne looked out of the window and checked her watch. She yawned.

"Did you sleep all right?" said Marnie.

"Well … I've slept better. I was thinking about the things we had to do for the journey and I didn't want to oversleep."

"Not much danger of that," said Marnie. "In any case, we weren't planning to leave too early. I don't want to go through the lock at Cosgrove in the dark. It could be very slippery and we don't want any accidents."

"Right," said Anne, standing up to look out of the window. "Actually, I think it's getting light. It should be okay by the time we get down to Cosgrove."

Marnie laughed. "Are you like this at Christmas?" Anne gave her a mock-withering look.

Minutes later, *Sally Ann* eased out of her docking area, reversing across the canal through the opaque water with its thin brittle crust and frozen patches at the margins. The engine chugged hesitantly at dead slow, smoke from the exhaust like clouds of breath, the faint smell of diesel in the air around Marnie at the tiller. Up front in the bows, where she had cast off the mooring ropes, Anne stood with the pole ready to fend off when Marnie put the boat into forward gear to bring the stern round. Waiting to play her part, Anne looked through the spinney and could just see the lights from cottage number one, where Jill and Alex were getting ready to go to work. *Blissful*, she thought. Yes. She could imagine how it must be for them, newly married, in their first home, the beautifully renovated stone cottage that they rented from Marnie. But for Anne, nothing could be as good as the life she had at Glebe Farm. She gripped the thick pole, ready for action, certain that there was nowhere else she would rather be, nothing she would prefer to be doing.

In fact, there was no need for Anne to fend off the shore, and Marnie brought *Sally*'s nose round smoothly into mid-channel. They were underway and the sky was beginning to lighten over to their right, above the buildings of Glebe Farm and, beyond that, the waking village of Knightly St John. Anne walked back along the gunwale, laying the pole in its place on the roof beside the boat-hook, to join Marnie on the aft deck. She checked her watch and stepped down into the cabin to enter the time on the log, carefully closing the doors and hatch behind her when she returned, to keep the warmth in.

Ralph's boat, *Thyrsis*, thoroughly checked over and locked up by Marnie and Anne, receded, its green paintwork turned to grey in the half light, and vanished in the gloom behind them. As they broke clear of the spinney and passed the last willow trailing fronds in the water, the fields spread out from the canal on both sides, stretching off towards the horizon, like a monochrome lithograph. As usual on a long journey, Marnie stood in silence at the outset, listening to the beat of the engine, getting the feel of the boat under her control, the balance of the tiller. Anne stood quietly beside her, taking in the sights and sounds, feeling the cold air on the tip of her nose. She saw a heron in the light of the headlamp, fifty metres away, apparently frozen solid on the bank, and even as she pointed it out to Marnie, it hunched forward and flapped off in a great circle over the fields. Now there was enough daylight to see sheep and cattle, humps in the landscape, clustered together on the slopes.

A few lamps were glowing inside the cabin, making a faint shadow of light that ran along the bank beside them. Anne wondered how they looked to anyone who saw them across the countryside, and almost at once she saw in the far distance a train, tiny and silent, a phosphorescent worm cutting through the dark landscape at a tremendous pace. There was no other movement to be seen. They were suspended outside the real world, and this could be any time, any place, ever. Anne felt so thrilled she wanted to jump in the air and shout, turn cartwheels on the roof of the boat, fly with the heron over the frosty fields. Instead, she took hold of Marnie's hand on the tiller in both of her hands, squeezed and smiled broadly into her face. Marnie smiled back and nodded, knowing. She had been through these feelings herself many times on *Sally Ann* during her journeys, especially when setting out on the first stage. She understood.

• • • • •

Forty minutes after setting off, they passed under the strange, ecclesiastical stonework of Solomon's Bridge, bringing a formal elegance to the functional beauty of the canal, and entered the village of Cosgrove.

Anne stepped down into the cabin and turned off the headlamp.

"After the lock at the other end of the village, there are no more until we've gone round Milton Keynes," said Marnie, dropping speed as they approached the first moored boats. "Watch out for ice or frost by the lock, and only open one gate, on the left. Take it slowly."

The lock was in their favour and the gate ajar, so that Anne's task was easy and Marnie brought *Sally Ann* through the narrow space and dropped a rope around a bollard to steady her against the side. Anne concentrated to keep her footing on the raised ribs as she pushed the gate shut, leaning the small of her back against the balance beam. The gate paddles turned easily and she crossed the lock without mishap, carefully holding the handrail on the top of the gates. While *Sally* descended in the lock chamber, Anne read the notice board for news of any sudden unannounced closures ahead. It was all clear. She put her full weight on the beam to tug the gate open and close it again after *Sally* had exited, and she stepped onto the aft deck a few metres along the towpath.

"Perfect," said Marnie, accelerating to half speed past the line of boats huddling at the bank.

"Of course," said Anne, checking her watch. She went down and entered the time on the log. "Coffee now or in half an hour?"

"Let's get through Wolverton ... unless you need one after your exertions?"

"No. Wolverton will be soon enough for me. Marnie ... what's that funny rattling sound?" They cocked their heads on one side.

"The mobile!" said Marnie. Anne fetched it from the chart table in the cabin.

"Walker and Co, good morning ... Hallo, Ralph ... Yes, we are ... Let me transfer you to the skipper on the bridge. See you soon!" She handed the phone to Marnie, who gave the tiller to Anne while she chatted. They picked up speed as they left the moored boats behind and floated over the river Great Ouse on the Iron Trunk aqueduct, looking down on the reeds swaying in the shallow water forty feet below them. Marnie pressed the "stop" button on the mobile and slipped it into her pocket.

"It's good to feel safe up here," said Anne, looking back at the aqueduct.

"I'm glad you think that," said Marnie cheerfully.

"Why are you glad?" A hint of suspicion.

"I seem to remember reading that the first aqueduct collapsed," said Marnie.

"Very comforting," said Anne. "I think I'll go below and put the kettle on."

"Don't look so worried ... that was a long time ago. It's fine now. Anne? Are you okay?"

"Yes, of course. I'm not really worried." She shrugged. "Anyway, we're over it now ... but I think I will go and put the kettle on." She turned to open the doors.

"Fine," said Marnie. But she wondered if it was fine. Anne had looked vague and off-colour and it surely had nothing to do with the aqueduct that they had crossed many times before.

• • • • •

"That smells good," said Marnie, taking the mug of coffee from the tray. "Biscuits, too! Is that allowed?"

"To keep our strength up," said Anne. "We use up much more energy in cold weather just to stay warm. I did it in a human biology project at school."

"Of course." Marnie sipped the coffee and took a biscuit. It was broad daylight now, overcast but bright, with scarcely any breeze. "You'd never think this was Milton Keynes, would you?" The countryside around them was heavily wooded, steep banks rising up from the canal on both sides.

"What did Ralph have to say?" said Anne. "Or was it private?"

"Just a few details about the Christmas arrangements." She was not going to say that he had wanted to talk about presents for Anne. "Oh, yes … he also invited me to a carol service. He's been able to get two tickets."

"*Tickets* for a carol service?" said Anne. "I thought the churches were so keen to get people in they'd stack them in heaps to get a good congregation."

"It's the parliamentary service at St Margaret's, Westminster. Usually just for MPs and their families." She lined *Sally* up for a narrow bridge, after which they found themselves running behind neat gardens sloping down to the water's edge.

"When's the service?"

"On the Monday before Christmas, just before the recess."

"We should be there in good time."

"He said he was sorry he could only get two tickets. They're always hard to come by."

"Oh, that's all right," said Anne. "I'll have plenty to do to keep me occupied." She clutched the steaming mug of coffee to her chest with both hands and looked at the trees and the gardens. In one of the houses someone had already put up electric candle lights at a window. "You know, Marnie, I think this is going to be a really memorable Christmas."

Part 04

Saturday 10–Sunday 11 December

As winter journeys go, it was a good one. They met few other craft and chugged without hindrance through the sleeping countryside. They may not have had many glimpses of the sun, but neither did they have to suffer rain or wind. There were no queues at the locks, and even though they had no fellow travellers to engage in conversation, or share the operation of gates and paddles, they had plenty to talk about between themselves, and progressed in easy companionship. In the months that they had lived together, they had become as close as sisters.

From sunrise to sunset they journeyed on without stopping, taking turns at the tiller and in the galley. They had meals on the go, lunch usually a mug of soup and a sandwich, hands clasped round the mugs to warm them up. The temperature stayed a few degrees above zero in the daylight hours and they ran the heating system on the lowest setting to maintain the level in the cabin. With two full gas bottles at the start, they had no worries about running out of fuel. *Sally Ann* was as well prepared for her winter journey as any boat could be, and Marnie felt glad to have Anne as her companion, knowing that she could depend on her in any situation.

They had planned the itinerary with their habitual thoroughness and Anne had drawn up a list of stop-overs where they could moor for the night, each one corresponding with a waterside pub where they would have an evening meal while the cabin warmed up. At two of the pubs, owned by Willards, Marnie had designed the interior decor and they were greeted like old friends, spending the evening chatting with the manager and locals beside a log fire. Anne would leave two small lamps glowing on *Sally Ann*, so that the boat was welcoming when they made the short trip back to the mooring through the crisp night air.

A few days into their journey, the temperature took a sudden dive and hoar frost clung to the boughs of trees while the reeds and rushes froze at the margins. The sun came out for a few hours and bleached the landscape, reflecting off the chilled branches, breathing a misty haze all around. The canal, the land and the sky merged into one opaque non-colour and Marnie and Anne stamped their feet on the deck in a vain attempt to keep out the icy cold. By late afternoon as the daylight ebbed away in the west and the sky turned pink, they decided to warm up the cabin with the fan heater. Anne lugged the generator onto the deck and connected it to the mains socket in the bulkhead. It came to life after two or three tugs on the starter cord and settled to its running speed, noticeably smoother than *Sally Ann*'s old twin cylinder diesel engine. Anne went down into the cabin to switch on the heater and was gone some time. Marnie expected that she would re-appear on deck clutching mugs of something steaming. After several minutes had passed, she pulled open one of the cabin doors and looked in. Anne was sitting in the saloon, head in hands, elbows on the table.

They were motoring in a long pound of about six miles between locks. Up ahead, they would make it through one last lock before a short stretch of two miles or so until they reached the pub where they would tie up for the night. A narrow bridge on an awkward bend took all Marnie's attention and she reached into the cabin to switch on the headlamp as a warning to any oncoming craft. As chance would have it, this time there was another boat, a broad-beamed Dutch barge already lined up for the bridge hole with no scope for manoeuvre. Marnie quickly raised a hand to re-assure the steerer on the barge and fell on the gear lever and throttle to halt *Sally Ann* and reverse her away from the bridge. In the commotion, Anne came quietly back on deck and stood at the side ready with the pole to fend off from the bank if they got caught on mud in shallow water.

The barge slid through the bridge hole with only centimetres to spare on either side and passed with engine growling and a wave of thanks from the steerer's cab. Marnie checked the approach and made a second run at the bridge, this time without hindrance, and Anne laid the pole back in place on the cabin roof.

"Just what we didn't need," said Marnie, straightening up and gathering speed. She looked at her watch and up at the sky. "A quarter of an hour of light if we're lucky. How far to our last lock?"

Anne checked the number of the bridge in the cruising guide and ran her finger down the map. "Should be less than half a mile, I reckon."

"It'll be dark for locking through," said Marnie.

"But if there's been no other traffic, the lock'll be set in our favour after the barge," said Anne.

"True. We can decide what to do when we reach it."

Five minutes later they saw the black and white balance beams of the lock gates ahead of them and the gates had swung partly open in the still water after the barge had gone through. The lock seemed to be inviting them in. Marnie picked up the windlass from the corner of the deck and offered the tiller to Anne.

"D'you mind if I do the locking? I've got stiff with standing on deck and the exercise will warm me up." She leapt ashore and jogged fifty metres along the towpath, leaving frosty footprints in the grass, before putting her weight against the nearest beam to pull one gate fully open. She waved Anne forward and the girl brought *Sally Ann* gently through the water and into the lock chamber, passing up a rope for Marnie to slip round a bollard. It felt good to be moving her limbs, and Marnie relished pulling the gates shut and turning the lock paddles with the windlass. She perched on the edge of a balance beam while the water rushed in and brought the boat up to the next level, and while she waited she thought about Anne who stood on the deck with one hand resting on the tiller, the other holding the rope to steady the boat in the swirling water.

It was dark when they drew up at the pub's mooring and there were no other boats in sight. They tied up and switched off the diesel, leaving only the gentle hum from the generator still running at the back of the deck. As usual, they sat in the cabin, now pleasantly warmed by the fan heater, and drank coffee while they planned the next day's journey. They sat in the saloon in sweaters and boots, poring over the cruising guide and map like submariners on a mission.

"We should make it to Leighton Buzzard by mid-morning," said Marnie, calculating the lock-miles.

"No probs," said Anne. "We can take on more stores at Tesco's and then on to the Tring summit."

Marnie grinned at Anne. "Your nose is bright pink."

"*You* can talk!" They laughed gently in the lamplight.

"Much more of this and we shan't need the headlamp at all," said Marnie. "Are you feeling better now?"

The question caught Anne off-guard and she took a sip of coffee to gain time before replying. "Sure. Fine."

"I ... happened to see you after you got the gennie going."

"I think it was the bending down to get it started," said Anne. "I just felt a bit wobbly ... had to steady myself ... vertigo, I expect."

Marnie put her hand on Anne's. "Look ... I'm concerned about you" Anne started to protest, but Marnie refused to be interrupted. "This isn't a holiday trip, Anne. It's quite a tough journey."

"But isn't that why you need me to be with you?"

"Not if you're not well. I shall be worrying about you in these conditions."

"So I'm a liability ... not able to pull my weight." Anne's face was the picture of misery.

"Of course not!" Marnie protested. "You could *never* be that." She chuckled. "Come to think of it, if we had to rely on your *weight*, we'd never get very far, would we?"

Anne tried to puff up her thin shape in her sweater to look bulkier than she was. She spluttered. "No. I suppose I'm not exactly Man-Mountain Super-thingy."

"You don't have to be. You're still my best member of staff ... after Dolly, of course."

"That's a *great* comfort," said Anne.

"So ... back to my question. How are you feeling?"

"Back to *my* question," said Anne. "How could you manage without me as crew?"

"I've done all my long journeys solo in the past," said Marnie. "I've got my system worked out. I can take it gently and the locks will help warm me up. That's not the important thing. Your health is the important thing."

Anne sighed and sneezed. "Right on cue," she said, reaching for a tissue.

"Any other symptoms?" said Marnie. "Apart from the dizzy spells ... "

"A few aches ... the occasional shiver ... a slight pain in the head."

"Are you aiming for martyrdom?"

Anne laughed. "Not deliberately. It just comes naturally."

"Okay," said Marnie. "We'll ring your parents when they get in from work and say you'll be home a little earlier than planned. If we stop by the shops in Leighton Buzzard, it's an easy walk. I can see you home."

"Are you sure you can manage without me, Marnie?"

"Don't worry about it. As soon as you're better we can meet in London and bring *Sally* back together. Everything will be fine."

· · · · ·

Marnie was right. After seeing Anne home at Leighton Buzzard, she set *Sally Ann*'s nose on a southbound course and was once again on her own. At first it felt strange not having Anne to share the running of the boat but, though colder than it had been, the weather stayed fair and she soon slipped into her old single-handed routine. The locks took longer and for the first day they were nearly all set against her, so that she had to work twice as hard to empty or fill them before she could drive *Sally Ann* into the chamber. Each evening she felt pleasantly tired after a run of around eight hours and she went to bed soon after supper, sleeping soundly until the alarm went off. They were crisp, sharp days with morning mist in the semi-darkness as she checked over the boat ready for departure, and evening mist in the dark as she went about the routine tasks in the engine compartment, checking the drop filter and turning the stern gland.

Marnie missed Anne's company as friend and crew member, but she rang her each evening to catch up on her progress. It seemed to be an attack of 'flu, and Anne was sensibly following doctor's orders to weather the storm and get back to full health as quickly as she could.

As on her solo journey of the previous summer, Marnie felt elated to be in command of her boat. She loved the cold air and the wintry landscape, the animals and birds, the pastoral surroundings and the freedom. She had had this feeling before, that she had escaped and was playing truant. She was travelling on a highway that led on to every waterway and ocean in the world. She could go anywhere and do anything. It surprised Marnie, not normally given to flights of fancy, that she could think like that. But travelling on the canals had this effect on her, especially when she was alone and her imagination was free to wander for hours at a time, while the engine chugged below her feet and the country slipped by.

The hours of daylight were imperceptibly growing shorter as she guided *Sally Ann* over the Chilterns and down through the rolling countryside of the Home Counties, descending steadily lock by lock, down towards the great city and the shortest day.

• • • • •

Friday 16 December

"This is the best time of the day here in winter," said Marnie, standing at the hatch and looking down the tree-lined banks of Little Venice. It was late Friday afternoon and dusk was falling. "It's beautiful to see the lights going on in the windows and the smoke coming from the chimneys on the boats."

"Talking of chimneys," said Albert, resident of longest standing among the boating community, "are you thinking of closing the door some time, or shall we just put our coats back on?" He spoke without malice.

"Sorry! Just wanted to admire the view." She pulled the door closed and turned back to the group of friends she had invited in for tea and biscuits. They were sitting round the table in the saloon with gin and tonics.

"I think it's the ice in this gin that's making me feel the cold," said Albert amiably.

"You poor old sod," said Roger Broadbent, Marnie's solicitor, who just happened to be looking in on *Rumpole* on his way home early from work.

"Cheers, anyway," said Marnie raising her glass. "Do you think those mince pies are warmed through?" she said to the fourth member of the group, Mrs Jolly, the old lady who lived across the road. She was the only person from the neighbourhood outside the railings who made the quantum leap to join the canal fraternity and she was as well known a character of Little Venice as any of the boaters.

"Any minute now," she replied, adding, "Isn't this cosy? I *do* love the old traditions."

"Like Christmas mince pies with gin and tonic?" said Marnie.

"Much loved in Palestine at the time of the Nativity, or so I understand," said Mrs Jolly unabashed. "I expect it was Gary who told me."

"A leading expert on all biblical matters," said Marnie. "Anyway, where is the old crook?"

"For anyone else, that would be libellous," said Roger brightly. "He's probably doing a deal with someone to rent them their own boat or offering them protection from accidental sinking while they're not here."

"It's a wonder he didn't appear when you opened the gin," Albert suggested, taking a large gulp from his glass.

"You know this really must be the prettiest stretch of the whole canal system," said Marnie. "It was lovely when I came down towards the pool and under the bridge by the toll house. I don't know how you keep your garden flowering so late in the year, Albert. Those tall pink roses are amazing ... must be all of nine feet tall."

"*Queen Elizabeth.* Had 'em for donkeys years. They often go on till Christmas. Which reminds me ... are you going to be here for the carols on Sunday, Marnie? You'd like that. The boats gather in the pool on the far side and they're all lit up with candles. Pity we can't sing ... but apart from that, it's a lovely occasion."

· · · · ·

"It's amazing how much gin can be consumed by so few people," said Mrs Jolly later, after the others had left, holding the almost empty bottle up for inspection. She handed it to Marnie, who was putting the washed and dried glasses away.

"Albert's liver has been replaced by a sponge," said Marnie, lining the glasses up in the cupboard. "It was the first transplant of its kind."

"Wonderful what they can do these days on the National Health," said Mrs Jolly, giggling. "I don't know why I'm feeling so flippant. Could it be the gin?"

"Surely not."

"No. I think it's because I'm starting to look forward to Christmas. I'm glad you'll be here for the carol singing ... and with your famous friends!"

"Oh, I hardly know them really. Only met them once. Still, I am looking forward to it. I only wish Anne could be here. Poor old thing."

"Never mind," said Mrs Jolly. "Can't be helped. She can come another year." She folded the tea towel and hung it on the front of the cooker. "You're quite right, Marnie. It is very special here ... quite magic, really. Do you have any regrets at leaving Little Venice for your country idyll?"

"I never have regrets about anything, Mrs Jolly. But when I see Little Venice, I know why I fell in love with canals and boats. I never dreamed it would change my life like this. You must come up to Knightly again – perhaps in the spring."

"And your plans are going well ... now that you're recovering?"

"Oh yes, now that the dreadful murder business is over. All I want now is some peace to get on with a normal life. I don't care how ordinary it is ... I've had enough upheaval and adventure to last me a lifetime. It's a quiet life for me from now on."

Part 05

Sunday 18 December

Marnie was half out of bed before she realised where she was. She blinked at her surroundings, the familiar sight of the cabin on *Sally Ann*, but something was different, something had happened to startle her awake. Outside, the wail of the siren echoed off into the distance down the Edgware Road. A fire engine. She rubbed her eyes, focused on the luminous hands of the alarm clock glowing in the dark and tried to remember what day it was. It must be Sunday. Six-forty. She yawned.

You are becoming a country bumpkin, my girl ... Brought up in London, Marnie was surprised at how quickly she had grown accustomed to the stillness of her new home, deep in the countryside. At Knightly St John, living temporarily on the boat, there were no sounds to wake her, even the early morning birdsong too faint to be heard through *Sally Ann*'s thick steel bodywork. Instead, she had woken at times in the night during her first week or two because of the intense, unfamiliar silence.

Sunday. Exactly one week to Christmas. The memory came back to her of a sound in the night, possibly an ambulance from the hospital round the corner at Paddington. She had never noticed any sounds before when sleeping in Little Venice, but now she was aware of cars going by, even at this time on a Sunday morning. London never slept. She reached across the cabin to turn up the thermostat on the heating and lay back to doze for ten minutes while the interior warmed up.

Sunday. The day of the carol singing. A day of rest. She had spent part of Saturday finishing her Christmas shopping in the West End and had been overwhelmed by the sheer volume of people in Oxford Street and Kensington High Street. She had had dinner with Beth and Paul and turned down their offer of a bed for the night to come back to *Sally*. There were last-minute jobs to be done, a few cards still to be written and sent off, an invitation to coffee with Mrs Jolly and lunch with Priscilla Barnes and Anthony James. After that, she would move *Sally Ann* round to join the other boats in the pool of Little Venice for the carols. All very festive. An ideal start to the Christmas season.

Almost ideal. Without Anne.

• • • • •

Heads turned in the restaurant as the couple made their way across to the table where Marnie was waiting for them. Opinions were exchanged on where they had been seen before and heads turned again to confirm recognition. For a few moments all the conversation centred on the man and woman whose faces were known in every living room in the land. They reached Marnie smiling, hands outstretched, asking if they were late, if she had been waiting long. They kissed her on both cheeks and took their seats. Marnie found herself wondering about fame, how it felt to be known wherever you went, the pleasure of meeting fans, looks of recognition, ingratiating smiles. How long before the novelty wore off, if it ever did? At what point did it become a bore, a nuisance? Certainly, the couple who now sat with her showed no sign of weariness with their lot.

"Did you know this place already, Marnie?" said Anthony. "We used to eat here quite often when we lived up the road."

"I've been a few times. It's handy for the mooring. Have you come down on your boat?"

"Not actually," said Priscilla. "Slight change of plan." She looked meaningfully at her husband.

"Er, yes," he began. "One of those things, I'm afraid. Sometimes your life's not your own in our business."

"Problem?" said Marnie.

"Oh, no, not really. I had a call on Friday asking me to appear on a TV talkshow this morning, that's all. Had to re-arrange the schedule at short notice. We're reviving a Noël Coward in the West End next month and the PR machine is rolling, so I get the odd invite to talk about it."

"Which means," said Priscilla, "that we don't have our boat here yet for the carol singing."

"Hence the change of plan," said Anthony.

Marnie had the feeling of being in the company of two players who had acted so long together that they could share each other's lines. She shrugged. "I'm sure we can be flexible. What do you have in mind?"

"Our son Marcus was going to bring the boat down for us, but now he thinks he'll only have time to get her to Camden Lock. So we'll have to go and collect her from there."

"Which means," said Priscilla, "that we shall have time on our hands this afternoon waiting for him to get there."

"Can't you just go and fetch the boat yourselves?"

"Not as easy as that," said Anthony. "He's already set off ... could be anywhere and there's no convenient place to meet on that part of the canal."

The waiter made his way over and flourished menus. "Ah, such a pleasure!" He beamed at his guests and three faces smiled up at him. "Marnie, how nice to see you again. It's been a long time since you moved. Too long." The dark eyes sparkled with real delight.

"Thank you, Luca. It's good to see you, too. And you have distinguished guests today." She indicated her companions.

"Oh, yes, of course." He bowed, kissed Priscilla's hand and shook the hand offered by Anthony. "I will tell Giancarlo to be on his best behaviour in the kitchen. An aperitif? Please, as my guests."

It was a good meal, fresh ingredients in fine regional dishes, imaginatively prepared and presented. Giancarlo was indeed on his best behaviour. Anthony suggested a bottle of Barolo, and Luca floated past from time to time to keep an eye on progress without crowding his customers. The conversation flowed as the meal went on. Marnie had a few acquaintances and clients who were actors and knew of their tendency to devote much of their conversation to themselves. She was pleased that her new acquaintances did not indulge in that habit and seemed to enjoy talking about boats and waterways, on which they proved to be knowledgeable, with a good supply of anecdotes. Marnie shared some of her own humorous stories and found it hard to believe they hardly knew each other at all. With the arrival of coffee, Luca offered them liqueurs and in the atmosphere of warmth and bonhomie it seemed churlish to refuse.

"We don't seem to have talked about the theatre at all," said Marnie.

"You can have too much of a good thing," said Priscilla with a smile.

"I wouldn't like you to think I wasn't interested in your work."

"Of course not," said Anthony. "It's nice to have a break from it now and then. Most often it's the only thing we have in common when we talk to someone for the first time, so it's understandable. With you, it's different. We share an interest in boats."

"Talking of which," said Priscilla, "we've got to get up to Camden Lock to collect ours."

"We've got loads of time," said Anthony. "Marcus won't be there for another hour or two."

"I wasn't thinking of the time. I was thinking of how much you've drunk." She spoke quietly but using the unmistakable tone of a television role she had made famous, a nagging landlady with a Gracie Fields accent. Marnie chuckled, delighted with the private performance.

"You know, you've got a point there, ol' gel. I ain't sure I could walk in a straight line if I could see it ..." The smooth, cultured tones of the classical actor had given way to the Cockney twang of Eliza Doolittle's father from *My Fair Lady*, a role Anthony had made famous on the London stage.

"There must be times when you find it hard to remember who you're living with," said Marnie.

"Most of the time," said Priscilla. "But we still have the problem of getting to Camden Lock. We can neither of us drive after drinking 'like this'."

"It's because of the pleasant ambience and Marnie's excellent company," said Anthony.

Marnie picked up the last remaining finger of a grissini breadstick from her plate and pushed it into the corner of her mouth. "So what yer saying is it's all my fault, is that it?" It was a very passable impersonation of Bogart and the actors grinned back at her. "You're trying to pin the rap on me, right? Well it won't wash."

"I hope you've got an Equity card," said Priscilla in mock reproof.

"I hope she *hasn't*," said Anthony.

"No," said Marnie in her normal voice, "but I *have* got a boat." They looked puzzled. "I could take you up to Camden Lock on *Sally Ann*. You could leave your car here and collect it tonight or tomorrow. I can get you there in good time. What do you think?"

"Mm ..." Anthony began. "We can't get breathalysed and lose our licences for being over the limit in charge of a boat, can we?"

"If we could, there'd be no one left on the canals," said Marnie.

• • • • •

Marnie was embarrassed that the two actors, whom she regarded as her guests in Little Venice, insisted on paying for lunch. They were charming but adamant and she had only acquiesced by making them agree to accept hospitality from her at some future date. This they promised to do, possibly while on a journey up the Grand Union past Knightly St John.

She hoped they would not find *Sally Ann* too modest compared with their own boat and recalled reading a magazine article about their boating exploits a few years before. It gave the impression that *Thespia* was the top of the range from one of the best boat-builders in the country. They climbed aboard and the visitors admired *Sally*'s classic – if dated – lines and praised even more the interior with its Liberty curtains, safari-style furnishings and oriental rugs.

There was still plenty of daylight but the air had a winter chill and Marnie equipped her guests with extra scarves and woolly hats for the trip. They grouped themselves together on the stern deck as they moved off from the bank and headed into Maida Hill Tunnel while the water heated in the galley for a reviving coffee. Soon they were passing through Regent's Park, chatting merrily while the condensation of their breath mingled with the steam from the mugs. Marnie offered the tiller to the actors and was surprised when Priscilla took the helm. Anthony explained that on *Thespia* his wife was always principal steerer, while he always handled the locks. She had a weakness in the back and they did not want to risk injury. Marnie thought of Anne at the helm while she dealt with the locks on the way down. She was sorry that Anne could not be with them and would ring later to see how she was. It would have been such a thrill for her to be travelling with the famous actors. She hoped there would be other times.

Leaving the zoo behind them, Priscilla slowed down for the approach to the tight left-hand corner at Cumberland Basin where the tall red pagoda restaurant towered up from the water among the trees on the bank. She had to bring *Sally Ann* to a halt as another boat nosed out from the bridge hole to turn towards them.

"Have you eaten at the pagoda?" Anthony asked Marnie. "I expect you're on first name terms with the owner here as well ..."

"Once or twice. It's very good, but I don't know the owner."

"Would it be first name or last name terms in Chinese, if you know someone well?" said Priscilla. "I'm not sure which way round their names go." Marnie laughed.

Meanwhile, the oncoming boat had straightened up and was advancing slowly to pass them. Instead of gathering speed, the steerer kept at dead slow and pointed at the group on *Sally*'s deck as he drew nearer.

"Now there's a famous face!" he called out. "Good to see you. Saw you on TV."

"Ah," Anthony muttered quietly through his scarf. "Sorry about this, Marnie. Hazard of the profession. Happens all the time. One gets used to it."

"Of course." Marnie stood back.

The steerer of the other boat leaned over as he came alongside. "It is Marnie, isn't it? You donated all those drawings to the museum. Wonderful gesture. Very generous."

"Oh ... yes, hallo." Marnie stepped nearer to the side of the boat. "Sorry, I don't think we've ..."

"Course not, but everyone knows *you*. Are you recovering?" The boats were now pulling clear of each other.

Marnie raised a thumb. "Much better, thanks. 'Bye!" The man turned to pay attention to steering his boat and glanced quickly over his shoulder for a final wave.

"You didn't know him?" said Anthony.

Marnie shrugged. "Complete stranger."

"The price of fame," said Priscilla, adjusting her woolly hat, lining *Sally* up for the blind corner.

Marnie walked along the gunwale to get a better view through the bridge hole. She signalled back to Priscilla that the way was clear and returned to the stern deck. Priscilla made a smooth turn and glanced at Marnie who was laughing gently to herself.

"What's the matter?" she said.

"I was wondering why the man on the boat didn't recognise *you two* ... until I looked at you. He'd have to be a nose-fetishist to know who you were. There's not much else of you visible." The actors looked at each other and burst out laughing.

"She's got a point," said Anthony.

"So have *you*," said Priscilla touching the end of his nose.

At that moment, the great Shakespearean actor, who had received prizes for his *King Lear* and his *Othello*, had won Emmy awards for his *Uncle Vanya* and his one-man show, *Rembrandt*, and who was tipped for a knighthood, began to sing. He had a strong baritone voice, rich and melodious, and hearing him, the two other members of the crew joined in to create a rousing three-part harmony. *Sally Ann* cruised along the canal between the towpath and the gardens of fine Regency houses, while the strains of *Rudolph the Red-Nosed Reindeer* lit up the wintry afternoon.

• • • • •

Sally Ann hove to in the middle of the channel where the canal widened at the entrance to the Camden locks, and the crew scanned the area for a sight of Marcus or *Thespia* like pirates reaching the shores of a desert island. The main difference was that this particular spot was far from deserted, with the bustling market on the towpath side and the usual heavy traffic crossing the canal on the road bridge ahead of them. Dusk was coming on and the lights from the stalls to one side and double-decker buses crawling over the bridge reflected jauntily across the water.

"I can see something on the far side of the lock," said Marnie, "but I can't make out what it is." She climbed onto the roof for a better view down to the lower level. "What colour is *Thespia?*"

"She's dark green with red and yellow markings ... seventy footer," said Anthony. Priscilla let *Sally* drift forward to improve Marnie's range of vision.

Marnie shook her head. "No. It's *Mary Rose*, one of the trip boats. I can't see any others." She slipped back onto the deck. "What time did you expect him to get here?"

"Hard to say," said Anthony.

Priscilla looked at her watch. "I thought he'd be here by now. It's not as if you can get lost on the canal."

"Shall we tie up and wait over there by the market? I could make some more coffee, or tea if you'd prefer." Anthony and Priscilla exchanged glances. "It's no problem," Marnie went on.

"Well ... that's very good of you, Marnie, but if we stay much longer, there's the risk of missing the carols. It's not fair for you to suffer on our account. You've travelled a long way to be there."

"I agree," said Anthony. "Look, let me make a suggestion. You drop us off here and head back to Little Venice. That'll give you plenty of time to line

Sally Ann up with the other boats in the pool. We'll follow as soon as Marcus arrives and we'll see you there."

"Tell them to save us a mince pie," said Priscilla.

Marnie frowned. "Are you sure? I don't like to leave you out in the cold … and it's getting dark."

"There's a café by the bridge overlooking the canal," said Anthony. "We can ensconce ourselves by the window and warm up. We'll be fine."

• • • • •

On the way back, at the approach to the bridge at Cumberland Basin, Marnie strained to detect any sign of a boat coming the other way round the blind corner. *Sally Ann*'s headlamp threw its beam forward, a narrow funnel of light that seemed to make everything outside its range even darker by contrast. She wished she had turned on some of the cabin lights to brighten the surrounding area, but it was too late now to leave the tiller even for a few seconds. As she eased *Sally*'s prow into the bridge hole, reflections and shadows seemed to flicker all around her like the ghost train in a fairground. To improve steerage Marnie pressed on the throttle and pulled the tiller over to take the bend in a smooth arc, the headlamp scanning the boats moored beside the bank ahead of her.

Once into Regent's Park, there were lamps casting pools of light along the now deserted towpath. At sunset the gates giving access from the surrounding streets were locked and Marnie was aware that her only company, albeit unseen, was the animals and birds in the zoo. She pulled up the collar of her jacket to keep out the cold and hunched her shoulders, stamping her feet on the deck in rhythm with the thudding of the diesel below her.

Ahead, something was floating in the water, a small dark shape in a patch of reflected light. Marnie automatically adjusted the steering to avoid it. Even a plastic carrier bag could get tangled in the propeller and cause a nuisance. It floated safely past and Marnie wished she had reacted more quickly, so that she could have hooked the bag from the water. She checked that the pole and boathook were conveniently placed in front of her on the roof, ready for next time.

Next time came soon enough. A dark mass was floating under the Macclesfield Road bridge, the 'blow-up bridge', and Marnie pushed on the tiller to take her round the obstruction, slowing down and reaching for the boathook. Even as she did so, she knew that this was not a carrier bag.

"Oh God, not again," she muttered, "not again."

• • • • •

Minutes later, Marnie paused for a moment to get her breath and collect her thoughts, kneeling at the edge of the water, panting with the exertion of turning the body and trying to pull a dead man out onto the bank. She had to rationalise her efforts. It seemed somehow indecent to let him lie there face up in the water in the dark shadow of *Sally Ann*, but she had to get the boat tied up and secure so that she could concentrate on the task in hand. She gripped the two mooring ropes and heaved with all her weight to bring *Sally* to the canalside, where she made her fast against the metal edging. There was no one in sight, no one to help her. It was eerie and surreal, the man obediently floating where she had left him, the boat's engine throbbing steadily at idle, a faint puff of grey smoke barely visible at the stern. Irrationally she wished she had turned the engine off so that the exhaust would not blow unhealthy fumes into the man's face. *Think, think, think. Get help. Yes.*

Marnie leapt on board and dived into the cabin to grab the mobile at the end of the bed. She pressed three nines, standing on the deck, looking down at the body as if she wanted to be sure it was real.

"Emergency. Which service please?"

"Ambulance and police."

It could only have been a few seconds, but Marnie could not cope with waiting. "Come on, come on!" It was ridiculous. She knew there was no hope, but she badly wanted someone else to be there, someone to share the responsibility, someone who knew what to do. "Come on, come on!" There was a click on the line and the operator's voice came back.

Marnie went through the routine of answering the questions posed by the calm, methodical voice of the woman at the other end of the line. She wanted to tell her how strange it all was, wanted to be reassured, spoken to like a real person by another woman who would understand what she was feeling. But the voice ploughed on, asking for details of the location, Marnie's name and phone number, telling her not to disturb anything until help came. After hanging up, Marnie thought of all the questions she should have asked. Was it all right to try to lift the body from the water? Was there anything she could do to try and revive him? How long would it be before anyone came? She took a deep breath and knew she had to get him out if she could.

Pulling at the man's shoulders, it all came back to her. She thought of the time she had first met Ralph, the previous summer in Oxford, when he had tried to commit suicide by drowning one night in the canal. Then, he had regained consciousness as she tugged at him and allowed himself to be pulled onto the bank in the boatyard. This man was never going to do anything ever again. She pulled one arm onto the canalside and struggled to get a hand under his other shoulder to gain leverage, but it was hopeless.

Could he have committed suicide, she wondered? Might Ralph have ended up like this, lying up to his ears in the murky water of the canal, with his mouth slightly open? What if it was not suicide? What if the man had been *murdered*? Squatting at the water's edge, Marnie glanced over her shoulder up and down the towpath. In the shadow of the bridge someone could be lurking even now, waiting to pounce on her. She shifted the weight on her feet, ready to spring up and run for it if anyone suddenly appeared. The engine made a reassuring sound, steady and reliable, the tang of the diesel faint in the evening air. But gradually Marnie became aware of another smell, something sweeter and richer. She lowered her face towards the man and sniffed. It was familiar. It was surely the smell of whisky. She sniffed again. Yes, no doubt about it. Perhaps he had had one or two drinks too many at an office party, slipped in the darkness, hit his head on a bridge column and toppled into the canal. Who could tell? He never would.

Minutes passed while she knelt with him in the cold and dark and waited, looking up and down the deserted pathway. Perhaps Anthony and Priscilla would come by on *Thespia*. Marnie strained to listen for the sounds of an ambulance or police car, but all she heard was the chugging of *Sally*'s engine. Even when she knew she would have to wait for the emergency people to arrive, she had not wanted to switch off the diesel, had not wanted to cut off her means of getting away.

The man's arm rested on the bank as if he was having a break from an evening swim. Marnie looked down at his face in the dim light. His eyes were closed as if he was resting, and she began to notice him as a person. The face had fine features, even in death, and his hair seemed well cut. This was no tramp like the ones she had heard about, who roll into the water in a drunken stupor, to their final sleep. He was wearing a dark coat, blue or grey, with a suit and tie, the edge of a light-coloured scarf just visible where she had tugged at his lapels. She put a hand to his cheek and, feeling completely foolish, patted it, at first softly and then harder. If he came round, she thought she would probably fall in from shock. But he did not come round and she hung her head dejectedly, wondering if she could have saved his life if only she had come along a few minutes earlier.

Somewhere in the background, in the world outside, she heard a siren wailing.

Part 06

Monday 19 December

"I believe you were involved in a murder enquiry just recently, Mrs Walker."

"Yes … but on that occasion, I was … well, the murder victim."

"Not often we get the chance to have a chat with the victim of a murder, Mrs Walker."

"Enjoy it while you can, Inspector. Actually, I thought this was rather more significant than just a chat."

"Quite so. A serious business. We shall be asking you for a statement, of course, but first I'd like you to describe the events of last evening. I'm going to record this interview if you don't mind. We'll use it as the basis for your statement."

Marnie nodded. "I don't really have anything to add to what I told your colleagues last night."

"That's all right. Sometimes there are things you remember after a night's sleep that you might've left out first time. Shock can have that effect on people."

At that moment a young police constable came into the room and placed cups of coffee in front of them on the table. It was a bare room and the aroma of the coffee did little to make it cosy. There was just a plain table end-on against a wall, with a tape-recorder, a few chairs, no pictures, no window, no carpet. The walls were painted grey-green. After serving the coffee, the constable went over to stand by the door. The inspector pressed the button to start the machine and a loud buzzer sounded for several seconds. The inspector stated who they were and what they were doing while Marnie cautiously took a sip of coffee. At least it was hot.

"Thank you for offering to come to the station this morning, Mrs Walker. It was good of you."

"I thought it would be easier than trying to do it on my boat. There's more space here." She could have added that she did not want *Sally Ann* touched – *contaminated* – by a police enquiry into a suspicious death. Memories of the murder investigation in Knightly St John the previous year were still fresh. Once was enough.

"Right. Now, in your own words, please, would you describe the events yesterday evening from the time you left your mooring in Little Venice."

Marnie began her narrative, keeping it succinct and to the point. There was nothing about feelings, nothing but the facts. When she reached the end, she sat back in her chair and drank the last of the coffee. The inspector did not turn off the recorder but sat in silence for a few seconds.

"That was most helpful, Mrs Walker. I wish all the people we recorded were as concise. Turning that into a statement will be easy. Are you happy that there's nothing you missed out? You saw no one else when you passed that way earlier?"

"No, just the man on the boat we passed. The towpath was deserted."

"And there's nothing you want to add?"

Marnie shook her head. "No, I think that's everything."

"You didn't recognise the man in the water?"

"*Recognise* him? Of course not."

"Why *of course not?*"

"Well … if I had recognised him I would've told you."

"So you'd never met him before?"

"I'd never met him before."

The inspector stood up and walked a few paces with his hands in his pockets. "I'd like you to think very carefully about this, Mrs Walker. How long did you wait with the body until the ambulance and police officers arrived?"

"I'm not exactly sure. Probably not many minutes, but it seemed quite a long time."

"*Quite a long time.* And you were close to him while you waited."

"I was kneeling beside him at the edge of the towpath."

"You could see his face?"

"Well … it was dark and he was partially in shadow, but I could see him reasonably well, I suppose."

"If it had been someone you knew, you're confident you would have recognised him at that distance in that light?"

Marnie was puzzled. "I suppose so, yes. But …"

"And you're quite certain he was completely unknown to you."

Marnie hesitated. "Well, I … I didn't recognise him."

"But now you're having doubts?"

"Only because of the way you're asking me the question. I assume you must have a reason for pressing me on this, but I honestly don't know what it could be."

"Mrs Walker, did you tell one of the officers last night that you had an engagement at the House of Commons today?"

"Yes, but only because I wanted to agree a time to come in this morning. It's a lunch engagement. I'd rather like not to be late for it."

"With whom did you have, *do* you have, this lunch engagement?"

"It's with Professor Ralph Lombard of Oxford and Michael Blissett … the MP."

"You know many MPs?"

"No. None, really. I've met one or two through Ralph. Just acquaintances. This afternoon we're going to the carol service for MPs and their guests at St Margaret's, Westminster."

"Can you give me your impressions of the dead man you found, Mrs Walker?"

It was ridiculous, but Marnie was beginning to realise that this was no simple interview. "Inspector … er …"

"Bruere."

"Inspector Bruere. Is there something about this business that you think I know that goes beyond my finding an unknown man in the canal last night?"

"You tell me."

"It's just that this feels more like an interrogation than taking a statement, which is the reason I offered to come here. If there's more to this than I realise, perhaps you should have suggested I might be joined by my solicitor."

Inspector Bruere shrugged. "I'm only trying to clarify one or two details in your account of what happened so that we have the full picture."

"I thought that's what I was giving you."

"Then shall we get back to my question? Your impressions of the dead man?"

Marnie pictured him lying in the dark water and suppressed a shudder. She took a deep breath. "I would say he was well dressed, wearing a dark coat, obviously good quality … shortish hair, well cut … his fingernails neatly manicured and clean … Oh yes, I noticed he was wearing two rings and what looked like a gold watch, a Rolex I think. It occurred to me that he hadn't been mugged."

"You're very observant."

"I was with him for some time."

"You were with him for some time … And you're sure you didn't know him?"

"Yes. Yes, I am. Quite sure."

"Does the name Tim Edmonds mean anything to you, Mrs Walker?" He watched her closely while she considered this for several seconds.

"It does seem to ring a bell, actually … I wonder … Tim Edmonds." She repeated the name slowly. "Or was it Edwards?"

A half-smile flickered across Bruere's face. "Edmonds."

Marnie nodded decisively. "I think I have heard the name … though I can't remember the circumstances. Is it someone famous?"

"Is that the best you can do, Mrs Walker? Think again."

Marnie shrugged. "It's not a case of the best I can do. You either know someone or you don't."

"Quite so." Bruere reached into his pocket and pulled out a small object. He slid it over the table towards Marnie. It was a transparent plastic envelope. "Do you recognise that?" Marnie picked it up and looked at the contents.

"It's one of my business cards. Where did you get it?"

"You're quite sure about that, Mrs Walker?"

"Of course I'm sure. It has my name on it and the name of my old firm. What else could it be?"

"Your *old* firm."

"Everett Parker Associates, yes. I worked with them for nine years before leaving to start up my own company last summer."

"So whoever had this must have known you for some time."

"Yes. Or rather … they must have met me some time ago. I give cards out all the time. That's why we have them … to give them to people."

"Would it surprise you to know we found that card in the wallet of the dead man … the man you say you didn't know?"

Marnie was visibly shocked. "I … I don't know what to say. I didn't recognise him at all. I'm *sure* I didn't know him. Who is he?" Bruere raised an eyebrow. Marnie looked down at the card. "Is he – or rather … *was* he – this … Tim Edmonds you asked me about?" Bruere nodded. Marnie shook her head. "No. I have no recollection of having met this person."

"Can I ask you to turn the card over, Mrs Walker." As he spoke there was a light knock on the door and a policeman walked into the room. He went across to Bruere and whispered in his ear. Bruere muttered something inaudible and the policeman left. Marnie turned the card over. On the reverse side, a single word was written: *dish!* "I do believe you're blushing, Mrs Walker! Ring any bells now?"

Marnie sighed. "It's a complete mystery to me. I can't explain it at all."

"Odd coincidence, though, wouldn't you say? You find his body, say you don't know him, and in his wallet is your business card with a rather personal comment on the back. To me it seems to suggest that you did know him and possibly rather better than just as a business contact. Does that sound a reasonable interpretation to you?"

"No! Look, I know when I know someone. The man I found last night was not someone I knew. Don't be in any doubt about that."

"That's your story and you're sticking to it?"

"It's not a story. It's the truth. And I think before we go any further, I'd like to talk to my solicitor."

"He's on his way," said Bruere. "There's someone waiting for you outside."

"Waiting for *me*?"

"You must have told someone you were coming here this morning."

"Certainly not my solicitor. I thought I was just coming to give a statement. I mentioned it to a neighbour in Little Venice – an old lady who lives opposite the boat – in case people wondered why I missed the carols last evening. I told her I was coming here and she invited me for coffee afterwards. Nobody else knows I'm here. Can I go now?"

"Of course. Thank you for your help. I'm sure you appreciate we'll need to see you again soon. How can we contact you, Mrs Walker?"

"I'll be staying on the boat for a few days. Let me give you my card – an up-to-date one. It's got my mobile number."

"Thank you. We'll be in touch."

As Marnie was escorted out to the entrance area, the duty officer pointed to the far side. She looked across to where several people were sitting and at first could not see anyone she knew. The person she expected, Roger Broadbent, her solicitor, was certainly not among them. Suddenly, from the middle of the group, a single person stood up and waved, with an expression that was half pleasure, half anxiety. Anne with an 'e' walked quickly and determinedly across the hall and greeted Marnie with a kiss on the cheek and a theatrical sigh.

"Honestly, Marnie, you shouldn't be allowed out! Are you all right?"

"Am *I* all right? *You're* supposed to be the invalid!"

"*Me*? No, I'm okay. It was just a touch of 'flu. I'm better now. Do we have to stay here or can we go back to Little Venice?"

Marnie took her by the arm and headed for the door. "Come on. Let's go and get a decent cup of coffee."

"Good idea," said Anne. "Mrs Jolly's expecting us. We're all due there in half an hour."

Out on the pavement, Marnie hailed a cab. "What do you mean ... *all*?" When they were in the cab driving away, Marnie repeated her question.

"Well, there's Ralph of course. He's coming by train from Oxford because it's quicker than driving. And Roger's coming too. He said he wanted to make sure everything was as it should be. Is it?"

Marnie wearily put her head back on the seat of the taxi. "I suppose this is what's known as the Bush Telegraph. One word to Mrs Jolly and the phone lines are melting all over the south of England."

"Well, *someone* had to do something and I was nearest, I suppose."

"And I'm really grateful ... but to answer your question, no, I don't think it is as it should be."

"It must have been awful for you, Marnie, but at least they can't try and pin it on you this time."

"Wanna bet ...?"

• • • • •

"Well, in any other circumstances I'd say how nice it is to see you all." Mrs Jolly was handing round biscuits to go with the coffee served in her best china. They sat in her living room like a family visiting a favourite aunt on a Sunday afternoon. Suddenly Anne delved into her shoulder bag and pulled out a slip of paper.

"Oh, I nearly forgot. This is for you, Marnie. It was tucked into the door of *Sally Ann*. I found it when I went on board this morning. Nice handwriting."

Marnie looked at the note addressed to her in a fine flowing hand. She opened it and read. "It's from Priscilla, asking if I'm all right. In the end they gave up waiting for Marcus and got a cab. They were surprised to find I hadn't made it to the carols. I'll phone them later."

Roger Broadbent leaned forward. "So ... they gave you quite a grilling. Strictly speaking, they should've suggested that you go along with your solicitor."

"Yes, but I would've said it wasn't necessary. At least until Bruere produced my business card and starting making all sorts of insinuations."

"Very odd," said Ralph. "And did he actually say it was Tim Edmonds that you found?"

"That's what I understood. Do you know him?"

"Oh yes ... fairly well. Don't you remember him? Could've been a high flyer at one stage in his career."

"He was my MP," said Roger. "I've seen him once or twice at public meetings ... very smart sort of chap, always immaculate."

"Classic English gentleman," said Mrs Jolly.

"You all seem to know him better than I did," said Marnie, "but I wonder if you'd have recognised him in the canal almost in the dark. Bruere doesn't seem to realise what it was like ... and somehow you don't expect to find someone you might know, or know of ..."

"My mum thought he was really dishy," said Anne.

"And that's a strange thing," said Roger. "That note on the back of your card. What was that about?"

"Beats me. I haven't a clue." Marnie turned to Ralph. "What was he like, this Tim Edmonds?"

"Mid to late forties ... as Roger said, very smart dresser, good with words ... quite a wit on his day, very good in debate. Came in at the '83 election, I think ... expected to go far ... quickly made PPS to the Attorney-General ... promoted to the Whips' Office a year later ... career set to take off."

"But it didn't?" said Marnie.

"Own worst enemy," said Roger. "Too fond of the good life ... went to his head."

Ralph nodded. "That's right. He was quite wealthy from all accounts, criticised for not trying hard enough, and a tendency to drink more than was good for him." Marnie remembered the smell of alcohol the night before. "Mind you, that was all behind him. Lately he'd been a reformed character, so much so that he was expected to be rewarded for his efforts in the next reshuffle."

"What efforts?" said Marnie.

"He was a key player in the PM's campaign, among other things. Since the scandal that brought him down, he'd got on with working for the party and that helped restore his reputation to some extent."

"Sorry to be so ignorant," Marnie sighed, "but what scandal?"

"He was cited in a divorce case about three years ago … an affair with the wife of a prominent QC …"

"Harold Larkin," said Roger.

"Right. Shortly afterwards his wife left him, accusing him of being a serial adulterer. It didn't help that she was the daughter of Michael Anstey, now Lord Anstey, one of the grandees of the Tory Party, former cabinet minister in the Heath government and a major contributor to party coffers. Result, as you can imagine, Tim Edmonds rapidly became *persona non grata*."

"There were lots of stories about his drinking habits in the constituency," said Roger.

"And in the House," said Ralph. "I remember one occasion when he was asked to withdraw by the Speaker and an opposition MP, Dale Campbell-Savours I think it was, suggested that his initials stood for 'Tired and Emotional'."

"I don't get that last bit," said Anne. "Or the bit about *PPS*."

Ralph turned towards her. "PPS is Parliamentary Private Secretary … it's like an assistant to a minister … good experience for high flyers. And 'tired and emotional' is a euphemism. According to the traditions of Parliament, the members cannot be described as 'drunk'. Instead, they use …"

"Oh, I see … T and E like his name."

"That's right."

"And you're sure he was no longer like that?" said Marnie.

"That's my understanding. When John Major announced the leadership campaign, Edmonds was one of his strongest supporters, did a lot of work behind the scenes as well as being up front in the hustings. It's well known that Major was not keen on the sound-bite approach, mainly because he's no good at it, but Edmonds *was* and fed him some good lines."

Roger chipped in. "The word locally was that he might be made a junior minister. He'd got a good reputation helping in by-elections and because the Conservatives kept losing them, he was regarded as loyal and dedicated to the party."

"So could rule out suicide," said Mrs Jolly. Marnie forced herself not to look in Ralph's direction. "It could only have been an accident or murder. And if the latter, definitely pre-meditated, if he hadn't been robbed."

A silence fell on the group as they digested this. It was the first time anyone of them had mentioned the word "murder" and now it hung in the air like smoke in the bar of a pub.

"Here we go again," said Marnie eventually. "Only this time I want to handle things better. I'm not going to make the mistakes I made last summer. If possible, I'd like to keep everything quiet."

"*Quiet?*" said Anne.

"Yes, if I can."

"Er ... that might be difficult ..."

"Why?"

Anne pulled a face. "I did mention to one or two people that ... you were being interviewed by the police ..."

"I see. And?"

"Well ... for a start the vicar's holding a prayer vigil in the church, the WI is organising a petition, the school's putting up posters all over the village, the local paper's running a Free Marnie campaign and the Appletons are sending you a food parcel from the shop ..."

"Ha ... ha!" said Marnie.

• • • • •

The cab was held up in heavy traffic for a few minutes at Marble Arch. It was twelve-thirty. Anne was on her way home on the train. Marnie and Ralph were heading for the Commons. The newspaper sellers were doing a brisk trade in the early lunchtime editions on the crowded pavements, the headlines proclaiming: 'MP DEAD IN CANAL MYSTERY'. Ralph checked his watch as the driver slid open the glass panel and leaned back.

"Christmas shopping!" he called over his shoulder. "Everyone's gone mad."

"Panic buying," Marnie suggested.

"Prob'ly. I could go through the park if you want. It'd be quicker but it's a longer route. Up to you."

"Go for it," said Marnie.

"Okay, love." He pulled over so that the nose of the taxi was half into the outside lane and edged up to the bumper of the car ahead. Marnie shuffled closer to Ralph on the seat and linked arms. She was worried about the effect on him of all the talk of drowning in the canal. He glanced at her and smiled.

"Are you okay, Marnie?"

"Of course." She squeezed his arm with hers.

"I'm sorry this had to happen. It must be awful for you after all you went through in the summer."

"We'll just have to see it through," she said. "At least we're not in the front line this time."

"I saw in the paper that the police believe there was a witness," said Ralph.

"A *witness?*"

"Apparently. The report said the police were trying to trace a tramp who was known to be living on the opposite side of the canal. There was at least one tramp there, it seems."

Marnie thought back to the times she had passed that way on *Sally Ann* and seen pallets covered with blankets and tarpaulins under the bridge set back on a mound rising from the water's edge. It was a well-known haunt for tramps and had provided shelter for years. But she did not know if they stayed there through the winter, and on the evening when she found the body there had not been a flicker of life or movement across the water.

"If they had a witness why were they giving *me* such a hard time?"

Ralph shrugged. "To see what else they could find out, perhaps."

"Yes. All because of that card, I expect. Well, I don't suppose the tramp will've gone far. When they've got his testimony that should sort things out. And once my statement's out of the way and we've resolved the card business we can bow out."

The traffic crawled forward and within seconds their taxi had eased into the outer lane and gained space as the lights turned to amber, racing across the empty road junction at the top end of the park to take pole position at the next set of traffic lights.

"I hope so," said Ralph.

"Tomorrow I'll give them my statement and that'll be that. No more grilling, no more trying to catch me out."

"You said they'd given you a hard time. *Did* they grill you?"

"It felt like it. I seem to bring out the animosity of the police. Do you remember Inspector Bartlett? He never believed a word I said. This one, Inspector … Bruere, kept calling me *Mrs Walker* all the time … very annoying."

"He was probably goading you to see if you were the violent type, the sort who could commit murder."

Marnie was indignant. "Yes. Well, he nearly found out."

Ralph chuckled. The taxi accelerated away and turned into Hyde Park where the traffic was thinner. "I was surprised you didn't know about Tim Edmonds. He was in the news quite a lot a few years back. Big scandal."

"I was probably having problems of my own at the time. Anyway, there's been so much scandal with this government, so much sleaze, it's been hard to keep up with everything that was going on."

"And yet he had your card in his wallet."

"I *know*," said Marnie. "It's *weird*. I've no idea how he got it." She shook her head.

"There's probably a simple enough solution," said Ralph. "We'll sort it out."

"Yes. Let's forget it for this afternoon. I just want to enjoy the day. Lunch at the House of Commons followed by the carol service sounds like excellent therapy to me."

• • • • •

By the time Marnie and Ralph took their seats in St Margaret's church the place was filling up rapidly and there was a hubbub of muted conversation, much of it no doubt centred on the death of Tim Edmonds. Marnie had a strange feeling. Here were all these people talking in shocked whispers about the dead MP while, unknown to them, the person who had discovered his body was sitting in one of the pews just a few feet away. They found themselves almost at the back with only one row behind them. Marnie leaned up against Ralph to murmur, "We were lucky to get in. Any later and we'd have been on the pavement. And I thought we were early."

"No danger of that," he muttered softly. "This is entry by tickets only. A lot of the front rows are reserved for members of the government. Half the cabinet and a load of other ministers from both houses are probably here. You're doing it again."

"What am I doing?"

"Rubbernecking."

"Am I? Surely not. Is that the Chancellor over there?"

Ralph gave her an old-fashioned sideways look and they settled down to reading the programme. Senior members of the main parties were doing the readings, including the Prime Minister and the Leader of the Opposition. A day of contrasts, Marnie thought. Interrogation by the police and now this. She had enjoyed lunch with Michael Blissett, punctuated by numerous handshakes as friends of his came past their table and wished them a Happy Christmas. He had not applied for a ticket to the carol service for himself ... *Not quite my scene* ... but had obtained them for Ralph as a favour. The organ struck up the opening bars of the first carol, 'Lo, He comes' ... and everybody stood up to sing as the procession made its way down the centre aisle. As the service progressed, Marnie let her thoughts drift over the events of the past year. She found herself wondering how she had dared to give up a secure career in London to set up her own design company in Knightly St John, renovating the derelict farm buildings to live and work in them herself and let the cottages and barns as a source of income. Amazingly, it was working out as well as she had hoped, with the support of Anne as her right hand. Her trusted right hand.

She admired the Christmas tree by the altar, so heavily weighed down with decorations, ribbons and lights that the green branches were scarcely visible, and she thought of the parish church of St John in Knightly, no less beautiful than this one, the scene of two terrible murders separated by 350 years, almost the scene of her own death a few months earlier. The thought made her shudder and she hoped no one noticed it as the congregation sang 'Hark the herald angels'. But Ralph seemed to notice and he moved closer so that their arms touched. She realised that he had a good baritone voice and sang in tune, unlike the woman behind her who sang flat, half a note later than everybody else. It was very off-putting, as Marnie, despite being a committed agnostic, wanted to do justice to the carols that she had known and liked since childhood.

The service must have lasted about an hour, but it ended too soon for Marnie. The congregation was asked to remain standing while the procession walked down the centre aisle and she tried not to stare at the famous faces as they walked past. The Prime Minister was smiling at everyone and their eyes met for a second. It seemed to be the norm for politicians to look straight in the eye, as if they were trying to impress people with their sincerity. The Leader of the Opposition was a few paces behind him, with a serious expression, his gaze straight ahead. As the guests of honour left the church, a muttering of conversation started up, half the congregation seeming to want to have a quiet word with the other half. Marnie recognised it as the way things were done in Westminster, to take someone aside for a *quiet word*. The church looked wonderful with its Christmas tree and candles and the organ, its pipes gleaming, softly playing an anthem.

Ralph turned to speak quietly to Marnie, as if he had been reading her thoughts. "Wouldn't it be marvellous ... if it was all true ..."

"What?"

"All this ... religion ... Christmas ..." His voice was barely audible.

Marnie looked at him carefully to make sure she understood what he was saying. He seemed genuinely moved at the thought. She replied quietly. "You mean … marvellous if it all meant something … literally?"

Ralph nodded. "Sorry, Marnie. Is that offensive?"

"Probably … but not to me. As something personal I think religion's fine, if you've got it. It's when people organise it that the problems come along."

They turned to move out into the aisle and Marnie had to hold back waiting for the shuffling crowd to move on before she could take her place. She bent down to pick up her order of service as a memento and, as she did, she noticed a man sitting alone at the far end of the back row, a distinguished-looking man in his fifties. It was his posture that attracted her attention. He was hunched forward and at first she thought he was praying, but instead realised that he was struggling to control his emotions. He looked desperately sad and she was sure his cheeks were damp as he stared in front of him, eyes downcast, with an expression of utter desolation, oblivious to everything going on around him. Marnie turned to ask Ralph if he recognised the man, but Ralph had already moved into the aisle and by the time they had the chance to speak, they were outside, someone she did not recognise was having a quiet word with Ralph and the moment had passed.

As Ralph made no effort to introduce her to the stranger, Marnie waited a few paces away, taking his action as a signal that he did not want to prolong the conversation. A minute later he turned to take her arm and they walked slowly down the path towards the West front of Westminster Abbey.

"Sorry about that, Marnie. That was one of the policy advisers from the Opposition. They want me to attend a meeting in the new year."

"I didn't think you got that closely involved with the individual parties."

"I don't. Anyway, I had an excuse. Even the new generation of whiz-kids don't expect me to cancel the White House to talk to them about monetary policy."

They stood on the pavement and the cold air swirled around them, whipped up by the passing traffic in Parliament Square, jostled by passers-by, shoppers, tourists, the never-ending London throng.

"It's funny," said Marnie, looking up at the ancient façade, newly cleaned and shining in the floodlights. "I thought we were going to be in there for the carol service, in the actual abbey."

"No, it's always held in St Margaret's. It's Parliament's parish church. Or did you think they'd renamed the abbey after Mrs Thatcher? Now there's a thought."

Marnie laughed. "I wouldn't be surprised." She took hold of Ralph's arm. "What now? You have to get back to Oxford for your committee?"

"Fraid so. Academic Board. Special meeting to talk about funding. If you like, you could come back with me, make yourself at home in my rooms and we could go out for supper afterwards?"

"You could eat another meal after that lunch?"

"Well, a drink then. I don't like to let you out of my clutches when I've got you."

"Sounds tempting, but it would be very late and I have to be here to see the police."

"Yes." Ralph sighed. "You're right, of course. Never mind. We'll have Christmas together."

They took a cab to Little Venice, where Ralph dropped Marnie off before going on to Paddington station not far away. She stood for a few moments looking down from the raised pavement over the railings at the boats. It had always struck her as a strange sight for the middle of London, the street lights reflected off the water, the gaily-coloured narrowboats drawn up along both banks like a gypsy encampment in the heart of the city. A romantic, almost exotic scene. It pained her to think that it was now touched by a murder enquiry and even more to think that she was involved in it. Marnie went on board to switch on the heating and switch on a lamp to welcome herself back before crossing the road to call in on Mrs Jolly.

"Come in, my dear. Let's go through to the living room. I've made a few things for a sort of late tea. We can sit by the fire and make ourselves comfortable."

It sounded as homely as if Marnie was back in Knightly St John. Taking a seat on a sofa opposite the fire, Marnie realised how tired she felt. It had been a long day and she was still not fully recovered from her injuries. The low table carried a traditional mixture of sandwiches and petits fours, with a Yule log and mince pies to add a seasonal touch. As a centrepiece, four advent candles were burning in a wreath of holly. Mrs Jolly re-appeared carrying a Royal Doulton teapot and settled onto her favourite armchair. She leaned forward to pour.

"I thought a nice pot of Darjeeling would revive flagging spirits, Marnie. There's nothing quite like it on a winter's day. Milk or lemon?"

"You must be a mind reader, Mrs Jolly. Lemon would be perfect."

"The slices are in that ramekin by the cucumber sandwiches."

Marnie almost purred with pleasure as the warmth and cosiness of the room enveloped her. The fire may have been of artificial coals, powered by gas, because of London's anti-smog laws, but it was near enough to the real thing. She sighed and sank back into the cushions.

"That's better," said Mrs Jolly. "Just help yourself to whatever you need and relax. If you feel up to it, tell me about your day."

Marnie smiled at the old lady. "Do you remember what I said about a quiet life ...?"

Part 07

Tuesday 20 December

It was before eight on Tuesday morning when the mobile rang. Marnie was sitting over a cup of coffee in *Sally Ann's* saloon, thinking.

"Marnie, it's Ralph. Sorry to ring early, but I knew you'd be up and about."

"No problem."

"Look, I've had a thought ... about your business card ... the one the police found on Tim Edmonds."

"All contributions welcome. I've drawn a complete blank."

"Could it be one of your team?"

"Who?"

"The *dish*."

"Go on."

"Well, the police seem to think it was meant to be *you* ... a logical and very obvious deduction."

"Thank you, kind sir."

"But could someone from your *department* have given him your card, or do they all have their own?"

She pondered. "It varies. Some do, some don't."

"So it's possible?"

"It's possible."

"Any idea who it could've been?"

Marnie thought about her old team. Most of them were young women and most of them were presentable, with good dress sense. But a *dish,* as in *dishy* ... that could only really be one of them. "I'll give Faye a ring ... Faye Summers."

"Does she measure up to the description?"

"In all departments. A good choice of words, Ralph. I'll keep you posted."

Marnie went back to her coffee and her thoughts. Through the window, she looked out on a grey day, dry and cold. She loved Little Venice, but really did not want to be there. She felt hemmed in and longed to be out in the country again, back in Knightly St John where she knew she belonged. Perhaps, after the police had taken her statement ... Suddenly, she nodded decisively and reached for the phone.

"Anne? Hi! How are you?"

"Fine, Marnie. Where are you ... in the dungeons? Do I have to saddle up the white charger?"

"Not yet. I'm still on *Sally*, but I'm thinking of escaping."

"Can you do that? Don't you have to get permission from the police?"

"I'm not sure, but I've had enough of London and I'd like to get home. How would it suit you?"

"Do you want me to come back down to London?"

"No ... I don't know when I can leave. But I could pick you up on the way."

"Right. I'll be on standby whenever you're ready. I'll go and pack."

Marnie knew Anne would be starting one of her inevitable lists before the mobile reached the table. Immediately it rang again.

"Marnie? It's Priscilla ... Priscilla Barnes. I hope it's okay to ring so early."

"Absolutely fine, Priscilla. I was going to call you. Thanks for your note."

"That's okay. What *happened* to you? Are you all right? We heard on the news about ..." She lowered her voice, "the body of the MP in the canal, and we wondered if you'd got involved in any way."

"I found him."

"Oh, my *god* ... You poor lamb! It must have been *awful* for you."

"Not very pleasant. Anyway, I'm giving a statement to the police and that should be the end of it."

"They said the police were treating it as a suspicious death."

"That's right, but I don't know what else they've found out. They don't give much away. Tell me, what happened to you and Anthony?"

Priscilla sighed theatrically. "Marcus had engine trouble ... condensation in the fuel supply, I think. We'd forgotten to keep the tank filled to prevent it. So he had to leave her on route. Marcus is not mechanically minded, I'm afraid. He works with special needs children. He's great with kids, not so good on machines."

"I'm glad he was okay."

"Keep in touch, Marnie, and have a good Christmas. We'll get together another time."

Finishing the last of the coffee, Marnie thought about her own fuel tank. *Sally Ann* consumed so little diesel that she hardly ever thought about checking. Time to write a list. *Anne would be proud of me!* she thought. Too early to ring Faye Summers at the office, she pressed another set of familiar numbers.

"Beth ... it's me. How are things?"

"Hi Marnie! Okay. What about you? Did you hear about that business of the body in the canal ... that MP?"

"Beth, don't get hysterical, right? There's something I've got to tell you."

"You're kidding! I don't believe it ..."

"I haven't said it yet ..."

"You don't have to. What happened?" Marnie gave a brief outline. "That's strange," said Beth. "The police didn't say a woman was helping them with their enquiries or anything like that."

"If they meant *me*, they'd probably say a woman was *hampering* their enquiries, as usual. Anyway, I just wanted to tell you that I'm here in Little Venice for the moment, I'm okay and I'm going back home as quickly as I can ... as soon as I've talked to the police. Sorry I haven't got time to see you. We'll have to sort out about the MG another time."

Marnie was surprised how well Beth had taken it. There was no doubt that Beth was giving her an easy ride since Marnie's brush with death in the summer. In fact, Marnie did not know what she found more difficult to manage, her sister's nagging or her understanding. She got up and crossed to the sink in the galley to wash her coffee cup. Through the slats of the venetian blind she saw a police car parked on the street the other side of the railings and two police officers staring down at her from the raised pavement.

When she had ushered them into the saloon, Marnie indicated chairs and they sat down. Chief Inspector Bruere was accompanied by a much younger man with a boyish, rather gentle face, who pulled out a notebook. Bruere introduced him as DC Knight.

"Usually I go through the ritual of offering coffee at this stage, but so far no one has ever accepted."

"Well I will, if you're offering, Mrs Walker," said Bruere. "It'll be my only breakfast today."

"For both of you?" The younger man smiled and nodded. Marnie lit the gas under the kettle and put four croissants in the oven. "You want to sort out my statement?"

Bruere nodded at his colleague and the young man took a document from his pocket, pushed it across to Marnie to read and sign. It seemed accurate enough. She signed it and gave it back to him.

"Have you managed to find the tramp they mentioned in the papers?" said Marnie.

"We're working on it."

"But it's true that you think there might have been a witness?"

"Like I said, we're working on it, Mrs Walker."

"Right," said Marnie. "So is this visit a good or a bad sign? For example, am I able to leave London? Can I head back to Northamptonshire?"

Bruere hesitated. "There are one or two matters we want to clarify, but … yes, you can go home. I think we've got your home phone number."

"It's on my business card. And I gave you my mobile number. You can reach me on it when I'm travelling if you need to. It'll take me four to five days to get home." Bruere raised an eyebrow. "I'm travelling on the boat, inspector."

"Of course." Both policemen looked around at the interior, taking in all the details of the saloon and the galley. Bruere seemed lost in his thoughts for a few moments. "Four or five days … right. Well, let's see if we can make some progress, shall we? The business card … the one we found on the body. Have you anything to add to what you said at the station?"

Marnie thought about Ralph's idea that *dish* could refer to one of her team, but she had not yet checked it out. "Look … er … I have an idea about that, but it's nothing definite. I'd rather wait till I have a clearer picture."

"Why not tell us now and let us decide?"

"It's quite possibly a blind alley. I don't want to waste your time." Bruere snorted and shook his head. Marnie made coffee and put the croissants in a basket on the table. She set down two plates, a sugar bowl and a small jug of milk. It was a very cosy scene. Almost. Bruere spooned two sugars into his cup and stirred slowly. "I wish I'd never found the body," said Marnie.

"So does Tim Edmonds," said Bruere. "And you still insist you can't explain about the victim carrying your business card in his wallet and you maintaining that you didn't know him. That's your story?"

Marnie sighed. "What have I got to do to get the police to believe me?"

"Just try helping us, Mrs Walker."

"But I've told you all I know."

"About your card?"

"Honestly, it's a mystery to me. I can't explain it, really. But I will do all I can to work out what it means. I'm going to ask my old team at Everett Parker. Somebody there may be able to come up with something."

"What makes you think that?"

Marnie shrugged. "Perhaps one of them used one of my cards. It's possible." Knight made a note. It was the first thing he had written. "You've got their address and details on the card you found on the body. You can check it out. There you are. That's all you wanted to query."

Bruere picked up a croissant and tore a piece off in his fingers. He frowned. Marnie wondered if he was not sure if he should dunk it in his coffee. He glanced over his shoulder towards the galley. Perhaps he wanted some jam. She was on the point of offering when he spoke.

"Who is MG, Mrs Walker?"

"Sorry?"

Bruere pointed with the croissant at the cork notice board on the wall of the galley. Anne had put it there for messages, lists, reminders. There were a few postcards, one of Anne's canal sketches, a list with some of the items crossed out. It gave a homely but purposeful impression. In the middle of the list were the two initials. "MG," he repeated. "Who is it?"

Marnie shook her head. "*What* is it?" she said.

Bruere scowled. "MG ... who is it, Mrs Walker?" He spoke slowly with a hint of menace.

"MG isn't a *who*, inspector. MG is a *what*. It's a *car*. The note is to remind me to speak to my sister about it. I have a pre-war MG sports car. It's taking up all the space in my sister's garage. I need to arrange to move it up to my place in the country."

Bruere looked at Knight who was drinking coffee to wash down his croissant. She had the awful feeling that he was going to splutter and she tried not to smile. That would have been a bad move. Even so, Bruere did not look pleased and seemed to suspect that Marnie was trying to be clever.

"Do you know Malcolm Grant?" Bruere said suddenly.

"Malcolm Grant," Marnie repeated. "Malcolm ... Grant. I think I have heard the name somewhere, but I can't place it."

"You don't know him?"

"I don't know him." This was beginning to sound familiar, she thought.

"His initials are MG."

"I've worked that out. But those are not his initials on my memo-board ... except by coincidence."

"We seem to have a lot of coincidences where you're concerned, Mrs Walker."

• • • • •

After the policemen had left, Marnie went around tidying the boat inside and out, as if she was trying to clean away the contamination of their enquiry ... their *murder* enquiry. While she moved around the cabin she laid her plans for the return journey. But first there were matters to be settled. On her list she wrote:

1. *Faye*
2. *Ralph*
3. *Diesel*
4. *Anne*

Satisfied with the boat, she reached for the mobile, rang Everett Parker Associates and asked for Faye Summers. A man came on the line, explaining that Faye was out all morning.

"Is that Andy? It's Marnie. Listen, I need to talk to Faye about a job we did ... or might have done, for an MP."

"Tim Edmonds?"

Marnie was taken aback. "Yes. Have the police contacted you?"

"The *police*? No. It was on the news and we were saying that we'd done a job at his flat."

"Who handled it?"

"Faye and Hannah. Hannah mostly, I think. It was while you were away that summer." *Of course!* That would explain it. Hannah was working part-time after having a baby.

"Can I speak to Hannah?"

"She left months ago, Marnie. Needed more time for the family."

Marnie arranged to ring later. While she was pondering her next move, she noticed that a message was waiting on the mobile. She pressed the arrow: *Please ring Ralph – urgent.*

"Hi, it's me."

"Ah, the system works! I never really trust machines."

"Sometimes they're more reliable than people," said Marnie. "At least they're there when you want them."

"Which is why I rang. Marnie, slight change of plan. I've got to come to London again. There's someone I need to talk to at the LSE. He's about to go to South Africa for a month, and I'm meeting him this afternoon. Could we have dinner together?"

"Ah ... that would be difficult. The police have been and told me it's okay to leave. Is there something urgent you want to talk about?"

"I want to try to get to the bottom of that question of the business card so that you can finish your statement and put this all behind you. And I wanted to see you again and give you moral support. But you really have to set off?"

"It's nice of you, but I must get *Sally* home before Christmas. If I don't go now, she could be stranded for months by lock closures."

"Would you be able to see me at lunch-time? I've arranged to meet Michael Blissett again at the House. Or is it too much of a rush?"

"No. In fact, I want to talk to you about the case, anyway. Perhaps I could just come for a chat and then leave you to have lunch with Michael? Sorry to be unsociable, but time's running out."

"That's fine. I'll be there by about eleven-thirty. Can you make that?"

"Okay. Ralph, do you know someone called Malcolm Grant?"

"Of course. Known him for years."

"Who is he?"

"An MP. Why?"

"The police were asking me about him. They took me by surprise. I couldn't place him, though I thought I'd heard the name."

"You'll probably hear it again, too. He was Tim Edmonds's closest friend."

• • • • •

By the time Marnie had changed – she wore a charcoal-grey jacket and skirt that she thought were suitable for the House of Commons – it was almost eleven as she emerged onto the stern deck of *Sally Ann*. Along the towpath the entrance gate clanged and she saw Gary reconnecting the padlock. He came towards *Sally Ann* with his usual walk, a cross between a swagger and the rolling gait of a seaman.

"Gary, what are you doing?"

He looked guilty but managed to keep the twinkle in his eye. His tone was defensive. "Nothin'."

"No, no. I mean what are you doing today?"

"*Ah*." The twinkle turned to a grin. "What do you have in mind, blue eyes?"

"I need the tank filling with diesel." Gary ran a working boat with a diesel pump that supplied most of the boats in Little Venice at a surprisingly reasonable rate.

"Oh. I thought my luck had changed."

"Could you do it this morning? I need to be away at lunchtime."

Gary thought about it. "Yeah. I've got to see a man about a dog, but I could do it before I go. How much do you need?"

"I don't know. Just put in as much as she'll take."

"How will I charge you if you're not here? Or more to the point, how will you pay me?"

"Good point." Marnie rummaged in her shoulder-bag. Cash or cheque were the only options. "I'll give you a cheque. If I sign it, you can fill it in when you've finished. Okay?" There was no reply. "Okay?" She looked up. Gary was frowning with his mouth open.

"Fine, Marnie. Er … fine. That's fine."

She signed a cheque and tore it out. "You won't let me down, will you? I want her filled up, so we don't get condensation in the tank."

"Trust me, Marnie. I'm a boatman."

"Good. Must dash. See you. Have a good Christmas!" She set off towards the tube station and looked back to see Gary staring at the cheque in his hand. "And I've got brown eyes!" she called out over her shoulder. If Gary replied, she did not hear it.

• • • • •

"Have you been waiting long?" Marnie met Ralph at the entrance to Central Lobby.

"Just arrived," said Ralph, kissing her. "You know, I still can't get over the new hairstyle."

"A lot seems to have happened since you first mentioned it. Have you announced our arrival at the desk?"

"Yes. Michael's on his way down. We're going to have a drink in the Pugin Room and then lunch. It's not too late to change your mind if you'd like to eat."

"I really ought to get back, but thanks for the offer. Can we have a quick word before Michael gets here? I've told the police that Edmonds could've got the card from one of my staff at Everett Parker. It's possible that he was given it while I was away the summer before last. He had his flat redecorated and a member of my team worked on the design. She was part-time, mainly working at home, so she may not have needed her own business card."

"Is that usual?"

"It happens. I'm going to speak to Faye about it later this afternoon. It would certainly help explain the mystery."

"Good. And what was that business about Malcolm Grant?"

Marnie shrugged. "The inspector saw 'MG' on my notice board and thought it could've referred to him."

"MG?"

"My old sports car. Beth wants me to get it out of her garage. It's been there for ... well, a few years, actually."

Ralph looked puzzled. "I wonder why they're interested in Malcolm."

"You said he was his closest friend."

"Yes ... I expect he's helping them, too."

"Well I hope he gets better treatment from the police than I do. They never seem to trust anything I say. What do you think they could be asking him about?"

Ralph shook his head. "Establishing his last movements, perhaps. I don't know. But they were very close. Neighbours too, more or less."

"Constituencies?"

"No. Quite the opposite, in fact. Edmonds was London Riverside. Grant represents one of the Lake District areas. But they both have places in north London. Grant was a terrific support to Edmonds at the time of the scandal. Rumour has it that he took Edmonds in hand and stopped him going completely downhill ... serious drink problem and all that."

"Sounds like a good friend to have ..."

"Ah," said Ralph. "Here comes Michael."

The MP greeted his visitors warmly and ushered them through to the long and ornate ground floor corridor leading to some of the restaurants and bars that give the Houses of Parliament the reputation of being the best club in Britain. The style of decor here too was Victorian Gothick, with rich colours, thick carpet, the walls hung with paintings of Parliament, an elaborate ceiling. It was the usual bustle with people thronging the corridor, some striding purposefully with pre-occupied expressions, others standing in pairs or in small groups having a quiet word with their colleagues. For a few moments Marnie's attention was distracted from her concerns. She enjoyed the atmosphere, the movement, the sense that important decisions were being discussed by people who had influence if not, according to Ralph and Michael, actual power. The dynamism of the place gave it a feeling of urgency, prevented it from seeming like a museum. The whole place was alive.

Towards the end of the corridor, Michael stopped and moved aside to let Marnie go in front of him. They were standing at the open door of a large high-ceilinged room with magnificent tall windows overlooking the Thames. It was furnished like a sitting room with groups of comfortable armchairs and sofas around small tables. To the left was a bar, and drinks were being served by a uniformed waiter. At eleven-thirty it was already half full.

"This is the Pugin Room, Marnie. He designed the interior of the House after the old building was destroyed by fire, as I'm sure you know, and ..." Before he could finish the sentence, a man passing behind them whispered in his ear and he spun round. Marnie thought she had seen the man on television in the news, but she could not put a name to him. She was thinking that she would have to pay more attention to politics and politicians if her relationship with Ralph was going to continue, when

Michael turned back to her. "Sorry, Marnie, won't be a minute. Alastair wants a quick word. Would you like to take a seat? We'll be with you directly." He indicated the Pugin Room and she went in. Ralph was drawn into conversation outside with the two men. *A quiet word,* thought Marnie, taking a seat at a table in the middle of the room.

She tried not to indulge in rubbernecking, but was sure she recognised some of the faces around her. With a sense of achievement she spotted a former Home Secretary at a corner table with a smartly dressed woman and two teenage boys. *Don't stare, Marnie. Be discreet!* She noticed the waiter hovering over her and glanced towards the door to see if Michael and Ralph were coming. Unsure what to do, she looked up at the waiter and smiled.

"I'm waiting for friends to join me." Instead of withdrawing, the waiter remained where he was and a frown crossed his face.

"Actually, madam, this room is reserved for –"

"It's all right, Simon, the lady is my guest." The voice came from behind the waiter, but it was not Michael Blissett's voice. This was more silky. Marnie strained to see who was claiming her and discovered that it was a man in his fifties in a formal pin-striped suit. He sat down opposite her. "What would you like?"

Marnie was flustered but determined not to show it. "A mineral water, please. Sparkling."

"Your usual, sir?"

"No. Nothing for me, Simon. I have to keep a clear head." He smiled at Marnie.

"You have a meeting?" she said.

"No," said the stranger. "A liquid lunch with the chairman of a Select Committee." He had good bone structure and looked fit for his age, like a City banker who kept up his jogging.

Marnie smiled. "My name is Marnie Walker. I'm actually waiting for Michael Blissett. He's talking to someone in the corridor."

"Shame on Michael. He's a good chap, even if he is on the wrong side. But abandoning you here shows appalling judgement. My name, by the way, is Malcolm Grant."

"Malcolm …" She held out her hand, struggling to contain her surprise. "… Grant. Hallo."

He looked confused. "I don't believe we've met, have we? I know I would have remembered."

"No. No, we haven't."

"Is something wrong? You seem … startled, if you don't mind me saying so …"

For a moment Marnie was uncertain about what to say. But then, remembering the problems she had had with the police in the past through giving an inaccurate impression, she decided on frankness. "Mr Grant, I ought to say to you that I was the person who discovered … Tim Edmonds in the canal. I know he was a friend of yours and I'm sorry."

Grant's expression faltered for just a second. He smiled grimly. "He was … he was indeed. It must have been an ordeal for you." Marnie nodded. "And no doubt the police have been questioning you, too."

"Twice," she said.

"Such a harrowing business. Still, we have to do what we can to help. At least once they've finished with their questions you can put it all behind you."

"Well, not quite, actually," said Marnie. "It's a little more complicated in my case."

"Really? In what way? Oh, sorry, perhaps I shouldn't be asking. They've no doubt told you not to talk about it to anyone."

The waiter arrived with Marnie's drink, giving her a few seconds to consider how to reply. "It's odd really, but I told them I didn't ... recognise the man in the water – it was dark and he was ... well, you know. Later they found my business card in his wallet."

"His *wallet*? So he wasn't mugged ... I see." Grant looked thoughtful, his mind far away. Marnie did not speak. The MP focused on her again. "In a way, that could be comforting ... if it could have been an accident, I mean. Do you think it was?"

"I just don't know." It was her turn to look thoughtful. She had assumed the man had been murdered. But why did she think that? He was wearing an expensive watch, his wallet was intact ... Perhaps she was expecting it to be a murder enquiry. *Suspicious circumstances* might mean anything. She recalled the smell of drink. Suppose he had had a drop too much and, stumbled and slipped on the towpath, hitting his head on the iron pillars of the "blow-up bridge" ... Everyone was going to drinks parties at this time of the year. She became aware that Grant was speaking. "Sorry, I didn't quite catch what you were saying."

"Your card ... it's just that, if you didn't know Tim, I wondered how he came to have your card in his wallet. Such an odd coincidence."

"That's what I said to the police. My firm did the redecoration of his flat in north London and one of my group must've given it to him."

Grant nodded. "Last year ... during the recess. Tim came up to visit us while they were doing it. I must say you don't look like a painter and decorator ..."

"I'm not. It's an architect's practice. I used to be head of the interior design group. I have my own firm now."

"Of course." He looked at his watch and glanced over his shoulder towards the door.

"I am sorry to hold you up," said Marnie. "Having to nursemaid me like this ..."

"That's all right. It's a pleasure. I was just thinking ... my own place down here ... it's a nice flat, but it could do with smartening up. Hasn't been decorated for ages. I wonder if you'd care to have a look and see what you think."

"Certainly."

"After the recess, of course. I'll be back down in early January. We only rise for a short time over Christmas and New Year. How do I reach you?" Marnie flipped open her wallet and gave him a card. "Walker and Co," he read. "Northamptonshire. Would this be too far for you, perhaps?"

"No. It's no problem." She saw Michael and Ralph in the doorway and nodded in their direction. "I think you're about to be rescued."

Grant stood up and shook hands with Marnie. "I'll be in touch after the recess. It was nice meeting you."

"Thank you again," said Marnie. He turned and walked towards the door, pausing briefly to say something to Michael and Ralph, wishing them a Merry Christmas.

"So ... you've met Malcolm Grant," said Ralph quietly, taking a seat beside her, while Michael had a word with a colleague in the next group.

"Yes. He obviously feels a lot of pain about the death of his friend. I had to say something ... I couldn't just pretend I knew nothing about it."

"Quite. Did he say anything of interest?"

"How do you mean?"

"Well, presumably one of you must have started the conversation and as you'd never seen him before, and don't usually go up to men in bars and ask them to buy you a drink ..."

"As it happens he rescued me from an awkward situation. I'll tell you about it later."

Michael rejoined them, apologising for keeping Marnie waiting. "I'm glad Malcolm looked after you. He's a nice chap."

"He said the same about you, Michael. I thought you were supposed to be on opposite sides."

"Oh, we are, of course, but he's all right, is Malcolm. I expect he was in here drowning his sorrows."

"Why do you say that?" said Marnie.

Michael glanced conspiratorially at Ralph and leaned over towards Marnie before replying. "I've heard it rumoured that Malcolm is going to the Lords." Ralph nodded thoughtfully. Marnie frowned.

"And that would make him unhappy?" she said.

"Of course," said Michael. "End of his political career ... no real chance of high office after that."

"And that's what he wants," said Marnie. "High office?" Michael shrugged. *It's what they all want,* she thought. "Is it always like this? All this rumour and gossip?"

"The place has gone mad this year," said Michael. "It seems to be even worse just now, before the recess. I blame the Prime Minister's leadership campaign ... I don't think the place has settled down since the summer."

"A hotbed of intrigue," Ralph muttered.

Michael nodded slowly. "There's a lot going on beneath the surface. You mark my words. There are still shockwaves in that party."

"Did the Prime Minister think he'd win the contest and get re-elected as leader?" said Marnie.

"Well, it was quite a gamble. Some people – in his own party – have said they thought he was almost past caring ..."

Ralph shook his head. "I suspect he'd done his calculations and was using it to consolidate his position."

"I knew you'd say that," said Michael, grinning. He turned to Marnie. "Ralph doesn't believe any politician would willingly give up power."

Ralph agreed. "After all, he was virtually running a minority government. Without the Ulster Unionists he would've been sunk and he needed to re-establish his authority in the Tory Party. I don't see why else he needed to do it. He was already PM. If he'd had enough, he could've resigned."

"And hand over to someone he hated?" said Michael.

"*Hated*?" said Marnie. "Surely, even if he'd lost, the Conservatives would still be in power but under a new leader."

"Exactly," said Michael. "An *enemy*." Marnie had the feeling that it was wiser to say nothing. Anything she said was going to make her seem naïve.

"I think you've made my point for me," said Ralph. "I don't think he would've risked it if he thought he was going to lose."

"So you see it as a kind of purge. A clever tactic."

"Clever?" said Ralph. "It was certainly unexpected. But I'm not sure it was *clever*. After all, it polarised opinion inside the party and forced his opponents to declare themselves in public."

"All the better to purge them," said Michael.

"The ones at the top were safe whatever the outcome," said Ralph. He turned to Marnie. "There was no way he could sack his main Cabinet rivals … he had to keep them on board because they led major factions in the party." Marnie sipped her drink.

"Well, whatever his motives, he's still there," said Michael, "as he's fond of reminding us. He's quite a decent chap, actually. And I expect he'll try to hang on till the very end before calling the General Election."

"I agree with you there. And the open divisions in their ranks will weaken them when they go the country."

"But they think people will have forgotten all this by then. The public has a short memory, Ralph. Mind you, I think this time they may have gone too far to get away with it. From what I hear, there are some very nasty things going on behind the scenes. You mark my words. It's not over yet, either."

When it was time for the two men to go to lunch, Marnie excused herself, and Ralph walked with her to Central Lobby while Michael chatted to the people at the next table in the Pugin Room.

"So it looks as if you're on the way to sorting out the business card. That should put an end to the matter."

"I hope the police will think so," said Marnie. She stopped and turned towards Ralph. "You know when you came in back there?"

"Oh yes, the *awkward situation* … What was that?"

"Apparently I had no right to be there unescorted, and I was about to be *thrown out* by the waiter when Malcolm Grant said I was his guest."

"Oh dear … I'm sorry you were put in that position."

"Yes, well, I was annoyed at first. It could've been very embarrassing. Michael should've realised. But it was interesting to see Malcolm Grant. You remember when we went to the carol service in St Margaret's … at the end when we were filing out, I saw a man in the back row in real distress. I'm sure he was in tears."

"You didn't mention it at the time," said Ralph.

"No, because you were ahead of me in the crowd and then someone wanted to talk to you outside. There seemed little point after we'd come out. Well, that man in the church … it was Malcolm Grant. I'm sure of it."

• • • • •

Emerging from the tube station in Little Venice, Marnie bought an *Evening Standard* from the news-stand on the corner. She was glad to clear her head, breathing in the cold winter air. The world around her seemed so simple and mundane compared with the plotting and jockeying in the

Houses of Parliament. She was relieved to be returning to the boat, with the prospect of the journey back up the Grand Union Canal to Knightly St John. But first, she had a call to make. It would be a quick visit, just long enough to say goodbye, hand over a small Christmas present and leave. She rang the doorbell at the house opposite *Sally Ann*'s mooring and was welcomed in by Mrs Jolly.

"A cup of tea before you go, Marnie?"

"Well, I really ought to be ..."

"I'll just boil the kettle. The fire's lit in the sitting room. I'll be with you in a moment. Oh, and I've made us a sandwich. You can't begin your journey on an empty stomach." Marnie surrendered and flopped into a comfortable armchair. Mrs Jolly came in a minute later carrying a tray.

"Are you feeling all right, my dear?"

"Yes, fine thanks. I'm well on the mend."

"Good, only I saw Gary this morning, and he thought you might be unwell."

"Did he say why?"

"Apparently you'd given him a blank cheque." Marnie laughed. "He said as soon as he'd filled your tank, he was going round to St Mary's Hospital to book you in for a brain transplant."

• • • • •

The next time Marnie was able to sink into a comfortable chair, she was several miles out of the centre of town. Dusk had fallen quickly as *Sally Ann* approached the boatyard at Uxbridge and Marnie was glad that she was well on her way and ready to go through the lock at first light. Supper was a bowl of hot soup – parsnip with a hint of curry spice – and a warmed roll, followed by a hunk of Wensleydale and a glass of Rioja. She felt a wave of contentment as she returned from checking the mooring ropes and pulled the steel doors shut to keep out the night cold. The aroma from the cooking was almost intoxicating after the hours spent on the chilly stern deck travelling through London's western suburbs. She lit the oil lamps in the galley and saloon and turned off the electric lights. Rather than listen to the early evening news programmes on the radio – she had had enough of politics for one day – she pushed a cassette into the tape machine and began supper to the accompaniment of Bach's fourth Brandenburg Concerto.

Making coffee, she spotted the newspaper and settled down for a lazy evening. Turning over the first page, there he was: Tim Edmonds stared out at her. The photo showed the MP looking drawn and troubled at the time of the scandal that had changed his life, but there was no disguising his good looks. The heading was 'A Life Full of Promise'. It was a quote from Malcolm Grant, "his staunchest friend and ally". The article revealed a privileged upbringing: the silver spoon, public school, Oxford. One page was organised like a scrap book of family photographs, with the big house in the country set in its own grounds, young Tim in Eton collar, in officer-cadet uniform, in white-tie and tails at a hunt ball with a society girl clinging to his arm; all the trappings of the upper classes.

Tim Edmonds had never known what it meant to lack anything. From university he had joined a City merchant bank owned by friends of the family. It was only a short step to nomination as a Conservative Party candidate and an eventual seat in the Commons. But then, after a flying start as PPS and junior whip, came the slide down the greasy pole for the young man who had so much. There was a blow-by-blow account of the divorce proceedings in which Edmonds had been cited and his subsequent disappearance from public view. For several weeks there had been no trace of him and it was widely assumed that he had gone abroad to escape media attention. Only afterwards was it revealed that he had been staying at the home of Malcolm Grant in one of the more remote areas of the Lake District. There was a photo of a house nestling among trees on a hillside overlooking one of the smaller northern lakes. It had been taken with a long lens and the caption explained that it stood about half a mile off the road along a private track.

Two whole pages were devoted to the story, with an account of the gradual climb back to favour of the disgraced MP. His wife had stood by him for a while despite everything, and Marnie found herself wondering what she would have done in her place. This scandal and Edmonds's disappearance had occurred shortly before the long summer recess, which had taken him out of the spotlight. Edmonds had not attended the party conference that autumn and there was the inevitable speculation that he would resign or be "encouraged" by the Tory hierarchy to quit.

The press had reported the "moral outrage" of leading members of the party, but this had stopped short of demanding his resignation. Some took the view Marnie herself had once expressed, that there was so much sleaze in the air that one mere divorce case seemed to make little difference, even if the wronged wife was the daughter of a Tory peer and the wronged husband a leading QC. Others were more pragmatic. The Conservatives had lost every by-election since 1983, they had ousted the redoubtable Margaret Thatcher in an internal *coup* and the new Prime Minister was trying to put the best face on the party in the run-up to a general election that most commentators thought they would lose. Nobody wanted a by-election that would probably depress the government's standing even further. Tim Edmonds was allowed to fade from view for the highest of motives … expediency.

Marnie poured herself a second cup of coffee and read on. The story outlined the MP's gradual return to public life. It was an extraordinary comeback that started in the most unpromising of settings. A by-election had been called following the death from a heart-attack of a popular Labour MP in a Yorkshire mining constituency. A young Tory hopeful had been selected to fight his first campaign without the slightest hope of winning or even keeping his deposit. Because of the popularity of the deceased MP and the shock of his sudden death, the government decided to mount only a token resistance and no major cabinet figures were going to take part. All the signs were that no one was willing to make a fight of it and, despite the reasons given by the leadership, there were murmurings that it looked as if they had no stomach for a confrontation and were throwing in the towel. Letters in the *Times* were asking what were the real reasons for not standing up to be counted, even if a victory was out of the question.

Then, without warning, Tim Edmonds had shown up at the local party offices as the campaign got underway and had begun simply by putting leaflets through doors along with the other party workers. He went out with the candidate offering him advice on tactics and briefing him on key issues, so that he was able to hold his own when faced with the most determined of hecklers. The "lad" spoke with respect of the deceased MP but asked for the right for another point of view to be heard. He even managed a few jokes at his own expense that raised a laugh at public meetings and he expressed the hope that the tellers would not merely have to weigh the Labour vote rather than count it on the day of the poll. When the word got round that Tim Edmonds was helping the "lad", people would turn up at meetings just to have a look at the man who had been front page news in the tabloids. The extra publicity raised interest in the election, raised the morale of the young Tory candidate and brought the full attention of the national media to the by-election that the Tories wanted to keep quiet. It was said that the leadership was furious and blamed Tim Edmonds for raising his head above the parapet and dragging them with him.

In the end, everyone praised the courage and dignity of the "lad", even though the result was the expected huge Labour majority. In his speech on the night of the declaration, the winner thanked his opponents for a fair fight and congratulated the young Tory on keeping his deposit. The next day, the serious press coverage centred on the role of Edmonds as the man willing to stand up for his party despite all the odds against them, while the tabloids called him "the only Tory with the guts to fight". A statement from Conservative Central Office described the result as "a moral victory of sorts" but made no mention of Tim Edmonds.

Marnie was surprised how interesting she found the story, and she read on to the end. From that day onwards Tim Edmonds became a stalwart of by-election campaigns, boosting the morale of the party even though they kept losing. By remaining in the background, he was able to put his experience at the disposal of the candidates. Simply by being there, he guaranteed media coverage and drew large audiences to meetings that would normally have attracted only a few of the party faithful. At the General Election he retained his own seat with an undiminished majority and was credited with influencing results in a number of key marginals.

When John Major surprised everyone by calling an election for the leadership of the party three years later while still in office as Prime Minister, Edmonds was one of the first to write a private letter offering to support him, "if it would not cause you embarrassment". The offer was accepted and Edmonds became a principal speech writer, working behind the scenes as part of the campaign team. His rehabilitation was complete with the announcement of the PM's victory over his rivals, and he was openly tipped in the press for a junior ministerial post at the next reshuffle.

Marnie finished her coffee and decided to have an early night. The occasional twinge reminded her that she was still not fully back to normal after the near-fatal injuries she had suffered not many months before. While she washed up, her thoughts were on the man she had found in the canal, on a life that had once again seemed full of promise. Malcolm Grant had made her wonder whether the death had been an accident after all. The smell of whisky, the evidence that it had not been a robbery ... The more she thought about it, the more uncertain she felt. But one thing was certain. In his career, in his private life and in his comeback, Tim Edmonds had made more than his share of enemies.

• • • • •

The next morning was heavily overcast with enough cloud cover to keep the canal from freezing, but there was a light wind with a cutting edge and Marnie was glad to pull on her ski clothes and get underway. In the silver and blue one-piece costume she knew was a strange sight, but it enabled her to keep going all day without discomfort and at that time of the year there were few to see her passing.

By the time she reached Rickmansworth the supermarket was open, and she tied up for a few minutes to take on fresh supplies. She used the mobile to call Faye Summers at Everett Parker Associates.

"*Dish?*" said Faye. "As in crockery?"

"More like *dish* as in short skirt," said Marnie.

"Not likely, not with Tim Edmonds around. Oh, sorry, I didn't mean to speak ill of the dead, but even so ..."

"Was he a problem? I thought he was a reformed character."

"To be fair, Marnie, he didn't actually try anything, but I always made sure I went with Hannah. He was one of those men who somehow makes you think twice before closing the door behind you. Mid-life crisis? You know what I mean?"

"Sure. We've all met them. But if he never tried anything ..."

"Well, he ..."

"What?"

"He did ask if I could go round one evening with the design and have a drink with him."

"And you went?"

"He said he was going on holiday and wanted to finalise everything before leaving. I didn't have much choice, and as it was in the evening I couldn't take Hannah. So I agreed to a quick meeting and said I couldn't stay long because I was seeing someone afterwards. That was true, actually."

"So what happened?"

"Well ... it could've got awkward. He asked me to stay for another drink and when I said I had to be going, he wouldn't take no for an answer. Anyway, I was just wondering how to leave without causing a fuss, when the door-bell rang. It was this other MP. All unexpected. I chatted politely for a minute or two and then got out."

"Was the other MP Malcolm Grant by any chance?"

"Yes, it was! How did you know that?"

"Just a guess," said Marnie. "It was in the paper that they were friends."

"That was him. Malcolm Grant. Very nice man. Now *he* was a different sort altogether, what my mum would call a *gentleman.*"

The lady is my guest, Simon, she thought. To Faye she said, "A rescuer of damsels in distress."

"That's right."

"Oh well," said Marnie, "Time to be on my way. Have a good –"

"Wait a minute! Did you say *dish,* Marnie? What about *dish* as in satellite?"

"How do you mean?"

"That was one of the problems we had. Tim Edmonds asked us to get a satellite dish installed. Said he wanted to get news programmes from Brussels ... more like hard porn from Holland, I thought ... Because his flat was in a listed building just by Regents Park, the planners wouldn't allow it. He was really annoyed."

"Ah," said Marnie. "That could be it … yes. It all makes sense."

• • • • •

For two days Marnie travelled steadily, taking *Sally Ann* up the long climb away from London and the Thames Valley, working her way through lock after lock to the Tring summit and the long pound in isolated, beautiful woodland over the Chiltern Hills. As the boat chugged along, Marnie thought about Tim Edmonds. He seemed to dominate her thinking for mile after mile, images of him haunting every waking hour, On one quiet stretch of water she phoned the police in London and told Inspector Bruere her idea about the *dish* on her business card. It made less impact than she had expected, and he only grudgingly accepted her solution to the mystery. She wondered if he was disappointed at not having something to suspect about her.

It was during the steep descent on the other side that Marnie became aware that something had changed. The weather had been grey for most of the time, with here and there an occasional glimpse of sun, and she had concentrated on managing the boat at a steady pace, the best way to make progress. She came upon a series of locks in her favour between the Wendover and Aylesbury arms and felt elated at her ability to run the boat, *her* boat, single-handed. While waiting for *Sally* to descend in a lock chamber, Marnie suddenly realised that she was no longer aching in her joints, no longer stiff in her movements. The journey, like her solo voyage two summers earlier, had made a new woman of her and she wanted to leap in the air and shout it aloud. *Sally Ann* had worked her old magic!

With Christmas just a few days off, Marnie had telephoned Anne at breakfast time and told her she would be in Leighton Buzzard by mid-morning, all being well. The plan was for them to take *Sally Ann* north together, sharing the rest of the journey. They expected to reach Glebe Farm on Christmas Eve, and Marnie would take Anne home that day to her parents. It seemed an odd arrangement, but Anne was keen to have another trip on the boat, Marnie welcomed her company and the journey would pass more quickly with Anne to help at the locks.

On that day the sun was ghosting in and out of the clouds, the temperature if anything colder, but the brightness in the air and the anticipation of meeting her friend raised her spirits. Chugging through open country, Marnie ran her finger up the line of the canal in the cruising guide and calculated three more locks in the next few miles before reaching the town. There she would take on water and tie up for an hour to buy provisions at the huge supermarket a short walk from the cut.

Ahead of her, Marnie saw the bridge by Slapton wharf. It was immediately followed by the first of the three locks. She hoped it would be in her favour with the gates already partly open. But the gates were closed and she pulled *Sally Ann* into the bank and made her secure between the bridge and the lock with a centre rope firmly attached to a bollard. She walked briskly to the lock, quickly turned the handle to raise the paddles and looked out over the countryside while she waited for the water to fill the chamber. When it was ready, she pulled open one of the gates and straightened up without a twinge. It felt good to be – *What!?*

Her mouth opened and Marnie was transfixed, unable for a few seconds to move. Coming steadily towards the lock on the exact course for entering the chamber, was *Sally Ann*. Marnie ran down the towpath, unclear as to how she would get on board to avert a disaster, at a loss to know how the boat had managed to free herself from her mooring rope, engage gear and steer herself away from the bank. Within a few yards though ... Marnie skidded to a halt, turned round and walked casually up to perch on the balance beam with her back to the boat. As *Sally* slid quietly into the lock, Marnie called over her shoulder.

"You might as well put the kettle on. We're probably both ready for coffee." In reply she heard a shriek of laughter and looking round she saw Anne, in red and white ski-suit, standing at the tiller smiling broadly.

• • • • •

That evening by the light of the oil lamps, Marnie was chuckling to herself as she put away the dishes after supper.

"Did you say something, Marnie?" Anne was carefully pouring water into the cafetière.

"No. I was thinking of you hijacking *Sally* like that and steering her into the lock. You had me fooled for a second."

"Just a second?"

"Well, two seconds, then," she said grudgingly. "You know, it was at the bridge after that one that we first met. You were trying to be invisible then, as I recall." It was a measure of how much things had changed that she felt she could mention that day without it causing pain. Anne had been running away from home to save her family the expense of feeding her when her father was made redundant. She had hidden on the bridge but Marnie had spotted her and eventually invited her on board for lunch.

Anne must have been reading her friend's mind. "We've come a long way since then, haven't we?" she said.

"Good times, bad times," said Marnie philosophically.

"Mostly good, some brilliant," said Anne. "And now here we are looking forward to our first Christmas at Glebe Farm. I feel as excited as a two-year-old." She pulled out the coffee table in the saloon. "Do you want this newspaper, Marnie, or shall I put it in the bin?"

• • • • •

Saturday 24 December

The following day was cloudier and less cold as they set off on the last leg of the journey back to the village they both thought of as home. The clouds grew thicker and denser, spreading a morning twilight across the country, and Marnie and Anne settled into a steady routine, waiting for rain that never came. When it was Marnie's turn to huddle at the tiller, Anne kept them supplied with hot drinks. At locks, Anne steered while Marnie worked the gates and paddles. Chugging along between locks, they chatted about Christmas arrangements, about the next phase of the works at Glebe Farm, about the plans for projects on their client list.

They talked intermittently about Tim Edmonds, his life, work and death.

Anne had read the article in the newspaper the previous evening and had spotted a reference to the fact that the police were still looking for a tramp who might have witnessed the 'incident'. Their description of the man they were seeking could have been any tramp anywhere.

Marnie filled in the rest of the story: the word *dish* on her business card; how she had met Malcolm Grant; her doubts about whether it was murder or really an accident after too much to drink. To lighten the conversation, she told Anne what Mrs Jolly had said about Gary thinking she needed a brain transplant after she had given him the blank cheque. Marnie was glad that they had the care of the boat to occupy them, the daily routines of keeping the engine running smoothly, checking the batteries, attending to the stern gland, securing the mooring ropes. For long stretches there were practical boating matters to claim their attention, the demands of navigating a fourteen-tonne craft through a winter landscape from early morning till night-fall. But again and again their thoughts returned to the body in the canal.

At midday on Christmas Eve, under a lowering sky, they negotiated the last lock and soon saw up ahead the graceful curve of the final bridge before Knightly St John. Within minutes they made out the roofline of Glebe Farm through the leafless branches of the trees in the spinney. As they approached home, Marnie turned to Anne.

"Let's put all that business aside now. Let's concentrate on making this a good Christmas. Here and at Ralph's cottage, we'll just get away from it all and forget about what's happened. Put it all out of our minds ..."

"Oh yes," said Anne. "Yes, let's do that." She became thoughtful. "Although ... I'm rather worried about you, Marnie. I thought you were fully recovered, but ... now I'm wondering if you might have had a major relapse."

Marnie protested. "I'm fine. Never felt better."

Anne shook her head. "I mean, giving Gary a blank cheque ... that's not a good sign! I fear the worst. I'd better order the forms to file for bankruptcy."

Laughing, Marnie put an arm round Anne's shoulder and they brought *Sally Ann* home to her dock at Glebe Farm in a flurry of sleet that they persuaded themselves was snow.

Part 08

Saturday 24 December

They secured *Sally Ann* in her dock and walked through the spinney, holdalls slung over their shoulders like seafarers, crunching the leaves underfoot, taking in deep breaths of cold fresh air, surrounded by silence.

"Oh, it's *so* good to be back here!" Marnie said. "I wonder where Dolly is ... over at the Burtons', I expect. Now, we can look forward to just peace and quiet ... a nice *lazy* time."

"Er ..." Anne began.

Marnie looked suspicious. "Er what? You've got one of those ... *looks*."

Anne pulled a slip of paper out of her top pocket and waved it gently, smiling.

"Not a *list*!" said Marnie. "Don't tell me it's your Do-It-Yourself Guide to Christmas."

"Just a few things we have to do," said Anne brightly.

They reached the office barn and Marnie put the key in the lock. "Stand by for the icebox," she muttered. She pushed open the door and went in. "Wow!" The office was warm and there were vases of chrysanthemums on the desks. Small holly wreaths laced with gold ribbon decorated the walls, and Christmas cards were strung around the beams. A swag of red tinsel draped itself nonchalantly across the photocopier. In the centre of the room stood a magnificent tree decorated entirely with gold and silver baubles, lit all over with tiny white lights.

"Blimey!" said Marnie.

• • • • •

There were more flurries of sleet and snow all afternoon and into the evening, and they swirled across the road making confusing patterns in the beams of the headlights when Marnie swung the Rover into the lane that led down to Ralph's cottage by the river. The trees and bushes pressed in on her in the darkness as she trundled the last hundred metres of the journey and pulled up under the low eaves at the side of the house. A security light came on, revealing the stone cottage with its porch covered in straggling growth that would be a mass of roses in the summer. Ralph opened the door, welcoming Marnie into the warmth.

"Welcome to my humble abode. Good timing. I only got here five minutes ago, myself. Supper will be ready in about half an hour. Let's have a drink by the fire."

"Poetry," said Marnie. In the sitting room Ralph took her coat as the first wisps of smoke began curling up the inglenook chimney and flames played around the kindling. "Is there anything I can do?" she said.

Ralph pointed towards the window and lit a candle on the low table in the middle of the room. "If you want some exercise, you can switch on the Christmas tree lights. After that, sit down and relax. You need to conserve your energy for a big decision."

"Easy. Three lumps of ice and go easy on the tonic," said Marnie. She admired Ralph's tree, but had to admit to herself that it was not quite up to Anne's standard. She flopped into the cushions of a deep armchair and stretched her legs, while Ralph went out to put her car in the carport. The cottage was just right for Christmas, with beamy ceilings, restful table lamps, shelves full of books, deep windowsills and chintz curtains. It had central heating and all mod cons, backed up by the traditional comfort of the inglenook fire. She heard Ralph come back, closing the front door to shut out the cold night. He went straight through to the kitchen and sounds reached her of glasses tinkling. Ralph had asked Marnie to let him provide everything, and she had agreed.

It was a cosy house and surprisingly homely, given that Ralph spent so much time away living in college for most of the week. Presumably this had been their home when Ralph's wife was alive. Perhaps it was strange for him to have Marnie there, or perhaps it was all so long ago that it did not occur to him to make comparisons. She yawned.

"I knew you were tired," said Ralph coming into the room armed with a tray of drinks and nibbles. Marnie's mouth snapped shut.

"It's a fair cop, guv," she said, taking the gin and tonic that Ralph offered her.

He put down small bowls of pistachio nuts, olives and cashews, checked that the fire was drawing well and lowered himself into the armchair opposite. They drank a toast to Christmas and absent friends.

"Ooh, this is *good*," said Marnie. "Just the right balance."

"For dinner, I've tried to keep it simple," said Ralph. "In my family the tradition was always to have fish on Christmas Eve, usually salmon. But I've opted for trout instead ... to start a new tradition. Baked with herbs and flaked almonds. Is that okay?"

"Absolutely."

"And a bottle of Orvieto to go with it?"

"Brilliant."

Ralph smiled at Marnie. "You're easy to please."

"Any woman will tell you that the best meal of all is the one cooked for you by someone else. Anyway, it sounds delicious and I know how good you are in the kitchen."

"I suspected you might just be too tired to cook for yourself at the moment."

"Yes, but I'm a hundred per cent better than I was. Thanks to good old *Sally*. That trip on the boat has restored me. I feel almost as good as new ... even after all the running around today."

They took another sip from their drinks and stared contentedly into the flames. Marnie turned and pulled something out of her bag, handing it to Ralph.

"What's this?" he said.

"I thought you might like to see Anne's Christmas tree and decorations. I was so impressed, I took Polaroids of them."

He looked mightily impressed. "When did she do all this?"

"She got her dad to drive her to Knightly before I picked her up."

"That tree's a masterpiece," said Ralph. "It's *amazing*. Isn't it rather a waste, though, as you're going to be away?"

"She'd thought of that. She told Jill and Alex they could have it as soon as we left. She just wanted us to have one because it was our first Christmas at Glebe Farm."

"I'm sorry not to have seen her," said Ralph.

"Never mind. You'll see her soon enough. I needed to take her home after we'd been for a drink with Jill and Alex. Anne had got them to switch the heating on yesterday to warm the place up and come back this morning with the tree so that everything was ready for our return. She's organised them to feed Dolly, too, while we're here."

"That girl is a genius," said Ralph. "She ought to be running the country."

"She is," said Marnie. "Hadn't you noticed?"

As if by a pre-arranged signal, Marnie's mobile began to ring in her bag on the floor beside her while at the same time the house phone joined in. Ralph got up to take the call in the kitchen.

"It's probably Anne now, checking up on us," Marnie muttered as she pressed the button. "Hallo, Marnie here."

"Good evening, Mrs Walker. This is Chief Inspector Bartlett. Sorry to bother you on Christmas Eve."

Marnie froze. It was a voice from the past, the officer who had led the murder enquiry that summer. "Hallo, Mr Bartlett. This is a surprise. What can I do for you?"

"We've been contacted by DCI Bruere at Lisson Grove. It's about ..."

"I'm sure I can guess what it's about."

"Yes. Bruere explained about your involvement and asked me to mention something to you."

"I don't think of myself as *involved*," said Marnie. "All I did was find the body."

"Quite. Well, he asked me to let you know that they've found the tramp who probably witnessed what happened."

"Thank goodness for that."

"Not really, Mrs Walker. They found him drowned in the cut at Limehouse."

"Oh, how awful. That's very sad. Do they know who he was?"

"They just said it was a tramp."

"*Just a tramp* ... he was a human being. He must have meant something to somebody, some time."

"I suppose so. The only name he was known by was Dodge. That's as much as you get with these people. All a bit academic now, though."

"Yes, now that he's dead. The poor devil."

"Fraid so. Will you be at home over the holiday, Mrs Walker?"

"No. I'll ... I'll be in Oxfordshire, at Murton, for a few days, until the 28th. I've got my mobile with me, of course."

"Just in case," said Bartlett. "Well, sorry to interrupt your evening. Good-bye. Oh, er ... happy Christmas."

Ralph came in smiling as Marnie slipped the phone back in her bag. "Was it Anne? Ah, no. I can see by your face that it wasn't." Marnie explained. "Well," said Ralph, "there's nothing we can do about it. It's a sad business all round. The best we can do is put it aside and let the police sort it out."

"Yes. It's the only way to cope. Who was that on your phone?"

"Randall Hughes. He just wanted to agree what time we're seeing him on the twenty-eighth. And he said he's looking forward to seeing us and wants to show us something he's done since becoming Rural Dean. Says he has a new lease of life. I suppose that's something we all have in common."

"So it was just a social call," said Marnie.

"Yes, just to wish us a happy Christmas."

"That's what Bartlett wished us," said Marnie.

"And that's what we're going to have." Ralph got up to check on the trout.

• • • • •

On Christmas Day Marnie woke to find Ralph already up. Sounds of activity in the kitchen reached her from downstairs. She drew back the bedroom curtains and looked out on a grey misty morning, the shrubs and trees in the garden dripping with dew, and spiders' webs among the branches. The mist was heavier away to the right of the garden where the river ran.

From the landing she called down and Ralph appeared in the hall. He smiled up at her. "Good morning and happy Christmas!"

"Morning, Ralph. Thank you. Same to you."

"How are you feeling? You look wonderful."

She laughed. "Too early to tell, but probably fine. Have I time to take a shower before breakfast?"

"Go ahead. I'll have it ready in fifteen minutes. Okay?"

"You're too good to be true."

In contrast to the antiquity of the house, the shower was state-of-the-art, with an adjustable head that ranged from a fine spray to powerful jets. Marnie luxuriated in her favourite Chanel shower lotion and used the jets to massage her back. The new short hairstyle was shampooed in a minute and she emerged from the bathroom towelling it dry, ready to face the world. From the wardrobe she took out a pair of black trousers and a white silk shirt and as she dressed, she became aware of the smell of bacon drifting up from below.

Ralph called out that he had laid breakfast in the conservatory, and Marnie walked in to find lighted candles on the table and a small pile of boxes wrapped in gold and silver paper at her place. He followed her in, carrying an ice bucket with a bottle of champagne.

"Now that's what I *call* a breakfast," said Marnie, kissing him warmly.

"You don't think it spoils the orange juice to dilute it, then?" said Ralph. He popped the cork and poured them each a Bucks Fizz. They sipped, kissed again and took their places at the table.

"This is wonderful," said Marnie. "I feel completely spoilt."

"Good. That's my master plan. Now, decisions again! Would you like breakfast or brunch?"

"I'm easy," said Marnie. "When would you prefer the turkey and pud? If we can't decide, I can ring Anne and get her to fax us a list."

Ralph laughed. "I knew you'd be lost without her to keep you organised. On the whole, given a choice, I think I'd rather prefer to have dinner this evening."

"So brunch followed by a walk in the country?" said Marnie. "Great."

Ralph went out to put grapefruit under the grill. As soon as he had gone Marnie nipped into the sitting room, took a small box from her bag and returned quickly to put it on his plate. She sat back to sip her drink and enjoy the view of the garden as the sun tried to break through the mist and clouds.

"Ready in just a few minutes," said Ralph. "Can I top you up?"

Marnie extended her glass towards him. "Just the champagne, please. One shouldn't overdo the orange juice on an empty stomach."

"Quite right. Are you going to open a present?"

Marnie picked up the box lying on top of the pile. It was about a foot wide, one inch deep and heavier than she expected. Intrigued, she undid the ribbon and gently eased it open while Ralph watched her face. Her mouth widened into a grin.

"It's perfect," she said, looking down at the model of a double canal lock, with moving balance beams, in polished brass. Earlier in the year Ralph had given her two model working boats in brass from the same series. "*Magdalen* and *Balliol* will have somewhere to sit. I'll keep it on my desk. It's gorgeous, Ralph. Thank you." She got up to kiss him.

"Open that one next," he said, pointing to a parcel that felt like, and proved to be, a bundle of books. There were four of them from the same publisher, all written by women who had served on working narrowboats during the war.

"The 'idle women'," said Marnie. "That's a really inspired choice."

"I wondered if you might find a mention of Iris Winterburn in there somewhere," said Ralph, referring to the old lady, one of the 'idle women', that Marnie had once met on her travels.

"I expect I shall. She was quite a character. Now, it's time you opened *your* present."

The package was small like a box for jewellery. Ralph untied the ribbon and pulled apart the sellotape. It was a watch, but not like the slimline version that Marnie knew he wore every day. This one was chunkier, with a case like pale bronze, and a tan leather strap. It had extra buttons on the rim and small dials for timing. The numbers were bold and the hands thick and luminous. It was guaranteed waterproof to a depth of a hundred metres.

"Marnie, you *really* shouldn't. It's … I don't know what to say. It's magnificent."

"Oh, it just fell out of the cornflakes packet and I thought of you." Ralph laughed, shaking his head. Marnie went on. "Actually, I thought it would be right for when you're on the boat. I know there aren't any canals a hundred metres deep, but at least it should be waterproof in any situation you're likely to meet. And you can time sections to plan journeys." For an instant Marnie saw the gold Rolex dripping wet on the wrist of Tim Edmonds in the canal and she blinked quickly to dispel the image, hoping that Ralph had not noticed.

Ralph undid the strap on his Omega and immediately put on the new watch to admire it. Suddenly he exclaimed. "Oh my god! The grapefruit!" He dashed out and Marnie heard the clattering of the grill pan in the kitchen. He returned looking relieved. "That was close. Another minute and … disaster. It was the thought of timing that reminded me."

Despite Ralph's misgivings, the grapefruit was good, enlivened by a dash of sherry and a layer of caramelised spiced brown sugar. While they ate, they made plans for their walk. Between courses Marnie was invited to open her last present, or so she thought. The smallest of her boxes contained a pair of pearl earrings that Ralph said was in honour of the new hairstyle. Marnie was intrigued to notice that the writing inside the box seemed to be Japanese and she remarked on this. To her surprise, Ralph looked perplexed.

"You may find it hard to believe this, Marnie."

"Try me. Did you buy them in Japan?"

"I didn't buy them at all. They were a gift." Strange thoughts raced through her mind. Could they have belonged to Ralph's wife? "I was given them five years ago ... by the Emperor of Japan."

"The ...?"

"Yes."

Marnie laughed in surprise and relief. "I didn't know he had toy-boys!"

"I'm serious. They were given to me when I went to Tokyo to collect a prize. Obviously, they assumed I would have a wife back home and one of the presents was these earrings. Until now I had no one to give them to."

"Well, you have now," Marnie said softly.

• • • • •

During their walk the sun made a partly successful attempt to appear. They had begun by setting off across a field and soon their route led them to the towpath by the canal between Oxford and Banbury. This was a deserted landscape, the canal wandering along a contour line between low hills that rose on all sides. For the first part of their journey they had walked arm in arm, but the path by the water was narrow and they went in single file, Marnie leading the way.

After brunch they had spent most of the morning in the sitting room with a blazing fire. There had been phone calls to and from a variety of friends and relatives, but otherwise it had been for both of them an uncharacteristically lazy time. Marnie had asked Ralph if he was at a loose end when he was not working.

"I suppose so, yes. I'm not really accustomed to having free time. Work has until now been the most important thing in my life. Even when Laura was alive I always spent most of the time working; so did she."

"That's fine if it's fulfilling," said Marnie. "I understand that."

"Up to a point it's fine," said Ralph. "But I must say I feel different after all that happened back in the summer."

"You feel differently about things?"

"Of course ... especially about you, Marnie. It isn't like my relationship with Laura. You're a more dynamic character, more active, in many ways more exciting ..." Marnie raised an eyebrow. "I didn't mean it like that ... well, yes I did mean it like that, I suppose. But I also meant you're more ... varied, capable ... not just an ideas person ... you're more active."

"Am I? I've never thought about it."

"You remind me of the 'idle women' on the boats in the war. You're the sort of person who can take care of herself in any situation."

"Which is how I came to be almost murdered and ended up in intensive care."

Ralph shrugged. "That can happen when you take risks." Realising that this conversation was likely to lead to upsetting memories, he added, "Were many of the idle women injured, actually?"

"I don't think so, but there were one or two near misses. At least I think that's what Iris Winterburn told me. We'll have to read the books you gave me."

They had walked for almost an hour when Ralph remarked that they had not seen a single soul all day. "Where is everybody?"

"It's obvious," said Marnie. "This is a major religious holiday."

"Of course," said Ralph. "So everyone is slumped comatose in front of the telly, wishing they hadn't had that second lot of Christmas pudding."

"Exactly. But you missed out one detail … they're probably watching a war film … a traditional Yuletide activity."

"*Inactivity*," said Ralph. "But you're right. I've never understood that. Very odd."

They stopped to decide on the rest of their walk by a lock beside a bridge two hundred years old, opposite a lock-keeper's cottage. In a window of the cottage stood a small Christmas tree with coloured lights flashing. The setting looked like a picture from a British Waterways calendar. Their alternatives were to retrace their steps or to go over the bridge and head off on a circuit that would take them through meadow and woodland in a loop back to Murton. They opted to stay by the canal and walk back the way they had come.

Standing there, Marnie thought back to the last time she had stood on a towpath by a bridge on a canal. For a few seconds she could see Tim Edmonds lying in the water and hoped Ralph was not reading her mind. He was not.

"Even after all this time, Marnie, I still get strange feelings when I look at the canal."

"In what way?"

"About the night I tried to kill myself. Now, looking back, I can't imagine what made me try to do it. I somehow feel that memory is there between us … spoiling our relationship."

"If I hadn't come along when I did, there wouldn't be any relationship to spoil. Anyway, who says our relationship is spoilt?"

"I just wish that incident wasn't there in our past …"

Marnie turned towards Ralph, taking hold of both his arms and looking up into his face. "Listen, Ralph, that is just the point. It is in the past. We can't change it. Don't keep looking back the whole time or you'll spoil the present and damage the future. Whatever that future might be, it starts now. Oh God, I sound like something that fell out of a Christmas cracker."

Ralph, who had been frowning while she spoke, suddenly burst into laughter and hugged her to him. Marnie laughed too, but inside herself she was annoyed that Ralph harked back again and again to an incident that she could see was obviously best forgotten; or at least not mentioned.

"Marnie …"

"I know what you're going to say, Ralph. But we have to put the whole thing out of our minds, put it down once and for all and agree never to talk about it again. Otherwise we're never going to break away from it."

"You're absolutely right," said Ralph. "It's time we, or perhaps I mean *I*, put it aside. Goodness knows, we have enough to keep us occupied in our lives as they are."

"That's how I feel, too," said Marnie. They linked arms and began walking slowly back along the path.

"Actually, Marnie, that isn't what I was going to say."

"Oh?"

He shrugged casually. "No. I was going to ask how you'd feel about marrying me."

• • • • •

Dusk was already falling by the time they returned to the cottage and, with a skill born of long practice, Ralph had smoke coming from the chimney at about the same time that steam was coming from the spout of the kettle. Marnie went upstairs to change out of her walking clothes. She put on a dress of blue silk and tried the pearl earrings. They looked good, and she went down to find the fire crackling, candles lit and the aroma of coffee from the pot standing on the table. Ralph followed her into the sitting room carrying an armful of logs that he dropped into the basket in the inglenook.

"Everything okay?" he said.

"Absolutely. You seem to have it all under control. I'm impressed."

Ralph poured coffee. "If everything in life could be so simple ..." He handed Marnie a cup. "Ah ... the earrings. They suit you. Are they all right? I'm not sure how you judge that sort of thing."

"I think 'exquisite' would describe them quite well, Ralph. They're much more than all right. I've put them on because of the special occasion."

"I didn't think you regarded Christmas as *very* special ... being an agnostic."

"I didn't mean that. I meant you talking about marriage."

"*That* special occasion. Right. Of course, I realise it's not as simple as running off to Gretna Green or asking a ship's captain to do the honours ..."

"*Narrowboat* captain in our case ..."

"Naturally. I hadn't thought of that." He knelt down to deal with the coffee.

"Now that's more like it," said Marnie. "A traditional proposal."

"You wouldn't be making fun of me, by any chance?"

Marnie slipped down to join Ralph, kneeling on the floor. She put her arms round him. "No. I'm not. And I agree with you that in our case things aren't simple." She kissed him lightly and got up to take her seat.

Still kneeling, Ralph handed her coffee. "I knew beyond any doubt how I felt about you even before I saw you lying there in the intensive care unit. Realising that you might not make it was unbearable." He shuddered. "How to resolve things is the conundrum. The last thing I wanted was to put pressure on you. The main priority was for you to recover."

"Which I have. Fully. I feel like a new woman."

"So do I," said Ralph, grinning. Marnie stuck her tongue out. He went on. "But our circumstances are more complicated than most people's. Between the two of us we have three homes, two boats and two careers."

"And one cat," said Marnie.

"Of course," said Ralph. "Given a simple choice, I'd ask you to marry me tomorrow ..."

"What's the matter with today?"

"The churches are closed. It's a Bank Holiday. And more to the point ... today, speaking metaphorically, you have things to do. I think we can only take one step at a time and try to work it out as we go along ... if that's acceptable to you."

"Yes. Absolutely it is." She took a sip of the coffee and stared into the flames.

• • • • •

Christmas evening was mainly spent over a long dinner in the conservatory, the light from the candles reflecting off the glass panes all around them and the glow from the fire visible in the background through the French windows. Ralph had found a long-forgotten CD of carols sung by Magdalen College Choir and the music drifted through the house like incense. Conversation was fixed firmly on the future with no harking back to the past. They prepared dinner together, working side by side in the country kitchen for the first time.

While Marnie chopped vegetables, Ralph occupied himself at the other end of the workbench. She found herself stealing glances at the man who had asked her to spend the rest of their lives together and she wondered how it could be organised. Was he the right person? They had known each other a relatively short time. But in that time both of them had come close to death and Marnie found that that helped focus the mind on essentials. Now here they were, quietly working side by side on the most basic domestic tasks like a married couple. Marnie hesitated over a Brussels sprout. Was this a panic attack? Was she ready to give up her career and move in as the wife of an Oxford don, going to sherry parties at the Warden's Lodge, dressing up for formal dinners where grace was said in Latin, having to entertain visiting professors whose special area was obscure and unpronounceable? She sighed and immediately tried to camouflage it with vigorous slicing that reduced the sprout to a pile of green shavings. She hastily pushed them to the side of the chopping board and took another. From the corner of her eye she saw Ralph half turn in her direction.

"Marnie?" He leaned against the workbench, looking thoughtful, holding a carton of cream. She waited. "I think it would be difficult for us to be together, I mean *live* together in the normally accepted way … you know …" He made a gesture with his free hand like the Queen waving from the back of a limousine.

"You mean being boringly conventional in a house somewhere?" she suggested.

"That sort of thing, yes. Or at least in our present circumstances."

"Well, given that we live about forty miles apart, that seems like a reasonable assumption."

"So something would have to change. Wouldn't it?"

"I suppose it would." She wondered where this was leading and had the growing suspicion that they were about to reach a turning point. "Do you have something in mind?"

"How about a glass of muscadet?"

"As a temporary measure it sounds okay to me." Ralph took a bottle from the fridge and pulled the cork. He passed a glass to Marnie and they admired the pale liquid. They both took a sip and Ralph turned back to his task, which seemed to involve pieces of smoked fish.

"Ralph, I have the distinct impression that our conversation did not quite reach its end. Or were you being enigmatic?"

"I was wondering how to explain what was on my mind." He took another sip of wine. "Do you know much about life in an Oxford college?"

"Er, well, I think I can guess … from what I've seen so far."

"Would it disappoint you if I weren't a professor there?"

"Are you planning to move?" Marnie realised that this could be a bigger issue than she had imagined. She knew that Ralph had been offered jobs in America, and she tried to grapple with the idea so that she would be prepared to give a sensible reaction.

"Hang on just a second," said Ralph. He quickly stuffed some ingredients into ramekins, poured on some cream and covered the top with grated cheese. He put the ramekins into the Aga, rinsed his hands and wiped them on a towel. "Ten minutes," he muttered, setting the timer. "Marnie, come upstairs."

Bewildered and without speaking, she followed him up to the landing where he led her into a small room without putting the light on. "I've had invitations like this before," she said. Ralph pressed the light switch. Standing in the middle of the room was a tall object covered with a sheet. "On second thoughts," she said, "I don't think I have had invitations like this before …"

"Pull the sheet off," said Ralph. "It's for you."

Muttering to herself, "I've always wanted a sheet," Marnie tugged carefully to reveal … a long-case clock. It seemed to be made of oak and the face was painted with scenes from country activities in each season. Ralph stepped forward.

"Do you see this picture here?" He pointed at a small illustration in the corner near seven o'clock. It showed what appeared to be a wagon piled high with hay, passing through tall grass. "Look at it close up."

Marnie craned her head forward. "Is it a boat, Ralph?"

"I think it's on a canal, possibly taking the harvest to the mill. I thought it would be just right for you and Glebe Farm."

Marnie put her arms round Ralph and kissed him warmly. "It's magnificent. I know the very place to put it in the hall. But it must have cost a *fortune*."

Ralph shook his head. "It didn't, actually. The case cost nothing. It was in the attic when we came here. I bought the workings in a junk shop for ten quid and got them repaired by a clockmaker in Abingdon."

"You sure know how to impress a girl," said Marnie.

• • • • •

The first course was the smoked fish in a cream sauce topped with melted cheese. It went well with the muscadet.

"Ralph, what made you suddenly think of the clock when you were starting to talk about possibly not being an Oxford don?"

"Well, it was the thought that you're very much based at Knightly St John, and I wasn't expecting you to give all that up. The clock just seemed to fit in perfectly with that part of your life."

"What about *your* life?"

Ralph sighed. "It's complicated, but there might be a chance of changing direction. I've not completely made up my mind, you understand, but I'd like to know what you think."

"I don't suppose this would have anything to do with your sabbatical on the canal, would it?" said Marnie. "Spending time on a boat can have a strange way of changing your attitude to life. Look what happened to me."

"Quite. And yes, in a way, that is part of the story. Another part was seeing you in hospital, thinking you were going to die. And then there was the thought that I've had the same job for all my professional life so far."

"So what would be the next step for you?" said Marnie. "Would you become head of a college, perhaps?"

Ralph shook his head. "Not really my scene, running a college, chairing committees, administration. Of course, there are all sorts of compensations ..."

"Such as?"

"Being on government bodies, travelling, meeting interesting people ..."

"But you do all that at the moment."

"Yes. Without being tied down."

"What is it you're thinking of doing, then?" said Marnie, wondering if being married would not seem to Ralph like another way of being tied down.

· · · · ·

Outside the air pressure was falling and thick clouds were piling up all over the countryside, dropping handfuls of wet sleet on the garden. Ralph put a few more logs on the fire and they settled down to roast duck, helped on its way by a bottle of claret.

"This is marvellous," said Marnie.

"Yes. I got a case from the merchants who supply the college cellars. You can't find this in the shops. It comes direct from a small chateau in Pauillac."

"No, not just the wine ... everything ... the whole meal ..."

"Good. Try and leave some room for dessert. It's my *pièce de résistance*."

Marnie was intrigued but could not remember anything else on the workbench and there was nothing in the Aga. She smiled across the table at Ralph. "So ... you were telling me about your mid-life crisis ..."

"No I wasn't!" Ralph protested. "At least, I don't think that's what it is. I just ... feel like a change."

"And you've had some interesting offers."

"Yes. I've got two books lined up after the one I'm working on now. My publisher's made me a good offer ... a *very* good offer, in fact. One of them could involve a TV programme, or even a series. And there are lecture tours on the continent and in the States, as well as consultancy work."

"It sounds as if you'll have a busy time."

Ralph shrugged. "That's nothing new."

"But you'd have to give up your chair at Oxford?"

"Not necessarily ..."

· · · · ·

Christmas that year was the most indolent time Marnie or Ralph had known for as far back as either of them could recall. For people accustomed to living their lives by the clock, working against deadlines, always having to think ahead to the next meeting, the chance to spend two whole days with nothing more to take into account than the time of the next meal and whether to go for a walk or stay by the fire was more than a luxury.

There were two main topics of conversation. The first was Ralph's *pièce de résistance*, his Christmas pudding made of ice cream. Marnie had been surprised when he had announced the pudding and then turned towards the freezer. It was a masterpiece and he would only drop vague hints about its recipe, a secret formula known only to generations of Lombards stretching back to the Middle Ages.

The second was how to manage the future. The more they thought about it, the clearer it became that Oxford was as central to Ralph's career as Glebe Farm was to Marnie's. If the university was willing to let him remain as a visiting professor with an agreed number of lectures each year, he would have the advantage of the title and prestige coupled with the freedom to pursue a wider range of activities. Marnie was worried that he might be thinking of giving up his life at Oxford on her account.

"No. Not really," he had said over coffee and brandy by the fire after dinner. "The other day I was sorting out one of the drawers in my desk. You wouldn't believe the clutter. I came across an old envelope that I'd put there when I moved years ago. On the back of it I had written a list of what I wanted to achieve while at All Saints. There were six items and the last remaining was … I know it sounds like vanity … to become a professor." He shrugged. "So that was that. I'd done it all. No better time for a change of direction."

"Vanity, ambition, call it what you like," said Marnie, "we all need something to motivate us."

"Not all of us are lucky enough to find that something," said Ralph. "And then for some, like the people I deal with, it can become an overriding passion, even an obsession."

"The politicians, you mean."

Ralph nodded. "Yes. Among others. There are also media people, celebrities in different fields, and academics of course, all striving to reach the heights as they see them. It starts as a goal in life and ends as the only thing they have to hold on to. You must see it in your profession, too."

"Of course. There are plenty of designers and architects chasing their own dreams. It doesn't bother me so much. All I want to do is run my own little corner of the market as well as I can. As long as the work keeps coming in and it's interesting, I'm happy."

"That's a credo that many would envy, Marnie."

"And you really want to change direction … it's not just … well, because I've come along? It would be soul-destroying if one day you realised you'd thrown away the most important part of your life on a whim."

"It's not like that. You're part of it all, but not in that way. No. If you're willing to accept me, then I'd like us to plan together."

From there it was a short step to the other topic of conversation. "I can't help feeling amazed that anyone would want to line up with me."

"Why not?"

"Everywhere I go I seem to run into trouble."

"Well," said Ralph, "you're certainly not boring!"

Tuesday 27 December

For Marnie and Ralph, everything about those few days was magic. Even waiting to meet Anne at Oxford bus station the day after Boxing Day brought a tingle of anticipation, and Ralph actually found a parking space for the elderly Volvo close by. They chatted about their plans for the day, huddled arm in arm in the draughty building smelling of diesel fumes, while they looked forward to seeing the sixteen year-old with her short pale blond hair, the thin, waif-like figure with her sharp features who had come to play such an important part in their lives. At two minutes past ten the Bedfordshire bus rolled into the station and drew to a halt in its allotted bay.

"Good timing," said Marnie, her breath a cloud in the chill air as they made their way out to the bus stop. The passengers were filing out and they found Anne at the rear of the bus by the open tailgate, dressed in jeans, boots and black blouson jacket, a long apricot-coloured scarf trailing almost to the ground. She was pulling a package out of the luggage bay. It was the size of a suitcase but thinner. Ralph pulled it clear and Anne immediately began pulling out another package of the same size and shape.

Marnie joined in and together they dragged it out. "What have you got here?"

"These were too big to go inside the coach." They hugged each other with their free arms, supporting the parcels with the others, before trooping out of the bus station to cross the road and find the car.

"Most girls just carry a shoulder bag," Marnie observed while Ralph delved in his pocket for the keys. "What have *you* got?"

Anne shrugged. "Just some essential supplies. You'll see." Ralph loaded both parcels into the voluminous boot and they set off for home.

"How was Christmas?" Marnie asked.

"Great. All the trimmings. Mum and Dad like everything to be traditional. And I had a couple of old schoolfriends round on Boxing Day. So I caught up on all the gossip."

"Good," said Marnie. "And how was your journey? Your bus was right on time."

"No probs. I was reading the paper and next thing, we'd arrived. Actually, there was an article about ... you know ... that MP. Did you know they found the tramp? It said he was in Limehouse Cut."

Ralph could see Anne's face in the rear-view mirror. Her eyes were like saucers. Marnie said, "Would you believe the police contacted me on Christmas Eve to tell me about it?"

"They *didn't!*"

"They certainly *did*. Inspector Bartlett rang me on the mobile at Ralph's."

"*Bartlett*? What's it got to do with *him*?"

"He's keeping a friendly eye on me for the Met, I suppose."

"Blimey. In the article it said that Tim Edmonds would've become a minister."

"That's what Malcolm Grant said on the box," said Marnie.

"Malcolm Grant," Anne repeated. "He was mentioned in the paper. I think it said he was going to be made a lord."

"Really?"

"I'm sure it did."

"Remember the rumour that Michael mentioned in the House last week," said Ralph. Marnie nodded.

"So they would both have been promoted together," said Anne. Ralph opened his mouth to speak, but changed his mind.

"Not far now," said Marnie, as the car turned off the dual carriageway and headed down a narrow country road. Soon they passed through the village and took the lane towards the river.

"Murton looks like a picture postcard," said Anne.

"Wait till you see River Cottage," said Marnie. They rounded a bend where the bushes overhung the track and scraped the side of the car before the cottage appeared ahead of them, half hidden by trees and planting.

"Is that it?"

"Welcome, honourable lady, to my unworthy home," said Ralph pulling onto the drive under the low eaves.

"It's *gorgeous*," said Anne. "Everyone's idea of an English country cottage. Has it got lots of beams and an inglenook fireplace?"

"Come and find out for yourself." Marnie and Anne unloaded the parcels from the boot while Ralph disappeared inside. By the time she shut the boot, Marnie guessed he had already put a match to the fire so that Anne would see it as soon as she walked into the living room.

Anne stamped her feet on the drive. "It feels cold enough for snow. My feet have been tingling all morning."

Marnie glanced up at the sky, heavy with grey clouds. "You could be right. Let's warm you up." They each took one of the unwieldy parcels and went in.

· · · · ·

Marnie handled the guided tour while Ralph made coffee. She began upstairs, warning Anne of the places where she would have to duck to avoid low doorways and beams. Anne took in every detail, and Marnie was certain that her friend was making a mental list of things she would like to do with the interior. No doubt they would compare notes later. The stairs creaked as they made their way down to the hall.

"Does it have a ghost?" said Anne.

"Haven't found one so far." Marnie pointed to the kitchen. "The ground floor is mainly three spaces, not counting the hall and the cloakroom. Kitchen, of course. Large enough for breakfast."

"Or supper if I'm eating alone," came Ralph's voice from the kitchen amid the clinking of crockery.

"What used to be the dining room is now Ralph's study." Anne peeped in to find a spacious room fitted with bookshelves, and a view over the garden. "And this is the living room." Marnie pushed open the door. The room was much larger than Anne had expected, furnished with comfortable sofas and armchairs, bounded by the inglenook stretching almost the full width, leaving just enough space for a small window in front of which stood the Christmas tree covered in white lights. The fire had already taken hold and the logs were crackling in the fire basket.

Anne smiled and shook her head. "It's super. Oh ... and there's a conservatory! You never said Ralph had a conservatory."

"It's always been the dining room since I took over the real one as a study," said Ralph bringing in the tray of coffee. "Come and make yourself at home. You haven't even taken your jacket off. You'll be warm by the fire."

Anne turned to hang her blouson in the hall and pulled a newspaper out of her pocket. "I don't need this any more. Can I put it somewhere? Unless you want to see the article about the tramp and so on ..."

"Perhaps I'll read it later," said Marnie. "Can you put it on the hall table?" When Anne went out, Marnie muttered to Ralph, "We'll not say anything about our plans yet, shall we? Perhaps we ought to get things sorted out first so we know exactly what we're doing. What do you think?"

"No rush," said Ralph. "We'll surprise her in our own good time."

Anne came back, showing off her new cream silk shirt, a present from her parents. She settled on the floor by the fire, leaning against one of the armchairs like a contented cat as Ralph passed her a cup of coffee. She accepted a Christmas biscuit and licked a crumb from the corner of her mouth. "So ... are you two a permanent item, then ... or what?" she said.

• • • • •

That evening, Marnie and Ralph stood smiling self-consciously at each other in the hall, waiting for Anne to call them into the living room. Marnie put her face close to the door and called out. "Are you going to keep us out here all night? We're dying of boredom!"

A muffled reply came through from the other side. "You shouldn't be. I've taken that into account ... part of my plan."

"What do you mean?"

"Open your eyes and you'll see."

Marnie was baffled until she noticed Ralph looking up at the low ceiling. Enlightenment dawned. Attached to one of the darkened oak beams was a tiny sprig of mistletoe.

"She has insights, that girl," muttered Ralph as he leaned towards Marnie.

"Psychic," Marnie said.

Anne's voice was heard again through the closed door. "Glad you found it ..."

"See what I mean?"

Ralph nodded. "What do you think she's up to in there? She's had us waiting out here for nearly five minutes."

Marnie shrugged. "You know what she's like. She wants to make her contribution ... show she's not just a passenger."

In fact, Anne's character had been stamped on that Christmas as soon as they sat down for coffee. Ralph had asked if there was anything special she would like to do and said he was flexible about meal-times. She suggested a snack lunch ("just something to keep us going"), some fresh air in the afternoon, returning for presents, followed by dinner in the conservatory. If they would let her, she wanted to make their second Christmas as enjoyable as the first. They let her.

Ralph suggested a walk by the river, and they had spent an agreeable couple of hours sauntering along frosty paths and tracks, wrapped up against the chill air, till their noses turned pink and they pointed them back in the direction of River Cottage. Fresh logs rekindled the fire while Ralph and Marnie prepared coffee in the kitchen and Anne was left for a few minutes in the living room. They returned to find her standing on the threshold of the French windows leading into the conservatory, a thoughtful expression on her face.

"I know that look," said Marnie. "What are you plotting?"

Anne's face was innocence personified. "*Moi?*"

"Did you say you wanted us to open presents now?" said Ralph.

Anne looked out through the conservatory windows. "It'll be dusk soon. Could we have presents after coffee?"

Ralph did not quite grasp the connection between dusk and presents. "Of course. Actually, I've got some champagne in the fridge. We could have that while we're doing the Santa Claus act. Or a Bucks Fizz. What do you think?"

After coffee, as dusk came down around the cottage, Anne asked if she could have a minute or two by herself in the living room, which was how Marnie and Ralph found themselves standing with a growing sense of anticipation in the hall. The feeling reminded them of their childhood.

"Ralph ..." Marnie spoke quietly. "I was going to ask you ... In the car, Anne said that Tim Edmonds and Malcolm Grant were both going to be promoted ... one a minister, the other a lord ..."

"Yes."

"You were going to say something, but changed your mind. Do you remember?"

"I was just going to say that becoming a lord isn't viewed by politicians as a promotion. I didn't say it, because I thought it would seem as if I was putting Anne down."

"They were really good friends, weren't they, Edmonds and Grant?"

"Oh yes," said Ralph. "Through thick and thin."

"Is that usual in politics?"

"It's not unusual. In their case I think they were both on the same national committee and spent a lot of time working together."

"Same interests, same views," said Marnie.

"Well ... not actually. That's the funny part of it. Edmonds was pro-Europe, Grant more of a sceptic. Edmonds liked Major, Grant preferred at least one of his challengers."

"So it was just a personal thing."

"Yes. They liked each other's company and I think they trusted each other. That's not always the case in politics."

"From what I've seen," said Marnie, "Malcolm Grant is pretty devastated by the death of his friend."

"No doubt about it," said Ralph. "In fact ..."

At that moment, the door opened. Smiling impishly, Anne beckoned them in. The room was transformed. The lights on the tree were candles. Candles flickered and glowed on the table and on the windowsills. Through the window they could see yet more candles reflected in the panes of the conservatory.

"It's marvellous," said Ralph. "I've never seen the house look so lovely. I'll just go and check my fire insurance policy."

Anne laughed. "Ralph, I don't think you're a real romantic."

"I'm learning."

Marnie walked over to the French windows. "I don't believe it!" she exclaimed. "Look at this." Anne took Ralph by the arm and led him across the room. The three of them gazed out towards the garden and saw the snow falling in large flakes, swirling gently in the breeze.

"All part of the service," said Anne. "Time for Santa?"

"I'll fetch the champagne," said Ralph.

Anne had arranged the presents at the base of the tree and positioned herself to pass them round. Marnie and Ralph were to open Anne's bulky gifts last. From Ralph, Anne received a copy of *The Water Gypsies* by A. P. Herbert. It was an old hardback, a signed first edition no less, and inside was the inscription: *To A.P. from A.P. with best wishes.*

"Who was the other A.P., I wonder?" said Anne.

Ralph shrugged. "No idea who the original was, but I know who it is now. How about *Anne Price?*"

"*Me!*" she exclaimed. "That's brilliant."

Next, she opened a gift from Marnie. It was a waistcoat in black velvet decorated with gold thread and beadwork. It went perfectly with her new silk shirt. Another small parcel from Ralph was opened to reveal a triple bracelet in gold of three colours, red, yellow and white.

"I'm overwhelmed, I really am." She hugged them both. "I hope you won't be disappointed with my presents." She placed one each in front of them and watched anxiously while they untied the ribbons and pulled off layers of corrugated cardboard and bubble wrap. Their expressions told her that they were not disappointed.

Marnie's was a watercolour of Glebe Farm as it had been when they first found it in ruins. The picture conveyed all the atmosphere of abandonment on the brink of total dereliction, but the lines of the old farm and the beauty of the setting seemed to hint at hope for the future.

"One day, Anne with an 'e', I shall have a wall worthy of your painting. Thank you. It is beautiful."

Ralph's was also a watercolour: his boat, *Thyrsis*, at her mooring by Glebe Farm, the trees in spring foliage, morning sunshine seeping through the spinney, an atmosphere of freshness and new beginnings. Ralph shook his head slowly.

"Sometimes, Anne, I think you can read people's minds and know them better than they do themselves. This is wonderful. Thank you so much and thank you for doing everything to make this a really memorable Christmas."

For once, Anne did not have a quick reply. Her eye fell on a last small parcel under the tree and she turned to pick it up. "What's this? I don't remember putting this out."

"Oh, that," said Ralph. "Er, that ... it's, um, a small gift for ... er, Dolly. I thought she could use a new collar and a tin of that special food for pampered cats." He looked at their faces. "Well, once or twice a year won't do her any harm ... will it?"

• • • • •

Wednesday 28 December

Anne awoke slowly and lay basking in the comfort of her warm bed. She thought back to dinner in the conservatory, relishing the way of life that she now enjoyed, a life she had scarcely imagined in her dreams. It was as if she was looking in on their meal from outside, seeing the three friends chatting together in the candlelight. They had tried to focus on pleasant subjects, Ralph's trip to Japan, Marnie's visit to her parents in Spain, new plans for the business, Ralph's ideas about a new direction. Anne laughed softly to herself at the thought of Ralph's Christmas pudding ice cream and its 'secret recipe'. It was she who had revealed that the recipe was contained in the December edition of one of the boating magazines. Ralph had coped very well with the ribbing he received from Marnie.

Anne sat up in bed. River Cottage was like Glebe Farm. There were no sounds to be heard and the world seemed far away in the silence. She wondered what time it was and thought it must be late. Already there was daylight showing at the window's edge. She slipped her feet into her slippers and stood up to open the curtains. The light was reflecting from the snow, the deep snow that covered the garden and was still falling in broad flakes jostled by breezes. There came a soft tap on the door.

Marnie, also in dressing gown, smiled at her. "Have you seen it?"

"Yes. It looks lovely."

"Ralph's out checking the road. He may be gone some time ... or rather, we may be here some time."

"You think we might be snowed in?"

"We'll have to see. How soon will you be ready for breakfast?"

• • • • •

Eating in the conservatory that morning was like being inside an igloo. Every time Anne looked out at the garden, where the snow was knee-deep on the ground and bent the boughs and bushes down with its weight, she felt like smiling for pure joy. It was everyone's dream, to be snowed into a warm house stocked with good food and drink in the best of company. Her only anxiety was the thought that she was supposed to be going home that morning, and Marnie and Ralph were due to visit Randall Hughes in Brackley. Now it seemed that all their plans would be disrupted. She hoped it was not an entirely selfish thought, but she did not care.

"It's not as if anything really important was at stake," said Ralph, pouring them all a second cup of coffee. "Shall I put on some more toast?"

"To be honest," said Marnie, "I love the idea of being snowed in. Nothing could be better. But I'm sorry if it causes problems for your parents, Anne."

Anne shrugged. "No probs for them. My worry is that you were going to see Randall and this will spoil it for you."

"We can go later," said Ralph reaching over to the toaster on the windowsill. "Anyway, the road outside isn't too bad, strangely enough. It must be a sheltered spot ... air currents or something. The problem is more likely to be the buses. I think we'd better assume that you'll be staying here at least for another day, Anne. I hope that's all right."

Anne put on her most enigmatic expression, like a poker player giving nothing away. She shrugged and nodded, convinced that she showed less emotion than the sphinx.

"No need to smirk," said Marnie grinning.

• • • • •

While Marnie and Anne cleared the breakfast things away, Ralph phoned the weather service, the AA and the bus station. He came into the kitchen and leaned against the rail on the Aga.

"Well ... the worst weather is to the south and east of us, we should not attempt to go in that direction unless it's really urgent and even if we did, there are no buses running until further notice."

"Which direction is Brackley from here?" said Marnie. "It's north, isn't it?"

"More or less. I thought I'd report back before we decided about Randall."

"Obviously Anne is snow-bound," said Marnie. "So no great problem, is it?"

Anne heaved a theatrical sigh. "It's tragic."

"Right," said Ralph. "You ring your parents, then I'll ring Randall. We'd better make emergency plans to withstand a siege. First priority ... fetch a bottle of claret from the cellar. Won't be long."

He rejoined them in the living room a few minutes later. He was carrying two bottles of claret. "We must be on the edge of the blizzard. Randall says it's not too bad over there. We may be able to go after all. And he'd be delighted to see all three of us. I suspect he wants us to help him finish the turkey."

• • • • •

"Help yourself to the bashed neeps," said Randall. "I think the ratatouille goes quite well." He sat at the head of the table in the well-proportioned dining room of his Georgian rectory in the centre of the small town of Brackley. The candlesticks on the table were silver, highly-polished and probably also Georgian. Tall and thin with dark curly hair and a sensitive face, he was wearing a deep blue velvet jacket and no dog-collar. The serving dishes in the centre of the table were Imari, and steam was rising from them as the guests served themselves.

"A very original menu," said Marnie.

Randall raised his glass and paused to admire the colour of the wine. "Well ... cheers and a happy Christmas to you all. Wonderful wine, Ralph. Excellent."

"I hope it complements the meal," said Ralph.

"Not exactly a traditional Yule-tide lunch," said Randall. "But when I knew that Anne would be coming, it gave me a golden opportunity to get the haggis out of the freezer."

"I hope I'm not being a nuisance," said Anne.

"Absolutely not. In fact, I was given the haggis, a *vegetarian* haggis, by one of my church wardens, a delightful lady from Aberdeen. Fiona Murray. She wanted me to have it for Burns night when she'd be away in Scotland."

"Why vegetarian?" said Marnie. "You're not a veggie, are you?"

"No, but Fiona suspected that most English people might not like the idea of a real haggis and these taste just as good, or so she told me. Quite rich and spicy, isn't it?" They all agreed that the combination of haggis, neeps and ratatouille was a success, especially washed down with a nine-year-old Pauillac.

"I should have brought a dozen bottles in case we get snowed in here as well," said Ralph.

"Hear! Hear!" said Randall. "In future, as soon as I hear a bad weather warning, I'll invite you over straight away." He replaced the lids on the dishes and transferred them to a heated server on the sideboard.

"You seem to have settled into Brackley very well," said Marnie. "The life of a Rural Dean obviously suits you."

"It does. And it gives scope to work on a broader scale than in a single parish. Since coming here I've been able to branch out."

"In what ways?" Marnie asked.

"Well, I'm organising a choral festival for church choirs in the area ... actually, it's in memory of Toni. She had a *wonderful* singing voice." Marnie remembered it well. *A voice like an angel*, Anne had said the first time she heard her singing in the church. "I've introduced a pastoral system for new clergy. We have three women vicars in the area now ... they're growing in numbers, unlike the men."

"How are they being received?"

"On the whole ..." he nodded thoughtfully, "pretty well ... Actually, there'll be a new woman vicar coming to Knightly. Did you know?"

"Mr Fowey told us," said Anne.

"Let's hope she's accepted by the village," said Randall. "Do you think she will be?"

"I do," said Marnie. "Toni's death made a huge impact on people ... so did her life. I'd rather think about positive things, if you don't mind."

"Of course," said Randall. "I'm sorry. I was forgetting about your recent experience. I hope it's not too distressing."

"What's this enterprise you're so keen to show us?" said Ralph.

Randall shrugged. "Nothing grand, really, but a minor victory for humanity in its way. It's just a drop-in centre for the homeless, people who can't cope with life."

"A sort of drop-in for drop-outs?" Anne suggested.

Randall smiled at her. "Yes. Exactly. Most of the ones who come are what would've been called 'tramps' years ago. They can stay for as long as they like, but they seem to spend a couple of nights with us and move on. It's their way of life."

"So they never have a permanent home?" said Marnie.

"Well, I'm no real expert, but the ones we have here tend to move around. They seem to come to Brackley at roughly the same time each year, I gather. And they usually have a special place they visit at Christmas. But I think the ones who live in big towns move around rather less than the country ones."

"What do the locals think of them?" said Marnie.

"They're very tolerant, actually. Some of the old boys have been coming to Brackley for years, apparently. They're no trouble."

"Where do they come from?" said Anne.

"Ah, that's difficult." Randall got up and fetched the second bottle of wine from the sideboard to top up their glasses. "That's something you can't do ... ask them questions. They're very private ... never talk about themselves, especially about the past."

"At least you've helped give them a present," said Marnie. "I mean a here and now."

"Yes, but it was a close-run thing. That's why I said it was a minor victory for humanity."

"Would this relate to a building by any chance?" said Ralph.

"You've guessed it. The old convalescent home was due to close. On closure it would revert to the trustees of a foundation, a small private trust bequeathed by a local benefactor at the turn of the century."

"They had plans for it?" said Ralph.

"Right. Or rather the chairman had plans for it. He's a great-grandson of the benefactor and runs a business here in town. His plan was to turn the building into a hotel and conference centre. It would make a fortune, or so I was advised by one of my churchwardens."

"But if it was a charitable trust …" said Marnie.

"Ah …" said Ralph.

"Ah …" Randall agreed

"Ah?" said Anne.

Randall nodded. "It would be a potential goldmine; a goldmine with jobs …"

"Jobs for the boys," said Ralph.

"Well-paid jobs," said Randall.

"Ah …" said Marnie.

"Ah …" said Anne.

"Never let it be said that the art of conversation has died in Brackley," said Marnie. "So what did you do to stop the master plan?"

"Briefly, after I heard about it from the churchwarden, I did some research on the trust documents and found that the building could only be used for medical or charitable purposes. That's what gave me the idea. So I lobbied the health authority and got them to agree to let the church take it over for a nominal rent to use for the benefit of the needy."

"What did the chairman of the trust think of that?" said Marnie.

"His views were rather less than charitable, I'm afraid. He virtually accused me of robbing him of his birthright. Anyway, when he realised he'd lost the argument, he quietened down. He had to, I suppose. He's a county councillor and he was standing for re-election. As a politician, he couldn't afford to let people know what he really thought."

"Now you're starting to sound like Ralph," said Marnie.

Ralph threw his head back and laughed. Anne looked thoughtful.

• • • • •

The hostel was in the high street not far from the town hall. The entrance was located in a narrow lane and the impressive Georgian front door was no longer used. Snow was falling lightly as they drove carefully in Ralph's car the short distance through the town from the rectory, preferable to taking their chances on the slippery pavements. Once inside the building, they were all surprised, except Randall, at the brightness of the interior and the absence of unpleasant smells. His visitors had expected the building to hum with the odour of dirty clothes and unwashed bodies, but they were greeted only with a faint aroma of cooking. Randall said he did not want the "guests", as he called the tramps, to feel they were being inspected, or subjected to a "Royal visit", so he suggested that they take coffee at a table on one side of the dining hall. One of the volunteers, a young woman student, greeted Randall and his friends warmly and poured the coffee into china cups with saucers. It tasted good.

At a few of the tables there were men sitting, some reading newspapers, a small group playing a board game. Most were middle-aged to elderly, though a few were young, and Anne whispered to Marnie that one of them seemed about her age.

"Why is he here?" she said quietly. "I suppose he has no home to go to?"

"Evidently not," said Randall. "But we never ask. If we asked questions, they'd leave and not come back."

"Do you know their names?" said Ralph.

"Usually. That's the one question we ask when they come. Just so we can address them in a civilised way. Whoever speaks to them gives them their first name and asks what *they* want to be called. Whether those are their real names or not, we don't know, and it doesn't really matter."

After coffee Randall showed them round. There was a TV room and another sitting room, with new furniture everywhere, no second-hand cast-offs. The bedrooms were divided into individual cubicles by partition walls almost up to ceiling height.

"We have nine staying overnight at the moment."

"All men?" said Marnie.

"So far, yes. There are few women on the road around here, or so I'm told."

"What about rules?" said Ralph. "It all looks free and easy. No notices up telling them what they can't do."

"We have some basic rules. No alcohol on the premises, no smoking upstairs. There are sprinklers in the bedrooms and they know they'll get wet if they disobey that rule. They can have fresh clothes and shoes if they want them. Shoes of course are very important to them. Their own things are taken and washed, and they all have a bath when they arrive."

"How do they feel about that?" said Marnie.

"Fine. No problem. They usually like to soak for an hour. We give them good meals and pleasant surroundings. No questions. Free to come and go when they want."

"I'm surprised they don't insist on staying," said Marnie.

"So was I at first, but they don't want to be surrounded by walls. They've left that behind them. A couple of days and they move on."

"How soon before they come back?"

"That we don't know. We've only been running for a couple of months, so we haven't had anyone return yet. We're keeping records, of course, though they don't know that. It's just for our own use."

"I bet you're very proud of this," said Anne.

"I'm not sure if pride is quite the feeling," said Randall. "But I'm glad we can help them. Especially at Christmas."

"Do you get to know them ... you know, as people?"

"That's a very good question, Anne. It depends on them. I think that nobody really looks at tramps. People tend to distance themselves. If someone comes up and asks for anything, you avoid eye contact. So you don't look at them. So you don't see them. But here, we see them as individuals, as human beings."

• • • • •

In the car on their way back to Murton, Anne was very quiet. She seemed to have withdrawn into herself. At the cottage, Marnie spoke to her while Ralph was putting the car away. "You're very pensive." To her surprise, Anne looked for a moment as if she was going to cry. She turned her head and went into the living room.

"Anne, are you thinking about the boy of your age?" Marnie had had the same thought when she saw him at the hostel. Anne had tried to run away from home. Marnie wondered if she had imagined herself ending up on the streets like that, wandering from hostel to night shelter, sleeping rough. But Anne shook her head slowly.

"I was thinking about the tramp who witnessed the death of Tim Edmonds ... What a life. He lives rough, sees something horrible like that and then drowns in the canal. It's awful. I think Randall's hostel is great."

Marnie put an arm round Anne's thin shoulders and stroked her cropped hair.

Part 10

Thursday 29 December

"Do you remember the first time we came to Knightly together, Anne?" Marnie turned off the main highway and pointed the Rover down the country road that led to the village, careful not to accelerate too hard through the slush. More snow had fallen in the night, not enough to prevent them from driving back to sort out the office.

"We couldn't find it, could we? Kept looking for the church tower and it kept disappearing!"

"Your folks didn't mind you coming back with me instead of going home for a few more days?"

"No probs. They know we have work to do. Anyway, I think of here as home now, as much as I do Leighton Buzzard."

They called in at the shop to stock up on basics and gossip. Molly Appleton told them the new vicar would be starting in January, the new *woman vicar*. There was no other village news, and it had been a quiet Christmas. They needed only a few provisions as Ralph was coming on later to sort out his papers on *Thyrsis*, and would join them for supper at the pub.

They found Glebe Farm none the worse for the heavy snowfall, leaving the office barn to warm up while they went through the spinney to check *Sally Ann* and *Thyrsis*. Twigs snapped under their feet and Dolly appeared at their side to be scooped up by Anne.

Back in the office barn, perched on desks and still wearing their jackets, Anne checked the answerphone and fax while Marnie opened the post. The background sounds were the rattle of the kettle heating up and Dolly's purring as she sat on Marnie's desk, washing her fur.

"Uh-oh ..." Anne, phone pressed against her ear, was frowning.

"What is it?" said Marnie.

"Inspector Bartlett wants you to ring him. *Urgent.*"

Marnie sighed and pressed the buttons on the phone. She was put through without delay.

"Thank you for responding so quickly, Mrs Walker."

"What can I do for you?"

"I'll come straight to the point. Is there any chance that you might have seen the tramp by the canal after all?"

"I've already told you. I had no idea anyone else was there. It was dark. I was squatting by the water. How could I have seen him? I would've mentioned it."

"Yes ..." He sounded disappointed. "That's what I thought you'd say."

"What else *could* I say?"

"It's just that, if past experience is anything to go by ... you might not have managed to tell us the whole story first time round."

Marnie gritted her teeth. Anne was watching her. "I suppose I deserved that, Inspector. But it makes no difference. That is how it was."

"Pity. We need someone to identify him."

"I thought he had been identified. If not, how do you know it was the same man? On the news it seemed definite."

"Yes, well ... it'd be nice to have more than the say-so of another tramp to go by. Never mind. Oh, one other thing, Mrs Walker. Do I understand you were planning to go abroad in the near future?"

"*Were* planning? I'm going to Spain next week."

"Business or pleasure?"

"To see my parents. Why?"

"Unless your visit's urgent, we'd prefer you to stay for the moment."

"Are you telling me I can't leave the country?"

"No ... no. I'm not saying that, Mrs Walker. I'd have to regard you as a suspect to order you to stay."

"But you *want* me to stay."

"Yes. It would help our enquiries if you were around to deal with any questions ... at least for the immediate future. You are the closest we have to an actual witness."

When Marnie put the phone down, Anne asked. "Problem?"

"Can you look up the number of the travel agent? My insurance had better cover this sort of cancellation or there'll be trouble ..."

• • • • •

"Stab him in the back?" said Anne, raising her voice. The waitress, who was at that moment setting down a plate of scampi and dips in front of her, looked shocked. Anne glanced up. "It's okay ... I was just speaking metaphorically."

"Oh, right," said the waitress dubiously. She placed grilled salmon in front of Marnie, and reached kebabs with rice across to Ralph.

"That's the point," said Ralph. "In politics it often happens that your opponents are in the party on the other side of the chamber; but your *enemies* are in your own party. That's why I say – and it's not just my view – that you're more likely to get stabbed in the back from someone sitting on the bench behind you than from someone on the benches opposite."

"I see. So they're all rivals." Anne pronged a piece of scampi and looked at it thoughtfully for a few moments. "What about Grant and Edmonds?" she said. "They were friends, weren't they?"

"It's not impossible, of course. But politics is about power, and people don't usually go into politics, especially not at Westminster, unless they want it pretty badly." He poured the wine, including half a glass for Anne who made hers into a spritzer. For a short while they concentrated on food and drink, each lost in their own thoughts.

"There doesn't seem to be much idealism about," said Anne. "I mean, when they're standing for election, it's all about wanting a better country and all that sort of thing. Big smiles for the camera. But really, it's just them wanting to be in power to tell everybody else what to do. Is that right?"

"I've probably made it seem worse than it is," said Ralph. "There can be idealism. Politicians often start from a position of wanting to make things better. They latch onto a philosophy and then it takes over their life, their whole way of thinking."

"That's why they're always convinced they're right," suggested Marnie.

"Do they all think they can be Prime Minister?" said Anne.

"I've often asked myself that question," said Ralph. "On balance, I think the answer is probably 'yes', or at least they think they can become cabinet ministers. That's what drives them on."

"Do you think Randall expects to become a bishop one day?" said Anne.

Ralph shrugged. "That's rather outside my field, I'm afraid. Though I wouldn't be surprised."

"And you wanted to become a professor?"

"Well, yes, to be honest, I suppose I did. But tell me, Anne. What's your ambition?"

There was no hesitation. "To be an interior designer ... like Marnie." She smiled at her friend across the table.

"And to have your own company one day?"

Anne shrugged. "I can't think that far ahead, but ... perhaps, one day. Who knows?"

"We don't have to stab anyone in the back to have that sort of ambition," said Marnie. "After all, there are lots of firms around, but only one Prime Minister."

"Yes," said Ralph. "The stakes are much higher. There's much more to gain and much more to lose."

"But you think we all in our different ways would like to get to the top of the tree," said Anne, glancing over to the decorations reflecting the flames from the pub's fire.

Ralph looked at the Christmas tree, the tinsel glittering from branch to branch, the stars and baubles looping their way up to the fairy perched above everything else, holding out her magic wand. He smiled at Anne over the rim of his wine glass. "You're speaking metaphorically, of course ..."

• • • • •

Friday 30 December

In the office barn Anne was snug and warm in her room in the loft. She went down to the shower they had installed at the back of the office and a few minutes later was pulling on her clothes. Instinctively she checked the answerphone and fax machine before setting off through the spinney on the short walk to breakfast with Marnie and Ralph who were staying on *Thyrsis*.

"No messages," she said to Marnie, pulling off her blouson jacket and looking approvingly at the breakfast table. "*Thyrsis* really is a civilised boat." She sniffed the air. "Hyacinths? Can I smell hyacinths?"

"There are pots of them in the main cabin," said Marnie. "Ralph always has them at this time of year, apparently. They remind him that spring is on the way."

"That coffee smells marvellous, too, Ralph."

"We know how to find the way to your heart," Ralph called out from the galley.

"I've had a message," said Marnie. "Bartlett rang. Inspector Bruere wants me to sign my statement."

"There's nothing on the fax."

"No, I have to go in person and sign it at the station – *their* station."

"In *London*? Then they should pay your travel expenses," said Anne indignantly.

"They offered to do just that."

"When are you going?"

"I told them I could come down early next week, when I go to the airport with Ralph."

On cue, Ralph came into the cabin with the coffee pot and set it on the table. Anne went out to fetch the basket of warmed croissants, covered with a yellow gingham napkin.

"Well," said Ralph pouring orange juice into glasses, "I suppose that's Christmas more or less over for another year."

"Next stop, hot cross buns," said Marnie.

"Even money says they'll be in the shops within a week," said Ralph. Anne laughed. "It's true," he said. "I'll bet you. It's the great rolling programme of the feast of capitalism."

"But they're not all like that," said Anne. "The church people, I mean. It's not their fault if business makes money out of their festivals. Randall isn't like that. Without people like him, who'd help the tramps?"

"True."

"Talking of which," said Marnie, "I've been wondering … Why did Bartlett ask me if I could identify the tramp who'd drowned? They knew I hadn't seen anybody that night."

"What are you saying?" said Ralph.

"Were they trying to trick me or something?"

"Or don't they know if it is the right tramp who drowned?" said Anne.

"Perhaps. On the news it said they'd identified the tramp as the likely witness."

"Supposedly," said Ralph, "some other tramp has identified the body as the man who lived in the park." They lapsed into silence.

Eventually, Anne said, "I'm not sure I follow all this. Did he drown or didn't he?"

Marnie shook her head. "It doesn't add up, does it? I'm not sure if there even was a tramp. I certainly didn't see anyone that evening. And the police must know that."

"What are you getting at, then?" said Anne.

"A hidden agenda," Ralph muttered.

"And this … going back to London to sign my statement … I could just as easily sign it up here. You know, I'm not sure they've ever really believed the explanation about the business card. I feel as if they're sort of … reeling me in."

"They *can't* believe you killed that MP," said Anne horrified.

"Perhaps not. But they might think I'm somehow involved. In which case … they might still have me down as a suspect."

• • • • •

It was one of those days when progress is made. While the rest of the world was still on holiday and thinking about their plans for New Year's Eve in the afterglow of Christmas, Marnie, Anne and Ralph were sorting out their lives in readiness for the next stage. Marnie was at her desk, deep in concentration over her designs for the coming phase of work for Willards. Anne was humming quietly to herself while she backed up files on the computer and waded through a mound of paperwork and correspondence.

Over on *Thyrsis*, Ralph was putting his papers in order, compiling the documents he would need in Japan and the briefing notes he would take to America.

Anne took down the planner for the old year and pinned up the new one to take its place on the wall by her desk. She was already putting in appointments for halfway through the new year. The new year ...

"Are you in a trance or can we get some coffee round here?" Marnie's voice brought Anne out of a dream. She jumped and turned to look across at her friend.

"Coffee? Oh, sure. I'll do it now."

"You okay?"

"Fine. I was just thinking about next year ... college and all that." She filled the kettle in the kitchen area at the back of the office. All the fittings had been chosen by Marnie when she moved in. The units were blond wood with steel handles. Modern and chic like the life Anne aspired to attain. Like Marnie herself. She stared at the kettle. It was almost like a chrome Volkswagen beetle with a black curved handle.

"You sure you're okay? Not going down with 'flu again?"

"Honest, Marnie, I was just having a quiet think."

"No problems?"

"No probs. I was just thinking to myself that at some point during this next year, I'll be starting a new phase in my life. I'll be somewhere else."

"Are you leaving, then? You mean ... I'll have to make my own coffee? This could be serious."

"I *am* being serious. It stands to reason. I'll have to study full-time, which means I'll be living somewhere else."

Marnie fell silent and Anne made coffee. When Anne put the mug down (designer mug) on the desk, Marnie looked up. "Where will you be studying, then? Have you got it all worked out?"

Anne perched on the corner of the desk, holding her mug in both hands as she always did. She shrugged. "A Levels ... some sort of college, I suppose. I don't want to go back to school. School was okay, but I've left all that behind now."

"I suppose there are colleges round here?" said Marnie. Anne shook her head and went back to her desk. Marnie persisted. "There *must* be. I'm sure I've seen one in Milton Keynes. And Northampton isn't far away."

"I think I'll have to live with mum and dad. I can't expect you to keep me when I can't work for you. It's not on. You need someone here." The implications seemed to weigh down on Anne and she sipped her coffee absent-mindedly. Beside her the phone rang.

"Walker and Co, good afternoon." She listened for a few seconds. "Yes, she is. Who's calling?" She looked at Marnie who was already reaching towards the phone. Anne pressed the buttons. "It's Malcolm Grant."

•　•　•　•　•

It started snowing again as the dusk came down in the late afternoon. Marnie waited till Anne was out taking the post up to the village before phoning Anne's parents. They talked for several minutes and when she replaced the receiver, Marnie was smiling. It was the first time she had felt cheerful since coffee. The thought that Anne might actually go back to her parents to live with them while she studied for the next two years had brought on a feeling of gloom. That waif-like creature had become a major part of her life and she could not imagine being without her.

With a flurry of chill air and the odd snowflake, Anne came into the office barn followed by Ralph. They stamped their feet on the doormat. "If it gets any worse, I'll be putting in for skis or a team of huskies," Anne said, hanging her jacket on the hook. Ralph put a bundle of files on the photocopier and undid his coat.

"Anne said Malcolm Grant rang."

"That's right. He suggested a meeting in London to talk about his flat. I said I'd see him next week."

"Are you both going?"

"No. Just me. I'll stay at Beth and Paul's for a few days."

"I've got some reading to do ... preparation for next year," said Anne. "A Levels. I'll have to find a college for September."

"I'll see if I can get you a Fellowship at All Saints," said Ralph.

Anne stuck out her tongue and smiled at him. "It's no good. They don't do my subjects and I can't do an Art Foundation course there."

"All Saints turned down by a sixteen year-old ... there'll be riots in Oxford when the word gets round!" He became serious again. "So you'll be seeing Grant alone? Where are you meeting?"

Marnie frowned. "He suggested that café in Little Venice – the one over the entrance to Maida Hill tunnel. You don't think it could be ... difficult, do you?"

Ralph sighed. "I suppose not. Will you be going back to his place?"

"We didn't talk about it. It's just an exploratory chat, he said."

"Good." Ralph seemed pleased that their meeting would be in a public place, but Marnie was not so sure. She had never had a meeting with a client away from the building to be discussed. She kept the thought to herself.

• • • • •

Saturday 31 December

It was breakfast time on Saturday. The last day of the year. "I've got my things packed," said Anne. "Before we go, do you think I've got time to take down the Christmas decorations? It'll seem like an anti-climax to find them still up when we get back."

"Sure. Good idea. I'll help you," said Marnie.

"Or you could just leave them up for next year," suggested Ralph, dunking a croissant. "Christmas cards will be back in the shops by February."

Anne laughed. "Next to the Easter eggs."

"Probably."

"Actually, Ralph, I think it all comes down to economics."

Ralph, the economist, professor of economics at a world famous college, author and adviser to governments on economic affairs, looked sceptical. "Not commerce, perhaps?" he ventured.

"No. Economics. You know you say how commercial it all is, and how lots of people can't afford everything?"

"Ye-e-s." He sounded suspicious.

"And there are Christmas things in the shops soon after the summer holidays."

"Give or take a day or two, yes."

"Well, I think it helps a lot of people."

"Helps them," he repeated. "Go on."

"I know an old lady in our street who buys something for Christmas every week when the things come into the shops. It spreads the load ... makes it easier for her to manage on her pension. If the Christmas things came out later, say in late November, she wouldn't be able to afford it all at once." Anne shrugged. "Economics."

Ralph thought of the folders of briefing notes on his desk and laughed softly. "Lessons on economics from a sixteen year-old ... for goodness' sake, don't tell the President!"

• • • • •

"Anne, I want to talk to you." Marnie swung the Rover out from the farm track after breakfast and headed towards the high street and beyond that the main road. She was taking Anne to the bus station for a short visit home. "I've got a proposition for you to consider."

"Right." Anne sat still and waited.

"I hope you'll like it," Marnie added, not wanting to cause anxiety. "It's about going to college."

"You can't keep me, Marnie. It wouldn't be fair."

"Just listen. I'm the boss. I give the orders."

"I'll write them out for you on a list," said Anne.

"Ha, ha, smartarse," Marnie muttered as she pulled out onto the dual carriageway. "Okay. This is what I propose. You find a college near here that has good A Level courses. You stay at Glebe Farm and work for me when you can ... mainly vacations and perhaps in your spare time. I keep you in return for that. Tell me it isn't fair."

"It isn't –"

"Not literally!" Marnie interrupted. "You're supposed to agree with me. It *is* fair. And you don't need to find a holiday job filling shelves in Tesco's or serving in a Little Chef. Plus you continue to get experience of the job. What do you say?"

"I'll need to talk it over with mum and dad."

"I've sort of done that already." Marnie was glad to be able to spring a surprise on her friend.

"I guessed you had," said Anne. "So they've agreed?"

"If you accept the idea, yes. What do you think?"

"What do I think?" Marnie glanced at her friend and saw the smile spreading across Anne's face. "I think it's great. I think everything is going to be just perfect ..."

• • • • •

Marnie was back by late morning and found Ralph in the office reading faxes. "I think I owe you about a dozen rolls of fax paper," he said.

"Be my guest." She walked over to her desk, spotted the red light glowing on the answerphone and pressed the button. There were two messages.

"Hi Marnie! It's only me." Anne's voice piped out of the machine. "Just wanted to thank you for a wonderful Christmas and for the super idea about next year. And don't forget to give Ralph an extra kiss from me when you see him off at the airport. Lots of love. 'Bye!"

"Why is it that the people who are most important in your life begin messages by saying 'it's only me' ..." Ralph nodded his agreement. The answerphone peeped again.

"This is DS Wallace from Lisson Grove police station with a message for Mrs Marnie Walker." Marnie's smile disappeared. "We'd like you to sign your statement as soon as possible, please, and there are one or two points we'd like you to clarify. Could you give me a ring to fix a day to come down?" He left a phone number and hung up.

"But I've already done that," said Marnie. "That message must have come in since I left this morning. Don't these people talk to each other?"

"Curious," said Ralph. "Do you know this Wallace?"

Marnie shrugged. "Don't think so, unless he was at the station when I was there. It was a constable who came with Bruere to the boat, I think. A young one. Do you think it could just be a way of putting pressure on me?"

"It does seem rather odd. I can't say I know much about how the police work. Are you going to ring back?"

Marnie looked at the phone. "No. I'm not playing games. They're messing me about. Have you any more work to do with those faxes?"

"No. They were just copies of papers for me to read."

"Right. How about a tootle on *Sally Ann*?"

"Sandwich and a glass of wine for lunch while we travel?"

"You're on. Let's go for it."

• • • • •

It was the last sunshine of the year as *Sally Ann* cut through the icy water between the sleeping fields. Dolly curled up on the hatch, purring while Ralph stroked her with his free hand – the other was on the tiller. Marnie uncorked a bottle of Aussie red and poured two generous glasses. There were herons on the bank at almost regular intervals and voles scurrying about at the water's edge.

"What will the weather be like in Japan?"

"Much the same as here," said Ralph. "This'll be my last dose of fresh air for a while, I expect. I don't go out for walks in Tokyo. Too much traffic, too little time between meetings." He took a bite of his sandwich, brie and black grape on granary bread, and mumbled his appreciation. Marnie sipped her wine and took over the tiller.

"It'll be nice to see Little Venice again. It's always delightful. I don't want this latest business to spoil it."

"No. You'll have to be careful about that. When are you meeting Malcolm Grant?"

"Monday morning when I go in from the airport."

"So, as soon as my back is turned, you're off with another man ..."

"Just like a woman," said Marnie. "Totally unreliable. I'm sure Inspector Bruere would agree."

Ralph was frowning. "I don't suppose you could arrange for someone to be with you when you see him ...?"

"You're not serious? You're not really jealous, surely?"

"Not in the least. I'm just a bit anxious about the whole situation. To tell you the truth, I don't like going off like this and leaving you to handle things on your own. Last time I went away ..."

"That was different, Ralph. All I'm doing is having a cup of coffee and talking about redecorating a flat. I'm sure I can look after myself."

"Yes, of course. I'm getting neurotic. But do be careful. Just bear in mind that Grant is probably a suspect."

"That makes two of us," said Marnie. "We have a lot in common. We should get on very well."

"I'm not joking."

"Do you really think Grant might have murdered his friend?"

Ralph drank some wine and stared thoughtfully into the glass. "No. No, I don't, not really." He smiled at Marnie. "The meeting of the two suspects. You're right, you should make a good pair!"

Marnie laughed. "Yes. Grant in scarlet-lined black cloak, complete with concealed dagger ... me in Mata Hari-style fishnet tights."

"Did Mata Hari wear fishnet tights?" said Ralph.

"No idea, but it seemed an appropriate image." They clinked glasses and cuddled together for warmth as *Sally Ann* chugged along in the pale winter light.

That evening they had supper on *Thyrsis*, a simple meal of pasta with smoked trout followed by cheese and dates, and they finished the red wine. Ralph produced a bottle of good cognac and they chatted over coffee about plans for the future to the accompaniment of *concerti grossi* by Corelli on CD.

"New Year's Eve," said Ralph. "Shouldn't we be out partying or throwing ourselves into the fountain in Trafalgar Square?"

Marnie shuddered. "I'd much rather be here. I've never been one for all that forced jollity." She sipped her brandy.

"I like the way they celebrate in Germany," said Ralph. "Everyone lets off fireworks on the stroke of midnight."

"I think I've got a packet of sparklers somewhere," Marnie volunteered. "If that's what turns you on."

"I don't need sparklers ... Marnie?"

"Ye-e-s?"

"Do you particularly want to stay up and see the new year in?"

"Not desperately. I expect the new year will still be there in the morning. How about you?"

"That's my view exactly. Tell me something. What was that you were saying this afternoon ... about fishnet tights?"

• • • • •

Monday 2 January

It was two days later, the first Monday morning of the new year, when Marnie drove Ralph to Heathrow. The pips were sounding for the eight o'clock news on BBC Radio 4 as they turned off the motorway and took the road leading into the huge airport. They had had a surprisingly good journey and now had over an hour to spare before Ralph's check-in time. At the end of the news bulletin came the item that brought their conversation to an abrupt halt.

"*... The government has announced the date for the by-election caused by the death of the MP for London Riverside, Tim Edmonds. It will take place on Thursday, 26 January. A memorial service for Mr Edmonds will be held a week later in his home town, Chichester. An appreciation of his life and work will be given by his close friend and fellow Conservative MP, Malcolm Grant, whose elevation to the peerage was announced in the New Year Honours list. In world markets the pound has continued to hold its own in the face of growing problems in the economies of the Pacific rim ...*"

"Do you want to listen to this, Ralph?"

"No. I've heard it all before." He smiled at Marnie. "Are you going to keep your hair short like that? It really does suit you." She shrugged and seemed not to be interested in the question. "Is everything all right?"

"I'm just concentrating on the traffic signs, plus the fact that several taxis are trying to fit into my exhaust pipes at the same time, and a maniac in a white van thinks this is the qualifying session for the British Grand Prix. Apart from that, everything's fine."

"Good."

"And ... you're about to go to the other side of the world when I've just got used to having you around. That might have something to do with it."

"Oh ..."

"Sorry." She gave him a quick smile and moved decisively into the lane for the short-term car park. "Didn't mean to hang the guilt thing round your neck."

"It's how I feel, too. Never mind. I'll be back next week."

They did not speak about what was really on their minds, and even when they eventually kissed goodbye at passport control, where Marnie remembered to give Ralph an extra kiss from Anne, neither of them mentioned memorial services, peerages or a certain dead MP. The nearest they came to any reference to their concerns was Ralph's last words before turning towards the departure lounge.

"Try to stay out of trouble ... at least until I get back."

Part 11

Monday 2 January 10.30 am

Marnie could hardly believe her luck. She had made reasonably good time to London from Heathrow after leaving Ralph and, as she pulled into Little Venice, a car was slipping out of a parking space immediately ahead of her, and not just any slot, one of the newly designated row of long-stay spaces. Making a New Year's resolution to think kind thoughts about Westminster City Council, she eased the Rover backwards to the kerb.

It was only a short walk to Warwick Avenue tube station, and Malcolm Grant came up the steps on the other side of the street within a minute of her arrival. Marnie stepped off the kerb and walked briskly towards him. He was wearing a camel-hair coat over a dark suit and sported a rather smart trilby. Marnie liked hats on men, especially when they wore them with a sense of style, like Malcolm Grant. He recognised her at once and smiled.

"I hope I haven't kept you waiting," he said. Marnie offered her hand. "Not at all. Is the café down the road okay for you?"

"It's fine. You lead the way. This isn't really my neck of the woods."

They set off towards the pool of Little Venice, walking briskly in the chilly air.

"I thought you lived near here."

"Other side of the park. I hardly know this part at all. In fact, I wasn't sure I was going to get here on time. I thought the tube'd be quicker. I came up from the House. I've got things to sort out in the office. Clearing my desk, you know."

"Oh, yes, of course. I should congratulate you ... on your peerage."

He made a sound like a grunt and muttered something. Marnie only caught the words "put out to grass ...".

"Has it happened yet? I mean, do I call you Lord Grant, or does that have to wait till you've been *elevated* or whatever happens?"

He shrugged. "I don't want to be stuffy about it. Do call me Malcolm, unless of course you like to keep relations with clients on a more formal basis."

"No, that's fine ... and please call me Marnie."

Still walking, he reached over to shake her hand. "That's agreed then. Marnie it is. Did you come on the tube?"

"No, not actually. In fact, I feel rather guilty about it, but I drove in. I invariably do. I'm afraid I've always used the car for business and it's become a habit."

"No reason to feel guilty about it. You have to do what's right for you – that's what the roads are for. It's called freedom of choice. Mind you, I'd have thought parking round here could be a nightmare. I wouldn't want you to get a ticket."

"*Tickets!*" said Marnie. "I could paper the walls with them ..."

Grant turned and smiled at her. "I was rather hoping for something a little more conventional for the flat. So where did you manage to park?"

Marnie pointed across the road. "Over there. Mine's the dark blue one."

He stopped for a few seconds as if focusing on it. "That sporty-looking Rover? Nice to see someone buying a *British* car ..."

They turned the corner and Marnie automatically crossed over to take the pavement that ran alongside the canal towpath. *Could he really be a suspect in a murder investigation?* she wondered.

"And is one of these boats yours?" They looked at the row of colourful craft lining the canal banks on the other side of the railings. Marnie knew them all and their owners and regarded them as friends.

"No. When I moved to Northamptonshire, I took her up with me."

Grant's eyes twinkled again. "Or the other way round, perhaps?"

Marnie laughed. "Yes. I suppose so." As they walked along in conversation, she found herself impressed by his curiosity about everything and the energy he exuded. *Could we both be suspects in a murder investigation?* she wondered. It occurred to her that he would probably be very formidable in debate in the Commons. He would make them sit up and take notice in the Lords, all right. He was asking technical questions about the different types of narrowboats when they arrived at the café perched over the canal at the entrance to Maida Hill tunnel.

Inside, two waitresses were chatting with another young woman behind the bar. One of them broke away to show them to a table on the balcony overlooking the water. She gave them each a menu.

"This is delightful, Marnie. Thank you for suggesting it." Grant's voice was warm and cultured, but not plummy. A trip boat slid quietly out of the tunnel immediately beneath where they sat, brightly painted in red and yellow and green, with a good number of passengers leaning out from under the awning even at this time of year, and they peered down to look as it emerged into the open and chugged steadily along the canal, heading towards the pool, while the guide's commentary drifted faintly up to them from the loudspeaker.

"So you've never been here before?" Curiously, Marnie found this surprising.

"No, never. Perhaps I've spent too much time in London's other most exclusive club."

"The House of Commons," said Marnie.

"Exactly." He looked over her shoulder. "Are you ready to order?"

Marnie became aware of the waitress standing behind her. "Just coffee for me, I think."

Grant nodded, looked up at the waitress and asked her a question in rapid, and what sounded to Marnie like very fluent, Spanish. The effect on the waitress was astonishing. She smiled broadly, a warm, full smile in a wide mouth showing perfect white teeth. Her eyes sparkled with pleasure, and for a few moments they talked animatedly together. Then, she turned and walked away.

"They have a speciality here, apparently ... almond pastries, made by their chef from an old Spanish recipe, possibly from Majorca. I've taken the liberty of ordering us one each, since she recommended them so highly. I hope you don't mind."

"Fine," said Marnie. "So she's Spanish, then?"

"Argentinian, actually, I think."

"Oh, is that what she was saying?"

"No. It was her accent."

"Her *accent?*"

"Yes, I think so ... it's quite distinctive. Now, where were we? Oh yes, you were telling me about the difference between a barge and a narrowboat. Do go on."

Marnie was drawn further into a description of boats in general and *Sally Ann* in particular, of trads, semi-trads, tugs and Joshers. Grant's questions were intelligent and perceptive, and she gradually came to realise that, for a man, and a *politician* at that, he was that rare species, a good listener. He seemed genuinely interested, and Marnie could not believe it was just the politician's technique of making someone feel that they were the most important person around.

"Marnie, may I just ask you something?"

"Like when am I going to get round to talking about redecorating your flat, for example?"

"Something rather less agreeable, I'm afraid. Are you going to be seeing the police during your visit?"

"I have an appointment in the morning ... to sign my statement. That's the other matter that brings me to London."

He nodded slowly and said nothing while the waitress brought their order. Another exchange in Spanish, a flash of the smile, and she was gone. Marnie cut off a piece of the pastry. It was light and delicious. They both agreed it had been a good decision.

"What about you?" said Marnie.

"I think it's very tasty."

"Your *statement*, I mean. Have you had to sign one?"

"Tomorrow morning for me, too."

"Inspector Bruere?"

"The very same." They ate in silence for a minute. Marnie wanted to ask Grant if he was treated like a suspect, but she could not find a way of asking without making it seem as if she thought so, too. It was Grant who broke the silence. "Actually, Marnie, I wonder ... if it would suit you, of course ... Do you think we might be able to look at the flat after going to the station? I have to go to a meeting very shortly, but perhaps you could come and see it tomorrow ... if you're still interested in the idea?"

"Well, yes. It's how I earn my living. That's why I'm here now."

He sighed and seemed almost weary. "Yes. But it can't be very pleasant for you having to associate with me. It must be a constant reminder to you about something you'd much rather put behind you and forget about."

"Forgetting isn't going to be easy ... not for a long time."

"No, but it can't help the situation having to deal with someone you know is a murder suspect."

Marnie choked on a piece of flaky pastry and quickly took a sip of coffee. Grant raised a hand and called across to the waitress in Spanish, and in seconds he was handing her a glass of water.

"I'm *terribly* sorry," he said, passing her his paper napkin. "I'm afraid that took you by surprise."

Marnie shook her head and croaked, "No ... not at all ... it was just the pastry." She coughed. Grant smiled. Suddenly they began to laugh at each other.

"I promise not to do that again, Marnie."

"It's a deal. And I'm sure they don't think of you as a suspect."

Grant shrugged. "From what I've seen of Bruere, he's probably had his grandmother rounded up for questioning, just to be on the safe side. Anyway, you think tomorrow might suit you?"

"I can meet you at the station, presumably ... unless you think we ought to be discreet about meeting."

"No. It's not a police state ... not yet. We still run most of our country, for the time being at any rate."

"And we'll have a look at the flat? I need to see it in daylight to get a feel for a choice of colour schemes. It'll depend on what *you* want, of course, but I want to get the best impression of what might be possible."

"You mean you aren't just going to provide what the Sunday supplements tell us are the *in* colours at the moment?"

Marnie shook her head. "It's *your* home. *You're* going to have to live with it. My job is to look at the flat, see how the light comes into each room, check out your taste in furniture. There are all sorts of practical questions."

"Such as?"

"Do you want to replace the curtains or do they all have to stay? What type of flooring do you have? If you spent a few thousand on carpets two years ago, I need to know your wishes. That sort of thing ..."

"It sounds fascinating, Marnie. I think I'm going to enjoy this."

"And it won't just be *my* ideas. It would help a lot if you thought about any changes *you* might want to make ... is there any part of the flat that you want to make brighter ... are there any features you particularly like and want to keep ... a certain colour on the walls or in the curtains? I always like clients to feel they have ownership of the scheme."

Grant nodded. "Right. I'll give it some thought. It'll help take my mind off things." He finished his coffee and looked at his watch. "I'm sorry to rush you, Marnie, but I ought to get going. Would you mind if I settled the bill now?"

"Oh, let me. I seem to remember I invited you here. This should be my treat."

"Nice of you, Marnie, but I'm rather old-fashioned about things like that. I hope you don't find it too off-putting. Excuse me a moment." He got up and went over to the bar. While he was away, the waitress came and cleared the table. Marnie glanced over her shoulder and saw Grant talking to the young woman at the till.

Marnie smiled up at the waitress. "Where do you come from?"

"I come from Argentina." She had a smile that any model or film star would be proud to own. "Do you know Argentina?"

"No. My parents live in Spain, in Almeria."

"Your lover speaks ..." The waitress stopped and put her hand over her mouth. "No ... is wrong. Sorry, I meant your ..." She searched for the word. "... *boyfriend?* he speaks very good Spanish, just like the Spanish. Sorry, I make mistake very much." She giggled charmingly when she saw that Marnie had not been embarrassed by her *mistake very much.*

Outside, Grant asked Marnie if he could give her a lift anywhere by taxi, but she explained she would be visiting a friend. While they stood on the pavement, turning their collars up against the cold, she told him about her conversation with the waitress. Grant chuckled.

"Oh well, it could've been worse … she could have said your *father*!" They laughed together again. He waved at a cab and they had to wait for it to perform a U-turn to reach them. Grant turned to Marnie and lowered his voice. "Marnie, it would be fine if you wanted to bring a colleague with you when you come to the flat … you have to be so careful meeting strangers in a house. Think of that poor young woman estate agent who disappeared in Fulham all those years ago."

"You're hardly a stranger, Malcolm." It was the first time she had called him by his first name.

"Nice of you to say so, but you must still be careful …"

Marnie was about to hold out her hand, when he raised his hat, smiled and climbed into the taxi. She watched it go for a few moments until the cab disappeared in the noisy traffic of the Edgware Road. *Could he really be a suspect?* Marnie looked down at her watch. It was twelve noon. She shivered in a blast of wintry air and walked off quickly to cover the short distance to a familiar front door.

• • • • •

"Oh, Marnie, come in out of the cold! It's *lovely* to see you." And Marnie was swallowed up in the usual warmth and hospitality of Mrs Jolly, who led the way to her sitting room where a fire was burning in the hearth and a bottle of wine was standing already opened, with plates and cutlery on a butler's tray-table. "Now you give me your coat and make yourself comfortable in here while I bring lunch through. With you in just a minute."

Marnie settled in an armchair, mentally bracing herself for turkey sandwiches. Mrs Jolly was as good as her word and re-appeared within moments.

"I bet you're expecting turkey sandwiches and a left-over mince pie …" She set down two plates and turned to go back to the kitchen.

"Oh, no …" Marnie began to protest, at least partly honest.

"Well don't you worry. No danger of that. Would you like to pour us a glass of wine? It's Australian. I got it at the supermarket. I hope it's all right." She was gone.

Marnie poured a little into one glass. It was deep red, a Shiraz Cabernet from South-Eastern Australia. The bouquet was wonderful. She took a trial sip. Mrs Jolly returned with salt and pepper and sat in the opposite chair while Marnie finished pouring.

"Any good?"

"First class. An excellent choice. Cheers and a Happy New Year!" They raised their glasses to each other.

"I hope it's all right, but I've done something very simple, a sort of post-Christmas, nothing-to-do-with-Christmas thing. It's only a so-called ploughman's lunch."

"If it tastes as good as it looks, it'll be marvellous."

"I baked the bread myself this morning, and the pear chutney's home-made … my mother's old recipe …"

"What's the cheese?" said Marnie. "It looks like … dolcelatte?"

"It's gorgonzola. I always get it from the little Italian delicatessen down the road. Beautiful mild creamy taste. I hope you like it."

"Why do I always feel as if I've come home when I visit you, Mrs Jolly?"

"I'm glad you feel like that, my dear. It's always a pleasure to see you … even it if is for just a pseudo snack lunch."

"*Pseudo?*"

"Well, it's not a real meal, a *ploughman's lunch*. There never was any such thing, of course, at least not when I knew ploughmen on the farms in Hampshire when I was a girl before the war. The idea was just an invention by the pubs for trendies and yuppies, oh sorry Marnie, don't take offence …"

Marnie laughed. "*Moi?*"

"Anyway, said she trying to change the subject and not put her foot in it again, tell me what you've been up to, Marnie. You certainly find yourself in some scrapes."

"Yes." Marnie sighed. "Where shall I begin?"

Mrs Jolly suddenly stood up. "Napkins. I always forget something. Won't be a minute." As she went out, Marnie heard her mutter, "Perhaps the question is – where will it all end?"

• • • • •

Tuesday 3 January 9.30 am

Marnie was escorted out to the reception area of the police station by a young WPC. It was the following morning. She looked at the people sitting around the walls, but Malcolm Grant was not among them.

"I don't suppose you know if Malcolm Grant is here?" she said to the policewoman.

"Not sure. I'll ask for you." She left Marnie and turned to speak to the desk sergeant.

"Would that be *Lord* Grant?" she said when she returned.

"Er, yes."

"He's in with Inspector Bruere, but he should be coming through any time now. Would you like to take a seat and wait for him here?"

Marnie found a place near the door. After a minute she became aware that a youth, pimply and with greased fair hair, was glancing repeatedly in her direction. She found this disconcerting, but then came to the conclusion that he was looking beyond her and sizing up the possibility of doing a runner. It almost made her smile to think that she might feel obliged to bring him down in a rugby tackle if he made the attempt.

Was this the right thing to do? she wondered. Or should she walk down the road and hope Grant would ring her on the mobile when he was free? She decided to give it ten minutes and imagined Bruere giving him the third degree, with spotlight in the face and chunks of lead-filled hosepipe being waved with menace. He was more likely being addressed as *My Lord* and having tea served in a china cup with saucer. That was how the British establishment worked. *She* had had a brief talk with DS Wallace with coffee in a throwaway plastic beaker and signed her statement. *He, his Lordship* (well, almost) was received by the Inspector.

She looked up from her watch to find Bruere coming towards her across the floor. Suddenly she felt nervous. She swallowed and stood up, wondering if there was something wrong with her statement, trying to conceal her anxiety.

"Mrs Walker, good morning. Can we have a quick word?" He gave a perfunctory smile, and seemed relaxed enough. They went into a small office down the corridor.

"Is there a problem with my statement?"

"No. It's fine. It's just that we need to be able to keep in touch with you."

"But I've told you all I know." She realised she was sounding like a cliché. It was just like the year before. Each time she spoke to the police, everything seemed unreal.

"You are a key witness, or at least the nearest thing to a witness that we have. We need to know where we can reach you. We've tried your home number and got the answerphone telling us your office is closed. We've tried Dr Lombard's home number and got no reply at all. We tried your mobile and it's switched off."

"Is it?" Marnie reached into her bag and brought it out. "Well, it seems to be on now."

"It was yesterday that we tried it."

"But I'm *sure* it was ..." She shook her head. "I must have touched the button by accident."

"So how do we contact you if we have to?"

"I'm at my sister's house in Chiswick." She gave him the number. "I'll be there for a few days and then back home to Knightly."

"I gather you've been speaking to Lord Grant." Bruere looked her steadily in the face.

"I'm planning the redecoration of his flat."

"Nice flat is it?"

"I don't know. I'm sure it is."

"You don't know?"

"I haven't been there yet. We're going this morning ... when you've finished with him." That did not quite sound the way she had meant it.

"You've known him long? Through Tim Edmonds, perhaps?"

"I never met Tim Edmonds."

"Of course, I was forgetting. You just mix in the same circles."

Marnie breathed in and spoke slowly. "I met Malcolm Grant by chance when I was at the House of Commons before Christmas."

"And he asked you to redecorate his flat ... the first time you met."

"It's a business arrangement. That's how I earn my living. I'd do yours if you asked me to." She had no idea why she said that, but Bruere was irritating her, twisting everything to make it seem suspicious.

"I'm sure I couldn't afford you, Mrs Walker. I'm not a member of that charmed circle. Tell me something. Your meeting at the House of Commons ... who organised it?"

Marnie thought back to the encounter when she had been left alone in the Pugin Room and Grant had come to her rescue. "It was pure chance."

"Pure ... chance." She knew he was thinking, *you come across a dead MP in the canal; he has your business card in his wallet; you say you never met him; a few days later you're in the Commons where you bump into the dead man's best friend and it's all just coincidence.* But all he said was, "Pure ... chance."

"I could find witnesses if you want."

"Of course you could."

"Inspector Bruere, tell me something. Is it true that Tim Edmonds was on his way to see Malcolm … Malcolm Grant the evening he died?"

"Yes."

"Can you tell me if Mr Grant is regarded as a suspect?" She was sure she knew what the answer would be.

"Anyone can be a suspect, Mrs Walker." She had been right.

"Including me, of course."

"In principle, yes. It's nothing personal. We learn that it isn't wise to rule *anybody* out, and you'd do well to think the same." His expression was very serious. "You should be careful about what you say and to whom you say it, Mrs Walker. This is a serious business. But then I don't need to tell you about murder, do I?"

Bruere left her in reception. Walking back to his office, he was wondering if anything was really pure chance where Marnie Walker was concerned. Standing by the entrance door, Marnie was looking at her watch again, wondering why the inspector had called her in to ask for her phone number. And how did he know she was at Ralph's? In fact, how did he know Ralph's home number, Ralph's *ex-directory* home number? She did not see Malcolm Grant until he appeared at her side.

"Marnie, good morning. Have you been here long?"

"Hallo. No, my interrogators have only just put the electrodes away." She hoped she sounded more light-hearted than she felt.

"I know just how you feel. Let's get out of here." Outside, it was even colder than before, with a wind-chill that cut through clothing. "Marnie, are you still okay about coming to see the flat?"

"Of course."

"I'll call a cab."

"We could get my car if you like."

"Are you on a meter?"

"Yes, one of the long-stay slots where it was the other day – I was lucky again."

"Then let's go by taxi. Pity to lose your parking place. They're not easy to find by the pool of Little Venice."

• • • • •

The flat was on the first floor, reached by an elegant curving staircase. Grant opened the polished mahogany door and stood aside for Marnie to go in. He took her coat and led her into the drawing room. It was just what she had expected. Tall ceiling, three long sash windows looking out onto the quiet tree-lined street. The furniture was antique sofas and armchairs in an assortment of deep colours now slightly faded, with a serpentine sideboard against the further end wall. Three oriental rugs were laid on the carpet. The walls were covered in a striped paper in cream and gold that was starting to show its age. Fifteen minutes from central London, the house seemed to stand in a serene corner where the sounds of the huge city could not penetrate.

"Why don't you just wander around while I make coffee. And I have to make a quick phone call. It won't take a moment."

"Fine." Marnie took out her notebook. "Would you mind if I took some Polaroids … or is the flat covered by the Official Secrets Act, or something?"

Grant came into the room carrying a tin of coffee. Marnie noticed it was from Fortnum and Mason. "Polaroids?"

Marnie pulled out the camera and held it up for him to see. "Instant photos. I normally use them when a job isn't on the doorstep. It helps me to have a record of all the details I might need to take into account when I'm planning a scheme."

"Right." He seemed hesitant.

"They just stay in a file in my office ... nobody sees them except me ... and possibly my assistant. Look, don't worry if you'd rather not. I'd quite understand."

"No. You go ahead, Marnie ... if you think it, well, necessary."

"You seem uncertain, Malcolm."

He shrugged and smiled. "I suppose I've lived too long surrounded by police warnings and security measures ... a hazard of the job, I'm afraid. You do what you need to do, if it will help."

"Are you sure?"

"Yes. It'll be fine. Really."

She made her tour of inspection and the more she saw, the more she became interested in the job. It would be a real challenge and a pleasant change from pubs and restaurants. Her notes grew alongside her list of questions and she had to rein herself in, knowing that the budget would have to be carefully worked out to keep within reasonable limits. When she returned to the drawing room, Grant had brought in the coffee with a plate of biscuits.

"I thought we might open these. They were in a hamper I was given by a grateful constituent." He began pouring the coffee into bone china cups. "Unless you're on an after-Christmas diet, of course. Mind you, I can't imagine why you should be ... you're beautifully slim."

Marnie heard a small alarm bell tinkling faintly in the distance at this first personal observation. She took the cup he offered her. "I think we're going to have to talk budgets at some stage in the proceedings, Malcolm. I've just spent the first million ..."

He smiled at her. "Good. I don't like half measures."

They talked for nearly an hour about colours and curtains and carpets. There were no further personal remarks and they sat on opposite sides of a low coffee table. It was all perfectly business-like and professional. Grant asked intelligent questions and gave helpful answers to Marnie's. Eventually, he looked at his watch. Marnie took this as a cue to bring the discussion to an end.

"We've made good progress," she said. "I wish all my clients were as well-prepared as you are. But now, you must have other things to do." She began gathering her notes and papers together.

"Not at all, Marnie. I was just wondering ... It's getting on for twelve o'clock. How's your parking meter?"

"I'm all right, as long as I get back by about one."

"Have you made any plans for lunch?"

"I hadn't given it any thought."

"Would you consider a sandwich in a pub? Of course, I don't want to force myself on you ..."

"Well, why not? I was only going to my sister's to pack. I'm going back to Knightly."

"Your sister won't be expecting you for lunch?"

"She's in Spain this week, visiting our parents. They retired to the south coast. Sun, sea and golf courses."

"So you're alone."

"A short break."

Grant stood up and Marnie took this as a signal to leave. Instead, he gestured towards the sideboard topped by a tray containing bottles of all shapes and sizes. "A quick aperitif before we go?"

"Better not, thanks. I shall be driving. And that's a beautiful sideboard, by the way." They both knew it was Chippendale, two hundred years old, but neither said so.

"Yes. One of the things I brought up from home. I think we've had it since new." Marnie smiled to herself at his reference to *brought up*, even though Cumbria was almost as far north in England as you could go. To Grant's class, London, the capital, was always *up*.

She admired the piece of furniture. It looked better than new, with the patina of age buffed by generations of care and polishing. She tried to see it in her imagination against a wall newly decorated with a vibrant colour. As she looked at it, she became aware that beside the bottles stood a small parcel wrapped in gift paper, gold and burgundy, a left-over from Christmas.

Grant was speaking. "It always makes me think of that painting by Winston Churchill, *Bottlescape*. Do you know it by any chance? It's at Chartwell, you know, his house in Kent, I think."

"Oh, really. I was just wondering about that present. You haven't opened it. It seems a shame."

Grant walked slowly towards the sideboard, his head bent. His voice was subdued when he spoke again. "It's not for me. It was the present I got for Tim. He was coming here that afternoon ... when he died. I was going to give it to him then." Grant coughed lightly. "Somehow I haven't had the heart to move it for some silly reason."

"I'm sorry. I shouldn't have mentioned it. Being nosy is part of the job. I didn't mean to intrude."

"You weren't to know. How could you?"

"I'm still sorry to stir up sad memories."

Grant walked over to Marnie and took hold of her hand. "You know I'm responsible for Tim's death, don't you?" Marnie could feel the colour drain from her face. She did not move. She was scarcely breathing. "If he hadn't been coming here that day, he'd be alive now. I blame myself." For a second she was convinced he was going to burst into tears. She put her free hand on his shoulder. The absurd thought came to her that it must have looked as if they were going to dance.

"You mustn't think that, Malcolm. You couldn't possibly know what would happen. No one can live like that. We can't know the consequences of our actions, especially simple things like inviting a friend round for a drink or whatever ..."

He raised his hand and touched her cheek, putting one finger against her lips. It was a gesture of extraordinary intimacy from a man she hardly knew, but she suddenly realised that she had no fear of him. They remained in that position for only a few seconds before Grant turned away. "Sorry to impose myself like this. Bad form. And thank you, Marnie, for what you said. If you don't mind, I should like never to speak about it again." He walked out of the room. Marnie shook herself mentally and went over to pick up her bag. When Grant re-appeared, he was holding her coat and seemed to have brightened up.

"I suspect you've probably had enough of me for one day. So if you'd rather not bother about lunch, I'd quite understand." He helped Marnie into her coat.

"Let's go and eat," she said.

• • • • •

Tuesday 3 January 12 noon

The taxi pulled into a quiet side street round the corner from the pool of Little Venice and drew up outside a pub that had a long connection with boating people. Marnie enjoyed being there again. "I feel guilty about dragging you around my old canal haunts, but I feel this is my part of London."

Grant paid the driver and turned to take Marnie's arm. "Did you actually live on your boat?" Marnie accepted his arm in the way she was sure he meant it: an expression of old-fashioned courtesy. For an older man, she was quite surprised that he never patronised her, never called her *my dear*, and never indulged in the kind of innuendo used by many men in their treatment of women they found attractive. They crossed the pavement and he held the door open for her.

"No. I had a flat in north London ..."

"Whereabouts?"

"In Hampstead, near the Heath." The pub was not yet crowded and they found a table.

"Lovely area," said Grant. "Probably the best part of London in my opinion." He took her coat. "Marnie, let's not talk about business or ... you know ... events. Tell me about your boat. If you don't think I'm prying, of course."

"Not at all. And strictly speaking, she's not my boat actually. *Sally* belongs to my sister and her husband. They lent her to me the year before last. I went away on her for the whole summer and I've been hooked ever since. In fact, I'm buying her now."

"I'd love to hear all about her ... and your adventures on her. Shall we first look at the menu?"

Across the floor, a man lowered his newspaper and looked over at Marnie and Grant. He liked what he saw. He had watched Grant help her off with her coat, which was long, black and dramatic. His gaze took in her short dark hair, the long grey tunic, tied Cossack-style with a belt at the waist, and the black loose-fitting trousers tucked into her boots. On the table in front of him sat a pint glass, almost empty. Marnie was vaguely aware of his stare, but was well accustomed to such attentions and paid no heed. Grant seemed not to have noticed him at all.

The menu was on a blackboard fixed to the wall, and Marnie and Grant studied it in silence for a few moments before choosing. "I know I suggested a sandwich," said Grant, "but don't feel obliged. Have what you will."

"A sandwich will be just right. They do a very good prawn salad here."

"Then I'll follow your example. And to drink?"

"Sparkling mineral water, please."

"Would you mind if I had a glass of wine?" said Grant. "It seems unfair, but I'm not driving and to be honest I've never quite got the hang of this trendy water business."

Marnie smiled. "Then perhaps I could join you with a spritzer."

"Excellent!" He headed for the bar. Marnie was surprised how well she enjoyed his company. After all, he was a Tory MP, and a Thatcherite Eurosceptic, too. But unlike so many men she had known, he did not ramble on and on about himself, or try to impress her with lavish hospitality and compliments. He listened and seemed genuinely interested in what she said. And he had kept in good shape. She was not surprised that he was regarded as one of the handsomest men in the public eye. He was very distinguished, with fine bone structure and touches of grey at the temples. She thought she had read in an article that he regularly played squash at the Commons and had been the Seniors Champion there for some years.

While Grant was ordering, the man at the other side of the saloon bar rolled up his newspaper, finished the dregs of his beer and stood up, taking a last discreet look at Marnie before leaving. It was approaching twelve-thirty and the lunchtime customers were arriving at a steady rate. Marnie thought there was just enough time to eat before she had to give up her parking space. Grant returned from the bar carrying two tall glasses.

"I thought I'd try a spritzer as well." He put them down and took his seat. "First time I've had one of these yuppie drinks ... Oh, is that rude of me? It wasn't meant to be." He passed a glass to Marnie.

"That's the second time in two days I've been bracketed with the yuppies," said Marnie.

"Oh dear, black mark Grant. What I meant was ... I think I'm rather set in my ways, and I thought it would make a pleasant change to try something ... different, a new experience."

"You mean you're rather conservative in your tastes," said Marnie. "Not surprising, really."

"Quite. Well, cheers. Here's to health and happiness."

"I'll drink to that. Happy New Year." They touched glasses and drank.

"Mmm. That's rather pleasant. I can see why you like this sort of thing. So, now, you were going to tell me about the good ship *Sally Ann* and your summer cruise the year before last ..."

Marnie explained about feeling stale in her job and wanting a break, how the partners had agreed to a spell of extended leave and how she came to be looking after *Sally Ann* during her brother-in-law's sabbatical in the United States. Grant gave her his complete attention, only interrupting the flow of her story to ask about points of detail, the size of the boat, what kind of engine, and so on. Marnie was enjoying herself, reliving that summer voyage. She was just explaining how she came to discover the ruins of Glebe Farm, now her home, when the air seemed to shudder, the glasses rattled at the bar, followed a second later by a thunderclap as loud as a storm directly overhead. A woman by the door screamed.

After a moment's hesitation, Marnie was on her feet in an automatic reaction, moving round the table to head for the door to investigate. Everyone seemed to have frozen where they stood or sat. She had not gone two strides before she was grabbed by the wrist and pulled to the ground. Grant had firm hold on her and was down on one knee, his arm lying across her shoulders.

"*Jesus Christ almighty*! What the *hell* was that? Pardon my French, Marnie." Marnie just shook her head, her mind racing with possibilities. "Stay here, keep down, don't move."

"But –"

"No buts. Trust me, Marnie. I know about these things. There could be secondary devices. Just stay put." Grant leapt to his feet and moved rapidly across the floor, pulling people away from the door. He turned in the doorway to face into the pub. "Everybody get down and stay there!" There was a murmuring among the customers. Grant raised his voice to a parade-ground bellow. "All of you! Now! Just do it!" Everyone reacted and hit the ground. Grant pointed at the barman. "You! Nine-nine-nine! All three services. Do it, man!" The barman needed no further prompting and rushed out of sight.

Grant slipped out of the door. Marnie raised herself and looked around the bar. There was a low murmur as the lunch-time crowd stirred, asking each other what they thought was happening. Nobody moved. Nobody except Marnie, who picked her way across the floor bent double, stepping over the customers. Heads were raised to watch her passing, but no one commented. It occurred to her that with her newly bought clothes, she could well have been mistaken for a Cossack dancer squatting, and she was aware how odd she must have looked in the circumstances. She reached the door and, still kneeling, eased it open, feeling the cold clean air on her face. She could see nothing and hear nothing. There was an eerie silence, no sound of traffic, no shouting, no movement. But at least, thank goodness, no wailing or screaming. She moved out far enough to look up and down the road. From somewhere nearby a faint rumble could be heard, like the diesel engine of a narrowboat as it emerges from a tunnel, steady and low-pitched.

"Shouldn't you stay in here?" It was a man's voice behind her, speaking softly. He was peeping through the gap of the pub door. A young man, his features pinched as if suffering from the cold. "That man, the soldier, he said we should stay put. I don't think you should be out there."

Marnie lifted her hand. "We're together. It's all right. Keep everybody inside. I won't be a minute." Like him, she spoke quietly. He nodded and turned back. Marnie skirted the fronts of the houses in the side street and moved carefully and quietly up towards the sound she could hear. Reaching the end of the street, she bent down on one knee and peeped slowly round the corner. Malcolm Grant was a short distance ahead, squatting behind a car, talking quietly and urgently into his mobile phone. Marnie leaned out further and saw smoke. She knew at once that the sound she had heard was the sound of burning. One second later, she realised that the fire was consuming a car, thick smoke twisting up into the air, air that was polluted by the stench of burning rubber and oil. Marnie tried to make sense of what she saw. Far off, she heard the faint wail of a siren. Suddenly she gasped and raised a hand to cover her mouth. The centre of the blazing mass of wreckage was her car.

Part 12

Tuesday 3 January 2.30 pm

Later – it seemed like days later, but in reality only two hours had passed – Marnie sat in a quiet room, vaguely familiar, in the police station that was currently featuring prominently in her life. She realised she was in a state of shock, but definitely not in panic. Even so, it came as a surprise to her to discover that she was sitting in front of a cup of tea, with a plate of digestive biscuits. She could not remember why she was alone in the room.

Since the explosion that had destroyed her car, much of the aftermath had gone by in a blur. It all seemed somehow unsatisfactory, as if she had been shielded from the full impact of what had happened, like a small child being sheltered from an unhappy event. This was not how she lived her life. Marnie Walker, independent self-employed woman of the world, did not need to have the truth kept from her. Nor did she want to be pushed into a siding while others sorted out her problems. She especially did not want a man, and a Tory politician at that, to be discussing *her* business with the police, as if she was incapable of fending for herself.

She picked up a biscuit and irritably took a bite. It was the first food she had eaten since … since … she could not quite remember. *Pull yourself together! Of course you can remember if you just make the effort!* Yes, it was in the café by the tunnel. Almond pastry from Spain … no, Majorca. She drank some tea and finished the biscuit. It was at the moment when her mouth was at its fullest that Inspector Bruere – *who else?* – chose to come into the room.

He did not look sympathetic. "It's just being typed up. It won't take long. How are you feeling?"

"What is?" Even Marnie was surprised at the aggression in her voice.

Bruere's turn to be taken aback. "Your statement." He looked bewildered. "The one you made ten minutes ago. Are you feeling all right, Mrs Walker?"

"I suppose I'm a suspect for blowing up my own car, am I?"

Bruere frowned. "I'm not with you."

"Were you ever?"

He shook his head. "Shall I go back out and come in again or what? I'm missing part of the jigsaw here …"

Marnie sighed and sipped the tea. It was in a china cup, not *best* china, but not plastic throwaway, and it had a saucer. Perhaps she had been promoted in the police vision of the world from suspect to victim. She tried to work out why she was feeling so much aggression, and put it down to shock. "I'm sorry. It's not your fault. For some reason I just feel so … angry."

"Hardly surprising, is it?"

"Don't tell me I'm in a state of shock. I can work that out for myself."

"Look, Mrs Walker, I can understand how you feel. If someone had blown up my car, I'd be screaming blue bloody murder and wanting to tear them apart with my bare hands …"

She knew she should not do it, but Marnie smiled, and the smile turned into a laugh, but it soon subsided. "It is shock," she said, cradling her chin in her hands, elbows on the table.

Bruere sat down in the chair opposite. He looked puzzled. "We've got a medic coming to have a look at you. Standard procedure ... and don't tell me you're not injured. Delayed shock can do strange things, and we don't want you going out of here and fainting under a bus. It would look bad."

"You're all heart."

"So I'm told. If you want, we can get you to hospital so they can give you a thorough examination. It's up to you."

"I'll be okay. Thanks." She picked up another biscuit and broke off a piece, pushing the plate across the table to Bruere. Without speaking, he took one and they nibbled together in silence. It seemed almost companionable. Marnie looked at Bruere. "So what's next?"

"Haven't you had enough?" His expression was deadpan, but it spread into a slow smile.

"I mean what do I have to do now? What about my car? Do you have any advice for me ... such as, what do you usually say to people whose cars have been blown up by a bomb?"

"It's usually something like *rest in peace*." He was not smiling. Nor was Marnie. "The truth is, there isn't any standard procedure. You've had a narrow escape. We have to find out who did it and whether it had anything to do with you."

"The fact that it was my car might give you a clue there." Marnie sounded more flippant than she felt.

"If it was terrorists, it might have been a coincidence."

"In whodunnits, this is where you ask me if I believe in coincidences and I say 'no' and you agree."

"Something like that."

Marnie was exasperated. "It's got to be related, hasn't it?"

"I would've thought so."

"So this is where you ask me again what it is that I'm not telling you, right? And I insist, and then ..."

"And then we finally believe you?"

"Why not? You've got to start believing me some time."

"Yes. You're right."

"Really?"

"As you said ... why not?"

"Blimey! Now I know I'm in shock. Is that offer of a complete examination in hospital still on?"

• • • • •

A WPC walked with Marnie and Bruere along the corridor from the interview room. She had made a gesture towards taking Marnie by the arm, but as she was moving closer, one glance from Marnie was enough to persuade her that it was not a good idea.

"Be careful, Rosemary. This one bites," Bruere had said with a rueful smile.

"I'll remember," said the WPC.

Bruere looked at Marnie as they reached the door at the end of the corridor. "You'll keep your mobile on, okay? Any worries and you contact us straight away."

Marnie nodded. "Your number's engraved on my heart."

"It's not too late to change your mind about protection. We can put you up for a while."

"I'm sure I'll be all right at my sister's. No one knows I'm there. And I'll drive home in the morning."

"How?" said Bruere. It was a timely reminder.

"Ah ..." said Marnie.

"Quite."

"I'll organise something, but it might take another day." They pushed through the door to the entrance hall. The WPC walked over to the desk and came back with a bundle.

"Your coat, Marnie. We had it sent from the pub."

"It seems a long time since I was wearing this. A lot seems to have happened."

Bruere helped her on with it. "There's a taxi waiting for you outside."

"You're spoiling me."

"Don't thank us."

Marnie climbed in and leaned forward to talk to the driver through the partition. Before she could speak, he called back. "Chiswick?"

Marnie felt a chill hand at her throat as the cab pulled away from the kerb. "How did you know that?"

"I had orders to take you to Chiswick, but you have to give me the address, love."

"*Orders*? Who from?"

"Mr. Grant. He booked me to pick you up and take you home."

Marnie gave directions and shifted back in the seat. *No one knows I'm there* ... She had not seen Grant since they were taken to the station. She knew he was having separate interviews, and a message had reached her that he had gone on to see some other officers, presumably at Scotland Yard. Now that she was out of the police station, she was starting to wonder whether she was doing the right thing. She was wondering what was actually happening around her. What should she do about the car? What would be done with the wreckage? Absurdly, she was worrying about a cassette that she had borrowed from Beth to play on journeys. She had put it in the glove compartment for safe keeping. Now there was no cassette ... and no glove compartment.

She looked out of the taxi window at London going by. Everything looked cold and ordinary. Nobody was paying any attention to her or her cab. But out there somewhere, someone was more than passingly interested in her, interested enough to want to destroy her. She shuddered. If Malcolm had not taken her to the pub, she would have been in the car driving to Chiswick when the bomb went off. *My god* ...

Marnie turned in her seat to look out of the rear window. Was one of the cars trundling along behind following her taxi? She had never looked out of a taxi's rear window before. It was surprisingly dark, tinted a smoky brown colour. She became aware of a voice and turned back to ask the driver to repeat himself.

"I said what address is it, love?"

Marnie hesitated before replying. She had a ridiculous image in her mind of the driver tied to a chair in a dirty garage while masked thugs threatened him with knives to make him reveal the address where he had dropped her. Absurd!

"Do you know Hamer Road?"

"Is that the Hammersmith end?"

"No. It's near the railway station, not far from the Polytechnic stadium."

"I've got you."

"You can just drop me on the corner when we get there, please."

"Mr Grant said I had to see you safely to your door."

"The corner's fine."

"He won't be happy."

"He won't be there."

"Fair enough, love."

They were making good time through the afternoon traffic. Marnie opened her shoulder bag to rummage for Beth's door key and noticed that the fronts of her trousers were still dusty from kneeling on the floor in the pub. She brushed them with her hand. Her new trousers. A new year. A good start! She pulled her long coat over her legs. She certainly did not feel like a Cossack and probably did not look like one, either. The trouble with her life just now was that nothing was probably what it seemed. She felt an overwhelming temptation to ask the driver to wait while she collected her bag from Beth's and then take her straight back to Knightly St John.

They turned into a side street and drew to a halt at the next corner. "Are you sure this is as far as you want go?"

Marnie climbed out. "This'll be fine. How much do I owe you?"

"Nothing. It's all taken care of."

"I can pay for my own taxi," she protested.

"No problem. Anyway, this isn't a taxi. You take care now." He drove off, and Marnie watched until he turned into another road and was gone. She walked more briskly than usual down the quiet suburban street, looking surreptitiously to see if there was anyone sitting in a parked car or standing under a tree. Everything looked normal. She opened the front door quickly and left it open while she made a rapid tour of the house. It was empty. While she was closing the door behind her, her mobile rang. It was Malcolm Grant.

"Are you at your sister's?"

"Yes. Just arrived. Thanks for the taxi."

"Sorry to have left you like that, but there were people to see, matters to attend to ... It took some of the pressure off you, I hope. How are you feeling?" His voice seemed strained.

Marnie tried to sound light-hearted. "How can I put it? Confused, shaken, anxious, angry ... you could try any combination of those. On the other hand, I'm still alive, probably because you suggested a pub lunch. So you could add *grateful* to the list."

"What are you planning to do now?"

"Something tells me you're about to give me your views on that. I've been planning to stay here and organise transport for tomorrow so that I can go home."

"Right ..." His voice was vague. He was thinking. Suddenly he snapped back to attention. "Okay. Look, Marnie, I can tell you that the advice here is that you should try to disappear from view for a day or two. Do you have friends where you can stay tonight?"

"Tonight? I'll be okay here."

"Does anyone know where you are?"

"Not unless they followed the taxi." The thought made her flesh creep.

"No one did. Look, if you have any problems, ring me at once on the mobile. Don't hesitate. Okay?"

After hanging up, Marnie considered her options. It did not take long. The house, a hotel, back to Knightly, police protection. She could probably stay with Anne or Mrs Jolly, but that would put them in danger, if there was any danger. Anne and Mrs Jolly. Other friends. They would hear about the bomb on the news. She reached for the phone.

"Anne, it's me."

"Have you heard the news, Marnie?" Marnie could imagine her friend's face, eyes the size of dinner plates. She was speaking quickly, everything coming out in a rush. "I couldn't believe it when I heard them say Little Venice, I mean —"

"I know. Listen, Anne, listen to me. Just listen. It was my car. I was nowhere near it at the time and no one was hurt. Got that?"

"Blimey, Marnie! But you could have been —"

"And I wasn't. Okay? It was lucky no one was passing at the time. But that's it. End of story. It was probably just coincidence that it was my Rover they chose to bomb." As she said the words, Marnie wondered if she really believed this.

"Okay. If you say so."

"Good."

"It's sad about the car. It was really nice."

"Sure. There used to be a time when you just got a ticket for staying too long at a meter. That's what I call a deterrent!"

Anne did not laugh. "Have you phoned Ralph to tell him? He's bound to see the news and worry about you."

Marnie hesitated. "Well, no, not actually ..."

"Of course. There's a huge difference in time, isn't there? I was forgetting. So what's happening now? Friendly chats with Inspector Bruere, is it?"

"Among others. There are all sorts of people who deal with bombings. I may have more interviews to come."

"So not back to Knightly just yet?"

"I suppose not. I'll keep you posted."

"What about transport? You'll need a car."

"Why do I get the impression you're already making a list of things to be done?"

Next call: Mrs Jolly.

"Marnie! Have you heard what's happened in Little Venice?"

"A car was blown up by a bomb. It was my car."

"Oh, you've heard, then. People are saying it's the end of the IRA cease-fire. Though why anyone should pick on this area no one can understand."

"Mrs Jolly, you didn't hear what I said. I said it was *my* car, my Rover that was blown up."

"Oh my *goodness*! Are you all right? On the news it said that no one was in the car at the time of the explosion."

"I'm fine. The car was just parked by the pool of Little Venice. I was in the pub having lunch when it went off."

Mrs Jolly suddenly sounded as old as her years. Her voice lost its vigour and seemed to quiver down the line. "Oh my dear. This is all very distressing."

"Well, I'm not hurt and nor was anybody else."

"Thank *god* for that."

"Right. And the insurance will take care of the technicalities. I just wanted to let you know."

"Are you somewhere safe?"

"Absolutely. Don't worry about me."

Marnie made coffee and helped herself to a cognac. While she drank, she made more calls: Beth and their parents in Spain, Jane Rutherford, Molly Appleton at the village shop, the Burtons in cottage number one, Philip Everett and Faye Summers. She told no one where she was staying and asked them not to try ringing her on the mobile. Cellphone calls could be intercepted. She thought she was becoming paranoid. So what? Better than becoming dead.

She did not try ringing Ralph. She had no idea what time it was in Japan, and in any case he would be in a meeting somewhere. Not the kind of message you could leave with a hotel receptionist.

A few times, she looked out into the street from an upstairs window without moving the curtains. She could not help thinking she was behaving like a fugitive in a crime movie. There was nothing unusual outside. But it was not impossible that someone knew where she was. After dark, things could be different.

To take her mind off these thoughts, she went out to the garage. She wanted to see the MG while it was still light. There was the familiar dust sheet that she had made herself and decorated with an MG octagon logo on either side. She lifted it off and was surprised how clean the car was. Despite their complaints, Beth or Paul had kept the old sports car dusted, its green coachwork shining, the leather upholstery and interior protected by another cloth. She looked under the bonnet. There was no battery, but the engine looked reasonably clean. An idea was beginning to take shape in her mind. From the glove shelf she took out a card.

• • • • •

"Harrison and Dent, good afternoon."

"Hallo. My name is Marnie Walker. You've done some work for me in the past on my MG. I was wondering if you could have a look at it and see if you can get it running."

"Walker did you say? Just a sec." Marnie could hear tapping on a keyboard, in the background the sound of grinding, the whirr of machinery. "TA, 1936, British racing green. Simon Walker. Finchley. That the one?"

"That's it. Only it's in Chiswick these days."

"Just down the road, then. But presumably you can't bring it in."

"That's the problem."

"Give me your address." Marnie hesitated before speaking. The man from the garage took the details. "How soon do you want it?"

"The usual."

"Yesterday. Right. Same as everybody else. Hang on a minute." Marnie could hear muffled voices. "Mrs Walker? We're not busy and you aren't far away. Could I collect it on the trailer after work? I could be round before six. Will someone be at home?"

• • • • •

Marnie spent the next hour or so writing notes about her work schedule for the coming months. There was plenty to keep Walker and Co busy, but she found it hard to concentrate. Her mind kept wandering. She asked herself if she really was in serious danger and saw the Rover blazing at the roadside. She needed a survival plan. She needed advice. It was nearly six. She picked up the phone. Roger Broadbent was still in his office.

"Happy New Year, Marnie. We can always live in hope. How are things? Is this a social call?"

"Roger, my car was destroyed by a bomb in Little Venice at lunchtime."

"Not a social call. *Christ!* Are you okay?"

"Yes. Luckily I wasn't in it at the time."

"Where are you now, Marnie?"

"That's the point. I'm at my sister's place in Chiswick. The police are advising me to keep out of the way. I don't think anyone knows where I am, but I can't be sure. I was wondering if I should go home."

"Hardly inconspicuous. Let me think." There was a pause lasting several seconds. Marnie heard a cup being replaced on a saucer. "Can you meet me at the supermarket at Kensal Green in about an hour?" The front doorbell rang.

"Sainsbury's? Yes, I can. What do you have in mind?"

"Bring your suitcase. All your things. I'd better get going."

The bell rang again, and Marnie walked to the front door. As she went to open it, her stomach turned, but she recognised the man from the MG specialists. He announced himself as Michael Dent, and she led him through to the garage.

He walked round the car, sticking his nose into every corner, kneeling down to peer underneath. "Doesn't look too bad. I was wondering what had become of it just the other day. We thought you might have got rid of it."

"There are some things you don't get rid of."

"Right. How's your husband by the way?"

"He isn't one of them."

A pause while the meaning sank in. "Ah. Sorry."

"Don't be. I'm not."

"On a practical note ..."

"The car belongs to me. The papers are in my name. I'll settle the bill."

"Fine."

"As you say, on a practical note, when can you have a look at it? I'm rather desperate at the moment."

He walked round the car again, looked in the engine compartment, checked the tyres were firm, pulled the handbrake. "Good foresight, taking the battery out and leaving the handbrake off." *Thank you, Paul.* "I can have a look at it in the morning. But I checked our records. We've done quite a bit of work on it already. That's an XPAG engine in there, good as new. Recon gearbox. Dodgy clutch. Pity not to be running it. How can I contact you?"

"That's difficult. I've got meetings. Can I ring you tomorrow afternoon?"

"Sure."

"One other thing. Do you think you could drop me at a tube station?"

• • • • •

Night had fallen as Marnie approached the supermarket. Her mobile rang.

"Marnie, it's Malcolm. I think we need to talk. I'm worried. We need to plan."

"I'm tied up just now."

"Okay. I don't think it'd be a good idea for me to come to Chiswick. Could we meet somewhere for dinner?"

Marnie felt things were moving too fast. "I'm not sure. It's been rather a tiring day, you know."

"That's why I suggest we talk. We can't do it on the phone."

"All right. But I don't want to be late."

"Fine. Where shall we meet? You choose."

"Do you know Albert's in Regent's Park Road?"

"Isn't that rather a long way from Chiswick?"

"That's okay. I'll be there at eight."

• • • • •

Marnie spotted Roger in the supermarket at the checkout. His trolley was full. "Are you planning for a siege, Roger?"

"No. You are."

"What do you mean?"

"Help me with this lot and I'll explain outside."

Instead of wheeling the trolley out to the car park, Roger turned left towards the canal. Between them, they lifted it over the grid designed to keep trolleys away from the water, and trundled along to where *Rumpole* was moored. They unloaded everything onto the deck, and Marnie took the trolley back while Roger ferried the bags and Marnie's case down into the galley. They cast off and pushed away from the path. Compared with *Sally Ann*, Marnie found Roger's boat as quiet as a whisper. The headlamp lit up the water ahead of them, and there was no other traffic on the canal that evening as they slipped between the houses and offices that lined the cut. Roger and Marnie stood close together with the tiller between them.

"This is all very mysterious, Roger."

"I've had an idea. You phoned me for advice, and I have some for you."

"I expected legal advice from my solicitor."

"I haven't got any. At least, nothing that'll help deal with your present circumstances. I've got help and advice as a friend, though. I think that's what you need right now."

Marnie put her hand on Roger's arm. "What do you have in mind?"

Roger explained his plan as *Rumpole* cut steadily through the dark water, heading down past Porta Bella dock and the Harrow Road towards Little Venice. "You can't stay at your sister's house, Marnie. Not if someone's looking for you. It's too easily traced. You can't return to Knightly St John for the same reason. And that applies to staying with friends as well."

"You're cheering me up, Roger. Should I just jump into the canal now and save us all a lot of bother?"

He reached over and put his arm round her shoulder, squeezing her gently. "Take the tiller for a minute. I'm making coffee." Standing alone on the aft deck, Marnie felt isolated and vulnerable again, though she realised that on the canal she was in a secret world outside the realities of life in general. Roger was soon back on deck. The coffee tasted good, and the warmth of the cup penetrated Marnie's gloves as she held it in both hands. Something else in the coffee penetrated more deeply too.

"Rum?"

Roger nodded. "Just the thing for a winter's evening."

"Go on about your help and advice from a friend. I don't think we've got to that bit yet."

"You need somewhere safe to stay. Simple as that."

"Yes. I'd worked that much out by myself."

"So where do you go?"

"Ah. That's the bit I haven't got sorted." She sipped the coffee for comfort.

"Do you remember Old Peter's mooring?"

"Down by Paddington Basin?"

"It's not been used much since he died. I cruised down there a week or two ago. The gap where he moored is still there."

"Not surprising. It's a dump."

"Apparently someone is renting it, but they're away for a while."

"You're suggesting I bring *Sally Ann* down here and live on the arm that leads to Paddington Basin?"

"No. You couldn't get her down here. Too many winter lock closures. Anyway, you might be spotted. I'm suggesting you stay on *Rumpole* and use Old Peter's mooring. No one would ever know you were there."

Marnie looked at Roger in amazement. "That's brilliant!"

After half an hour they passed under the bridge by the canal office and entered the pool, turning right past Browning Island and easing their way into the narrow channel leading to Paddington Basin. Even on a bright day, this was a gloomy stretch, with office buildings keeping out the light, and grimy bridges criss-crossing the murky, litter-filled water. But in the dark of a January evening, with no light but the headlamp on *Rumpole*, it was a sad and depressing place. It seemed unconnected with other parts of the city and as undesirable an area as Marnie could imagine. She thought the rats hereabouts would probably go around in pairs for safety.

"What do you think?" said Roger.

"It's beautiful."

• • • • •

After Roger had left, Marnie unpacked and took stock of her new base. *Rumpole* was spacious and better equipped than *Sally Ann*, with a modern shower room, plenty of storage – now filled with provisions – and an efficient diesel-fired heating system. Because Roger and Marjorie mainly used the boat for relaxation and entertaining, much of the cupboard space was empty. Marnie rationalised most of Roger's tackle into one cupboard containing cleaning gear, tools, spare ropes and a child's fishing net. This came as no surprise, since most boaters carried a net for retrieving objects lost over the side in the shallow water of canals. But Marnie found herself smiling. In her mind she had an image of Roger, big burly solid Roger the solicitor, sitting on the side of the boat with his trousers rolled up to his knees. He had a handkerchief knotted on his head to protect his scalp under its light down of thinning hair, and was holding the fishing net, looking like a garden gnome. Chuckling quietly, she began to unpack her clothes.

They had agreed on two major policy decisions. The first was that Marnie would not use the solid-fuel stove in case the smoke from the lum betrayed the presence of someone on board. The second was that Marnie would not use her mobile phone except in an emergency. This introduced a sinister element into the equation that disturbed her, with worries about surveillance and the monitoring of calls. But she knew she had to agree. And there was a phone on *Rumpole* that she could use in safety.

Outside, the bank was surfaced in concrete bounded at one end by a bridge, enclosed by a high brick wall. The area extended alongside the moored boats, leading down to Paddington Basin half a mile away. A door set into the wall opened onto the street where traffic rolled by on its way towards Paddington station. High above the scene loomed the huge mass of the elevated urban trunk road known as the Westway, which blotted out the light and cast this short branch of canal into a near-constant gloom. This was a neglected and forgotten place.

In the corner, an elderly caravan huddled up against the bridge. It looked as if it dated from the fifties. Marnie had been inside it once before, when Roger Broadbent had explained the contents of the will of Old Peter, bequeathing her the drawings and papers of the great canal engineer William Jessop that had been lost for two hundred years.

So this was her temporary home. Marnie sat in the saloon and tried to think through her situation. It was simple. She was in hiding. The question was: from whom? Answer: whoever had tried to blow her up. She found it hard to believe that anyone could wish to destroy her. She had found a body, but apart from that, she had no other involvement in the matter. The problem was that someone else took a different view. As long as the murder of Tim Edmonds remained unsolved, she was in danger. As long as she kept out of sight, she had a chance of surviving. Thank goodness for Roger. At that moment the phone rang. It was a gentle ring, but it made her stomach churn.

"Hallo?"

"Marnie, it's Roger. Sorry to startle you, but I've been in touch with the British Waterways office in Little Venice. I spoke to Jack Stevens, the man in charge. I told him I'd had a spot of bother with the engine while I was running back from Paddington Basin. He agreed I could leave *Rumpole* there until I got it sorted out."

"Nobody needs the mooring?"

"No. Not for some time, with any luck. No one's going to bother you."

"Roger, I can't thank you enough."

"No need."

"There is one thing. I said I'd have dinner with Malcolm Grant this evening. Do you think I should cry off?"

There was a pause. "Where are you meeting him?"

"Near Primrose Hill. I don't really want to go out, but I can't stay hidden indefinitely."

"Do you think you can trust him?"

"It's not that … after all, he saved my life. It's just leaving here that worries me."

"You should be okay if you can get a taxi. After all, no one knows where to look for you. But do you want to see him? That's the point."

"I feel drawn, Roger. He's the only person I can talk to about what happened. And he's got connections. He stands a better chance of finding out what's going on than I do by myself."

"Seems to me that you've made up your mind."

After the call, Marnie stared at the mobile in her hand. *This is really weird … somebody out there seems to know everything about me … where I am … what I'm doing … even what I'm thinking.*

She changed into her darkest clothes, adjusting to a new way of life, trying to think like a fugitive. It meant planning every move in advance. It meant creating a backup system, taking precautions. One part of her thought it was an adventure, until she remembered the body of Tim Edmonds floating in the canal. Another part thought it was all absurd, until she remembered her car, mangled and blazing at the roadside. To keep her thinking positive, she decided to make one phone call.

"Anne? Hi! It's me."

"Are you safe? I've been worrying about you all day."

"I'm okay, but I have to be brief. Listen, I'm not staying in Chiswick. I'm … somewhere else."

"How can I contact you? How will I know if you're all right?"

"I'll phone you every day. Whatever you do, don't ring me on the mobile. If you want to get in touch, try this number late in the evening or early in the morning." She gave the number of the phone on *Rumpole*. "If you get no reply, it takes messages. If you don't hear from me within a reasonable time, contact Roger Broadbent. I'll give you his number."

"I've got it already."

"Of course. I should've known."

"You're not going to tell me where you are, are you, Marnie?"

"Better not to, just now."

"What about your plans? Anything I can do?"

"I'm having dinner with Malcolm Grant this evening. I think we've got to put our heads together to try and sort things out."

"Do you trust him, Marnie?"

"Do I have much choice?"

"Does he know where you're staying?"

"No. Only Roger knows that."

"What about Ralph? Have you spoken to him? I meant to tell you, he's left three messages on the answerphone at the office. You'll have missed him now. He's on his way to America. He seems okay and just assumes we're at meetings."

"Did he leave a number?"

"Only a hotel in Tokyo. It's too late to reach him there now. Perhaps he'll ring you on the mobile."

"Ah …"

"What?"

"It's switched off. And I don't really want anyone using it at the moment."

"Okay. I'll monitor the answerphone and let you know if he leaves a contact number."

"Fine. Good idea."

"Marnie, you really need me with you. You shouldn't be facing everything alone like this. Don't forget I'm here."

Afterwards, Marnie sat in the saloon, planning the evening, working on an idea. She checked her wallet. Luckily, she had plenty of cash. Next she checked the mobile. It took her several minutes to remove all the stored numbers from its memory until there was nothing that could connect it with her.

Turning off the lights before opening the hatch, she went out into the cold night. A distant street lamp lit up the scum on the canal. None of the other boats showed any lights. There was not a wisp of smoke from their chimneys. *God!* she thought, *what a forsaken place. And thank goodness for it.* She unlocked the door in the wall and slipped out, walking quickly towards Paddington station. One or two cabs passed her in the traffic, but she kept her face down and ignored them.

Inside the great vaulted space of the main line station, she found a newsagent and located what she was looking for. The pay-as-you-go mobile phones were in a display near the entrance. She read the instructions on the box. It was just a matter of registering, and it could be used straight away. She presented the cash to the man at the pay desk, a cheerful Indian with a ready smile.

"You can be a real yuppie, now, my lovely. Ring all your friends, tell them you're going into a tunnel." He had a sing-song voice and flashed a smile of brilliant white teeth in a dark face as he laughed at his joke. Like all attractive women, Marnie had become accustomed to the attentions of men, most of which she ignored. But at that moment, she could have hugged this one.

"If I switch it on," she asked, "does it give off a signal just by being on?"

"It gives a signal all the time, even when you don't switch it on. That's how the company knows where to find you. It's like Big Brother."

"I'm not sure I understand."

The newsagent called one of his staff to serve the next customer. "Look, it's like this. The phone is always awake. It is telling the firm where you are. It tells the nearest cell your exact location. That's why it's called a cellular phone. But it's not really Big Brother. It just has to know where you are, so you can receive your calls."

"It sounds rather sinister to me."

The Indian lowered his voice and tapped the mobile's box. "My brother-in-law works for this company at head office. They often deal with the police tracing the movements of people over a period of time to find out where they've been."

"Can anyone do that?"

"No. Just the police ... or people like that. But you don't have to worry. You don't look suspicious to me." Another flash of the big smile.

After this conversation, Marnie had a change of plan and headed toward the departures board. *Going into a tunnel,* she thought. Cardiff, Swansea, Fishguard ... That looked promising. Better still, there was one train heading for Exeter, Plymouth and Truro. Even further. She quickly consulted the timetable. It took ages to get to the end of its journey. Platform nine. The train was there, but a ticket collector was checking everyone that approached it. Fortunately, the station did not have barriers, and Marnie found it easy to pretend she was going for the train on the adjacent platform where no one was watching. Halfway down the platform, she stepped across to the Cornish train and quickly boarded at the nearest door. It was more full than she had expected. Trying to appear like any normal passenger looking for her reservation, she walked down the aisle, her heart pounding. In fact, she was scanning the carriage for something special. It was in First Class that she found it. Here, there were fewer passengers. She took a seat by the window, praying that the train would not leave before she could get off.

Satisfied that no one was observing her, she slipped the old mobile out of her coat pocket and wedged it firmly between the seat and the carriage wall. She stood up and checked. It was completely out of sight.

"Do you require dinner, madam?" The voice behind her made Marnie jump. "A table for one? We're now taking bookings."

Marnie struggled to keep her composure. "Actually, I was just starting to get worried. This is the train for Fishguard, isn't it?"

"Oh no, madam. You're on the wrong platform altogether." He pointed through the window. "That's the South Wales express over there. You'll have to hurry."

She thanked him and set off at high speed. At the top of the platform, she turned towards the taxi rank and stood back to let a man take the cab at the head of the queue so that she could have the one behind it. As it pulled away, she saw the Cornish train close its doors and begin moving off. Somewhere inside it her old mobile was hidden, silently giving off its signal to anyone who had the technology to be able to check where she was going.

If anyone was tracking her, they were tracking her to Land's End.

• • • • •

When Marnie arrived at Albert's, Malcolm Grant was there before her, sitting at a table with a glass of Scotch.

"Am I late?"

"Not at all. Spot on." He kissed her lightly on the cheek.

Nearly all the tables in the bistro were occupied, and Marnie glanced at the other diners while she perused the menu. They were mostly couples, apart from a group of six people in the opposite corner. The atmosphere was friendly and intimate. A low murmur of conversation. A normal evening surrounded by normal people. Malcolm noticed her eyes wandering.

"Just what I was thinking, Marnie. Nice place. Good choice. Would you like something to drink first, or are you ready to order?"

"I'm ready to order, I think. The trout with almonds is usually very good, but I expect you're a steak man. I ought to warn you, if you have the mushrooms à la grècque as a starter, you'll have to keep clear of other people for at least three days."

"Strong on garlic?"

"Nuclear."

It was during the starter course after the first sip of wine that they began to unwind and talk. They kept their voices low.

"This claret's rather good," said Malcolm. "It seems ages since our last meal together."

"Lunchtime." Marnie felt the memory flood over her, and her stomach tightened. "Although, of course, we didn't actually eat anything. It's been a busy day."

"Best to try and put it behind you."

"It was nearly my last. I almost put it behind me permanently."

Malcolm reached across the table and touched her hand briefly. "A dreadful shock, but you've come out of it, and you have to move forward. It's the only way."

"Easy to say."

"I know. But I do understand. I was there too."

"You were amazing. Totally unflapped. I think they call it *cool under fire*."

"Let's just say I'm used to certain types of situation. I was in the army for a long time. You were the amazing one. Most people go to pieces and hide under the table."

"Most of them did, the sensible ones."

"But not you, Marnie. You wanted to get out there and see what was going on."

"Take the high ground. It nearly got me killed last time I did that. Some people never learn."

"It's in your blood. I saw it a lot in the army. You could call it character ... or breeding. Sometimes the least likely men could show real bravery in action."

"I didn't mean to be brave. Curiosity probably got the better of me, that's all."

"Oh, I didn't say you were brave – *foolhardy* springs to mind." He smiled at her over the rim of the wine glass. They laughed quietly together. "You know, Marnie, it's funny meeting you like this, all on account of what happened to Tim. I think you would've liked him."

"I don't really have much impression of him, apart from what I've read in the papers."

"The papers, yes. Well, you won't get much of an impression there. Though he was always good at handling the media. He could do these *soundbites*. Most of our lot can't. We try and say too much, I suppose. All brought up writing essays at Oxbridge. But Tim could do it. That's why Major used him in his campaign."

"I thought Major was quite good with the media. His soapbox and all that."

"Useless."

Marnie was surprised at the bitterness. "Don't you think he came over as quite a sincere person?" She was amazed to find herself defending a Tory Prime Minister ... and to a Tory MP.

Malcolm did not even look up. He just sat there shaking his head, muttering. "No sense of leadership. No charisma."

"Not even on the soapbox?" Marnie said lightly.

Malcolm snorted. "Blessed soapbox. Silly stunt." There was derision in his voice. She remembered what Ralph had said about enemies in your own party. The plates from the first course were cleared away. Malcolm poured some more wine.

"Tell me about Tim Edmonds."

Malcolm shrugged. "The PM used him to keep himself in office. Tim could make up for the things he lacked himself. He went on using him."

"I meant as a person … as your friend."

"As my friend. They don't come much better, Marnie. We hit it off from the start. We met while serving on a committee, had a drink afterwards. It went on from there. He was good company, no bullshit."

"I suppose you had the same ideas and a lot in common."

"Same ideas? What gave you that impression?"

"Well, you were both MPs in the same party. It's a reasonable assumption."

"Actually, we disagreed about a number of fundamentals."

"Such as?"

"Oh, the usual … Europe, monetary policy. Tim wasn't as keen on Maggie as some of us. I thought she was the best thing to happen to this country since Churchill. *He* wouldn't have kow-towed to the bureaucrats in Brussels."

"But she still signed all those treaties, the Single European Act and all that."

"Expediency, Marnie. Anyway, we had different views. So what? We all have our own views. We all think we're God's gift."

"Do you all think you can be Prime Minister one day? Really?"

"Of course. What else do we have? Egos and ambition. Only a fool would deny it. Now Tim's gone. What a bloody waste."

Marnie began on her next course and took a sip more wine. Tentatively, she asked, "Do you think he was murdered?"

"No! I don't know. I really don't. I'm seeing someone at Scotland Yard tomorrow. I'll try to find out what's going on. I'd like to think it was a dreadful accident. He was keen on his drink was Tim. He could've slipped and hit his head and fallen in the canal."

"I think he did possibly smell of drink, actually," said Marnie.

"Did he? Did you tell that to the police?"

"Not in so many words. It's hard to be sure. There was the smell from the engine, you see. Diesel's quite strong. But I think I could smell something else. It might've been alcohol."

"I think you should add that to your statement, Marnie."

"Won't they find that suspicious? I mean, if I suddenly alter my statement."

"The police find everything – and everyone – suspicious. It's just part of their job. I think you should tell them."

"But the autopsy will've revealed whether he'd been drinking, won't it?"

"It may depend on how much water he ingested. I still think you should mention it."

"Okay. I will."

"Tell me, Marnie, do you have any ideas about what happened that evening? Did you see anything or anyone there or nearby, anything at all that might help?"

Marnie shook her head. "I might've had an inkling of someone on the towpath, but it was dark and I was busy with the boat. I saw nothing that would help when I tried to pull him out of the water. The police said a tramp might've seen something."

"A witness?"

"Maybe, but he was found floating in the canal himself at Limehouse a few days later. Apparently he'd fallen in and drowned. Probably drunk."

"Poor sod. So that's all you know?"

"Yes. Not much to go on."

"I don't think anyone will ever – "As he spoke, a faint warbling sound interrupted him. Malcolm reached into a pocket with a muttered apology. "Grant ... I don't think so ... Look, I can't talk now, I'm having dinner with a friend ... Yes ... I don't know ... What time? Very well. I'll be there at ten." He folded the phone, the smallest Marnie had ever seen. "No peace for the wicked, as they say." He smiled at her.

"Problem?"

"Apparently there's to be a division at ten o'clock. All hands to the pumps. That's the trouble with soldiering on with a wafer-thin majority, I'm afraid."

"So you have to go. Of course."

Malcolm looked at his watch. "Not immediately. I have a little time. Where were we?"

"Agreeing that we're not getting anywhere, I think. I wonder what happens next."

"I'll talk to the Commander at Scotland Yard in the morning, see if I can find out what progress they're making, if any."

"In my experience of dealing with the police, they don't give much away."

"Well, I'm on a police policy committee and being an MP sometimes has a few advantages, even if we have no actual power, despite what people might think."

"That's what Ralph says ... Ralph Lombard. You saw him with Michael Blissett in the Commons that day."

"Oh yes. Everyone knows Lombard. Ralph. I only know him slightly, but on the whole I think he's quite plausible. Perhaps a little suspect at times."

"In what way?"

"Perhaps he leans a touch too far to the Left for some of us, but I'm sure he thinks he's being objective. He has the reputation of being a bit of a know-all. Believes he's one jump ahead of the rest of us. Do you know him well?"

"Quite well."

"But he's not around at the moment?"

"He's in the Far East on a lecture tour. He's talking about an impending crisis that's going to affect the 'tiger economies'."

Malcolm raised his hands, palms upward. "I rest my case, m'lud." He smiled.

"I still don't know what happens next."

"I can let you know how I get on tomorrow. Can I ring you at your sister's?"

"I might be out. Things to do. I've got to arrange transport. I'm in a mess."

"Of course. On your mobile, then?"

"Look, why don't I ring you at a given time? That may be easiest."

"Fine. Say about eleven? I'll be out by then."

There was the usual argument about the bill. Marnie insisted that she had chosen the restaurant and it was her turn to pay. As usual she lost, faced with Malcolm's firm belief that a gentleman pays the bill when with a lady. She found this tiresome, but tried to appear grateful and put it down to experience. They left the restaurant and emerged onto the pavement just ahead of another couple. Two taxis were passing and Malcolm managed to wave them both down, signalling to one to wait. He opened the door of the first cab for Marnie, but she refused.

"You go first. You're in a hurry. I'll take that one."

"If you're sure." He kissed her on the cheek and got in.

Marnie walked slowly back to the waiting taxi as Malcolm pulled away. She opened the door as his cab performed a U-turn, and he raised a hand as he passed. His taxi turned the corner and headed off towards Primrose Hill. Suddenly, she called in to the driver. "Sorry. I've left something behind. I have to go back." She waved to the other couple who were standing at the edge of the pavement. "You can have this one if you want it. I can't go just yet." They accepted and she went back to the restaurant, standing in the doorway until the taxi was out of sight. Secretive behaviour was becoming a habit. For a few minutes she watched while one or two taxis went by. As another one came into view on the opposite side of the road, she moved out quickly and hailed it from the roadway. It pulled in.

"Are you a taxi?"

The driver gave her the weary look of cab drivers the world over. "The sign on the roof's meant to be a clue."

"I meant are you free? I couldn't see if your light was on."

"Sure. Where to?"

"Paddington station."

"You're on."

Marnie spent the journey trying to resist the temptation to look out of the rear window at the following traffic. The first time she looked, she realised it was a waste of time. Car headlights looked like car headlights. She thought about suddenly getting the driver to stop so that she could change taxis, but dismissed this as paranoid. It also occurred to her that she would be an easy target standing at the roadside if someone was following her with malicious intent.

"Driver, could you go via Little Venice, please?"

"Little Venice? It's not very direct from here."

"I know, but I'd like to see the boats."

"You're the boss."

Before long, they swung off the main road, and there seemed to be no other vehicles immediately behind them. They ran along the canalside past *Sally Ann's* old mooring, past friends who had no idea that Marnie was in hiding just around the corner. The taxi was lucky to take the left turn over the bridge by the pool of Little Venice just as the lights were turning red. It joined the road coming down from the Westway in light traffic and aimed towards the station, parallel with the arm of the canal leading to Paddington Basin. Marnie opened her wallet and took out a tenner, enough for the journey with a generous tip. She passed it through the partition by the driver's head.

"Can you drop me just before the flyover, please? This is for you. Keep the change."

The area looked deserted and unwelcoming. "You sure you want to be dropped here?"

"My ex-boyfriend's pestering me. I don't want the hassle."

"Fair enough."

Marnie got out quickly and the taxi pulled away. She stood in the shadows for a few seconds beside the door in the wall. Nothing strange happened. Several cars passed. Two huge juggernauts buffeted the air around her, engines roaring as they changed gear. At any other time she would have regarded these surroundings as hostile, not the place for a lone woman at night. Now she saw them as her camouflage, her sanctuary. No one would expect to find a solitary woman in a place like this. At least not a woman in her right mind.

On board *Rumpole*, Marnie checked that the curtains and blinds were drawn and put on the light. Everything was in order. She took out the new mobile and rang a familiar number. Anne's mother answered, her voice anxious. They were not used to having phone calls at ten o'clock at night. Their life was normal. Marnie apologised and Anne was summoned down from her room.

"Are you all right, Marnie? I was wondering about you."

"That's why I thought I'd touch base. I've just come from dinner with Malcolm Grant."

"How did it go?"

"Okay. I think he's as bewildered as I am."

"Remember Ralph said not to trust anyone."

"Ralph isn't here." She wondered if he would ever be around when he was needed, but rejected the thought as unkind. "I'm ringing Malcolm tomorrow. He's going to Scotland Yard to see some bigwig, and we might find out what's happening."

"Then what?"

"Well, I'm getting tired of the cloak-and-dagger routine. And I don't really think anyone's following me. If they were serious professionals, they'd have caught me by now. The car bomb probably was just a coincidence. I think once I've heard from Malcolm I'm going to head for home."

"I'll be ready when you are."

"Okay. I'll try and sort out a car. What are your movements tomorrow?"

"Shopping with mum in the morning. Back for lunch."

"Expect to hear from me."

"I'll start packing."

"Of course. Anne, I'm sure things will be all right. There's nothing to worry about."

"Good."

Marnie pressed the stop button, glad that she had reassured her friend. She was pleased that one of them was not worrying.

Anne put down the phone and sighed. She noticed that Marnie was still not telling her where she was staying.

Part 13

Wednesday 4 January 9.00 am

Marnie waited until her patience was exhausted the next morning before ringing the MG garage at around nine. She got through to Michael Dent.

"We were just talking about you. Or about your car to be precise."

"You've got trouble?"

"Well, not really. You do realise we did quite a lot of work on it when it was here a couple of years ago. It obviously hasn't been driven since. In fact, it was booked in for a new clutch and never turned up."

Marnie thought back to the turbulent days of the end of her marriage. A new clutch on the MG had been the last thing on her mind. "I'm sorry. There was a lot of turmoil in my life at that time."

"I quite understand. The point is, there isn't all that much to do to get her on the road again. She'd benefit from being used, actually."

"What do you have to do? How soon could I have it back?"

"Basically, it's the new clutch and replacement of most of the pipes and hoses. They've gone brittle and rotted. A day's work."

"How long to get the parts?"

"Mrs Walker, we are the stockists."

"I see. And when can you fit the job in?"

"Do you hear that?" In the background was the sound of an engine running. Michael Dent came back on the line. "That was your car."

Marnie was incredulous. "You've got it going?"

"Not actually moving, at least not until we get the clutch in. But that's not a big job and we're never busy at this time of year. If all goes well, you can collect her in a day or two."

"So I'll be able to drive it straight away?"

"If we could have her here for a few days we could make sure everything's okay. A car that age needs looking after. And then you'll need tax and insurance, of course. Oh, and one other thing ... you may have noticed that it's winter. Brass monkey weather out there. The car has no heater."

Through *Rumpole*'s porthole window Marnie could see that a thin crust of ice had formed on the canal in the night, trapping the film of scum and debris on the surface into swirling patterns. She scribbled a list of jobs to do and thought of Anne with her constant supply of sticky yellow notes. First stop was her insurance broker. Not good news.

"This is a tricky one, Marnie."

"You think it might not be a write-off? I could put the remaining bits of the Rover into an envelope and post them to you to save the loss adjuster a journey if you like."

"It's not that. The problem is: what was the nature of the explosion?"

"My recollection is a sort of loud bang followed by burning and a lot of smoke."

"Marnie, I'm being serious. Was it vandalism? in which case you are covered. Was it a terrorist attack? in which case it counts as an act of war, and you're not covered."

"*What!* You mean the insurance might not pay up?"

"I'm working on it, believe me, but it's not straightforward."

"What can I do in the meantime? I've got to have transport, otherwise I'm stranded."

"You can hire a car for up to five days. I'll give you a phone number. Quote your policy reference and they'll bill the company direct."

Marnie arranged the hire on the phone, surprised how easy it was, and glad that something was going right.

• • • • •

Beth and Paul's house looked quiet from the outside as Marnie parked the hired Ford Escort on the drive. The inside was just as quiet, and there was no evidence of any intrusion, planting of bugging devices or hidden cameras. Paranoia, paranoia, she muttered to herself, walking through to the kitchen and the door to the garage. It looked empty with the MG gone. Beth would be pleased.

Marnie surveyed the wall of shelving and from the top took down a bulky cardboard box that was dusty but intact. She blew the dust off at the back door and opened the box on the kitchen table, before taking the contents upstairs to Beth and Paul's bedroom. Standing in front of their full-length mirror, she tried on the items. They were a trifle big for her, but not excessively so. The leather bomber jacket with its sheepskin lining was highly fashionable, though this one had never seen the King's Road, Chelsea. It had been issued to a Lancaster navigator, a cousin of her father, at an airbase in Berkshire in 1944. The flying helmet, also of leather and well-lined, was a reasonable fit, if slightly eccentric. Marnie did not care about making a fashion statement. Her aim was to make herself unidentifiable. With the aid of her scarf and dark glasses, she achieved just that. She also wanted to keep out the cold while driving an open sports car in January.

She bundled the clothing back into its box, stowed it in the boot of the Escort and drove into town. On the way, she stopped at a phonebox to ring Malcolm.

"How was your discussion? Interesting?"

"Yes. Quite interesting, but not the sort of thing to talk about on the phone. Can we meet?"

"I have a lot on today, but we could get together."

"Unfortunately, I've got a lunch engagement that I can't put off," said Malcolm.

"If you buy me any more meals, they'll change your title to Lord Egon of Ronay."

"It's my pleasure, Marnie, but today's a problem. Now, where shall we meet? My lunch appointment's near the Commons. Are you able to come into the centre?"

"I've got a hire car. Parking will be difficult."

"That's no worry. I can park it in the Commons. It's only the restaurants that aren't open this week. The car park's available."

They agreed to meet in Whitehall and have coffee round the corner from Parliament. Malcolm took the car in through Carriage Gate while Marnie walked slowly to the St Stephen's entrance to meet him. He guided her to a small café a few minutes away, and they settled into a corner where they could talk.

Marnie sensed at once that something was troubling Malcolm. He had shaken her hand when they met, seemed to be avoiding eye contact, and was more distant than usual. She waited until after the coffee arrived before speaking.

"What's happened, Malcolm? You seem rather preoccupied. I don't mean to pry, but was it anything that came up at your meeting?"

"Marnie, I was thinking that with all that's happened, your car and so on, perhaps it would be an idea if we put the redecoration of my flat on hold for the moment ... until things have settled down."

"Oh ... I see." She did not see. "Actually, Malcolm, I don't understand. The bombing of my car can't have anything to do with decorating your flat. How could it?"

Malcolm stirred his coffee. Marnie realised that someone had got at him. "Well ..." he began.

"Surely you don't think I have anything to do with terrorists?" she said. "You don't really believe I'm involved in anything like that?" Or did he think she could be involved in the death of Tim Edmonds? That was a question she could not bring herself to ask.

Malcolm looked up. "No. I don't believe that."

"Well, you're right. I had absolutely no connection with it. It was just by chance that I happened to be passing, just as it was purely by chance that I met you in the Commons."

"And just by chance that your car was targeted for a bomb? You must admit, Marnie, it all looks very odd, to an external observer, to say the least."

"You said you believed me."

"I do. But to the suspicious minds of the police, it must seem that you're connected with something very strange. Most people don't just find bodies of VIPs and then get their cars blown up shortly afterwards. Surely you see that, Marnie."

She suddenly saw her position from the outside, as the police must see her. It all looked highly suspicious, and she wondered what action the police might take next. "But you believe me?"

He hesitated. "Yes, I do. The problem is what the police think."

"I see. Do you think they could cause trouble for me?"

"Not while I'm around." He put his hand on hers across the table.

Marnie eased her hand away and sat up straight. "I'm not sure you should get too involved."

"I am already. And the more I think about it, the more convinced I become that Tim's death and the bombing of your car can be no coincidence."

Marnie felt trapped. It was like being drawn into some dangerous game that she did not want to play, with rules she did not know or understand. It was all unfathomable and seemed so unfair. "What has any of this got to do with me?"

"Have you ever had any contact with terrorism, Marnie?"

"What kind of question is that? Of course I haven't. I'm an interior designer, for God's sake. People don't get that violent about soft furnishings. They just ask us to choose a different colour scheme. We're not normally regarded as a bad insurance risk. Talking of which, my insurance company could cause problems if they can claim the bomb was a terrorist weapon.

I'm sure they'll try and screw me if they can. Oh, sorry, that must have sounded really vulgar."

"You could never be vulgar, Marnie." Malcolm had a twinkle in his eye. He touched her hand again. "But you've never had contact with terrorists before?"

"The nearest I've come is a restaurant I'm doing. It was partly burnt down. The police suspected arson. I've been there once or twice. That's all. It's absurd to think I could be involved with terrorists. I'm the victim, remember. It's my wretched car that was destroyed." While protesting her innocence of any link with men of violence, Marnie felt a strong desire to hit Malcolm, preferably with a blunt instrument.

"I agree, though of course ..."

"Though of course what?"

"Well ... you do associate with Ralph Lombard."

"*Ralph?* So?"

Malcolm spread the fingers of one hand. "He is known as a radical."

"Nonsense!"

"Marnie, he wrote several articles and books about student revolts in Europe in the 60s. He was popular with the underground left and was a personal friend of some of the leaders of the Provos in Amsterdam – he wrote a book about them just before he produced *We're Going Wrong* – and that was a blatant Marxist tract."

"But that doesn't link him with terrorists. You don't think he would have done this to me?"

"No, but his enemies might, as a means of getting at him."

"Why?"

"The underworld is riven with factions, Marnie. I think you may be out of your depth. There's more going on here than meets the eye. We'll find out more when the army have had a chance to look at the bomb."

"But the car was blown to bits. Surely there'll be nothing to look at."

Malcolm looked at her quizzically.

"I am out of my depth," said Marnie. Malcolm nodded.

• • • • •

There was a chilly wind gusting up Victoria Street as they made their way back towards the Commons. They walked with heads bent forward.

"I'm sorry the police aren't making more progress," said Marnie. "I really want them to find out who did it. I wish I could help more."

"So do I. I keep asking myself if there is something I could do that would help."

"If what you told me is all you know, I don't see how you could provide any more information. You were really only involved on the periphery."

"I've thought about almost nothing else since it happened, Marnie. But I must say I've thought a lot about you these past days. It's been good to have you around to share it all, though it does seem unfair on you."

Marnie was unsure how to take this. "What does your wife think of all this?"

"Of course, I've talked to Pauline about it ... mainly on the phone, but it's not like having someone around who knows about things from close range. Cumbria's a long way away."

"Was she also a good friend of Tim?"

"Not really. They got on okay, but she always had a reservation about him after the scandal."

"Doesn't she come to London?"

"Hardly ever. She's a county councillor and prefers life in the Lake District. A country girl at heart." They paused at the kerb, waiting for a gap in the traffic. Malcolm looked at Marnie with a serious expression. "You do realise that talking like this could lead you into danger ... I mean, getting a politician to talk about himself could be terminally boring ..."

Marnie smiled. She found herself liking him more each time they met, as if he was a pleasant uncle. She hoped his view of her was suitably avuncular. "I'd been thinking that I ought to talk to your wife about the decor of the flat ... when we eventually get back to that subject ... if we do. She'll have views about colour schemes and things, I expect."

The traffic lights changed and they moved off across the road. "Oh no, I don't think so," said Malcolm. "Pauline's not in the least interested in what goes on down here. We tend to lead separate lives. We're very compartmentalised."

"Is she excited about being Lady Grant? Sorry to pry into your private life."

"That's all right. I expect she likes the idea of the title more than I do ... goes down well with the tweed jacket and pleated skirt brigade, and the various county committees. Pauline has her own life up there. It suits her. I prefer to be here. I feel that you and I have the same approach. You could say we're in the same boat ... that's quite appropriate for you, really."

I'm not even in the same boat these days, Marnie thought, pulling up her collar against the cold air.

Malcolm suddenly stopped in the street. "Marnie, there's something else I should've told you."

"It can't be any worse than telling me I'm suspected of being mixed up in terrorism, or that I have a friend who associates with violent revolutionaries."

"I think I'm a suspect in Tim's murder," said Malcolm.

"Is that something new? I thought we both believed we were being regarded as suspects."

Malcolm shook his head. "It's one thing to have an idea that the police are treating you as *involved* in a matter. You can tell yourself they treat everyone like that ... force of habit, or just their way of working. Realising they actually suspect you ... that's something else."

"I see. Did they tell you that at Scotland Yard?"

"Not exactly, but the tone of the meeting left me in little doubt."

"What *did* they say? Did they accuse you of anything?"

"They questioned me about that evening, the evening of his death."

"But you weren't there, were you?"

"I couldn't prove it, Marnie. Even you said you thought you might've seen someone on the footpath. Who's to say it wasn't me?"

"It was just a fleeting impression. It might only have been a shadow. I may have been wrong. If there was someone, the police can't prove who that person was."

"Which gets us nowhere and still leaves me as a suspect."

"Can't you prove you were somewhere else? Is there no way of demonstrating that? Where were you in fact? ... if you don't mind me asking."

"Look, we can't stand here like this in the street."

"No. And you've got your lunch appointment, don't forget."

Malcolm took Marnie by the arm and guided her towards the West Front of Westminster Abbey. Leading her along the pavement beside the great cathedral, he nodded in the direction of St Margaret's church. "Let's go inside for a few minutes. We should be able to get some peace and quiet." Marnie let herself be led, thinking *peace and quiet, some hopes!*

Inside, the church was empty, and they sat at the end of the last row of pews. It was exactly where Malcolm had been sitting, head bowed and grieving, when Marnie had first seen him at the Christmas Carol service.

Malcolm began, his voice little more than a whisper. "They asked me to explain exactly what I was doing that evening. I told them Tim was coming to see me in the flat, and I was there waiting for him to arrive. When he didn't turn up after about an hour, I rang his home and left a message on the answerphone. That was how the police knew I was expecting him. My message led them to me."

"It's a pity you did that, really. If you hadn't sent it, they would never have made the connection."

"Maybe not, but I would've told them about our meeting when they asked people to come forward with information."

"I suppose so. Were you worried when he didn't show up?"

"Not especially. I just wanted to check we both had the right day. Things crop up all the time in our world, it's not unusual. But I suppose I thought it was odd he hadn't rung to let me know."

"Not in character for him to be negligent when you'd invited him round?"

"Actually, Marnie, I hadn't invited him. That made it even stranger. He'd asked if he could come and see me."

"For a particular reason or was it just a social call ... deliver your Christmas card and have a drink, perhaps?"

"No idea. I never found out. He didn't say what it was. I didn't even speak to him. He sent a message."

"Did you get the impression it was something urgent?"

Malcolm looked into the distance. "Come to think of it, that is possible."

"Can you remember what it said?"

"I knew he was going on a skiing holiday with a girl-friend, and I think he said he wanted to talk to me before he left. It was something like that. Not much to go on, really."

"I don't suppose you've got this note?"

"Doubt it."

"Pity."

"Why do you say that?"

"Well, it would prove something, I suppose ... corroborate your story."

"In what way?"

"It would bear out your statement that he'd asked to see you. And, combined with your answerphone message, it would show that you were likely to be waiting in your flat. What kind of message was it? A betting slip?"

"No. Typed, I think."

"Signed or pp'd?"

"I think it was signed. Tim's secretary was on maternity leave, so he had a series of temps. They wouldn't have permission to pp any of his correspondence."

"Do you know her name?"

Malcolm shook his head. "It'd be Charlotte or Samantha or whatever. Our lot are always called something like that. Somebody's daughter."

"I know it's not much proof, but if the message was signed by Tim, that must mean something. It would all hang together, wouldn't it?"

"I see what you're getting at, though it wouldn't really prove anything as such."

"Better than nothing," said Marnie. "A kind of moral support. But if you don't have the message ..."

"I hadn't really thought seriously about it. Perhaps it could still be there. In the bin in my office, perhaps."

"From before Christmas? Wouldn't it have been emptied?"

"Not necessarily."

· · · · ·

Malcolm's office was in a different part of the House of Commons from Michael Blissett's. They made their way up to the second floor in an ancient and cramped lift and walked along narrow corridors and up winding staircases until they reached a broad landing. Malcolm's door was of dark solid wood and while he reached in his pocket for the key, Marnie saw the sign: *This door to be kept locked at all times.*

The office was bigger than Michael Blissett's and reminded Marnie of an old-fashioned solicitor's, with panelled walls and shelves of books around an old mahogany desk. They seemed to be in a tower, and through the window she could see the river and Westminster Bridge.

"Nice place."

"Yes. From the time when I was in favour with the whips. I came here when Maggie was in charge, of course."

"Will you be able to stay here when you go to the Lords?"

"No. This is strictly for the Commons." He bent down and picked up the waste bin. It was stuffed to overflowing. "If the note's still here, it could also be somewhere on my desk, I suppose." The desk was similarly cluttered with files, notes and bundles of correspondence. Marnie wondered what Linda the redoubtable PA would make of it all. Or Anne, come to that.

"Why don't I search the bin and you do your desk?" said Marnie. "That way, I'll only handle items that have been thrown out, and you can deal with papers that might be confidential."

"Very diplomatically put, Marnie. Let's do just that."

Marnie sat in a chair and spread out an old copy of *The Times* on the floor beside her. Onto this she began laying the scraps that she picked out of the bin. "Why has your office been left like this over Christmas?"

"I've been on a committee investigating Members' interests. Very delicate matter. I only let the staff in to clean when I'm here. It's quite normal practice in the House."

Marnie nodded and continued with her search. There were betting slips, circulars, lists. She even came across a note on paper with the heading '10 Downing Street', and it took all her willpower not to read it. She put it face down on the floor and ploughed on.

"I keep telling myself I've got to do something about this desk ... tidy the blessed thing, but somehow –"

"Hey!" Marnie's cry interrupted him in full flow. "Sorry, Malcolm, but I think I've found it. Look at this." They stood in the middle of the office and read the note.

Malcolm,

I need to see you before the recess. There is a matter that has to be settled and it cannot wait until we return in the new year.

I am heavily committed this week, but could see you on Sunday if that suited you. Could I come to the flat at around 5.00 pm? Can you confirm if that is okay?

The note was clearly signed 'Regards, Tim' in a bold firm hand.

"Well, that rather supports your story, I think," said Marnie. "You must definitely show that to the police."

"You think it helps?"

"It backs up what you told them. They'll have to give you the benefit of the doubt when they see this. It shows you were telling the truth, if nothing else. I don't see what more you can do."

"I'll certainly give it to them, Marnie. But don't hold out too many hopes."

Marnie read the note again. "Have you no idea what he wanted to talk to you about?"

"How could I? I never saw him again ... except to identify his body."

"Oh, I'm sorry. I didn't realise. I just wondered if it might've had something to do with your peerage, perhaps."

"The peerage? Why should it? That kind of thing's handled by the PM's office in Downing Street several weeks in advance."

"Well, it must have been something important."

"I suppose I'll never know."

● ● ● ● ●

In the Houses of Parliament it is relatively easy for a visitor to move around the building, provided they are heading towards an exit. Unaccompanied movement in any other direction is invariably questioned by the police officers who are stationed at every turning point. So it was that Marnie was able to drive the hired Ford Escort out of the car park without challenge.

They had separated on better terms than when they had met that day. Malcolm had accompanied her down through the labyrinth of passageways and corridors leading to the escalator off Star Chamber Court. They had taken a lift to go down two more floors, and it had surprised her to learn that there were five floors of underground car park. He had kissed her lightly on the cheek like an old friend.

"Just follow the arrows to the surface, Marnie. Go round the courtyard and through Carriage Gate. You'll come out in Parliament Square."

"Right. You will give that note to the police, won't you?"

Malcolm patted his coat pocket. "I'll see them after lunch. I hope to God we can get this wretched business sorted out once and for all."

"I wonder if we'll ever know the truth," said Marnie.

"Keep in touch. I'll let you know what I find out. How do I contact you?"

"I'm thinking of going home tomorrow. There's no reason to stay in London."

Marnie drove up to the surface, leaving the car park by the steep ramp that brought her out beside the huge Christmas tree still standing in New Palace Yard. It seemed a long time since she had anything to celebrate. She drove across town to Little Venice and found one of the long-stay parking spaces. It was opposite where she had parked the Rover on the day of the explosion. The street had been tidied, but there were scorch marks and blast damage on the trees and the front wall of the nearest house was charred black. When she shivered while locking the Escort, it was not just because of the chill in the air.

Subterfuge was becoming second nature to her now, and she quickly walked along to the tube, went down the stairs into the station, crossed the booking hall and re-appeared up the stairs at the other exit on the far side of the road. A brisk walk led her to the pool where she went down to the waterside and hurried round the path over the bridge and back up to meet the road further along. Three minutes later she was opening the door into her refuge. There was no disturbance on *Rumpole*.

Marnie kept her coat on while she waited for the heating to warm up the cabin. She put the kettle on and made a sandwich. There was a call to make. Anne answered straight away.

"Everything all right?"

"Fine. Listen, I don't want to talk for long, but I've just seen Malcolm. I think we've found something that at least corroborates his story. I'll explain when I see you."

"Okay. Marnie, I've got some news for you. I've spoken to Ralph this morning."

"How did you do that? I thought we didn't know where he was."

"After we spoke last night I had an idea. I rang our office and altered the message on the answerphone. I said for urgent matters to ring my number here. He phoned at midday. It must have been breakfast time in America. I didn't tell him about your car ... I wasn't sure what to say about that, but I said you were down in London and wanted to contact him. He gave me his hotel number. He's there all morning, so he's there now." Anne gave her the number.

"You're a genius. I think you'll go far, starting with Knightly St John."

"When are we going?"

"Tomorrow. I've got a hire car."

"Okay. I'll be ready and waiting."

"Probably a good idea to alter the answerphone message to the usual wording."

"I did that after Ralph phoned."

"I should've known."

Marnie got through to Ralph without difficulty. There was concern in his voice.

"Is everything all right, Marnie? Anne said she couldn't give me a number where I could reach you. Where are you?"

"I've borrowed a friend's place in London, but we're going back to Knightly tomorrow."

"So, how are things?"

"Well, they have been better. The edited highlights are that opinions vary as to whether Tim Edmonds was murdered or had a ghastly accident, somebody's tried to kill me –"

"*Kill you?*"

"Yes. My car was blown up."

"*What?* My God! Were you hurt?"

"No. Luckily I was in a pub having lunch with Malcolm Grant when it went off."

"That's dreadful, Marnie. I must come back at once."

"You can't, Ralph. Look, I'm all right. Just finish your work. You can't leave now."

"Are the police protecting you?"

"I think they still have me down as a suspect."

"You're joking."

"No. I'm in hiding."

"From the police?"

"No. From everybody else. But I've had enough of this and I'm getting out of London. The bad news is that if the insurance company can prove it was a terrorist bomb, they won't have to pay up for the car."

"Act of war?"

"Something like that."

"Well, at least you weren't injured or … Look, Marnie, I'm going to alter my schedule here and come back. Can I ring you somewhere?" Marnie gave him the new mobile number. "What happened to the old one?"

"That's a long story … several hundred miles long, in fact."

One last call. Marnie rang Roger and told him her plans. She mentioned the possible smell of alcohol.

"You didn't tell this to the police when they took your statement?"

Marnie sighed. "No. I wasn't sure. But now I think of it, I'm fairly certain there was a smell other than just diesel fumes."

"It won't do any harm to mention it. Explain it as an afterthought that's just come back to you. Say you told me and I advised you to raise it with them. It might be important if his lungs were full of water."

"Right. Will do. Roger, I can't thank you enough for all your help. Having a safe haven here's been a lifeline to me. I'm so grateful to you."

"I'm in no hurry to have *Rumpole* back just yet, you know. Why don't we leave her there in case you have to pop down again?"

"What about you?"

"Up to my eyes in work at the moment. Not a chance of using the boat. Anyway, it's not the weather for boating. Keep the keys with you, Marnie. Use her any time. You never know."

"Are you sure, Roger? You're not just making it up?"

"Trust me – I'm a lawyer."

"I trust you all right, but I don't believe a word you say!"

Marnie was surprised to find she was hungry and enjoyed the sandwich and coffee in the now warm cabin. While she ate, she made a list of things to do the next day and switched on the radio for the hourly news bulletin. There was a report about the bombing of her car.

"*Scotland Yard has confirmed that the bomb that destroyed a car in Little*

Venice, in central London, yesterday was not of the kind used by any of the terrorist groups, and no advance warning had been given. A spokesman stated that this was a much simpler device and had been attached under the car's fuel tank to cause the maximum damage."

So not terrorists, thought Marnie. At least that makes the insurance situation easier. She was just thinking of clouds and silver linings when the implications of the news dawned on her.

• • • • •

"Can I speak to Inspector Bruere, please?" Marnie waited to be transferred.

"This is Sergeant Wallace, Mrs Walker. Chief Inspector Bruere's out. Do you want to leave a message?"

Marnie explained about the alcohol. She also told Wallace about the note they had found in Malcolm's office. He promised to pass on the information, and was writing the message on his pad when Bruere walked in.

"Marnie Walker's just been on. It seems she thinks she smelled alcohol on Edmonds when she found his body. *Just an afterthought*, she says. And guess what? She and Grant found the note from Edmonds arranging the meeting for the evening of the murder."

"I know. I've just seen Grant, and I've got the note." He pulled out a transparent envelope. "Very convenient."

"Two new items," said Wallace. "But they don't add up to much. We knew about the alcohol from the autopsy, and we knew Edmonds was going round to see Grant. What does it prove?"

"It shows that those two are talking to each other. For a woman who doesn't know any MPs, Marnie Walker's surprisingly well connected."

• • • • •

Marnie decided to have an early night. She had a busy day ahead. It was while she was tossing a salad that the mobile rang.

"Ralph. Great to hear from you. How are things?"

"Lunch break here. I'm trying to wrap things up. What about you?"

"Supper time here. I've just been packing things up. Ready for an early start."

"Any news or progress?"

"All quiet at present. On the news I heard that the police are saying the bomb that blew up my car wasn't the sort used by terrorists."

"Not terrorists ..."

"No." Marnie knew what Ralph was thinking. "Stupidly, I was quite pleased at first. Then reality took over."

"You were pleased?"

"The bad news could've been that some terrorist nutters picked on my car by chance. Bad news for my insurance policy. The good news could be that some hired assassin was trying to kill me, so my insurance cover will pay for the next car for him to blow up."

"Oh, Marnie ... This is a mess. Don't you think you should go to the police for protection?"

"Who do you think's top of my list of suspects? No, only joking. But I'm certainly not popular with them at the moment. Was I ever? Talking of the police … Ralph, did you know the Provos?"

"The provisional IRA? Marnie, my subject is economics."

"No, the Provos in Amsterdam, back in the 60s and 70s."

"Yes, of course. But I thought we were talking about terrorists. Why do you ask?"

"Someone was talking about radicals the other day, and I wondered if you'd had contact with them."

"I wrote a book about the Provos and other radical groups. And several articles in journals. It all followed on from my doctorate – economic impact on Europe of the French Revolutions of 1789, 1830 and 1848. I wanted to look at upheavals in modern times."

"Are you still in touch with them?"

"Not really. They don't interest me much professionally these days. I still see Piet Bax and Henrik de Jong at conferences, of course. I'm not sure why you think this might be relevant."

"There's speculation about who could be planting bombs when there's supposed to be a cease-fire."

"Well, it certainly wouldn't be the Provos of Amsterdam. Violence was never their scene. And most of them are respectable solicitors or media tycoons these days."

"It was just a thought."

"I don't see how it could have anything to do with what's happening around you, Marnie. Just keep your head down below the parapet. I'll be back as soon as I can."

Part 14

Thursday 5 January

It was a strange drive the next morning back to Knightly St John. The usual easy flow of conversation was missing. The usual sense of anticipation as they returned home was buried somewhere below the surface. Silence filled the car for miles, as Anne looked out of the window at the fields and trees under an overcast sky, and Marnie concentrated on the road. Everything was different now. Their way of life seemed to have been poured away. Everything they had worked to create had been thrown out. The anticipation of returning home had been replaced by uncertainty about what they would find there. The smallest details of their lives had been changed so that they felt like strangers in their own world.

Anne reached into the glove box and took out the mobile phone. It was the first time she had handled the new one, and she had to study the layout before she could make it work. "Where's the memory on this, Marnie? I want to let Jill and Alex know we're on our way."

Marnie replied vaguely, "Oh, I'm not sure. I haven't put the numbers in." Anne put the phone back in the glove box and turned her head to gaze across the empty fields. She flipped open the road atlas on her lap and looked down at the familiar route.

"I know what you're thinking," said Marnie.

"Mm?"

"But it will be the same again one day. Once we've put all this behind us."

Anne nodded slowly, as if she almost believed it. "I don't want anything to –"

"Nothing is going to spoil it. I won't let it. You know, Anne, I'm sick of things coming in and taking over our lives. I moved up here – *we* moved up here – to make a fresh start and do our own thing. Up to now it's been great."

"Apart from you getting murdered, almost."

"Yes. That small detail aside. Well, I'm damn well not going to let other people and their horrible lives get in the way of our happiness. And our success. This is our time and we're going to do things our way."

Anne smiled for the first time that day. "Yes." Her voice was choked so that the word scarcely came out. Marnie glanced at her friend. Anne was blinking, her eyes moist. She cleared her throat. "I'm so glad you said that, Marnie. I was beginning to think –"

"No. We have to press on and get things back to normal."

"But what about Tim Edmonds and all that?"

"I don't give a damn about him or any of them." Even Marnie was surprised at the venom in her own voice.

"Right," said Anne. "Right."

"Well, of course, I do really. I mean, I'm sorry he died. You can't hold that against someone. I know that. But I didn't want to get mixed up in it. I didn't ask to get involved."

"It's a bit difficult to get out of it, though, isn't it?" Anne said quietly.

When they reached the village and drove down the High Street, it looked normal enough. Lights were on in the shop, but they drove past. Anne had bought some basic provisions that were stacked in a box on the back seat. Lights were visible in the school, where someone was getting ready for the start of the new term on Monday. Life was going on behind the scenes.

Marnie turned off the road through the gates at the top of the field track, and at that moment, for both of them, it felt like coming home. Marnie smiled quickly at Anne and reached sideways to touch her hand. Anne muttered something, but Marnie could not make out what it was because there was a rushing sound in her ears. She took a deep breath and felt free for the first time in days.

The car rolled to a halt beside the office barn. The farm buildings shone faintly in the cold wintry light. This was her place, their place. Marnie got out of the car and looked around at the complex of farmhouse, cottages and barns that seemed to welcome them with every stone, timber and slate. Anne climbed out and reached into the back for the box of groceries. Marnie turned to speak to Anne as she reappeared on the other side of the car. Anne's expression, looking beyond Marnie, stopped her before she uttered a sound. Marnie turned and saw Jill Burton standing in the doorway of cottage number one. If she was pleased to see them, it did not show in her face.

Marnie watched with misgivings as Jill came across the cobbled farmyard towards her. "Morning, Jill. How are things?"

"Hallo, Marnie. Morning, Anne. Well, it's all a bit strange actually."

"Let's go into the office and you can tell us about it. It's too cold to stay out here." Marnie took Jill by the arm and guided her inside. Anne opened the shutters and put the kettle on while Marnie sat Jill in a chair. She perched on the corner of her desk. "Tell me what's bothering you."

Jill looked uncomfortable. "First of all, Dolly seems to have gone missing. We haven't seen her for the last two days. I fed her Tuesday morning, as usual, and she went out on her rounds. You know she likes to go in the spinney. Usually we don't see her for hours and then she appears for her next meal ... like she had a wristwatch."

"And you haven't seen her since then."

"No. I've hunted high and low in the spinney. Alex too. We went to the boats, up the track, we checked the road. No sign of her anywhere. She's not caught up a tree ... you know what she's like for climbing. We wondered if she could've got inside one of the other buildings and got trapped somehow, but they're all locked up and there's no way in that we could see. I am sorry."

"Don't worry, Jill. It's not your fault. We'll have a think."

"And then there's the other thing ..."

"What's that?"

"I don't know quite how to put it." Jill searched for the words she needed. Marnie waited. "While we were out looking for Dolly ... I thought someone was out there ..."

"Out where?"

"Just out there ... around the farm. You could see where the undergrowth had been trodden down, as if someone had been moving about."

"An animal perhaps?" Marnie said, wondering at the same time about what might have happened to Dolly. "A stray dog ... a fox?"

"I showed Alex, and he said there were footprints in the ground. It's not as hard under plants as in the open. I know you'll think I'm being silly, but once or twice I've had the feeling that there was someone near the farm."

"Just these past few days?"

"Yes. While we've been out searching for Dolly." Jill shook her head. "It's probably a daft idea, but Alex wondered if there might've been a tramp or someone like that, a vagrant, you know, looking for shelter. It's been bitterly cold the past few nights. Alex has been out checking the windows and doors on the farm and the cottages. We've looked in the barns, but there's been no sign of anyone trying to break in. We've checked at night and then again first thing in the morning. To tell you the truth, Marnie, it's made me feel really nervous. I'm glad you and Anne are back."

"Right. And apart from this feeling you've had, and the trampled undergrowth, has there been any actual trace of a person?"

"Apart from the footprints, nothing else really. Oh, there was a cigarette butt, but it could've been dropped any time."

"Did you pick it up?"

Jill looked puzzled. "No. Should we have?"

"No, of course not. I've been dealing with too many police officers. I'm starting to sound like them. Where was the cigarette?"

"Up at the back of the farm by the old kitchen garden."

• • • • •

Marnie came to lean up against the draining board as Anne washed the coffee cups. "Did you hear that? It was Jill's mini. I think she's gone shopping."

"Nice little car, that. Just right for her."

"We'll have to think about getting one for you some time. You'd like that, wouldn't you?"

"Wow!"

Marnie began drying the cups. "While she's out ..."

"Ye-e-s."

"No need to sound suspicious."

"It was the way you said it ... like a conspirator."

"I was just going to suggest we had a look round the farm."

"Yes. I was going to go on a hunt for Dolly."

"Let's do it now," said Marnie. "While the coast is clear. I wouldn't want to worry Jill."

"Why should she worry?"

"Well, it must be a disappointment. Just married, moved into her first home with her husband, and feeling under surveillance from a prowler. That's not what they expected at Glebe Farm."

"So this isn't just about looking for Dolly."

"We'll see."

The trouble with Glebe Farm was its scattering of outbuildings, barns and sheds, the heaps of materials for the construction work. There was no shortage of places to hide. Marnie and Anne picked their way carefully round the farmhouse to the old kitchen garden, anxious to disturb nothing. It was Anne who found the first trace of intrusion. They kneeled down and examined the ground. Marnie pointed. "I think this is what they saw. All the other trampling was probably done by Jill and Alex. Pity."

Anne stretched forward and reached into the flattened planting. She pulled out a cigarette butt.

"What do you deduce from that, Watson?" Marnie said, trying to sound more flippant than she felt.

"Someone's been smoking here," said Anne with a deadpan expression on her face.

Marnie inspected it closely. "It doesn't look as if it's been here very long. It seems to be fresh."

"And it's smoked right down to the filter," said Anne. "That's how kids smoke."

"Or someone on surveillance who's bored out of his skull and has nothing else to do?"

"You could be right."

Marnie surveyed the area for some time before speaking. "No, I'm not ..."

"Was that a trick question, then?"

"No. Seriously, Anne. Look at this place. What does it tell you?"

"Am I back to being Watson again?"

"If you like. What do you see? Look at it."

Anne stared all around her and glanced at the cigarette. "Oh, yes. I see what you mean."

· · · · ·

For lunch, Marnie made a mixture of tuna and mayonnaise and sprinkled it with black pepper and lemon juice while two pittas warmed in the oven on *Sally Ann*. Meanwhile, Anne put together a small salad and tossed it in vinaigrette. Marnie stuffed the tuna and salad into the pittas while Anne opened a bottle of designer mineral water.

"So you think I'm right?" Marnie said to Anne, as they began eating.

Anne nodded agreement and chewed steadily. She swallowed. "Yes, definitely. This is delicious, Marnie."

"I think your balsamic vinegar makes all the difference." Marnie said, taking a sip of sparkling water. "I'd prefer a spritzer with it, if I'm honest. Look, coming back to the intruder ... if that's what it was. That was definitely not a pro."

"No."

"A professional of any sort, police, terrorist, or whatever, was not going to leave the place trampled underfoot like that. It's too obvious."

"And the cigarette end was a give-away," Anne joined in.

"If it came from the same person."

"And you think it did."

"I think the butt was fresh. If it had been out there long, it would've rotted. So, yes, I do. At least there must be a fair chance that it did. And no pro is going to be watching somewhere with a lighted cigarette in his mouth. For a start it glows in the dark."

"And it smells," said Anne. "And leaves traces of ash."

"We'd never find that," said Marnie. "They must just think of us as hopeless amateurs, not worth even the basic precautions."

"No, but if they did something and the police came to investigate, *they* might find it."

"Right. So what do we have? You think it was someone more your age."

"Seems logical."

"But why?" Marnie said. "What would be the point?" They ate in silence for a few moments. "Unless ..."

"What?"

"There is that other possibility. Perhaps it was a tramp, like Jill said."

"Looking for somewhere to sleep, somewhere sheltered?"

"Maybe. We'll have a look for signs of occupation in the barns. There isn't much real shelter down here, though. And I think tramps know where to look, usually. And they wouldn't stand out there in the same place for long. Surely, a tramp would be searching around for somewhere to go."

"So that knocks that idea on the head," said Anne.

"Although ... there might be another reason."

"For it to have been a tramp? What do you think?"

"What if he was trying to see us ... get in touch, make contact?"

After lunch, they resumed their search of the buildings and grounds, becoming increasingly aware of their anxiety about Dolly. Of intruder or cat, there was no trace, and they turned back towards the office barn, neither feeling inclined to settle down to work. A faint sound behind them caused Anne to look over her shoulder.

"We've got company, Marnie."

Approaching slowly down the rutted field track was a familiar, dark green Range Rover, shiny as new. The car drew up behind the hired Escort, and Marnie greeted George Stubbs with a handshake. He in turn patted Anne gently on the shoulder, and she smiled through her desire to pull a face.

"I heard you were back, my dear. You were spotted as you drove through the village."

"Even in a strange car?"

"Of course. Townsfolk notice the car. Country people look for the person in it. Quite a difference, you see."

"Yes. Well, George, what brings you here? Have you time for a cup of tea or coffee?"

George looked quickly at his watch. "Much as I would love to, I'm afraid this is only a flying visit."

Marnie led him into the warmth of the office. "Fire away. What can I do for you?"

"It's more in the way of what can I do for you, Marnie. I'm on my way to a meeting of the constituency management committee. Gerald will be there."

"Gerald?"

"Sir Gerald Cornforth ... you know, your local MP."

"Oh, right. I see."

"I was wondering if you needed any help?"

"From my MP?" Marnie wanted to say that she had seen enough MPs to last a lifetime.

"Yes. He's a good chap, Gerald. Knows his way around where it counts. Good connections. If there's anything you need to know ..."

"That could cover just about everything, George. The police aren't exactly forthcoming. I never know where I am with them."

"I suppose not. Can't be easy running an investigation."

"Actually, I have had some help from an MP. Do you know Malcolm Grant?"

"Of course. I've met him at functions a few times. That's what I call a man. Salt of the earth is Malcolm. Great fan of Maggie, too. Fine chap. Peer now, you know. Shame really. I thought he'd go far."

"But you have a high regard for him."

"Absolutely. First class. Top drawer. And he's helping you, you say?"

"We've discussed the case of Tim Edmonds a few times."

"Good. Good. Oh well, I'd better get along. If there's anything I can do, just shout."

Marnie walked with George out to his car. "George? If there was a stranger hanging around in the village, do you think someone would know about it?"

"Bound to, I'd say. You can't have secrets in a place like Knightly. What sort of stranger?"

"I'm not sure. A tramp, possibly?"

"That's most likely Woody."

"Woody?"

"Nice old stick ... been coming through for years. Mind you, I'd be surprised to see him at this time of the year. Usually he's around in the spring."

"Where would he be at this time?"

"No idea, Marnie. Sort of thing you don't ask, really. We give him some food, bit of cooked ham, some apples from the loft, fill his water bottle. He's pleasant enough. Does no harm. You look surprised."

"Sorry. I just couldn't imagine you knowing a tramp. It seems so odd."

"You get all sorts in the country, Marnie. Can't pick and choose."

"I suppose not. Then, if it isn't this Woody, who else might be around?"

George shrugged. "Search me. But I'll ask in the village if a stranger's been seen. You never know. Nothing else I can do?"

"Thank you, George, no. Oh, except ... I don't suppose you've seen our cat, Dolly? She seems to have gone for a wander."

"Big black cat," said George. "Fine-looking beast. Odd time of year to go off."

"Yes. We're getting worried about her. She's been missing for two days."

"Mm." He lowered his voice. "I'll have a word with the dustmen."

"Dustmen?"

"Yes. They sometimes ... you know ... on the road and all that ..."

"Oh ... yes."

"Don't look so glum, my dear. She'll turn up. Nine lives, you know. I'll keep a lookout. And if I hear anything about strangers in the village, I'll call by. Remember, anything you need, don't hesitate."

Back in the office barn, Anne was sorting the contents of her in-tray into priority order. "Have you got enough to keep you occupied for now?" Marnie said. "There are one or two jobs I want to do on the boat."

"Sure. I'm just getting organised."

"Okay. I'll see you in a while."

Marnie drew the zip on her jacket up to her throat as she set off through the spinney. It would freeze again tonight, she thought. Reaching *Sally Ann*, she went on board only long enough to pick up a woollen hat, that she pulled down over her ears. Slowly she walked along the bank, scanning the surface of the canal as she went. After ten minutes, she turned back towards *Sally Ann*, and began walking in the opposite direction. Less than five minutes later she saw the small dark shape in the water on the opposite side of the cut. A lump came to her throat, and a wave of anguish swept over her. Somewhere behind her, she heard Anne calling, and began to retrace her steps as quickly as she could. Anne appeared from the trees.

"I wondered where you were when I looked on the boat and saw you weren't ... What's the matter? What's happened?"

"Er ... nothing ..."

"Marnie, you look upset. Are you all right? What is it?"

Marnie shook her head and must have glanced towards the canal. Anne looked past her and her eyes focused on the water. She stepped forward and stared.

"Is that ...? Oh, no ... It isn't, is it, Marnie? It's not Dolly, is it?"

Marnie put a hand on Anne's shoulder. "I can't quite tell."

"But you think it is ..."

They stood in silence for several seconds until Marnie made a move. "Come on," she said quietly. "Let's get *Sally* and find out."

The diesel engine clattered into life at the first touch of the starter, and they eased *Sally Ann* out into mid-channel to slip slowly towards the shape in the water. Marnie edged the boat over towards the far bank and throttled back to coast the last few metres. She looked over the side while Anne stood behind her. There was no mistaking the small body floating half-submerged in the frosty water. It was a tiny lamb. A black sheep. Marnie raised a hand to her forehead and burst into tears. With a sob, Anne rushed forward and stared down.

"That's not Dolly!"

Marnie rested both elbows on the roof of the boat with her face in her hands. Anne turned towards her friend and saw tears falling onto the deck. She put an arm around Marnie's shoulder.

"But it's not her, Marnie."

Marnie coughed. "I know." Anne reached into her pocket and pulled out a paper tissue. Marnie took it and dabbed her eyes. "Sorry, Anne. This is ridiculous. I should be the one comforting you."

"It isn't as simple as that," said Anne quietly. "Is it? You've been closer to the action than I have. It can't be easy having to be brave the whole time. You've been under so much strain. And you know more about what's going on."

"Do I?" said Marnie. "I wonder."

• • • • •

That afternoon, in his office in the House of Commons, Malcolm Grant reached forward and switched on the lamp. The green glass shade glowed pleasantly and its brass stand shone, bringing the papers on his desk back into focus. He was surprised how gloomy the room had become even though it was still light outside. He had been sorting through papers when his mind had wandered off, thinking about his interview with Bruere, thinking about Marnie. She was often in his thoughts these days, too often for his own peace of mind.

He tipped the contents of the waste paper bin into a black plastic sack and felt sorely tempted to push everything from his desk into the bag as well. All his political career could be dropped into that bag and thrown out with all the other rubbish. *House of Lords! Huh!* Geriatric ward to make old buffers feel they still have somewhere to go, somewhere they can feel important.

"Why had your bin not been emptied over Christmas, Mr Grant ... or should I be calling you *Lord Grant*?" Malcolm remembered Marnie telling him how irritated she was by the way the police used her name all the time. He had kept a straight face and explained calmly to Chief Inspector Bruere that he was technically still a commoner and that the cleaners would not enter his office without his permission, and that when he was not there he could not give that permission.

"Is that normal, sir?"

"Yes. With all these so-called 'researchers' about the place, you never know who might walk in and take a look at what you've got on your desk."

"You think New Labour would do such a thing?" Bruere looked as sceptical as a Tory backbencher in a debate on European integration.

"Who said anything about Labour? We've had a leadership contest, remember? It's better not to take chances."

Bruere had said pointedly, "A contest in which you and Mr Edmonds took opposing sides."

"We are allowed to think for ourselves here, you know. Tim and I had differences of opinion on several policy issues. We respected each other's points of view. Hardly a motive for ... Or do you see things differently?"

"No, sir."

"Good. So where do we go from here?"

"Can you think of anyone who *would* have a motive for killing Mr Edmonds?"

"All politicians have enemies of one sort or another, Chief Inspector. Don't you think it could have been a mugging that went wrong?"

"If it was, it went quite badly wrong, sir. His wallet was in his pocket, containing cash and credit cards, and he was wearing a gold Rolex."

"And you don't think it could have been an accident?" Bruere had got up to leave. "I can tell you one thing is certain," Malcolm said.

Surprise me, thought Bruere. "What's that, sir?" he said.

"This business has nothing to do with Marnie Walker, nothing whatever."

"Thank you, sir. That's very reassuring."

Malcolm looked up at the clock, amazed to find that another half hour had gone. It would soon be dark outside. In front of him on the desk was a note from the Serjeant-at-Arms. He had a week in which to clear his office. He would have to apply for an office in the Lords. Even if they could find him one, it would not be like this. He would be starting from zero. *Zero.* He crumpled the note in his fist and dropped it into the rubbish bag.

• • • • •

Thursday 5 January – afternoon

"If we don't go soon, it's going to get dark." Marnie was looking out of the office window as she pulled on her jacket.

Anne put her lamp out and stood up. "I just can't think where she could be. Cats can get into such small places." She opened her desk drawer and took out a torch.

"That's a good idea," Marnie said. "I'll get mine from the car as we go out … ah."

"No torch," said Anne.

"No car," said Marnie. "Or at least not the one I was thinking about."

"Shall I fetch the torch from *Sally Ann*?"

"We can go that way. It'd be just like Dolly to come and meet us as we go through the spinney."

"I wish," said Anne.

They walked quickly through the trees without speaking, collected the torch from the boat and returned, skirting the complex of small barns from behind. Anne was opening her mouth to remark on the stillness surrounding them, when Marnie grabbed her arm. They stopped in their tracks. Marnie put a finger to her lips and pointed ahead of them. Anne strained to see what Marnie had spotted. It took her a few seconds before she realised that about ten metres ahead of them someone was standing in amongst a small clump of bushes that gave a concealed view of the buildings around the farmyard. The watcher was wearing a hood that concealed his face.

Anne was uncertain about what they should do, but Marnie was in no doubt and in no mood for holding back. With a cry of "Hey, you!" she charged forward, brandishing the steel torch, leaving Anne to try to keep up. The watcher, taken completely by surprise, glanced quickly in the direction of his assailants and turned to run. He managed one step before colliding with a tree, bouncing backwards and falling to the ground with a bump. Before he could gather his wits, Marnie was standing over him, pulling back the hood.

"Who are you and what are you doing here?" Marnie said in as hard a tone as she could produce. She looked down at the intruder. He was little more than Anne's age. He raised a hand to his forehead where a cut above his eye was starting to bleed.

"Sorry, I … I … can I get up, please?" His voice was trembling, and Marnie's fierceness evaporated. She reached out a hand to help him to his feet.

"Now don't you try and run off. You've got some explaining to do … and it had better be good."

"I don't feel like running anywhere." A trickle of blood ran out below his hand and down his cheek.

"The first aid kit's in the cupboard in the office," said Anne.

• • • • •

Marnie dabbed the wound with cotton wool soaked in TCP. The intruder winced and jerked his head back. Marnie dabbed again. "It isn't much of a cut. No need for stitching."

"I'll put the sewing machine away then," Anne said, pulling an antiseptic wipe from its packet. Marnie took it and mopped the boy's cheek. He glanced towards Anne.

"Have we got a plaster to cover this?" Marnie asked.

Anne inspected the medical kit and produced a plaster. The boy looked at it. "That's not very big," he said softly.

"Don't worry," said Marnie. "Size doesn't matter." The boy's cheeks turned pink. Marnie got up, went to the sink and washed her hands while Anne put the first aid box away. They came back to sit on Marnie's desk, looming over the intruder like inquisitors. "So ... what's the story? Why were you spying on us? You'd better start with your name."

He hesitated. "Ronny."

"Is that your real name?" He nodded. "Okay. Ronny what?"

"Ronny Cope."

"Where do you come from?"

"I live in the village. The other side of the church. Martyrs Close." Marnie and Anne knew it, a small exclusive development of executive homes.

"Go on." He looked awkward. "How old are you?"

"Seventeen."

"And why were you watching us?"

"I was just ..." His voice faded. "I come down here sometimes ... to go for a walk."

"The truth," said Marnie. "You weren't walking, you were hiding in the bushes. I'd call that 'skulking'. The police might call it prowling or even stalking."

"The *police*?" Panic showed in his face. Marnie was already getting the picture.

"Do you smoke?"

"Sometimes. It's not illegal. I'm over sixteen."

Marnie sighed. "Do you feel like a cup of tea?" Anne got up and crossed to the kitchen area. To her back Marnie called out. "Anne, I think you've got an admirer." At the sink, Anne missed the spout of the kettle that she was filling from the tap and sprayed herself and her surroundings with water.

• • • • •

Friday 6 January – late morning

Anne looked up from checking the invoices file. "I keep worrying about Dolly. What can have happened to her? I don't believe she's run away."

Marnie put her pen down on the drawing board. "No. Definitely not. Though I could accept that, if I knew she had found a good home and was all right."

"She couldn't find a better home than here. Shall I make coffee?"

"Good idea. But without creating the interesting office water feature this time, if possible."

"That was your fault," Anne protested, filling the kettle with inordinate care.

"I did feel badly about the cut on his head ... once I knew he wasn't spying on us."

"I wonder what he told his parents about it."

"Probably that he was wounded in the pursuit of true love, I expect," Marnie said. Anne stuck out her tongue. "Seriously, though, it is quite flattering. Had you seen him before?"

Anne shook her head. "I don't think so."

"Well, he seems a pleasant enough boy, and it's nice to have an admirer."

"Talking of which," Anne said, "what time are you collecting Ralph from the airport tomorrow? I haven't got a time in the diary."

"About eleven in the morning, I think. What about you? Have you any plans? Do you want me to drop you in on your folks for the weekend?"

Anne concentrated on making the pot of coffee. "I hadn't thought about it, really. Are you going on to Murton?"

"Actually, we've had to change plans from what we originally thought. Ralph needs to sort out his college work and his jetlag, and I have to do something in London, so I'm just going down to meet him, have lunch, or whatever meal it is for Ralph, and put him on the coach to Oxford."

Behind her there was a knock on the door. This was strange, and Marnie immediately became wary. She had heard no footsteps outside. "Come in." Perhaps she had imagined it. In a louder voice, she repeated, "Come in."

The door swung slowly open, and into the office walked a bedraggled, but still sturdy black cat. Two voices called out in unison, "Dolly!"

From behind the door appeared Ronny Cope, proud and pleased to think that he had found a way of making two women happy at the same time. Beaming broadly, he looked up from the cat, who was now sitting washing herself in the middle of the floor, to find himself confronted by two people with tears streaming down their faces.

• • • • •

That night, the best brushed and fed cat in Britain lay contentedly purring in her basket in the saloon on *Sally Ann*. In the sleeping cabin, Marnie put out the light and began drifting off to sleep. Her last thoughts, for the first time since the start of the new year, were pleasant. Dolly had returned, and the thought made Marnie smile to herself in the darkness.

Part 15

Saturday 7 January – late morning

"You look much better that I thought you would."

"What did you expect?" Ralph was still holding her firmly in his arms in the arrivals area at London Heathrow airport.

"Red-eyed and yawning, I suppose. All jetlag and stubble."

"I'm glad you have such high expectations of me, Marnie. I think I'm running on adrenalin at the moment … seeing you again. It seems ages."

"Come on. Let's go and feed you before you nod off." They kissed again and headed for a restaurant. Marnie swung Ralph's smaller bag over her shoulder while he guided a larger suitcase on wheels through the crowd.

"Anne sends greetings. She's looking forward to seeing you."

"She's running the office this morning? And the rest of the country as well?" They stepped onto an escalator.

"Actually, she's entertaining a visitor for lunch. Anne has an admirer."

"A boyfriend!"

"Not quite. At least not so far. They only met yesterday."

"How romantic," Ralph said.

"Not exactly. We attacked him with blunt instruments, and he made the confession while we were trying to stop his wounds bleeding."

"Really. I'm glad your usual reticent charm hasn't completely faded in my absence. Talking of wounds …"

"Oh, I'm much better. Good as new."

"You certainly look it. Better than ever, I'd say."

"I can't be sure if you really mean that or if you're just scared of my … reticent charm. Look … there's a place over there. Are you hungry?"

• • • • •

Unable to decide what meal this was for his body-clock, Ralph opted for scrambled eggs and smoked salmon with toast and coffee. Marnie, who had not eaten that morning chose the same. As they ate, Marnie brought Ralph up-to-date. He frowned throughout her narrative, only brightening up when she explained about Dolly and Ronny Cope.

"So he found her in a shed. Presumably not one of yours."

"No. Right up in the village by the old people's bungalows. He just went round calling her name and she responded. We'll never know how she came to be locked in there. It's the one bright interlude we've had since you left."

"And it doesn't seem as if any real progress has been made with the Edmonds investigation," Ralph said.

Marnie sighed. "I don't know. The police never tell you anything. Or if they do, you can't tell if they mean it or if they're trying to trip you up."

"I'm surprised they haven't been a little more forthcoming with Malcolm Grant. He's one of the Law and Order brigade."

"He said they have him down as a suspect. Well, perhaps things will change now they've got the note from Tim Edmonds."

"Mm … it doesn't prove much, Marnie. Though I suppose it does corroborate his story … if the note is genuine, which I expect it is. It'd be too easy to detect a forgery. I wonder how far the police have got with solving it all."

"No idea," Marnie said. "I think about it all the time."

"That's only natural."

"You know when you see a detective film on television ... Morse or Dalgliesh or Poirot ... the story seems to follow a recognisable pattern, one incident leads on to the next, and at the end it all somehow falls into place ..."

"That's how they write them, I suppose."

"Yes. And you know what's going on because you get clues and evidence. Well, with this business, just like the murder in the village last year, I have no idea what's happening. Every now and then the police turn up, I get a glimpse of what they're doing and then I get dropped."

"Would you expect them to take you into their confidence?"

"No. In fact, I'd rather have nothing to do with them at all. But of course I can't choose that because of finding the body and being part of their evidence. But what gets me is that I could possibly be of more help to them if I knew what they were thinking. I'm not even on the outside looking in ... there's nowhere for me to look."

"And Grant's no wiser? I'd have thought he would get some impression of what's going on. He's certainly got connections."

Marnie sighed and shook her head. "I don't know what to think, Ralph. I'm not even sure if he really trusts me. The whole thing's a confusing mess."

• • • • •

"Do you like trout?"

"Sure. I eat anything."

"Good. I should've asked you first, really." Anne opened the fridge and took out a bottle of Orvieto. "Do you drink wine?"

"Yeah. Well, I like it, but I don't drink it often. Do you?"

"Not every day, but quite often. Just a glass ... usually a spritzer if it's white."

Ronny looked puzzled. "A what?"

"Spritzer. White wine mixed with sparkling water. It's nice. Wanna try one?"

"Great." Ronny finished laying the table in the saloon on *Sally Ann.* "What shall I do now?"

"You can uncork the bottle if you like. Lunch'll be ready in five minutes." Anne busied herself scooping the pips out of a melon. Behind her, she heard the pop of the cork being extracted. Ronny laughed softly. She turned to see him smiling, reading the label on the bottle. "What's so amusing?"

"Dunno ... everything, really. Being on the boat like this ... having a meal here. You ... everything."

"You find this funny?" She inspected the pan of new potatoes on the hob.

"No. It's just so different. No one's ever made me lunch before ... apart from my mum. It's like eating out on holiday. Do you do this kind of thing a lot?"

Anne bent to check the flame under the pan as she turned down the gas. "We have friends to eat with us, yes."

Ronny smiled and shook his head. "You're just like your friend ... you know, Marnie. You're just like her."

"Am I? I suppose that's a compliment." She put two bowls on the table, each containing half a melon, and handed Ronny a blue gingham napkin as she sat down. "It was meant as a compliment, wasn't it?"

"Oh, yes. I suppose so."

"Right," Anne said. "You don't seem very sure."

"Well, it's just ... you're not like other girls I know."

"In what way? You've noticed I've got two heads, is that it? Most people spot that straight away."

Ronny laughed. "Apart from that. You're just ... I don't know ... you're like Marnie. You're sort of ... trendy."

"*Trendy*? Nonsense!" She shook out her napkin and put it on her lap. "Well, *bon appétit!*"

• • • • •

"You keep trying to change the subject." Marnie smiled at Ralph.

"What do you mean?"

"Every time I mention your visit to Washington, you steer me away."

"I don't mean to. It's just that I'm more concerned about you."

Marnie raised a biro towards her mouth like a long cigarette holder and put on a sultry expression with hooded eyelids. Her accent when she spoke was middle European with a hint of Marlene Dietrich. "Presidents ... I can take zem or leave zem. Zey're all ze same to me ..."

Ralph laughed. "Idiot!"

Marlene Dietrich said, "Tell me about your secret talks wiz Clinton ... spill ze beans."

"I'm trying to be serious about a serious matter, that's all." He reached across the table and took her hand.

Marnie said, "I know, but I'm sick of this thing hanging over me the whole time. I want it all sorted out. I want to get back to a normal life, while I can still remember what normality is like. I'm not kidding, Ralph, I've been going round like a fugitive, skulking in the shadows, covering my tracks. I'm not James Bond. I'm just an interior designer trying to earn a living."

"And the world won't let you."

"No, it won't. All I did was find a body in a canal. It could've happened to anyone."

"But it happened to you, Marnie."

"Lucky me ..."

• • • • •

Anne carefully forked the remains of pink flesh from the bones of the trout and tipped them onto a saucer while the kettle boiled. "Dolly will love this." On cue, and recognising the action in the galley, Dolly stretched languidly and walked over towards her, rubbing her flank against Anne's jeans, purring. Ronny had to step over her to put the dishes in the bowl in the sink.

"She's a nice cat. Very clever. She kept answering when I was calling her name by the sheds until I found her."

"She's lovely. We think the world of you, don't we, Dolly?" Anne bent down and put the saucer by the cooker. The purring continued while Dolly buried her nose in the fish. "It's getting sunny outside. Shall we have coffee on the deck? We can put jackets on."

"Anne? Can I ask you something?" Ronny's voice was tentative.

Anne turned to face him. Her voice was serious. "What?"

"You and Marnie... what's it really like being mixed up in this ... in this murder?"

"Depends what you mean by *mixed up*."

"Well, in the village some people are saying it's odd how Marnie ..."

"Go on."

"Like last year she was involved in the vicar's murder ... you know."

"We both were. It was horrible. Toni was our friend."

"And now ..."

"Ronny, what are you trying to say? You're not making much sense."

"Some people think it's a weird coincidence that Marnie found that body."

"It was. What else could it have been?"

"Oh, I know. But it is strange, isn't it?"

"Of course it's strange. But it's not as if Marnie's taken this kind of thing up as a hobby. What do you think we are, a pair of witches?"

"Christ, no. I mean, sorry, no, nothing like that. 'Course not."

"We're no different from you or any other people, Ronny. And don't forget, you're the one who found our cat ... our *black* cat."

"Bloody hell, Anne. Don't make it sound creepy. It was pure luck. I just went out looking and found her, that's all. I was trying to find her and I did."

"And you could say that body found Marnie. She wasn't looking for anything, just minding her own business."

• • • • •

Ralph came back to the table with their second cup of coffee. Marnie was writing a list of things she had to do that day.

"So you were impressed by the President?"

"He's certainly running a strong economy. America's never been so prosperous."

"And it's not just a boom?"

"Not in the usual sense of a boom-and-bust cycle, no. If he can keep it on course, he'll go down as one of the most successful presidents of all time."

"And what's he like as a person?"

Ralph looked thoughtful. "Mm ... Impressive, in a very American way. His style's quite informal. You know that folksy, homespun way they have ... first names and all that. But he's certainly sharp ... shrewd, even. Of course, I didn't speak with him for long, about half an hour in all, but I gained a fair idea of how he works."

"So America is in good hands." Ralph did not reply. "Isn't it? Ralph? What's the matter? That's what I thought you were saying."

"Well ... it's just that ... there are rumours."

"What kind of rumours?"

"About his private life. I heard one or two things."

"I can't imagine you listening to gossip."

"Oh, this wasn't idle tittle tattle."

"Even so."

"Marnie, when thinks happen around the most powerful man in the world, heading the world's biggest economy, economists like me have to take notice. It could have an impact on everything."

"But if they're just rumours ..."

"We shall see. But the world of politics is never what it seems. There's always something going on beneath the surface."

"Tell me about it," Marnie said. With irony.

· · · · ·

The faint winter sun filtered through the trees of the spinney, bringing dappled light and shade all around the docking area as they sat on deck wrapped up against the cold, drinking their coffee. They gripped mugs in both hands to keep their fingers warm, and the steam rose straight up from the drinks in the still air. The water in the canal shone, reflecting a faded blue sky. A few birds were singing. There were no other sounds, no cars, no aeroplanes, nothing to intrude.

"Anne?"

"You're not going to spoil it, are you?"

"I was going to say sorry."

"You don't have to."

"I didn't mean that you and Marnie were ... you know."

"Good. We're not crooks, or witches or anything."

"No. This has been really nice. I've enjoyed it."

"I'm glad. So have I."

"I'm going to help with the dishes when we've finished coffee."

"No need."

"I want to. I do at home."

"All right. Thanks."

"Can I come and see you again?"

"Sure."

· · · · ·

Ralph paused while lifting the coffee cup to his lips and stared at Marnie. She blinked. "What is it?" she asked.

"As they say in America, can you just run that past me again?"

"Why? It's not so difficult to understand. I need transport. It's there, it's mine, and I can use it straight away. What's the problem?"

Ralph put the cup down on its saucer. "But don't you think it a little ... unusual?"

"Perhaps, just a little. But that doesn't make it a bad idea."

"So you're going to use your MG, a 1936 sports car, to travel around in ..."

"I have to have a car, Ralph."

"This is the person who covers her tracks so as not to be noticed, who goes into hiding on a friend's boat ... *somewhere in England* ... sends her mobile phone on a train journey to Land's End and whose sole aim in life is to blend into the shadows."

"Well ... since you put it like that ..."

"Driving around in a rare open sports car in the middle of winter. Marnie, you don't have to be a rocket scientist –"

"Or a leading economist …"

"Or a leading, somewhat bewildered economist, to spot a slight inconsistency in your approach there."

"But I'll be unrecognisable, Ralph. Trust me. When I'm all togged up in my gear, my own mother wouldn't know me."

"She's not blind, by any chance?"

"Ralph!"

"Sorry."

* * * * *

After seeing Ralph off on the Oxford Express, Marnie turned the Ford Escort towards central London, stopping briefly to pick up the box of flying gear from Chiswick. She checked in at the Rentacar office and felt a twinge of unease as she handed over the keys of the very inconspicuous family saloon, probably the most common car on the roads of Britain. She took a cab to the garage of Harrison and Dent.

Michael Dent was on the phone in his office when she walked into the workshop, and he waved through the window in a gesture that he would not keep her waiting long. Marnie put the bulky cardboard box down on the concrete floor and spotted the car standing at the other end of the large brightly-lit space that was filled with the paraphernalia of auto engineering and smelt of fuel, rubber, steel and lubricants. Her MG was lined up in a row with two more modern sports cars. Compared with them it was narrow, angular and eccentric. The bodywork in British racing green was shining. The chrome of the headlamps, bumpers and wire wheels was gleaming.

Michael Dent came out of the office at speed. "Sorry about that, Mrs Walker. She's all ready for you." He walked Marnie across the garage. "We're very pleased with her. I hope you are." When they reached the car, he pulled open the bonnet to reveal the engine compartment. He beamed at her. "What do you think?"

It looked as good as new. It looked like an antique on wheels, the kind of car that would turn heads in every country in the world. It could not be more noticeable if it tried. Marnie smiled. "It's perfect. Just what I wanted."

* * * * *

Anne noticed that she was humming to herself as she put away the dishes from lunch. It was a strange, unexpected day. Ronny had gone home, promising to come back soon. From the window in the saloon on *Sally Ann*, she had looked out and seen him skipping through the spinney in the pale afternoon light, and she half expected him to run into a tree and injure himself again. *Funny boy,* she thought. Anne was unaccustomed to having a *devoted admirer*, as Marnie had described him. It was all very curious. He had appeared from nowhere. She shook her head.

"Well, Dolly, what do you make of that?" From her basket in the corner of the saloon, the cat looked up, momentarily interrupting washing behind her ears. She resumed the task, having given only brief consideration to the question. Anne continued. "How odd that I'd never seen him before. He arrived just like that, out of the blue." She closed the cupboard door and hung the tea towel over the rail on the front of the cooker. For a few moments she stood at the sink, staring in front of her, thinking. She turned to sit on the nearest chair and leaned forward with her elbows resting on her knees, her hands dangling loosely before her.

Why hadn't I seen him before? she thought. *And if I hadn't seen him, how had he seen me?* Dolly stepped out of the basket and came to sniff at Anne's hands, which she'd clasped in front of her. Anne stroked her absent-mindedly and the purring engine started up. *Where could he have seen me without me noticing? It's only a small village. Am I being paranoid? Am I right to be paranoid?* She stood up and looked out of the window again. The light was slowly fading, but she could clearly see that the spinney was empty. She walked through to bolt the entrance door at the stern.

• • • • •

"Do you think I could ask you a favour, Mr Dent?" She gave him a cheque to cover the work on the MG.

"Call me Michael, Mrs Walker. Thank you for this."

"Marnie."

"Right, Marnie, what's the favour?"

"Is there anywhere I could change my clothes here?"

Michael Dent led her to an empty office behind his own and closed the venetian blinds. "This do you?"

"Just right."

Minutes later she emerged into the workshop wearing heavy-duty jeans, flying jacket and scarf, carrying the airman's helmet. A pair of tinted glasses hung round her neck. The group of men was standing around her car and, seeing her, they broke into spontaneous applause.

"Marnie, that's terrific! Where did you get that amazing gear?"

"I inherited it from an uncle."

"Did he have a shop in the trendy end of Covent Garden?"

"I'll have you know this is the real thing, a bomber jacket from Bomber Command."

Michael Dent inspected her enthusiastically from head to foot. "You know, Marnie, I think I believe you. It certainly looks authentic. What's it for?"

"I'd have thought that was pretty obvious. I'm going to be driving a pre-war open sports car with no heater and no creature comforts of any kind. A girl's got to look after herself in this hard world, you know." She knew she was playing up to her all-male audience, even mildly flirting, and she was honest enough to know that she liked it. It made a pleasant change from being interrogated by the police or fleeing from real or imagined enemies. She was remembering that she was an attractive woman, worth more than a second glance, and she revelled in it.

"Well, we've been thinking about that, and we've got some ideas in that direction, too."

"I'm listening."

Michael gestured towards the MG. "Come and see. We've come up with a solution to the heating problem." He placed himself between Marnie and the car.

"You've fitted a heater? Wow, that's really ..."

"No, not quite, actually. We've produced something based on thermo-hydraulic principles, rather like the system used on the new Mercedes SLK range of supercharged two-seaters."

"I'm impressed. Bewildered, but impressed. How did you do it – whatever it is – in the time?"

Michael Dent raised a disappointed eyebrow. "We are specialists, you know," he said in a pained voice. "You're in the hands of professionals here."

Marnie gave him a blast of the hooded eyelids. "Okay, I'll buy it. Amaze me."

With a flourish, Michael stood aside and pointed into the cockpit. Marnie peered in. She looked down at the driver's seat to find a bright red hot-water bottle nestling on the old leather.

· · · · ·

Anne walked back through the spinney more quickly than usual while it was still light. She opened the office barn and pulled out the vacuum cleaner, intending to give the whole place a thorough going over as she waited for Marnie to get back from London. Instead of attacking it with her customary energy, she found her mind wandering. It wandered mainly in the direction of Ronny Cope.

Part of her was flattered that someone should fancy her so much that he came and watched her from a hiding-place. She put down the cleaner and walked to the back of the office where a mirror hung near the workbench. An honest appraisal. Face not unpleasant. Skin clear, if rather pale, but no spots. Eyes blue, but not cold. Pointed chin, nose not too long. Even teeth. Lips could be fuller, but not really thin. That was more than could be said for the rest of her. Everything could be fuller, and she was thin. *Boyish*, she thought, and turned to catch her outline reflected in the windows. *Thin*, she admitted, in an outbreak of honesty.

So what was so appealing that it brought a boy of seventeen, apparently with good eyesight and no evidence of mental abnormality, down to this remote corner of the village in the middle of winter, to look out for her? *Flattering*, she thought. *But strange*. What attracted Ronny Cope, from the executive four-bedroom-with-en-suite end of the village, obviously from a good home, in Martyrs Close? *Perhaps I've become irresistible without noticing it …*

She pondered this possibility for two seconds and on an impulse picked up the phone, pressing three buttons. "Directory, Jackie speaking, what name please?"

"The name is Cope, C-for-Charlie-O-P-for-Peter-E."

"Cope, and the address?"

"Martyrs Close, Knightly St John, Northamptonshire. The nearest town is Towcester. I don't know the house number."

"One moment, please." Anne glanced over towards the window, wondering if she had heard Marnie's taxi arrive. She assumed Marnie would come from the station by taxi. "Caller, I have no number listed for that name in Martyrs Close. Are you sure of the address?"

"Could it come under Milton Keynes? That's the nearest large town."

"I have the street and the village, but no one called Cope, I'm afraid."

"Could they be ex-directory?"

"I'm sorry I have no record of the name. Nothing's coming up at all."

"I see. Thank you." Anne replaced the receiver and stood wondering. Had she mis-heard him? No, he had definitely said Martyrs Close. She decided to keep busy until Marnie returned, and plugged in the vacuum cleaner. Before switching it on, she went to the outside door and turned the key in the lock. As an afterthought she pushed home the bolt, half smiling at her concern. But only half.

• • • • •

It had taken Marnie just a few minutes to decide that the hot-water bottle was a good idea after all. She had reached across to the passenger seat and dragged it over, first setting it on her lap, then slipping it round against the small of her back. It was very comforting. On the whole, she was surprised how little cold penetrated her airman's clothes, and thought the Lancaster bomber must have afforded all the comforts of a flying fridge.

The little car ran well and was sensitive to every movement of the steering wheel, gamely pulling away from traffic lights and gripping the road firmly on corners, the whole drive accompanied by a throaty exhaust note. Top-end performance was lacking, and the steering was heavy, but the MG more than made up for those deficiencies by the sheer fun of driving it, and as she pulled out of London Marnie chose to avoid motorways and pointed the sports car north on the open road.

Being exposed to the elements gave Marnie the impression that she was travelling faster than she was, and it was the gradual change in light that made her realise the journey would take her into dusk. She tried to remember how the lights worked, but found little time to study the switches as the car's lively steering demanded all her attention. On a stretch of dual carriageway, she pulled into a lay-by and turned off the engine. The switches were clear, but she decided to check that everything was in working order and climbed out to make sure the lights were on. It was good to stretch her legs, and she pulled off the helmet, enjoying the feel of the cold air around her ears. Full beam ... fine. Dipped headlights ... okay. Sidelights and tail-lights ... all present and correct. She smiled at herself, wondering if this was how the early women aviators felt when checking the flimsy planes in which they flew round the world and set records seventy years earlier. Marnie was exhilarated by the open-top car and could not believe she had abandoned it for so long. It made her forget her troubles, at least for a while.

She was only vaguely aware of other cars around her as she concentrated on the job in hand, and so it was with surprise that she discovered a man approaching from behind.

"You lucky devil!" Marnie stood up from squatting to examine a tail light for a suspected crack in the glass. "Oh, sorry ... I thought you were a bloke." The man laughed. "The clothes fooled me for a minute there."

"An easy mistake," Marnie said casually. The newcomer was about the same age as Malcolm Grant, wearing an expensive-looking coat over a suit and tie. Beyond him, Marnie saw a Jaguar saloon parked further back in the lay-by.

"Takes me back to my youth." He nodded at the MG. "I had a TC like this in my twenties. Actually, is it a TC? Looks different somehow."

"It's a TA." Marnie pulled open the door.

"Now that's rare. Don't see many of those around."

He looked set for a chat about sports cars, but Marnie wanted to get on. "No. I want to get it home before it gets too dark. Not sure how good the headlights are."

"Right. No. Don't blame you. Well, have a good journey. Going far?"

"Quite a way." She pulled the door open, smiled and climbed in. The man stood watching while she turned the key and pressed the starter button. He grinned when the engine sprang to life and Marnie blipped the accelerator. Expertly, she slipped the car into first without crunching the non-synchro gears and gave a brief wave, easing forward, at the same time pulling on the flying helmet and fastening the strap under her chin. The engine growled when she drew out onto the highway and took it up through the gears to cruise at close to sixty. She slipped on her tinted glasses and tucked the silk scarf close round her neck to keep out the cold.

Marnie kept an eye on the rear-view mirror and very soon spotted the Jaguar coming up behind her. There was a knot in her stomach as the powerful saloon car kept station about twenty metres back. *Just a car enthusiast?* Her fugitive instincts sharpened as the two cars travelled in convoy for the next mile. Up ahead, Marnie saw a roundabout and was aware that there was little traffic on this section of the road. She gripped the wheel tight and gritted her teeth, easing off the accelerator on the approach and braking gently for the turn, double-declutching to drop into third gear. The Jaguar held back and swung with her through the roundabout at a steady pace. As Marnie straightened up on the exit, there was a flash of headlights from the Jaguar and the car pulled smoothly into the passing lane and ran alongside. She glanced quickly across while changing into top. The Jaguar driver gave her a thumbs-up followed by a blast on his horn as he accelerated past and set off into the distance. For the next ten miles Marnie looked at every car pulled up in a lay-by and took careful note of every vehicle on the road ahead and behind.

Soon the signs came up for the roundabout where she would be taking the Northamptonshire turn. Marnie changed down to third, blipping the throttle between clutch movements and drove two laps of the roundabout before choosing her exit. As she pushed the lever into top gear, a car on the opposite side of the road flashed its headlights and the driver raised a hand. She waved back. Minutes later a Porsche approached and flashed. Marnie waved again and was immediately flashed by the car behind the Porsche.

Very inconspicuous! she thought, as she hurried north in the fading light.

• • • • •

Dusk was well advanced when Marnie turned off the high street of Knightly St John onto the field track leading to Glebe Farm. *Let George Stubbs tell me anyone recognised me in this gear!* she thought, as the wheels caught the first hard ruts in the ground. She needed all her attention to steer a straight course down the slope and stopped the car at the back of the office barn.

Seeing lights on in the barn, she walked quietly up to the door and knocked twice. She stood waiting for some moments still wearing her fur-lined leather helmet, bomber jacket, boots and gloves. She put on her tinted glasses and pulled the silk scarf up around her mouth so that all areas were covered.

The door swung open and Anne found herself confronted by the apparition. For three seconds there was silence. Anne opened the door wide. "Hi Marnie. How was Ralph? There's a message for you on the answerphone from Beth. Do you feel like a cup of coffee?"

"Do I look like a cup of coffee?" She walked into the middle of the room as Anne closed the door behind her.

"Well, to be honest, you look more like the abominable snowman." Anne smiled at her friend.

Marnie pulled off the glasses and flying helmet. "How did you know it was me?"

"I gave you that scarf for your birthday."

Part 16

Sunday 8 January – morning

"Oh, hi Anne!"

Anne looked up from the planning diary. It was eleven o'clock on a grey Sunday morning. "Oh, hi Ronny! Just happening to pass by?"

"Yes."

"On your way to ...?"

He looked blank. "Well ..."

"Really?"

"Are you working?" Anne inclined her head towards the diary on her desk. Ronny protested, "But it's Sunday."

"Marnie says that because she's self-employed, she has total freedom to work seven days a week. She allows me that freedom, too."

"Is she back, then?"

Anne nodded. "She's in the garage barn with her pride and joy. Do you want to see?" She led him outside to the next barn where Marnie's rear end, clad in tight-fitting overalls, was protruding from under the bonnet of the MG.

"Nice!" Ronny exclaimed. Anne gave him a sharp sideways glance. "Er ... nice ... car," he added. "Very nice."

Marnie turned to greet Ronny. She looked purposeful in her boat overalls, a rag hanging out of a side pocket.

"You lucky devil!"

"Good morning, Ronny." She looked at Anne. "Men are programmed to say that when they see an old car. It's built into their psyche at birth."

"I'll make a note of it. What are you doing?"

"Checking everything, oil and fluid levels, tyre pressures, wiring, leaks, connections, just a general going over." To Ronny she said, "I brought it up from London yesterday to give it a run. It hasn't been used for a few years."

"And is everything all right?" he asked.

"Seems fine. One or two things needed tightening, that's all. The spark plugs are clean ... always a good sign."

Ronny walked round the car. "It's beautiful. I've never seen one this close up before."

Marnie said to Anne, "All males are also programmed to wear that sort of smile on their faces and nod their heads up and down when looking at old cars. Experience will teach you these things."

"Thank you," Anne said.

"But it *is* beautiful," Ronny protested. "Anyone can see that, not just *males*. It's your car, Marnie. You're not male."

Marnie wiped her hands on the rag, closed the bonnet and turned both handles to lock it. "Sure. How about a hot drink? I'm starting to freeze up."

They began to make their way to the office barn, but Ronny held back to look in the cockpit. After a few moments he ran up to join them. Suddenly, from behind, there was a hissing sound that made them stop in their tracks. As they turned, a series of bangs rang out like muffled gunfire. Anne screamed and jumped, running into Ronny who caught her in his arms.

Marnie muttered, "What the hell ..." She quickly pulled an adjustable spanner from her pocket but lowered her arm as she watched the jumping cracker springing about on the ground. "Ronny ... this is your doing, I take it?"

Open-mouthed, Anne gaped at the firework as it completed its antics and fizzled out. "Ronny! I nearly had heart failure!"

Ronny began to laugh. "It was only a joke." He smiled at Marnie.

Anne gave an exasperated sigh. "You can let go of me now."

"Oh, right."

Marnie shook her head, smiling. "Coffee," she said.

They were all glad of the warmth in the office barn, and Anne switched on the kettle while Marnie washed her hands. She kicked off her boots. "Ronny, can you help me to get out of my overalls?" He hesitated. "They're rather a snug fit. I'll undo the buttons. If you can help me get my arms out, I can manage the rest."

"Oh, er ... sure."

They struggled with the overalls, and Marnie stepped out of them, leaving her wearing a sweater and jeans. She slipped on a pair of shoes. "That's better. Thanks. So what brings you down to this end of the village on a frosty morning?"

"Just a social call. Is that all right?"

"Sure. And you've come all the way down from Martyrs Close?"

"Yes."

Marnie checked her hair in the mirror. Casually she said, "Have you lived there long?"

Ronny said quietly, "A while."

Marnie went on. "I'm trying to think who we know in Martyrs Close. Which is your house?" There was a pause. "You did say Martyrs Close, didn't you?"

"Number twelve."

"That must be at the top, backing onto the church."

"Yes." He was much more subdued compared with the boy who had let off the firework a few minutes before.

Anne muttered something about milk and went out. Marnie brought the tray over and put it on her desk, returning to the kitchen area to fetch the coffee pot. "How do you have your coffee, Ronny?"

"Milk and one sugar, please."

Outside, standing beside the garage barn out of earshot of the office, Anne pressed buttons on the mobile phone. After three rings she heard a familiar voice. "Hallo?"

"Mrs Appleton, it's Anne. Sorry to bother you."

"No bother, my dear. We're just back from church. What can I do for you?"

"Do you deliver papers to Martyrs Close?"

"Yes."

"Do you know the people at number twelve? We can't remember their name."

"Let me think now ... number twelve ... number twelve ... oh yes, that'll be the Wolstenholmes."

"Wolstenholme."

"Yes. They're at number twelve."

"Thank you very much."

"Oh, is that it?"

"Yes, thank you. We just wanted to check. Thank you. 'Bye."

Anne went back to the office and hurried over to the fridge. She joined Marnie and Ronny, put the milk jug on the tray and poured herself a cup of coffee. Ronny did not look up. Anne added a note to Marnie's jobs list and sat down. Marnie glanced briefly at the list and leaned over her desk to alter the calendar. "Coffee all right?" she said to Ronny.

"Yes, thanks."

"You know, it's funny, but I've been thinking ..." She took a sip of coffee. "I had it in my mind that the people at number twelve, Martyrs Close, were called Wolstenholme. Odd, isn't it?" Ronny looked up, his face solemn. Marnie continued. "Have I got that right?"

"Yes."

"Wolstenholme ... not Cope."

"No."

Marnie's voice was calm and reasonable. "I'm sure there's a simple explanation ... I'd be interested to hear it."

Ronny cleared his throat. "My step-father. My parents got divorced. I kept my own name." He put his cup down. "Thanks for the coffee. I'd better be getting back now."

• • • • •

The atmosphere at Sunday lunch on *Sally Ann* was sombre. The cheerful Greek-inspired starter of houmous and tzatziki with warm pitta bread had been intended to brighten a winter's day with thoughts of warmer climes, but it was eaten in near silence. It was Marnie who eventually spoke. "This paranoia thing is a real drag ... suspecting everybody all the time."

"It's not very pleasant," Anne agreed. "I felt sorry about Ronny."

"Yes. I felt sorry *for* Ronny ... how he must have felt."

"What he must've thought of us," said Anne. They sighed in unison.

"He must've planned that firework stunt to make you react like that." Marnie smiled ruefully.

"Like what?"

"Jumping into his arms, of course." She smiled at the memory.

Anne said, "And while he was planning that, we were planning how to catch him out."

"Yes. Well, I'm sorry to spoil your friendship. A real shame."

Anne looked up. "Oh, it wasn't me ... it was you he ... *admired*, as you say."

"Nonsense! To a boy like Ronny, I'm an old lady. Next stop zimmer frame, pension book and false choppers."

"No, I mean it, Marnie. I saw how he looked at you. He couldn't take his eyes off you."

"Don't be silly."

"It's true. And when you asked him to help you out of your overalls ... I mean, well ... actually help you *undress* ... I thought he was going to pass out."

Marnie laughed. "Good god! Really? Oh dear ..." She shook her head. "No. Trust me, Anne. I know about these things. Over thirty is definitely over the hill. You're the one."

"Ralph's over forty," Anne said, "and I don't think he's over the hill. I think he's great."

"Yes, well, hands off. I saw him first." Marnie smiled. "Come on, cheer up. We'll get in touch with Ronny and invite him down for tea or something. We'll do it soon and apologise. He'll understand if we explain the situation we're in."

"Okay. Talking of Ralph, when will we be seeing him?"

"When he's slept off his jetlag. He'll probably ring this evening."

"Good."

By the time they moved on to baked sea bass with roast peppers and glazed carrots, they were in better spirits, chatting about the week ahead and their plans to complete cottage number two. There were meetings in the diary with new clients, and Marnie had to decide when to see Malcolm Grant again to discuss his project.

"Are you definitely going to do his flat?"

"Yes. I don't see why not. I want to try to get everything back to normal with Malcolm." The phone rang and Marnie picked it up. "Hallo?" There was no reply. "Hallo?"

"Oh, Marnie ..."

"Ronny? Hallo."

"I don't know how to say this ... I'm sorry about how I left this morning ..."

"No. I'm the one who should apologise. I was going to ring you. We owe you an explanation."

"No, you don't. The firework thing was silly and then I got embarrassed about my parents. It's just ... I didn't want to have a different name. I wanted to keep my own name."

"Ronny, that's a private matter for you and none of our business, but there are things you don't know that I'd like to tell you about. Then you'd understand about this morning. But I can't do it on the phone."

"I was going to come down, but I saw you had a visitor and thought I'd phone instead."

"No, that'll be someone for the Burtons. Anyway, we'll check the diary and ring to invite you down again. We'll do it soon."

"I'd really like that."

"Good. We need to sort out some arrangements. We'll probably be going to London for meetings, but we'll be in touch."

"You're always doing interesting things, Marnie. You're not boring like other people."

Being a murder victim, finding a murder victim, having your car blown up, being a murder suspect ... again ... certainly makes for a full and eventful life, Marnie thought as she put the phone down. She reached for the bottle of wine.

"What was that about the Burtons?" Anne asked.

"The Burtons?"

"You said something about the Burtons. Only, they're not in. They've gone to friends for the day."

Marnie pondered this. "Then we've got a visitor, it seems." She stood up to look out of the window.

• • • • •

They stepped quietly out of *Sally Ann* and took the path through the spinney that led to the back of the office barn, to the place where they had first seen Ronny. Neither of them spoke. Their breath clouded in front of them as they stepped carefully over fallen twigs and patches of dry leaves, trying not to make a noise. They circled the whole property but found no one. Glebe Farm and all its outbuildings were deserted. They paid special attention to the MG and the garage, but it looked undisturbed, and a thorough examination revealed no interference.

"I wonder what he saw …" Marnie muttered.

Anne shrugged. "Perhaps he was mistaken."

"Well, he must have seen *something* to make him definite enough to change his mind and turn back. Was it a person or a car, I wonder? I wish I'd asked him. Come on, let's check out the office."

Marnie unlocked the door. It looked no different from usual. They stepped inside, and while Marnie looked in all the spaces on the ground floor, Anne climbed up to her attic room. "Nothing up here." She came down the wall ladder and as she turned at the bottom, something caught her eye. "What's that? Is that a piece of paper behind the door?" They found a small note that had been pushed aside by the door as they had come in. Anne bent down to pick it up and gave it to Marnie.

"Ah … end of mystery, I think." She read, "*I expect you are having lunch. Will look in later in the hope of seeing you. Regards, Randall.*"

Anne laughed with relief, and after a few seconds, Marnie smiled.

• • • • •

They strode out across the fields that afternoon, both of them needing the fresh cold air to blow away the cobwebs. In jackets and boots, with woolly hats pulled down over their ears, they walked briskly, chatting happily together about the countless details that made up their life at Knightly St John: projects on the drawing board, new schemes to launch, the grand design to renovate the whole of Glebe Farm. For an hour they marched on, and life seemed all it used to be before finding the body of Tim Edmonds. Marnie intended to keep thoughts of that event and its after-shocks at the back of her mind, trying for Anne's sake as well as her own to restore some version of normality to their world.

They took a route they had not trodden before, a well-signposted public footpath that carried them through fields on gentle slopes, with occasional views down to the canal and distant sightings of villages miles away, the spires and towers of their churches standing out like markers in the landscape. It was the setting in which they had come to build their life, full of expectation and fulfilment.

They had taken a circular pathway that brought them back towards Glebe Farm from the opposite side to the way they had set off. The afternoon light was just beginning to fade, with cloud cover hastening the onset of dusk. Approaching the complex from an unfamiliar angle, they looked down on their base from a few hundred metres away, saw the Burtons' car parked to one side and lights in the windows of cottage number one. The buildings were obviously still being renovated, but especially in this failing light, the whole development, nestling among its trees, had a reassuring homeliness about it, and Marnie and Anne felt their spirits lift.

They stopped for a few moments to take in the view, and Marnie reached across to give Anne's hand a quick squeeze. Without a word being spoken, they were resuming their walk when another light flickered into view. They stopped again, this time less certain that all was as it should be. The headlights of a car had appeared on the other side of the farm, making its way slowly down the field track. Anne suddenly felt the need for another squeeze of her hand, while Marnie felt in her jacket pocket for the solid steel casing of the torch she carried.

"Isn't that a Beetle?" Anne said.

"Could be."

"Oh, good."

They set off with renewed speed to meet Randall.

• • • • •

The three converged on the front door of the office barn at the same time, Randall wearing a sheepskin jacket over his cassock.

"Hi Randall! We got your note. Is this a flying visit or can you stay a while?"

"Well … I wouldn't want to impose on you, Marnie, arriving uninvited like this."

"What I mean is, do we put the kettle on for coffee?"

Anne said, "Is the Pope a Roman Catholic?"

"Actually, Anne, that's a very interesting question. It might take me some time to answer it …"

"Right," said Marnie. "We put the kettle on. Come on, we'll go on board *Sally*."

Anne took the coats and hung them on hooks behind the door of the heads, except for Randall's bulky jacket which she laid on Marnie's bed near the door from the stern deck. They trooped through to the galley and saloon, Randall stooping to avoid bumping his head on the ceiling. At six foot two he was an incongruous sight in the cabin of a narrowboat, a tall slim figure austere in his long black robe and dog collar, with black wavy hair, sharp features and intense dark eyes. But Randall was an incongruous sight anywhere in the cassock, buttoned all the way down the front, that harked back to an earlier age. He exuded the air of a man who knew where he belonged in the scheme of things and had the strength of character to defend his point of view against all comers. In his chosen career he had not infrequently had occasion to do just that. Now, in his late thirties and Rural Dean of Brackley, he was regarded by many as the future candidate for a bishop's chair. Not all his fellow churchmen liked that idea. But despite his ultra conservative appearance, Randall had no problem with the ordination of women priests, just one example of his independent mind. He lowered himself into a chair while Marnie lit two oil lamps on the galley workbench.

"So, what's it to be, Randall? Tea, coffee or something stronger?"

"It had better be tea, I think. After the communion wine this morning, anything stronger might take me over the limit."

Marnie laughed. "Surely the police wouldn't pull you up on suspicion, not in your clerical gear?"

"Acting on a tip-off from the Archdeacon they might."

"You haven't fallen out with someone have you, Randall?" Anne asked primly.

"*Me*? What an extraordinary thought!"

When the oil lamps had reached their full strength, Marnie switched off the electric lights and Anne put a candle on the table in the saloon. The effect transformed the cabin, with a softer light no less bright than before, but much warmer. Randall sat back in his chair enjoying the ambience of the boat as much as the company of his hosts.

"This is very pleasant, Marnie. I've never been on your boat before. It's really quite charming."

"And what brings you back to Knightly? Not just a social call?"

"This part of my visit is entirely social, but I came over to see Jim Fowey to talk about handing over to the new vicar. He said he'd been down to see you."

"He told us it would be another woman vicar and he thought it would be no problem this time."

They all three fell silent for some seconds at this reminder of the death of the previous vicar, Toni Petrie, back in the summer. In her short time in Knightly she had become a friend.

Randall broke the silence. "Angela Hemingway is her name. Nice name, nice young woman. A curate in Northampton. She'll be starting in a week or two. I know you're not churchgoers, but I've no doubt she'll come to see you. You'll like her, I'm sure."

"And you like her too," Marnie said looking steadily at Randall.

"Yes."

Anne shot a glance at Marnie, who got up to turn off the gas under the kettle and make tea. "Darjeeling with lemon?"

"Excellent."

"Randall, I don't suppose you saw anyone near the farm on your way down?"

He looked at his watch as if thinking of an excuse to keep his uninvited visit short. "No, but perhaps I shouldn't stay long. Are you expecting visitors? "

"That wasn't meant as an unsubtle hint. I just wondered."

"Do you mean now, as I came down from the village?"

"Now or earlier."

Randall reflected, steepling his long fingers together. "I don't think so. Are you expecting someone?"

"Not really. Don't you have evensong today?"

"My curate's in charge this evening. Martin. A very earnest young man. Very keen, if a little ... pedestrian."

"And the drop-in centre?"

Randall looked at his watch again. "You're sure I'm not ..."

"No, no. I just thought that if you were free, you might like to stay on and have supper with us."

"That's kind, but I didn't expect to just turn up out of the blue and intrude on your evening."

"Good. That's settled, then." Marnie stirred the pot while Anne set out cups and saucers.

They spent a convivial evening together, interrupted briefly by calls from Ralph, who planned to come to Knightly the next day, and Philip with news of meetings in London later in the week. Supper was an impromptu affair of cheese soufflé and salad with a bottle of Shiraz Cabernet, over which they talked about mutual acquaintances, Ralph's trip, Marnie's plans for the farm, Randall's work in his new job. Anne asked, "Do you have a lot to do? I mean, it's not just services on Sunday, is it? Do you have more work as Rural Dean than when you were the vicar here?"

"I have my own parish with all that that entails, plus my wider pastoral role as RD. Then there's the centre on top of that."

"Do you get ... I mean, does that count as extra work, part of your job?"

"You mean do I get paid more. No, I don't. The pay's lousy, but the perks are good. Riches in heaven for eternity." He winked at Anne. "No, seriously, I get enough to live on and the house ... and the rest is the satisfaction of the job. It may sound idealistic, but that's how it works."

"And you're very busy?"

"There's the usual stuff, services, sermons, choir, PCC, running an ancient building on a shoestring. There are weddings, baptisms, funerals, visiting sick and elderly parishioners, hospital visits, helping other vicars in my patch. Then there are the extras."

"Like the drop-in centre," Anne said.

"Of course, and completing my thesis."

"So you'll be Doctor Hughes. When will that be? We'll have to celebrate."

"Maybe later this year."

"It's amazing all the things you do," Marnie said.

Randall tapped the side of his nose. "Hidden depths, Marnie. You'd be surprised."

"Really? And what do you do in your spare time?"

"I dine out with charming ladies who ask polite questions about my work. This wine is very good. Is it Australian?"

"Not polite questions," Anne said. "I really wanted to know what you do. I don't know much about vicars, and I'd never heard of a Rural Dean before. Is there anything else that you do?"

"Well, I'm organising an annual church choir festival in memory of Toni Petrie, and there's twinning with churches of other denominations in Europe. You're making me feel tired at the thought of it all."

"And you really like working with the tramps, don't you?"

"They're very undemanding. They don't have high expectations of life, and they regard any kindness as a bonus, though that doesn't stop them being suspicious of it."

"Do you think they appreciate what you do for them?"

"Probably not in the way you mean, Anne. I think they're wary of people, as if those of us who belong to normal society are part of the opposition. They just try to keep out of the way and hope they'll be left in peace."

Marnie said, "They seemed happy enough in your centre."

"I think they are. But they're very suspicious of authority or contact with other people except in a very limited way, on their own terms. It'd be all too easy to frighten them off."

After supper, with encouragement from Anne, Marnie agreed to show Randall her new gear. She disappeared for a few minutes to the other end of the boat, returning transformed by the flying clothes and helmet.

"That," said Randall, "is quite something. I've never seen anything like it, apart from in war films. You seem to be held together with zips and press studs."

"Yes. It's rather like a pit stop in a motor race."

"You mean you feel like a racing driver when you wear those clothes?"

"No – it needs a crew of three to get me in and out of it all."

"Sounds like fun," Randall said.

"*Rural Dean!*" Marnie said prudishly. "I didn't think you were supposed to have ideas like that."

"Hidden depths, Marnie. I did warn you."

•   •   •   •   •

That evening, they were making up the inflatable bed in the saloon when Anne who was kneeling on the floor, stopped and stared momentarily in front of her. Marnie came from the locker carrying a pillow and looked down at her friend. "Penny for them?"

Anne shook her head. "I was just thinking about Ronny." She smiled. "His face when you asked him to help you out of your overalls ..."

"I certainly didn't mean to shock him." She threw the pillow to Anne. "He's a nice boy. And he's got a sense of humour, too. That trick he played with the firework ... You should've seen *your* face!"

"I know."

"That was well planned, if you ask me," Marnie said.

"So that I'd jump in his direction?"

"Of course."

"Do you really think so?"

"Well, it worked didn't it?"

Part 17

Monday 9 January – morning

"Hallo, Marnie Walker."

"Morning, Marnie."

"Ralph, hi! How are you? Feeling more human again?"

"Well, let's not exaggerate. I've had a restless night, but I think I've caught up with you. It is Monday, isn't it?"

"Yes. Congratulations. Happy Monday. So, what's new? Any plans, or would that be going too far?"

"I was thinking that I might come over this afternoon."

"Great. At this very minute, Anne is on *Thyrsis*, getting the boat aired and warming her up. Actually, she's been gone about half an hour. I was just starting to wonder what had happened to her."

"Have you had any more suspicious incidents or strange visitors?"

"Randall came yesterday and stayed for supper."

"I don't think I'd count the Rural Dean of Brackley as a suspicious character."

"From what Randall tells me, the Archdeacon might disagree with you there."

"That doesn't surprise me."

"And we had a visit from Ronny, Anne's admirer. I mentioned him to you."

"*Another* visit. Must be keen."

At that moment, Anne came into the office, her cheeks pink from the cold. "Anne's back, Ralph. She's heading straight towards the kettle like a heat-seeking missile. It's an impressive sight." In mid-step, Anne blew a kiss in the direction of the phone. "And she sends greetings. Before you go, there's something I just want to ask you. It's been on my mind these past few days. Do you know anything about Harold Larkin?"

"Larkin, the barrister? I've met him a few times, but I couldn't say I knew him well. Why do you ask?"

"I think Harold Larkin could have had a grudge against Tim Edmonds because of Edmonds having an affair with his wife."

"Sounds like a reasonable assumption, Marnie, but from what I've heard, more than just Harold Larkin could have that sort of grudge."

Within a few minutes of hanging up, the phone rang again. It was Beth. She yawned.

"Don't tell me you've got jetlag, as well. It's only just over two hours to Malaga."

"No. Our flight was delayed. We didn't get in till half two this morning. They made some excuse. Probably the wrong kind of clouds, I expect."

"But otherwise you're okay and everything's normal?"

"Fine. Paul's gone into college to see if his research budget has survived the vacation. That's fairly normal. And I thought I'd say hallo. Actually, there is something not quite normal ... the garage seems strangely deserted without your MG cluttering it up."

"Ah, funny you should say that ..."

• • • • •

Monday 9 January – afternoon

Ralph seemed to be in remission from jetlag. On arrival, he had suggested they go on board *Thyrsis*. There was something he thought they should see on his satellite television. They sat in the saloon with the TV running in the background and the sound switched to mute.

"So you think they really are heading for a recession in the Far East?" Marnie asked.

"Definitely. All the signs are there."

"But not everybody sees them … or agrees with you."

"You know how it is, Marnie. If you laid all the economists in the world end to end, they'd fail to reach an agreement."

"But if all the signs are there," Anne chipped in, "why doesn't everybody see the same thing?"

"Economics is about theories, Anne. The key difference is in how you interpret the facts as you see them."

Marnie said, "Malcolm Grant mentioned you the other day and said you were regarded as rather a know-all."

Ralph laughed. "That has to be a recommendation."

"Don't you mind him saying that?" Anne said.

"Of course not. If he and his lot agreed with me, I'd think I'd got it all wrong. And in any case, economists are supposed to be know-alls. That's what we're here for. It's our job to tell everybody else what's going on and what they ought to do about it."

"Then why didn't you go into politics and run everything, instead of telling the politicians?" Anne asked.

"That's a complicated question. The main reason is that I got interested in the ideas when I was your age. Now I interpret situations … I elaborate theories. It's like studying a pure science. I find it fascinating."

"Not frustrating?" Marnie said. "You don't mind seeing the politicians actually running the economy?"

"Ask politicians who runs the economy and you'll get all sorts of strange answers. And don't forget, on average they spend as much time out of office as in power. The political life is full of frustrations and missed opportunities."

"So you like to travel the world talking to powerful people and helping to influence things," Anne said.

"That's part of it. At least some of the time."

"And you invent theories that make them want to listen to your ideas."

"That's what I try to do, yes."

"Is that what you've been doing on your sabbatical?" Marnie asked. "Developing a new theory?"

"It's rather … I've been working up something that's been on my mind for quite a while. I've written one or two articles about it, and reaction's been good … on the whole." He glanced up at the television and reached for the remote control. "Look. I think this is what we've been waiting for." Ralph pressed a button and the sound came up. A commentator was speaking in a hushed voice.

"… some disquiet among MPs that there has been so little progress reported in the investigation of the death in suspicious circumstances of

Tory MP for London Riverside, Tim Edmonds. The question is being raised by Sir Gerald Cornforth, MP for Northamptonshire South. I understand that the person who found the body and has been helping the police with their enquiries, is one of Sir Gerald's constituents."

Anne glanced hurriedly at Marnie. Ralph said, "Did you ask him to do this?"

"No, but I think I know who did. It was probably George Stubbs." She fell silent as the portly shape of Sir Gerald Cornforth rose to speak. He looked younger than Marnie expected, with pink pudgy cheeks and an air of self-importance, in dark pinstripe suit, striped shirt and striped tie. Marnie could not help thinking that he needed a makeover. She forced herself to concentrate while the MP asked the Home Secretary about the state of the inquiry.

"... and for the sake of all concerned, most importantly of course the deceased's family, his friends and, not to say the least, in the interests of all who are currently involved in assisting the police with their investigations, we need to know when we can expect a definitive statement on progress from Scotland Yard and if possible an indication of when matters might be resolved." He sat down as the Home Secretary whispered in the ear of another minister sitting beside him on the front bench.

"Did all that just mean – *what's happening?*" Anne said to Ralph.

"You've got it."

The Home Secretary stood up. "I'm grateful to my friend, Madam Speaker, for raising a question that has been on everybody's mind since the distressing death of the member for London Riverside in December. Indeed, this is a matter on which we would have been making a statement in this House at an earlier date had the Christmas recess not intervened. I would like to add my own expression of sadness and condolence to the family. He leaves behind a devoted wife and –"

"Is this actually his answer to the question?" Anne said.

"Believe it or not."

"He's just listing more or less everybody who ever knew Tim Edmonds," Marnie said.

"He doesn't want to be accused of insensitivity or, more importantly, of his speech making political capital out of a tragic situation," said Ralph.

"Would he think of doing such a thing?" Anne asked.

"That will come next, I expect."

The Home Secretary was now in full flow. "Members on both sides of this House will be aware that for many months I have been taking decisive action to secure additional resources, not just for the Metropolitan Police but for forces up and down the country ..."

"You were saying, Ralph ..." said Marnie. Ralph shrugged.

"How did you know he was going to do that?" Anne asked, shaking her head.

"He's a know-all, that's why," said Marnie. "It's his job."

Ralph laughed. "You don't have to have extraordinary powers to know what these guys get up to. I watch this kind of thing every day."

"And will he in fact answer the question?" said Anne. On the screen, the Home Secretary resumed his seat.

"Apparently not."

Several members stood up on all sides of the chamber. The Speaker called Sir Gerald Cornforth again and the others sat down. "I'm grateful to my Right Honourable friend for his expressions of sympathy, and no one could call into question his commitment to the cause of law and order in this country." Mutterings, apparently of dissent as well as agreement, could be heard in the chamber as Sir Gerald continued. "No Home Secretary has done more in living memory to reduce the level of crime on our streets and –"

"It'd be easy to forget that there's somebody dead in the middle of all this," Anne said bitterly.

"I'm not likely to forget it in a hurry," said Marnie.

"This sort of thing could get verbosity a bad name," Ralph muttered, as the MP continued. Eventually he repeated his question about progress with the police investigation and sat down amid calls of "Hear! Hear!"

"They sound like a flock of sheep bleating," Anne said.

"This is supposed to be democracy in action," said Ralph. "You're meant to be impressed."

"No wonder a lot of MPs didn't want it to be televised," said Marnie.

"What will he do now?" Anne asked. "Will he answer the question?"

"He'll probably stall."

The Home Secretary once more stood up and leaned forward, placing a large notebook on the despatch box. "Madam Speaker, I can assure my friend that I have been in constant touch with the Commissioner of the Metropolitan Police throughout the course of his investigation. The most urgent inquiries are still in progress and many leads are being followed. It would not be appropriate for me to comment in detail at this stage, and I will make a further statement to the House in the near future."

"Smartarse," said Marnie. Anne giggled.

"Thank you," said Ralph.

"Did you write the script for this, Ralph?" said Marnie.

Ralph smiled at her. "I think that's it." He reached for the remote control.

"Hold it!" said Anne. The Speaker called Sir Gerald again, and he rose still exchanging words with the MP sitting beside him.

"Madam Speaker, I appreciate the need to give the Commissioner time to complete the investigation, but I should be grateful to my Right Honourable friend if he could at least inform the House whether the police have yet been able to establish the cause of death of the member for London Riverside." Shouts erupted all over the chamber. Above the uproar, Sir Gerald bellowed, "Are they treating this as a case of murder?" It was pandemonium.

This time the Home Secretary was on his feet before Sir Gerald had sat down. He strained to make himself heard over the din. "I cannot make any further comment at this time, Madam Speaker. I have promised ... I have ... I have promised a statement in due course and I will return to this distressing subject again shortly." He took his seat, looking pointedly over his shoulder in the direction of Sir Gerald, who did not move.

The atmosphere in the chamber was stormy, the Speaker on her feet shouting, "Order! Order! This House will come to order!"

Anne and Ralph both spoke in unison. "That's interesting ..." Ralph pressed the Mute button on the remote, and the scene became a hideous mime of bawling faces and waving papers.

"What is?" said Marnie.

Ralph spoke first, a surprised frown on his face. "I don't think the police know what happened. They don't know if it's murder or not."

"Is that what you were thinking?" Marnie said to Anne.

"No. I was going to say that the MP sitting next to Sir Gerald whatsit – the one he was talking to – that looked like your Malcolm Grant to me."

"You're right," said Ralph. "It was."

• • • • •

By late afternoon normality had returned to Glebe Farm. Marnie was finalising the design for a client who would be back from a holiday in the West Indies and no doubt itching to have her drawing room and conservatory transformed. Anne had spent a happy hour or two bringing the financial records up to date ready for the accountant, preparing the regular invoice for Willards Brewery and was now writing a shopping list. At four thirty she stood up and pulled on her jacket. "I'm off to the shop!"

Marnie looked up from her concentration. "Right. We ought to get the next invoice off to Willards soon."

Anne placed a document on the desk. "Sign here, please. Same as usual. No change from last month." It was a familiar chant, and Marnie shook her head smiling as she scribbled her signature.

Anne inserted the invoice into an envelope and sealed it down. "Marnie? Why was Malcolm Grant in the House of Commons today?"

"It's part of his job."

"But I thought he was supposed to be a Lord."

"It can't have happened yet. There must be procedures, I imagine ... the Chiltern Hundreds, or something. Ask Ralph, he'll know." As an afterthought she added, "But ask gently. The 'know-all' joke may be wearing a bit thin."

Anne laughed. "Yes. Perhaps I'll just look it up in a book somewhere. It was Malcolm Grant who called him that, wasn't it?"

"Sure was."

"Do you like him, Marnie?"

"Malcolm?" She hesitated. "In many ways I suppose I do."

"You sound surprised."

"He's a Tory MP. Not my usual circle of friends, despite what Bruere thinks."

"But he treats you nicely, you said."

"Did I? Well, he is quite gentlemanly, if you see what I mean ... opens doors, helps me on with my coat, things like that. It's pleasant if it's not overdone. Why are you asking this? Is there a special reason?"

"I wondered if he was the one getting Sir Gerald thingy to ask those questions to get the police to stop putting pressure on you."

Marnie chewed her pen for a few seconds. "Or on him as well. We're both in the same boat." She looked up at the clock. "Talking of boats ... you'd better get to the shop. We've got Ralph coming on *Sally Ann* for supper tonight, don't forget."

Anne turned and accelerated for the door. "I'm as good as there."

• • • • •

The mobile rang in the saloon early that evening while Marnie was in the galley slicing red peppers. "Anne, can you get that? My fingers are sticky." It was Roger Broadbent. Marnie wiped her hands and took the phone.

"Marnie, did you know questions about Tim Edmonds and the police were asked in the Commons this afternoon? I've just heard it on the news."

"We watched it live on satellite. It was the local MP."

"And you're still planning to come back to London?"

"I have a life to lead and a living to earn, Roger."

"I knew you'd say that. Then for goodness' sake keep a low profile. Use *Rumpole* and if you're approached by the media, say nothing."

"I know, trust you ... you're a lawyer."

"I mean it."

"Should I be expecting media attention? It's hardly hot news."

"Are you kidding, Marnie? You've got off lightly so far. Every news editor in the country is looking for an angle on this. You are highly newsworthy for all sorts of reasons. Getting out of London when you did may have been a wise move."

"And now I'm planning to move back."

"I hope you know what you're doing, Marnie."

"So do I."

After the call ended, Anne asked, "What was all that about?"

"Roger thinks I should stay away from London."

"But what about our meetings?"

"I know. He says I have to lie low."

"Wouldn't that be easier in London? I mean, you're easy to find out here. There's nowhere to hide, is there?"

The phone rang again. Two pairs of eyes watched it. Nobody moved. "It can't be the press," Marnie said. "Nobody knows that number apart from a few close friends."

"One way to find out," Anne said and picked it up.

"Randall here, Anne. Have you seen the news?"

"Yes we got live action this afternoon. Let me hand you over to Marnie."

"I was going to ring you anyway, Marnie, to say that Angela would like to meet you and will be in touch."

"Fine. I'll look forward to seeing her. I'll be going to London on Wednesday for a few days."

"Do the press know that you're the constituent they were talking about on the news?"

"Not yet."

"There'll be quite a bit of interest, won't there, when they find out ... after what happened to you last year? You've managed to keep out of the limelight so far, but things are bound to change now. I think you've got to protect yourself as much as possible."

"I've made plans, Randall. I'll just have to hope for the best and see how things turn out."

"If there's anything I can do to help, just let me know."

"How about letting me claim sanctuary in the church?"

• • • • •

Monday 9 January – evening

"Ralph, can I ask you a question?" Anne was mopping up the sauce from the roasted peppers on her dinner plate with a piece of bread.

Ralph reached for his glass of wine. "Ye-e-s."

"It's all right. I'm not going to ask about any state secrets."

"Good. I don't know any. I just have this strange feeling that I'm about to have another lesson in economics."

"Anne did get an 'A' in GCSE Business Studies," Marnie said. Anne gave her the death stare.

"How could I forget?" said Ralph. "Okay, ask your question."

"I just wondered what you went to tell them in Japan. Why did you have something that they wanted to know about? I know you're brilliant and all that, but what was it that actually made your advice more important than the opinions they get from other economists?"

"Nice easy question," said Marnie.

"Er, right. Well, they know about my theory because of some articles I wrote. They attracted interest from economists around the world, including some who know me in the Far East. In particular, there are two people I know in the Japanese Ministry of Trade and Industry, and an old friend in Washington DC."

"And this isn't a whole new theory?" Marnie asked.

"It's more a reflection on existing methods of analysis and forecasting."

"A mathematical model?" Anne suggested.

"In a way, that comes into it." Ralph hesitated as if reluctant to continue.

"You don't have to give away your secrets if it's all confidential. I was just interested because it must be important if you get invited to talk to the President of America about it. I expect I wouldn't be able to understand it, anyway."

"It's not that it's secret, Anne, as you put it. It's just that I could bore for Britain on this subject. It's one of my hobby horses."

"Okay. But I'm sure it wouldn't bore me."

"Is there some way you could give us an inkling of what it involves?" Marnie said. "A potted version?"

"Well, if you're sure you won't be bored stiff, I'll just give you the concise three-hour lecture." He smiled at them across the table. "It's called 'hindsight theory'."

• • • • •

Marnie took a bottle of Courvoisier out of the 'cellar', otherwise known as the cupboard under the workbench in the galley, and put two brandy goblets on the table while the coffee was brewing. Ralph poured the cognac.

"I didn't think that was boring," Anne said, as she cleared the dishes from the table. "And you worked on that theory while you were travelling around on *Thyrsis?*"

"It was the perfect place to work … no interruptions, phone switched off when I wanted to be left alone, maximum privacy. No one at college even knew where I was with any certainty."

"So you worked out a system for analysing past events and situations and built a – what did you call it? – a conceptual model that you could apply to current circumstances."

"That's the basic principle behind it, yes."

Anne spoke slowly. "That means you take the situations leading up to an event in history and examine them in relation to each other. You then work backwards to identify the key events and analyse why they were more influential than others in shaping the outcome."

"Correct."

"And that's really new, is it?" Marnie said. "I thought we were all wise after the event."

"It was that kind of consideration that set me thinking. I tried it out in relation to a number of events in recent years to see if it was possible to achieve a scientific analysis, what you called a 'mathematical model', Anne."

"And you found it worked," said Marnie.

"I tinkered about with it, of course. Eventually, I found that you could attach a mathematical value to events in proportion to their influence on the circumstance being examined. Each aspect of a situation is given a coefficient of influence. If you apply that to the circumstances, you can see how the systems work to shape events."

"That's the part I find difficult," Anne said.

"Not difficult. Look at it like this … at the heart of every complex idea is a simple proposition. At the heart of hindsight theory is the understanding that some factor is the main cause of what happens. Opinions might differ on what that factor is, and factors will change as a situation develops, so I wanted to try to devise a scientific way of working things out. My model helps me to do that in economics. That's why it has to be mathematical."

"But if it wasn't used for economics, it could be different?"

"Of course. It's just a way of working out what is important, focusing on the key factor."

"So you could apply the idea to anything," Marnie said.

"Within reason, yes. Remember the purpose is to analyse data and determine what has happened. That's all there is to it, really."

"So history isn't bunk," Anne said. "We did that at school … Henry Ford."

"He meant it in a particular way. Perhaps you shouldn't take it out of context."

"No, but you'd say it isn't bunk if you can put it in a framework of some sort."

"Exactly."

Anne stood up and poured more coffee. In unison, Marnie and Ralph took a sip of cognac. "Would you say it was a sort of 'chaos theory' for economics, Ralph?"

"That's not a bad way of looking at it. Are you sure you want to stay an interior designer, Anne?"

"And you're in great demand for information on this from banks, financial institutions, even governments," said Marnie.

"They seem to find it helpful."

"Good old *Thyrsis* for giving you the seclusion to work it all out."

"Absolutely. Which is why I'm keen to go on working on the boat … marvellous environment. Total privacy and I can just publish my material when I'm ready. No leaks." Anne laughed. Ralph looked blank. "Did I say something funny?"

Anne rocked with laughter. "You wouldn't want leaks on a boat would you?"

• • • • •

Monday 9 January – night

That night, Marnie came back on board *Thyrsis* and bolted the centre door behind her. Ralph emerged from the sleeping cabin in pyjamas and dressing gown, stifling a yawn.

"Anne did a good job getting the boat aired. She's made up the bed with fresh sheets, too. Did you know?"

"I guessed. She was here long enough to do an overhaul on the engine this morning."

"Is she okay on *Sally Ann*? She wouldn't rather be on *Thyrsis* or in her room in the barn?"

"I offered her both, actually, but she said she was happy down here on *Sally*. She's got the mobile if she gets worried about anything."

"Right. I'll keep my phone on the shelf by the bed. The bathroom's all yours. Oh, by the way, what's that big cardboard box in the saloon? I asked Anne but she just said to ask you."

"That," said Marnie, "is my disguise." She tried to look enigmatic.

"Why are you looking enigmatic like that?"

"Am I?"

"Yes. Tell me more. I'm very curious. Can I see it?"

"Now?"

"Why not? No time like the present."

"Well, it is quite a business getting it on and off."

Ralph laughed. "Sounds like fun."

"Why do all men react to it in the same way?"

"How many men have had this conversation with you?"

"To be honest, only one … Randall. And I suppose strictly speaking, he doesn't count, because he's a man of the cloth."

"You obviously read the wrong Sunday papers," Ralph said. "Well, do I get the show or are you going to keep me in suspense?"

"Okay. I'll go and change." She smiled seductively.

While Marnie turned towards the saloon at the front of the boat, Ralph picked up his mobile from the eating area and headed for the sleeping cabin. Marnie unpacked the box and laid the flying gear out on the sofa, slipping off her sweater and skirt and pulling on the jeans, shirt and bomber jacket. She wound the silk scarf round her neck, carefully zipped herself in and fastened the press studs down the front of the jacket and at the wrists. Finally she put on the fur-lined leather flying helmet and pulled the goggles into place, settling them on the front of the helmet above her eyes. She pulled the jacket down at the sides and raised the back of the collar, wriggling herself in the close-fitting uniform until she was comfortable. There was no mirror in the saloon, so she pulled apart the curtains and looked at her reflection in the window.

Muttering, "Phew, what a palaver!" she made her way through to the rear of the boat. The door to the sleeping cabin was ajar, with only the dim bedside light burning. In a soft voice, she called. "Here I am ... coming, ready or not ..." She pushed the door gently open to find Ralph, still in his dressing gown, sprawled out on the bed, breathing steadily, fast asleep. She looked down on him. "Hallo, Jetlag Lombard," she said quietly. With a tug she unfastened the press stud under her chin and loosened the helmet. She sighed. *I might just as well stay in this gear all night.*

Part 18

Tuesday 10 January – morning

At around seven the next morning, Marnie was in the galley on *Thyrsis* when there came a tap at the window. She went to the centre doors in the saloon to open up for Anne. As she passed the sleeping cabin she glanced in at Ralph. He was still sleeping as peacefully as she had left him half an hour earlier when she had slipped soundlessly from the bed to take her shower. She put a finger to her lips when Anne climbed down into the boat, and they made their way in silence to the galley, pulling the door closed behind them. Anne had a bundle of newspapers under her arm and she put them on the table. Marnie could feel the cold radiating from Anne's jacket.

"Where have you been to get this cold?"

"Oh, I walked up the field track with Ronny. I didn't want to come over too early in case Ralph was still asleep."

"Ronny? Ronny's been on *Sally Ann*?"

Anne smiled. "Marnie, you sound like a Victorian governess. Of course Ronny hasn't been *on Sally* ... he came down *to Sally*. He brought these papers to show us. Then we went to the office barn to collect our *Guardian* and I walked up to the road with him. Actually, you're not going to like this." She pointed at the newspapers on the table and turned to take off her jacket.

Marnie picked up the top paper and read. It was *The Times*. The next one was the *Daily Mail*, followed by the *Mirror* and the *Sun*. At the bottom of the pile was the *Guardian*. As she read the headlines and front page articles her face clouded. "Where did Ronny get all these?"

"His brother does a paper round for Richard Appleton, and when he saw the headlines he went straight home and told Ronny. So he went to the shop and got these for us." Anne looked sheepish. "Er, I think he told Mr Appleton to put them on our bill ... hope that was all right."

Marnie's voice was distant as if she was somewhere else. "Fine. Very ... enterprising." She opened one of the papers to read an inside article spread over two pages.

Anne said, "Shall I make breakfast?"

"Yeah." Marnie sat down at the table and opened another paper. Under her breath she muttered, "Blimey!"

The door swung open to reveal Ralph in his dressing gown. He smiled. "Good morning."

Marnie looked up. "I've got to go."

"Was it something I said?"

"Look at these, Ralph." She handed him a paper. "Front page on all of them ... *Is it murder or isn't it?* ... *Police baffled* ... *Home Secretary covers up police bewilderment* ..."

"Why does this make you think you've got to go?"

"Try this one." She passed him the *Sun*. Half the front page was taken up by the headline: LOOK WHO'S HELPING THE POLICE. The other half was a series of photos showing Malcolm Grant emerging from the police station. In one shot he was standing by the open door of a taxi, leaning forward as if to kiss a woman who was beside him on the pavement. Her head was partly concealed by Grant's. She had very short dark hair. The caption read, "And look who's helping him … who is the mystery woman?"

"This is you?" said Ralph.

Marnie nodded. "We'd both been interviewed the same morning. He was in a hurry to get to a meeting, so he took the first taxi. Perfectly innocuous. The photo makes it seem more than it was."

"The camera always lies."

"Does it?" said Anne, picking up the papers.

"Of course. It only shows one side of the story."

Marnie said, "What I want to know is how did the photo get taken in the first place? How did they know we'd be there? Was someone following Malcolm? Or me?"

"I doubt it," Ralph said. "Probably a freelance acting on his own initiative … recognised Grant … took some shots."

Anne looked at the photos. "Why didn't he get more of Marnie? That could be anyone. It's not really recognisable unless you know her."

"It looks as if he's shot these from across the road with a telephoto lens. With all the traffic, buses and so on, these were no doubt the best he could manage. What did you do next, Marnie?"

"Got into a cab, I think."

"That's how he lost you."

"And now they'll be trying to find me."

"Yes."

"It's only a matter of time. I've got to go. I'll leave today instead of tomorrow."

"You think it's wise to go back to London?"

"There's more camouflage in London and that's where it's happening. There's nothing I can do here, and I could be traced if I went to your house. Anne can go back to her parents for a few days. The press won't be able to find out anything here. They'll soon lose interest and give up."

Anne pulled toast from under the grill and put the slices in a rack on the table. "I'm not going home, Marnie." Her voice was matter-of-fact. There was no reaction. She bent down to take rolls out of the oven and put them in a basket. "I'm not sure if you heard that. I said I'm not going home. You need me with you. Ralph agrees with me."

"Well, now –"

"See?"

"Anne, I didn't –"

"You can't," said Marnie. "I don't want you to get involved. It could be dangerous."

"You're going into hiding, aren't you?" said Anne.

"I'll be keeping under cover, yes."

"And you think they – whoever *they* are – won't be able to find you, right?"

"That's the general idea."

"And what about me?"

"What do you mean?"

"How long do you think it'll take them to track *me* down? As soon as they find out about you, they'll find out about me. One look in the phone book under the name Price in the Leighton Buzzard area, and they'll have located me. I'll be a sitting duck."

Marnie looked at Ralph. He stared back at her. She sighed. "Why do I never win an argument with Anne?"

"Welcome to the club." said Ralph.

• • • • •

Ralph pulled back the blanket covering the cockpit and heaved Marnie's bag and Anne's rucksack into the space behind the seats of the MG. Marnie had warned him to be careful not to trip over the wires running across the floor. He discovered one fan heater humming away in the driver's foot well and another under the car trained up towards the engine. It was seven forty-five, still dark, and they had packed in a hurry. The simple but effective heating system was Marnie's idea, a trick she had remembered from times past when she and her husband ran the MG all year round.

Marnie and Anne appeared from the office barn. In the beams of the outside lights, Ralph could not help thinking they looked like astronauts starting off on a mission. Marnie was in full flying kit and was talking into her mobile. Beside her, Anne was togged up in boots, jeans, her thickest jacket and a baseball cap, her apricot scarf wound several times round her neck. She carried a plastic carrier bag. As they drew nearer Ralph could hear Marnie's conversation.

"... and you're sure that's okay? ... Sure, sure ... I will ... Of course I will ... No. Anne's coming too ... You try stopping her ... I know ..."

Anne said to Ralph, "Marnie wanted to let Roger know we were coming, make sure it was all right." He nodded.

Marnie finished her call. "Right, then. Let's get going. Sorry to dash off, but I think we've got to be away before anyone can get to us."

Anne cleared away the fan heaters while Marnie and Ralph hugged. From the carrier bag she took two hot-water bottles and dropped them onto the seats. She was smiling when Ralph turned to kiss her goodbye.

"Look after yourself, Anne. And look after Marnie."

"You bet."

They bumped up the hard ruts of the field track, Anne with a road map, a file of papers and the inevitable list on her lap, the seats still warm from the fan heater, the hot-water bottles pressed into the smalls of their backs. It was an icy, misty morning, the first hint of light showing on the horizon away over to their left, the glow from the headlamps picking out the tufts of grass between the bumps, catching a glimpse of the tails of rabbits scampering for cover.

"Why don't we put the hood up?" Anne asked.

"More trouble than it's worth. And it doesn't make much difference. The wind just buffets around under it. We'll use it if it rains, though."

"Right. How long will it take to get there in this?"

Marnie glanced across at her friend. "You don't 'get there' in a classic MG ... you *motor* ... and it's not a 'this' ... it's a thoroughbred performance car."

"Oops! Sorry. I'll try again. How long will it take us to 'motor' down to London in your classic sports car?"

Marnie hesitated as they reached the top of the track where it joined the road. She revved the engine briefly and pushed the lever into first gear. "We should do it in under a fortnight ..."

• • • • •

As the morning grew lighter, Anne was surprised how long the journey seemed to be taking. The little car gave the impression of speed, but everything on the road seemed to overtake them, especially coming out of roundabouts. Even lorries swept past them on the straight, buffeting them with a bow-wave of air pressure and flooding them with turbulence in their wake. Anne had to pull a second scarf out of her rucksack and tie it round the baseball cap to keep it in place.

Several cars paused and ran beside them for a short distance while overtaking, driver and passengers peering out at them and smiling. Some gave a thumbs-up before pulling ahead. Marnie realised she looked like a remnant from the Battle of Britain. Quite a few cars coming from the opposite direction flashed their headlights, and Marnie waved back. One modern MG sports car gave them a friendly blast from its horn, its driver punching the air like a racing driver winning a grand prix as he swept past. Marnie hooted back and flashed the headlights.

Anne shouted in Marnie's ear. "I thought we were meant to be inconspicuous. We've been waved at by just about every driver in the south of England!"

"Trust me," Marnie bellowed back. "I know what I'm doing."

Anne shrugged. "You're the boss. You're in control."

"Don't exaggerate."

The car seemed altogether more complicated to drive than the modern Rover, and Anne watched Marnie's strange ritual with the gear lever as she changed down for roundabouts. She noticed that Marnie changed first into neutral, blipped the accelerator, then slotted the stubby lever into gear. Once or twice there was a grating sound that made Marnie wince, but mostly the operation was smooth. With the sounds from the engine and other traffic there was little chance of prolonged conversation. After an hour, Anne tried not to think about the cold. The draught coming from the floor was making her feet numb, and she lowered the hot-water bottle into the footwell to combat the chilly blast of air. At least it stopped some of the wind whistling through.

By the time they reached the edge of London, Anne was thinking back with longing to the times when they would travel down in the Rover, the engine barely audible, the temperature warm and comfortable, carpet under their feet, a CD playing softly, the instrument panel glowing in different colours. This car felt like a faster version of the narrowboat.

While waiting at traffic lights on the North Circular, Anne leaned nearer to Marnie. "Where to first, your old office?" Marnie nodded in reply. "And we're leaving the car at Chiswick tonight?" Another nod. "It's very nice of Beth to agree to you leaving the MG in her garage again."

"Ah."

With Marnie now wearing dark glasses, and the scarf drawn up round her chin, it was difficult for Anne to read her expression. "Ah? You mean, 'ah' as in she doesn't know?"

"She does know."

"What then?"

"Agree isn't quite right." Marnie engaged first gear and accelerated away as the lights changed to green.

• • • • •

Tuesday 10 January – morning

By the time Marnie turned into the car park at Everett Parker Associates, all the spaces were occupied. She drove round to the side door and drew up outside, blipping the accelerator twice before switching off the engine. They climbed out, grabbed their bags and went in, glad to feel the rush of warm air inside the building.

Anne pulled off the baseball cap and ran a hand over her hair. "Can you just leave the car there, Marnie? Are you allowed to do that?"

"The worst that can happen is that someone will drool over it. It'll be fine."

In the reception area Marnie asked for Faye Summers and Philip Everett, and while they waited, Anne walked around thawing out, looking at the drawings and photographs lining the walls. The colour scheme was off-white with grey carpet and steel furniture. Anne whispered to Marnie. "One day we'll have something like this, won't we?"

"You like the style?"

"Mega. Who designed it?" Marnie gave a slight bow. "Really? It's great."

"It's also time they changed it. Anyway, I thought you liked our office the way it is."

"Oh, I do, but it would be nice to get some more pictures up. I'll do it when we get back."

"Okay."

Faye Summers came through a door at the back of reception and stared at them. "Wow, Marnie! Is that really you?" They hugged and Marnie introduced Anne. "Good to meet you at last, Anne. I've certainly heard a lot about you. Come through to the office. Everyone's dying to see you, Marnie."

"I'll look in after seeing Philip. We're running a bit late. I just wanted to say hallo."

"And show off your new gear. Did you fly down by Tiger Moth?"

"More or less. We landed in the car park."

"You look amazing, as if you've just stepped out of *Vogue* ... 1939 edition! Who said fashion's all in London? Every time we see you, you're setting a new style. Brilliant, Marnie! I'm absolutely green."

"Green wouldn't go with that sweater."

Behind them there were footsteps on the stairs and Philip joined them, ushering Marnie and Anne up to his office. "I like the gear, Marnie. It looks like battle dress ... quite appropriate for you, I'd say."

For an hour they discussed projects while Anne took notes. Philip passed them a series of letters, briefing details and photographs. Marnie gave an update on progress with the Willards Brewery jobs.

"You've landed on your feet with Willards, Marnie. It's set you up."

"Thanks to you giving me the work."

"They wanted you anyway. It made sense to cooperate. And it was just the right time to start up on your own."

"It seemed a big gamble when I took the plunge."

"Yes, but with hindsight we can see that you were in the right place at the right time."

Marnie said, "With hindsight everything falls into place. And not long ago I found myself in the wrong place at the wrong time ..."

"What do you mean? ... Oh, the Tim Edmonds thing, yes. That must've been pretty horrible. Dreadful business. Have the police sorted it out yet? I only know what I read in the papers."

"Same here. We're none the wiser."

"It's funny that ..." Philip began. "You know how it is when you hear a name or a word that you'd never heard before, and then you just keep hearing it all the time. The name Tim Edmonds came up in conversation only the other day, and I'd never heard anybody ever mention him."

"Someone talking about the case, after seeing it in the news?"

"No. It was at a meeting. I was talking to a site agent and a clerk of works, Ray Curtis, who turned out to have done an extension on Edmonds's house."

"A clerk of works for a house extension? That's rather unusual, isn't it?"

"His house in Esher ... *mansion*, I should say. Grade Two star listed building, late eighteenth century. They certainly weren't hard up for a bob or two."

Marnie saw the gold Rolex gleaming in the dark water. "I don't suppose he really knew Edmonds ... not a lot in common."

"Ray seems to have got on well with him. Apparently he was very free with the drinks after a meeting. They'd go into the house and talk over the project, usually armed with a good single malt."

"I'd be quite interested to meet this Ray Curtis."

"Meet him?"

"I'm interested in anything or anyone who could cast some light on what happened to Tim Edmonds."

"If you're serious, I could get a number for you. Are you going down to see your old team?"

"Just briefly. I've got a lot on today. I may try to pop back and see them later in the week ... if that's all right with you? I don't want to disrupt work too much."

"That's fine, Marnie. Any time. I'll dig out the number and let you have it. Anything else we can do for you while you're here?"

"Just one thing. Can we refill our hot-water bottles?"

· · · · ·

Downstairs, reunited with her former group, Marnie asked if she could make a phone call to check her answerphone. She was still not using the mobile except when necessary. There were three messages. The first was Malcolm Grant just 'touching base', asking Marnie to ring when she had a moment. The second was the builders' merchant reporting that he still did not have a date for the delivery of the radiators. The third was a surprise.

"Hallo, Marnie. This is Priscilla Barnes. We've been thinking about you a lot, and we hope you're okay. We'd love to see you again. If you come to London, give us a ring and we'll get together."

· · · · ·

In the lobby by the exit they pulled on their flying gear, ready to brave the elements again. Anne was in heaven and felt that she could float naked through the streets of London without noticing the temperature. But she nonetheless grasped her hot-water bottle as a precautionary measure.

"And they really said I could come, too?"

"Of course."

"That's amazing. Tea with Priscilla Barnes and Anthony James at the Ritz. I can't believe it. I can't wait for tomorrow afternoon. Shall I wear my new skirt?"

"Good idea. And talking of luggage, I think we'll go down to Little Venice and drop off the bags on *Rumpole* before we take the car round to Beth's."

They climbed into the MG, positioned their hot-water bottles, and Marnie started the engine. "Everything we do is magic," Anne said dreamily. Marnie smiled, but her thoughts were somewhere else. In her pocket was the number where she could reach Ray Curtis that afternoon.

• • • • •

At the first attempt to stop, they had a lorry on their tail and Marnie had no choice but to keep rolling under the elevated motorway and go round for a second lap. Seeing the volume of traffic approaching the junction, she turned off back towards the way they had come and pulled into a side street near the bridge by the canal, outside a pub.

"This is going to be tricky. There'll be no easy place to pull over with all this traffic."

"What can we do?" said Anne.

Marnie shook her head. "Dunno. Let me think."

"Why don't I carry the bags round while you wait here with the car? We're never going to be able to park there, or even stop."

"No. And the kerb's too high for me to mount it. I'd risk damaging the spokes on the wheels."

Anne got out and reached behind the seat for the rucksack. Marnie passed her the key-ring. "The big key is for British Waterways locks only. For *Rumpole*, it's the smaller one here. Don't go in at the back like *Sally*. Use the side doors like *Thyrsis*." As an afterthought she added, "And don't worry about the caravan. It's all locked up and empty. There's no one there."

"Okay." Anne pulled out Marnie's bag and slung the strap over her shoulder, gripping it in both hands.

"Can you manage the two of them like that?"

"No probs. Back in a minute." Anne set off but almost immediately stopped and turned round. "Caravan? Did you say caravan?"

"Yes ..." Marnie caught on. "Oh, right! How stupid. Presumably it didn't get there by boat."

Anne put the bags back in the car, set off at a jog and was back in under five minutes. Marnie was walking up and down the pavement to keep warm. Anne's nose was pink, but she was smiling.

"There's a gate just a bit further on. I think it'll be tricky ... it's right on the junction. You'll probably have to reverse in. I tried the BW key and it fits the lock. The gates are a bit stiff. I don't think they've been opened for a while. You can drive in all right. The surface is okay and it's clear."

"What about somewhere to park?"

"I don't think you can get in beside *Rumpole*, but you'll have room nearer to the gate. You won't be blocking anybody in."

"Let's go for it."

This time it was easier. Marnie waited for a clear run at the junction, and was able to move over and reverse the MG off the road while Anne leapt out and dealt with the gates. Once inside with the gates locked behind them, they were able to park the car up against the wall by a pile of timber stacked under a tarpaulin. Marnie surveyed the scene.

"The car can be seen from those offices down the cut." She pointed.

"Does that matter?"

"I don't know. I just don't like to take any chances. You never know …"

Anne looked at the stack of timber. "You see this tarpaulin, Marnie? It's very big, big enough to cover the car."

Marnie grimaced. "It's also very dirty. Filthy, in fact."

"Right. So no good?"

"Ideal, I'd say. Come on, let's get a couple of blankets from the boat."

They returned with a sheet and a blanket that they used to cover the MG. Next, they pulled the tarpaulin away from the timber and draped it carefully on top of the car, covering every part of it so that it was unrecognisable.

"What now?" Anne said.

"What do you think? Look at the pair of us dressed up like stalwarts of the British tradition. There's only one thing for it … we must have a cup of tea."

Anne laughed, and they turned towards *Rumpole* with a spring in their step.

• • • • •

Tuesday 10 January – afternoon

Lunch had been simple fare, cheese sandwiches and coffee. Afterwards, they settled down to study the briefing papers that Philip had given them that morning. Business was obviously thriving, and Marnie was pleased at the prospect of keeping up the connection with her old firm as an outside consultant.

When they had worked for nearly two hours, Marnie got up and checked the store cupboard. She took out a box of pasta, a jar of olives and a tin of tomatoes with garlic and herbs. Anne volunteered to buy fresh salad, bread and yoghurts. They decided to go together while it was still light, dividing their efforts once they had crossed the bridge by the pool of Little Venice. While Anne headed for the shops, Marnie went to a call box and phoned Ray Curtis.

"Philip Everett told me to expect you," he said in a pleasant London accent. "How can I help?"

"Well, I'm really trying to find out as much as I can about Tim Edmonds. I don't know if Philip mentioned it, but I was the one who found his body in the canal."

"Yes. He did say that. What do you want to know?"

"To be honest, I'm not actually sure. I just want to find out about him, his friends, his contacts, associates, allies, enemies, anything." There was a silence at the other end of the line. "I'm not sure if there's anything you could add to what I already know. I suppose I'm clutching at straws. But I think I ought to tell you that the police have been treating me as if I were a suspect, and frankly I don't like it."

"No. Of course not. I'd like to help, certainly I would ..."

"But there's nothing you can tell me. I do understand."

"Look, I think there is something I can do, but it's not the sort of thing to talk about on the phone."

"No. I'm in a call box."

"I don't mean like that. I mean, there is some way I might be able to help, but we'd have to meet."

"Okay."

"Would you be free the day after tomorrow, Thursday evening some time?"

"I could be, yes."

"Where can I find you?"

"Give me a place to meet and I'll come there."

"All right. Fulham Broadway tube station. Eight o'clock?"

"Fine."

"I'll be in a red Mondeo estate, parked in the side street facing you directly opposite the exit."

"I'll find you."

"I'll give you my mobile number in case you have any problems."

Marnie took down the number. "Thanks. We'll look forward to seeing you, then."

"We?"

"Yes. My friend Anne and I. She works with me. We're in London together for a few days." There was no reply. Marnie filled the silence, "I call her Anne with an 'e' ... it's a sort of nickname."

"Sorry, Marnie, no extras ... it'll be tricky enough as it is. I can only take one. Even then I'm chancing it a bit."

"*Tricky*? How will it be tricky?"

"I can't say. You'll just have to trust me, I'm afraid."

Trust, Marnie thought. *I haven't got much of that in the store cupboard these days*. "So no Anne?"

"Sorry. Definitely no Anne, with or without an 'e'."

• • • • •

Marnie walked round towards the shops to meet Anne, keeping her expression as calm as possible.

"Oh dear, what's the matter?" Anne said as soon as they met. Marnie told her about the conversation on the phone. "He said you had to *trust* him?" Anne was incredulous. "After all you've been through? I shouldn't think you could really trust *anyone*, apart from a handful of us."

"I doubt I could even spell the word."

Part 19

Wednesday 11 January – morning

An early night had done her good. Marnie woke feeling refreshed after eight hours of sleep. Even the rumble of London traffic on the other side of the high wall had failed to disturb her in the night. She sat up in bed and parted the curtain with a finger. It was still dark but in the background light from the overhead motorway she could make out oily patterns on the surface of the canal. As always, she began thinking about the day ahead. She would spend some more time that morning going over the schemes for Philip and talking them through with Anne. They would both enjoy that. Later there would be tea at the Ritz with famous friends. They would certainly enjoy that. And later … She tried to put out of her head the events planned for later in the week. That was the part she was less likely to enjoy, at least in anticipation. She felt a tingle of anxiety pass over her and wondered about calling off Thursday's meeting with Ray Curtis.

"Marnie?" Anne was calling from her cabin.

Marnie thought: *She can probably hear my brain working … she's got radar, that girl.* She called out, "Yes. I'm awake."

Anne came through in her dressing gown. "Are we going to be very busy this morning?"

• • • • •

While *Rumpole's* engine warmed up, Marnie walked along to check the MG under its camouflage. All was well. On the way back to the boat she looked up at the sky, now turning a lighter shade of grey. Anne had especially wanted to see dawn come up as they travelled along the canal through Little Venice. She had tactfully suggested taking the arm towards Paddington, but Marnie had opted for a run in the opposite direction through Regent's Park. It was a prettier route, she had said, with gardens running down to the edge on one side and then the zoo to left and right of them all the way to the turn for Camden Locks by the Chinese pagoda restaurant. She had not mentioned the Cumberland Road Bridge, the famous, now infamous, 'blow-up bridge' where she had found the body.

Marnie untied the mooring ropes and pushed the boat away from the side, letting Anne take the tiller. *Rumpole* pulled smoothly through the murky water under the last bridge and into the pool of Little Venice. On their left the waterbuses were at rest, lining the bank in their maroon and cream livery. Ahead of them was Browning Island, with the main line of the canal crossing from left to right behind it.

"Are you sure about Regent's Park, Marnie? It's not too late to change your mind." There were clouds of condensation from her breath as she spoke.

Marnie tried to sound more chirpy than she felt. "Come right full rudder, number one. Half speed ahead. Go easy by the bend under the bridge."

"Aye aye, skipper," Anne said, playing along. Marnie set off on the gunwale to the bows to check that all was clear up ahead as they approached the blind corner. She gave Anne a thumbs-up, and they accelerated round into the arm leading down to the Maida Hill tunnel and on towards the park.

Both sides of the canal were lined with brightly painted narrowboats, attractive in the dappled street lighting that flickered between the trees on either bank. This was where Marnie had first kept *Sally Ann* and where she still had friends. They cruised by Mrs Jolly's house before entering the tunnel entrance below the café where she had eaten with Malcolm, and soon found themselves gliding under road and train bridges to enter Regent's Park, with the sky now perceptibly brightening by the minute.

"This is beautiful," Anne said. "How far shall we go?"

"How about down to the pagoda and back? That should make a nice run. About half an hour."

"Okay. And breakfast? Could we tie up somewhere in the park?"

"I think, strictly speaking, that isn't allowed, but I don't see anyone around to stop us."

"Great." Anne steered a straight course down the middle of the canal through the zoo, where the kudus looked down on them from their compound and unfamiliar foreign birds preened themselves on high branches in the aviary. "This makes a change from the sheep and herons back home," Anne laughed. "It's all so exotic for a narrowboat on the canal. Everything's usually so ordinary and English." Marnie let Anne stay at the tiller for the turning manoeuvre by the pagoda, waving her friend on from the bows, glad to see her enjoying herself so much. Privately, she was thinking: *but not always so ordinary ...*

After making the turn, Anne asked if Marnie was ready for breakfast and where they should stop. By now the sky was bright and it was almost full daylight. Marnie suggested tying up in the zoo for the novelty of the occasion, and Anne offered her the tiller while she went below to make a start on breakfast. Alone at the helm, Marnie could not help but think back to the last time she had travelled that way. Some distance ahead she could see the bridge where it had all happened and she knew she should pull in to the side and moor, but something compelled her to keep going. She wondered if it was a kind of exorcism, to return and find it as it had always been, just a bridge standing high up over the water. Twice now it had been a scene of tragedy. Once at the time of the explosion that gave the bridge its nickname, and now the death of Tim Edmonds. Marnie was surprised to find herself slowing down as she neared it.

Anne emerged from below. "The kettle won't be long. I've put the croissants in the oven." She noticed where they were. "Oh ... Isn't this where ...?" she began slowly.

"Just down there," Marnie said simply.

"Are we moving on a bit further, then?"

"I suppose so. I wanted to ... I don't know, actually, what I wanted. It just seemed a pity that every time I came this way, I'd have that hanging over me. I hoped I might be able to get it laid to rest. Can you understand that, Anne?"

"Absolutely, I can. When we came by on the way out, I just tried not to think about it."

"Me too. But it was somehow different going that way. Coming back I saw the bridge from the direction I was going on that journey. It brought it all back. It's such a pretty place. I found myself resenting Tim Edmonds for spoiling it. As if it was his fault. Mind you, it has painful associations of its own, of course. That's why it's called the 'blow-up bridge'."

"It was an accident, wasn't it?" Anne said. "I read about it in the cruising guide. A munitions boat exploded and killed the crew and a boy who was walking on the towpath."

"Yes. Over a hundred years ago. They rebuilt the bridge and turned the columns round to even out the wear. You see the grooves on the water side? They were from when the columns were the other way round."

"So this place has its own ghosts from way back," Anne said quietly. "Was the zoo here then, or did it come later?"

"It was here. In fact, I seem to remember reading that some of the animals had nervous breakdowns because of the noise of the blast ... the elephants, I think it was."

"Are you serious?"

"I don't feel very jokey in this place, Anne."

"Why don't we go on a bit further, then?"

"Sorry. Am I being spooky? I didn't mean to scare you."

"That doesn't matter. I was thinking it would be nicer for you. For me it's just a pretty place."

"Then let's stay here for breakfast and lay my ghost to rest once and for all. Is that all right by you?"

"Sure. Let's be practical. Shall I make mugs of coffee or a whole pot?"

Marnie smiled. "You're indomitable. Let's have a pot to warm us up."

"You're on." Anne went down to the galley leaving Marnie to make the boat secure against the bank.

On the towpath, Marnie went over the events of that evening. She found she was calmer now than she had expected. The sighting of the body, the desperate '999' call, the bitter cold of the water and the sheer weight of the man that she could not lift out, all these came back to her. She could see him clearly again in her mind. Walking along the towpath, she tried to recall the state of the bank. Had it been slippery with ice or frost? It had been close to freezing as night came down. She wanted to believe that it had been an accident, that the MP, perhaps a little befuddled by one or two Christmas drinks too many, had just slipped at the edge in the semi-darkness and caught his head on the column, knocking himself out so that he had drowned while still unconscious. He was a fit man, and no trace had been found of any other cause of death. She suddenly remembered Malcolm Grant sobbing silently alone in the back pew of St Margaret's church at that carol service, while the Great and the Good filed out, basking in recognition and looking forward to the recess. Those were sincere tears. Of that she had no doubt. And she knew she herself was innocent of any suspicion.

At that moment she knew with complete certainty that it really had been an accident. That was why the police had not been able to arrest anyone. That was why the coroner had recorded an open verdict. There was no evidence of 'foul play' on which to make a case. *Foul play* ... how the British see the world! A set of rules laid down by men in striped blazers. The Establishment. Men like Tim Edmonds and Malcolm Grant, soon to be Lord Grant of Somewhere. He would probably take a title from his part of the country, the Lake District. Lord Grant of ... Cumberland ... Cumberland

Road Bridge. Marnie realised she was rambling and refocused her thoughts. An accident, yes. That's what it was. A wave of relief swept over her, and she was glad she had come back to this place, glad she was here with Anne. For all its bad memories, it would always now be just the scene of a sad accident, the place where a promising career had been cut short as it was about to take off again.

Marnie stepped back onto the counter, the small platform for the steerer on *Rumpole*, and called down to Anne. "How's it going?"

"Won't be a minute," came the reply.

Marnie felt a reluctance to go below, enjoying the sharp wintry air. It promised to be a bright day, and she had the feeling that it would be a new start, another small new start in a life that had become a series of new beginnings. She was happy that she had left the firm and branched out, happy that she had found Anne, happy that she had Ralph. These positive thoughts helped her cope with the less pleasing sides of her life, the death of Toni Petrie last summer, her own near fatal brush with murder, the finding of the body here, the blowing up of her car … *the blowing up of her car* … Where did that fit into her surmising?

Anne's face appeared in the hatch. "Are you ready? I've laid the table. It's looking nice. Marnie, what's happened? You look somehow different. Have you laid your ghost to rest?"

"I think maybe I have."

"That's wonderful. And isn't it a lovely day? We've got a real treat this afternoon, too." Her smile was wide and joyous.

"You know, Anne, you make things pretty wonderful yourself. You're a tower of strength to me."

"Blimey! What brought that on? I've only made a pot of coffee and warmed up some croissants!"

"And I suspect you've made a list of everything we have to do today."

"You bet! It's almost too good to go inside this morning, isn't it? Shall I bring the coffee and things up here?"

"Why not? We can go in if it gets too cold. Good idea, number one."

"Aye aye." She vanished from sight.

Marnie had noticed that in the time they had been tied up no one had come by, but now one or two joggers were trotting past, headsets on as they listened to their music or the morning news. Glancing towards the opposite bank, a movement caught her eye. In the dark under the bridge was a clutter of pallets with covers like tarpaulins. More careful inspection revealed them to be blankets, and from one of them someone was standing up. From instinct, perhaps the traditional greeting of the boater, Marnie raised her hand. The man, for man it was, stopped and stared across the water at her. He made no other move, but simply looked over towards her.

Just then, Anne came up holding the coffee pot in one hand and two mugs in the other. She followed Marnie's stare and saw the man. She spoke softly to Marnie. "Is that one of the famous tramps we heard about?"

"I suppose it is."

"Do you think he was here when … you know …?"

"When Tim Edmonds had his accident?" Marnie said. "Who knows?"

Without warning, Anne called out, "Hallo!" Marnie jumped in surprise. She was even more surprised when the tramp nodded back.

"Good morning," she said. The man mumbled something indistinct, but not unfriendly. "Anne? Can you untie us? We're going on a visit."

• • • • •

Afterwards, Marnie could never quite work out what had prompted her to take the boat to the other side of the canal to talk to the tramp. She guessed it was probably part of her need to bring the episode of Tim Edmonds to a close. The tramp might have been able to help, she had thought. As things turned out, he had been a greater help than she could have imagined. At closer range, the man looked as if he could be any age between forty and sixty. Not surprisingly, it had been Anne who had broken the metaphorical ice once they had crossed to the other side of the cut. She had walked along the gunwale and spoken to him.

"Hallo. I'm Anne. My friend's called Marnie." The man squinted at her and eyed the coffee pot on the hatch.

"Would you like some breakfast?" Marnie said.

"Breakfast? I don't know when I last 'ad breakfast, not proper breakfast."

"How about coffee, a croissant, toast with butter and marmalade?" Anne went below.

"Anythin' in the coffee?" the tramp said.

"That depends. We can start with milk and sugar, if you like."

The tramp looked suspicious. "Depends on what?"

"What can you tell me about the man found in the canal before Christmas?" Anne returned with a tray that Marnie took from her and placed on top of the hatch.

"You can't be the law." He still looked suspicious.

"The *law*? No, I'm not the law. In fact I was their prime suspect until someone here corroborated my story. I'm the one who pulled him out. Are you Dodge?"

The tramp took a step back. "What's your game?"

"No game. The police told me there was a witness whose name was Dodge. They said he'd drowned at Christmas in Limehouse Cut."

"Well, they don't know everythin', do they?"

"You're not dead."

"If you say so."

"But you are Dodge." The tramp looked at Marnie and said nothing. "You told the police you saw me?"

He narrowed his eyes, sizing her up. Eventually he said, "Yeah. I told the law you just come along and found 'im ..."

"So you were my alibi."

Dodge looked pointedly at Marnie. "So you owe me."

"Probably, but first what can you tell me?"

"You was on that boat ... posh bird with the lovely arse." Anne put a hand to her mouth, trying not to laugh

"How do you know that?" Marnie said. "How can you be sure?"

"You 'ad that little short jacket thing on. It only came down as far as –"

Marnie and Anne smiled openly. "I meant what made you say I was posh?"

"I 'eard yer, didn't I? You was on the phone. I could 'ear yer plain as anythin'."

"What did I say?"

"You was saying 'Come on, come on!', all urgent, like. I thought you was talking to the bloke in the water till I saw the phone. I knew he wasn't goin' to do nothin'."

"You heard me saying that?"

"Yeah. You said it over an' over. I could 'ear yer clear as anything."

"And the police took a statement from you?"

"Law didn't believe me. Said I just made it up to stop 'em suspectin' me. Tried to make out it was dark, said I was drunk ..."

"Well, it was dark," Marnie said.

"An' I was drunk."

"Just like the police to try and twist everything."

Dodge drank half the mug of coffee in one go and began eating. Anne had spread thick butter and marmalade on a slice of toast. He ate quickly but neatly, taking care not to drop crumbs. He wiped his mouth on the gingham napkin when he had finished. "The law said no one'd believe my evidence. Said the defence'd make mincemeat out o' me ..." He invested this last statement with special meaning, looking at the plate of mince pies. Anne took the hint and passed them over. The atmosphere was improving by the minute.

"Please help yourself," Marnie said. To her surprise, Dodge lifted the plate to her first. She took one, and he offered the plate to Anne. The three of them had breakfast together like friends, Marnie and Anne perched on the roof of the boat with their legs dangling over the side, Dodge sitting on a mat on the sloping bank.

Marnie swallowed a piece of mince pie. "I believe what you said. You must've been the nearest thing they had to a witness. So something made you want to keep out of it. Then, when the man was found in Limehouse Cut, you let it be known that it was you."

Dodge nodded and took another mince pie. "Don't remember the last time I 'ad breakfast made for me by a woman ... *two* women." He winked at Anne, who smiled back at him. "Even if one of 'em is just a skinny bint with no tits." Marnie almost choked on her mince pie, embarrassed for Anne, but Anne spluttered with laughter. "Well, nearly none," Dodge added generously.

Anne spoke quietly to Marnie, inclining her head towards the cabin. "George Stubbs?"

Dodge at once looked suspicious again. "Who? Who's there?" He made as if to get up.

"No." Marnie raised her hand. "There's no one there. A neighbour gave us some bacon. He's a butcher. That's all."

"Would you like a bacon sandwich?" Anne said.

"You serious?" Anne smiled and went below.

"Dodge, tell me what you saw, or think you saw. Please."

The tramp sat in silence for several seconds, narrowing his eyes. Marnie waited. When he spoke, his voice was distant. "I'd been on cider. Does yer 'ead in, that does. Strong stuff. There was two of 'em come along. Stood talkin' over the other side under the bridge. Couldn't see much, wasn't really lookin', just 'eard voices at first."

"Raised voices? Were they arguing? Was it a quarrel? A mugging, perhaps?"

Dodge shook his head. "No. Just talkin' ... quiet."

"Could you hear what they were saying?"

"No. They weren't arguin'. Weren't jokin' neither."

"Did you see their faces?"

"No. Too dark. Shadows under the bridge."

"Did anybody else come by?"

"Not after a while. They lock the gate after it's dark. Nice after that. Quiet. No one around."

"This isn't much to go on," Marnie said.

"Tell you what ... they 'ad some booze on 'em. Talkin' of which ..."

Marnie frowned. "Dodge, this man was an MP. He'd hardly be out drinking in the street. It does seem a bit unlikely. Are you sure you saw them drinking? It was getting dark."

"See? Now you sound just like the fuzz ... They didn't believe me ... didn't want to. You're just the same."

"No, I'm not. More than anybody I *need* to believe you. It's just that the person who was killed wasn't the kind of man to be out here in the dark drinking on the towpath. It just wasn't in keeping with his character. You must see that. I *do* want to believe you, but what you're telling me seems odd."

"But it's true. That's what 'appened. Look, it was like this, right? I got up to have a ... well, to go over there by that tree. I looked over, didn't want 'em to see me ... I'm entitled to some privacy. They didn't notice, but I could see them and I saw their 'eads goin' back ... 'eard 'em say 'cheers' or somethin' like that." Marnie frowned again. "Look, love, you can believe it or not. It makes no odds to me. But I know when I see people drinkin' booze out of a bottle ... which reminds me again ...this is nice coffee ... got anything to go with it?"

"Maybe. I'll have a look. But tell me everything first."

"That was it ... honest."

Marnie sighed. "Think carefully. People don't just casually fall into canals for no reason. Was there a scuffle?"

"Not really."

"Did you hear him fall in the water? There must've been quite a splash."

"No splash ... maybe a cough or a grunt. That's all. Then a bit later I saw you come along on the boat. It wasn't this one, was it?"

"No. You're right, it wasn't. But did you see the man actually go into the water?"

"No. I weren't watching 'em the 'ole time. I keep to meself."

"Tell me anything you can remember about them, anything at all."

Dodge thought back. "They was toffs. Posh voices like yours. Couldn't 'ear what they were sayin', but they definitely 'ad posh voices."

"And they didn't fight."

"No. Just chattin', like. Definitely not fightin'."

Anne came out with a bacon sandwich on a plate, uncertain which caused Dodge the greater surprise, the food or being served it on a real plate. While he ate, Marnie went below. She reappeared to find Anne and Dodge in conversation about Randall.

"Do you ever get round Brackley way in your travels?" *Typical of Anne, she thought. She can make polite small talk with a tramp.*

"No. I stick around 'ere."

"Well, if ever you do decide to go that way, look in on Randall Hughes in Brackley. He's got a really nice place to stay for a while. You'd like it."

"Right." But Dodge was rapidly losing interest as he saw what Marnie was carrying. She held up a half bottle of Scotch. He stared at it. "That's a single malt. You're never givin' me that ..."

"Here you are." She passed it to him, and it went straight into his pocket. "Late Christmas present." Anne stared at Marnie but said nothing.

"You're a real mate, love," said Dodge, grinning.

Marnie held out something else. "Will you do something for me?"

The grin disappeared. The eyes narrowed. "Is this the catch?"

"No catch. This is my business card and this is a phonecard. If you think of anything else, anything that might help me know what happened that evening, I want you to give me a ring on those numbers. Keep trying till you reach me. Will you do that for me? My late Christmas present?"

Dodge stared at the cards for several seconds. "All right."

• • • • •

It was after they had gone through the tunnel and emerged in Little Venice before Anne spoke. "Why did the police think he'd drowned? Why wasn't he identified properly?"

Marnie shrugged. "Just another vagrant, I suppose ... a statistic. It's not as if they were interested in him. He was no use to their case as far as they were concerned."

"But he really was a witness."

"He certainly was."

"But not a very good one, though?"

"What do you mean? His testimony changes everything. It proves it can't have been an accident. At least I think it does. There were definitely two people there. It doesn't sound much like an accident to me."

"But do you believe what he said about them drinking? It didn't seem right. And the police didn't believe him."

"Correction: the police didn't think they could make his evidence stand up in court. I think that's different. Why would he lie? He had nothing to gain, or lose come to that, by saying what he saw."

"But he could've been so fuddled by drink that he couldn't see properly," Anne suggested. She was steering *Rumpole* very slowly in mid-channel past the moored boats.

Marnie was leaning against the hatch. "I think he could see all right. He saw what I was wearing." They smiled at the memory. "And don't forget, he remembered what I said on the mobile. He even recognised that I was on a different boat."

"Do you think someone tried to scare him off?"

"Doubt it," Marnie said. "Or why would he have come back?"

"He was telling me he liked it there. Said it was sheltered and safe on that side of the canal. But why didn't he see what happened?"

"It's probably very simple. He just wasn't looking, that's why. He didn't know he was going to witness something."

"No, that's right. He probably wanted to get back to his cider. Actually, Marnie ... I was a bit surprised ... about the whisky."

"Surprised? I know it was Roger's, but I'll get another bottle to replace it."

"No, I meant ... that you gave it to Dodge."

"Ah ... do you mean you were surprised or shocked?"

"To be honest ..."

"I know. You think he'll drink himself to death."

"Well ..."

"I realise that, but frankly what difference will it make to his quality of life? One half bottle won't do any more harm than the stuff he'll be drinking anyway."

Anne sighed. "I suppose not."

"Look at it like this, Anne. You wouldn't have been shocked if I'd given it to someone else who liked a drop of scotch, who may well have a tendency to drink too much ... someone like an MP, for example. But it seems different because he'd be dressed in a smart suit."

Anne looked thoughtful. She handed the tiller back to Marnie while they turned under the bridge by the old toll house to come left round Browning Island and take the arm back to their gloomy mooring.

• • • • •

Wednesday 11 January – afternoon

Waiting to be shown to their table, Marnie whispered to Anne, "Ralph accused me of rubbernecking when we were in the Commons."

"What's that?"

"Twisting your head round to look at famous people ... like the Prime Minister and members of the Cabinet."

Anne looked puzzled. "Why are you telling me this? ... Oh ... is that what I'm doing?"

"No, not really. I couldn't blame you if you did. It's not every day we have tea at the Ritz. But your eyes have grown two sizes bigger and they are out on stalks."

Anne giggled. "I've never seen anything like it. It's so ..."

"Opulent?"

"Absolutely. I'll try to push my eyes back in."

A waiter led them across the restaurant, Anne determined to look in front of her, noticing that one or two heads turned in their direction as they walked by. She could understand why. Marnie looked stunning in a dove-grey suit and pink shirt, the new hairstyle revealing simple pearl earrings in a gold setting. She had noticed a look on Ralph's face when out with Marnie, a blend of pride and confidence, and she knew how he felt. It did not occur to Anne to feel jealous.

Anthony James and Priscilla Barnes stood up as they approached, kissing Marnie on both cheeks, shaking hands with Anne. The waiter moved chairs for them to sit, handed them menus and withdrew.

Priscilla said to Anne, "I understand you're the organiser in the team."

"Marnie teases me because I write lists of things to do, but it helps me not to forget, and it's fun ticking off the jobs when they're done."

"So you're the office manager," said Anthony.

Marnie said, "Anne is training to be a designer. She'll be going to college in the autumn. I give it five years before she's running the firm."

"It's really kind of you to let me come with Marnie."

"Our pleasure," said Anthony. "Have you been here before?"

"Gosh, no. It's amazing. In fact, this has been a day of real contrasts."

"In what way?" Priscilla asked. As they spoke, the waiter reappeared beside them.

Anne said, "Well, we had breakfast on a boat in the park with a tramp." They laughed.

The waiter bent forward and spoke quietly to Anne. "Breakfast with a tramp, miss ... tea with a knight of the realm."

"Knight of the realm?" Marnie said. Anthony made a modest, self-deprecating gesture and asked the waiter to bring them all the full afternoon tea.

Priscilla smiled. "Anthony was given a knighthood in the New Year's Honours List."

"Oh God," Marnie said, "how embarrassing. I didn't know. I've been too preoccupied with other things to take in the news these past few weeks. Congratulations."

"I think we all understand you've had other things on your mind," Priscilla said, "and you've been in the news yourself, too."

"Almost in the news. My car being blown up, and then part of my head being the 'mystery woman' in the newspaper."

"So it *was* you," Anthony said.

"Yes, but nothing like what they were suggesting. Malcolm Grant was going off to a meeting. That's all it was."

Priscilla looked genuinely sympathetic. "You must have had a very trying time, Marnie. We know what it can be like when the media are after you. We've seen it happen to people we know in the past."

"I think I've got off lightly so far. Strictly speaking, we're in hiding just now. Anyway, you two are among the whole country's favourites. The press are always nice to you. And this latest news must make you very happy."

Anthony smiled and shrugged. "It's rather humbling, actually, when it happens to you. You realise a lot of it has been good luck. The world is full of actors, most of them out of work." The waiter interrupted the flow of conversation by arriving with a trolley laden with food and pots of tea.

When they had settled down again, Anne asked, "What happens when you get a knighthood? I mean ... how do they tell you about it?"

"The first intimation I got was a phone call from Downing Street. A man asked if I were offered an honour would I accept it. I was so stunned I just said *yes, of course*. After he hung up, I realised I hadn't even asked what it would be. A week later a letter arrived offering me the knighthood. I wrote back to accept and that was it."

"Now we have to wait to be given a date for the ceremony," Priscilla said.

"So you're not quite a knight of the realm yet?" Marnie said.

"That depends ..."

"On ...?"

Anthony smiled. "How desperately I need a table in a restaurant when they say it's full. I think that's probably the main advantage."

"Plus I get a new dress for the visit to the Palace," Priscilla added, also smiling.

"When did you first get the news?" Marnie asked.

"About a month before Christmas. We were just starting to rehearse the Noël Coward."

"So you knew all about it when we first met at the Commons."

"Yes."

Marnie stirred the lemon in her tea, but something was bothering her, and she had to be asked twice before accepting a scone from Priscilla.

• • • • •

Wednesday 11 January – evening

They double-checked everything around *Rumpole* before settling in for the evening. The MG was snug under its coverings. They opened up the caravan to make sure it was empty and untouched. They walked round the boat, including the gunwales, to make sure all the windows and hatches were secure. Armed with a glass of wine, Marnie sat back in Roger's favourite armchair to glance through a clutch of design magazines, while Anne reclined on the sofa looking at photographs that Marnie had taken for their projects. A tape of Handel's *Water Music* from Roger's small collection was playing softly in the background.

Anne looked up. "Cottage number one looks really good, doesn't it?" She held up one of the photos that Marnie had brought to show Philip and the others.

"Mm. I'm quite pleased with it."

"The front door looks brilliant in that dark green."

"Not too Laura Ashley?"

"No, just right. It sets off the light colour of the stone."

"Good."

A lively hornpipe filled the cabin, giving it a festive atmosphere. Marnie was reading a feature about an artist in Rome who had made a wonderful apartment in an ancient tower overlooking a square in the city centre. Her mind was filled with vaulted stonework, city roofscape views and deep cream sofas. Anne was leafing through photos, taking occasional sips from a glass of pressed orange. Suddenly she looked up.

"Marnie?"

"Mm?"

"The towpath in Regent's park ..."

"What about it?"

"Dodge said it was locked after dark."

"It is."

"That other man ... the man with Tim Edmonds ... do you think he could've been on a boat?"

Marnie dropped the magazine onto her lap and sat upright. "I hadn't thought of that."

"It could explain why he was there ... and how he got away."

"Yes ... I suppose it could. But that's all it does explain. I mean, why would he be meeting Tim Edmonds? If we believe Dodge, the two men were friends. That's why they were chatting and drinking together ..." Marnie shook her head. "No ... it doesn't add up. It just doesn't make any kind of sense."

"No?"

"Can you imagine someone like Tim Edmonds meeting someone and drinking with them on the canal towpath in the dark on a winter's evening? It's all so improbable. Can you imagine someone like, say, Ralph or Anthony James, doing such a thing? It can't be right."

Anne said, "I was just trying to think of other possibilities. You remember that Sherlock Holmes story where Holmes says after everything's been discounted, whatever's left has to be the truth?"

"Yes, but I don't think we've exhausted all the possibilities yet. There's probably some simple reason that we haven't thought about, that's all."

"I suppose so," Anne agreed reluctantly.

They lapsed back into silence while a slower movement of the *Water Music* wafted over them. They went back to their reading. After a few minutes, Anne spoke.

"Can I interrupt you again, Marnie?"

"Sure. But don't expect any clever theories about how the mystery man got out of the park."

"No, it's not that. I wanted to ask you something about Malcolm Grant."

"Go ahead."

"I thought you said you didn't meet him until after Christmas."

"That's right. Don't tell me you're doubting me as well."

"I'm not ... I never would ... but this photo ... it looks as if it was from before Christmas."

Anne held up a Polaroid from Malcolm's flat. Marnie looked across. "I took those the day after I drove Ralph to the airport, whenever that was ... second or third, I suppose. Why do you think it's from before Christmas?"

Anne passed it over. "Look at the sideboard. What do you see?"

Marnie studied the photo. "Bottles, a decanter, a soda siphon ... give me a clue."

"Look next to the decanter ... on the left. What's that?"

"Oh yes ... something shiny. I can't see it very well in this light. What do you think it is?"

"It's obvious. It's a Christmas present."

Marnie stared harder, moving the photo closer to the lamp. "Yes. You're right." She thought back to that morning in Malcolm's flat, the solitary present in its elegant wrapping on the beautiful Chippendale sideboard. The Christmas present that Tim Edmonds had never received.

Part 20

Thursday 12 January – morning

"... so we'll begin the forecast with the south-east, including the London area, East Anglia, the East Midlands and Lincolnshire. The morning will be mainly overcast with occasional breaks in the cloud giving a few glimpses of sunshine. Brighter weather will gradually spread from the south-west. Temperatures will be a little higher than of late, around the seasonal average of eight to ten degrees. There will be a fine evening and a clear sky tonight, bringing the risk of frost in sheltered areas ..."

Marnie was in the shower-room brushing her hair. She called out to Anne in the saloon. "I should've thought to get my hair trimmed while I was here. Be nice to see Julie again."

"Why don't you?"

"No time. Anyway, I'd never get an appointment at such short notice."

"You could try telling her you were a Knight of the Realm," Anne suggested.

Marnie laughed. "It would have to be a Dame of the Realm in my case. It doesn't have the same ring to it, somehow." She walked through to the saloon, pulling on her black Cossack coat. "Can you imagine the receptionist at the salon ..." Marnie put on her best Cockney sparrow voice. "*Julie, there's some dame on the phone wants a cut and blow-dry ...*"

Anne shrieked with laughter. "Does she really sound like that?"

Marnie flashed her the heavy eyelids and the Marlene Dietrich pout. "In Hampstead ... are you kidding? They're all Sloane Rangers up there." Marnie put on her fur hat – imitation fur – and adjusted it carefully. "How does that look?"

"Terrific. You look like a film star." Anne beamed at her.

"Seriously."

"I mean it."

"It's not too late to change your mind. You're very welcome to come with me."

"No. I want to stay here this morning. You go round and see your friends. I'm going to have a shower, wash my hair, and not have to rush, just relax. I want to read through the things we got from Philip so that I know all about the projects. Pity I haven't got any files here or I could book them all into our system. Never mind, I'll clip them together all ready to file when we get back. And I want to work out some ideas for designs."

"That's your idea of a relaxing morning, is it?"

"I'll be fine, Marnie." She did not need to add that she had no wish to get in the way when Marnie chatted with her old team at Everett Parker Associates.

"Right. See you later. You're in charge, number one."

"Aye aye, skipper."

• • • • •

An hour later, Anne gathered the last of the papers together and put them in their folder. She was thinking about them while she got up to make coffee. For the first time during her stay on that arm of the canal, a boat went slowly past. She watched it through the galley window, but moved back out of sight as the steerer came into view. A reflex action. Anne moved quickly through the boat, checking all the windows and hatches. Everything was secure. She went into Marnie's cabin and found the mobile phone on its cradle, the light glowing to show it was fully charged. She picked it up and took it into the saloon.

Automatically, Anne switched on the mobile, plugged in the external aerial, opened the window and attached the magnet base of the aerial to the roof of the boat. She opened her notebook and dialled the office at Glebe Farm to access the answerphone. A friendly voice told her she had two messages.

Beep. "Marnie, it's Roger. I hope you pick this up. You seem to have *Rumpole's* phone switched off. Slight snag, I'm afraid. John Stevens from BW has been on to me about using that mooring. It appears that Jonathan and Michelle are coming back earlier than expected. Something to do with the boatyard where they were having repairs done. Anyway, they've already set off and will be there some time tomorrow, that's Thursday. Sorry about this, but there's nothing we can do about it. I suggest you take *Rumpole* back to my mooring tonight. Give me a ring when you can."

Thursday. That's today! Anne thought. Perhaps the boat that went past was them. What could she do? Before she could think more about it, the beep sounded again.

"This is Malcolm ringing on Wednesday at about four o'clock. I hope you're okay, Marnie. Haven't heard from you for a while. Assume you're at home. I've been moving offices and I've got a new number in the House. Would you like to ring and compare notes when it's convenient? Thank you. My new number is as follows ..."

Anne scribbled the number on her pad. There was a final beep and she pressed the button to save the messages for Marnie to hear later. So that was Malcolm Grant, she thought. He had a pleasant voice, calm and polite, but it sounded strained. An anxious voice tinged with melancholy.

Anne stood up and opened the side doors giving on to the bank. She climbed the steps and looked around like the periscope of a submarine. The air was less chilly, though her breath clouded, and it was refreshing to be out in the open after the enclosed warmth of the cabin. The boat that had passed had disappeared from view in the direction of Paddington Basin and St Mary's Hospital half a mile away. If that boat had been Jonathan and Michelle, presumably the owners who were returning to their mooring, they could have gone up to turn round. But Anne convinced herself it could not have been them. That boat had passed without hesitation. No one had slowed to investigate *Rumpole*. They would surely have come alongside and made contact. She had time to think and plan.

She thought through the possibilities. It was obvious. Marnie had to be told about the change of plan at once. From the file she checked the Everett Parker Associates headed notepaper for their phone number and pressed the buttons on the mobile, asking to be put through to Faye Summers.

"You've just missed her, Anne. She went out a couple of minutes ago."

"Right, I'll wait till she gets back. Thanks."

"No. I meant she went out to a meeting. One of the clients came in and

Philip suggested they go out to have a look at the job as Marnie was in town. She may be gone for a while."

"Oh, I see."

"Is it urgent? You could try Marnie on her mobile."

"I'm using it for this call. Can I ring Philip's mobile? Do you have his number?"

"*Philip's*? He hasn't got a mobile. Hates them. Philip's in the dark ages as far as technology's concerned."

"What about the client? Do you have his phone number?"

"It's a *her* ... and the flat doesn't have a phone yet. The conversion's not finished. Still a building site."

Anne sighed. "Back to the drawing board ..."

"The designer's motto. You're learning, Anne."

Anne was determined to be positive. If the people came back wanting their mooring, she could move *Rumpole* herself. *No probs.* So that was all right. She could not ring Roger, because she did not have the office address book and did not have his numbers. That would have to wait until Marnie was back. Okay so far. The one number she did have was for Malcolm Grant. Her first thought was that she should wait for Marnie to deal with this. But there was something in his voice, a weariness, a sadness, that made her want to do something to help. She remembered how Marnie had seen him weeping at the back of the church, alone and grief-stricken. Now the police were treating him as a suspect, like Marnie. She desperately wanted to help. It would be just a quick word to let him know they had received his message and that Marnie would be in touch soon. There could be no harm in that, and she would not say they were away from home.

After three rings the answerphone cut in. It was an impersonal woman's voice, the official voice-mail machine inviting her to leave a message. "This is a message for Mr Malcolm Grant. I'm phoning from Walker and Co on Thursday morning. Marnie Walker is at a meeting just now and will be asked to phone you back when she returns. Thank you."

That should do the trick for now, she thought, and ticked the item off her list.

• • • • •

Thursday 12 January – afternoon

The sound of the gate shutting brought Anne to the window, dropping her magazine to the floor. She opened the doors and stood aside to let Marnie climb in.

"Have you eaten, Anne?"

"I had a sandwich. What about you?"

"We had something in a pub. This client turned up while I was with Faye. There were complications with the job, so Philip suggested we go and see the site for ourselves."

"I know. It's okay. Faye told me when I rang."

Marnie slipped off her coat and draped it over a chair. "You rang?"

"Yes. We've got complications here, too."

"*Damn!* I knew I should've phoned you ... I'm trying not to use the mobile.

What's the complication?"

Anne gave Marnie the mobile to listen to the messages. While listening, Marnie muttered, "There's a third message, a new one." She listened in silence. After switching off, she said, "Well, that's some good news, at least. Or should I say at last? The radiators are coming next week. Hurray! We can get number two going again."

Suddenly they froze as two bangs thudded on the side of *Rumpole*. Marnie leapt to the window to see a boat pulling slowly alongside. At the bow she saw the name *Magician*. Anne climbed up the steps through the cabin doors and looked across the roof. It was an old, scruffy boat, dark green and dull black, in need of a repaint, inching along beside them. Standing on the near gunwale was a young man with a pony tail. At the tiller was a pretty young woman wearing an army greatcoat. Both were smiling. Marnie appeared next to Anne.

"You must be Jonathan and Michelle? Sorry to be on your mooring. We'll move right away. Do you fancy a cup of tea?"

• • • • •

"You could solve all the problems in the whole world like this," Michelle said in a dreamy voice as they sat in the warm, comfortable saloon on *Rumpole*. She had her feet curled up under her on the chair.

"With tea and biscuits?" Anne suggested.

"Tea, coffee, a pint, a spliff … anything'd do." She smiled like a cat in the sun.

• • • • •

Marnie decided to swing the boat round the big weeping willow on Browning Island where the swans nested, to line up for the toll house bridge on the run back to the mooring. Even in the middle of winter this was a magic place, with a terrace of tall white stucco houses looking down on the pool over the finely wrought black railings. She straightened the tiller passing the art gallery barge moored on the towpath side of the island and set their course to take *Rumpole* home.

"I liked Jonathan and Michelle," Anne said, turning her collar up against the cold breeze.

Marnie nodded. "Pity they had to come back now, though. That was a good place to stay. Nice and secluded."

"Not their fault they had to leave the boatyard due to that barge needing the dry dock."

"No, and they could hardly stay there with all that banging and welding going on around them. Never mind." She set the speed to dead slow for the last hundred metres, as they passed the boats lining both banks.

"Marnie, there's something I forgot to tell you." Anne pulled a face. "You may not be very pleased with me."

"Unless you've given details of our hiding place to a sinister foreign power bent on our destruction, I doubt there's anything that would trouble me overmuch."

"Ah … Guess what … I used the mobile to leave a message for Malcolm Grant." Anne grimaced.

"Well," Marnie said, "I don't think that'll do any harm. In any case, we're not there now, so no one could trace us if they tried."

"I suppose not. Are we just going to stay on *Rumpole*'s mooring, then?"

"Actually, I was wondering about that … I have a suggestion. Suppose I go to see Ralph for a few days?"

"I could go home for the weekend. Mum did say she's got some clothes washed and ironed for me."

"Right. You wouldn't mind?"

"Course not. You've hardly seen Ralph since he got back. What about Malcolm Grant?"

"I'll phone them both from a call-box and I'll arrange to see Malcolm one day next week. Perhaps he's got some more information."

They were approaching the gap in the line of boats, and Marnie slowed down using reverse gear. With skill born of experience, she slotted *Rumpole* neatly into the mooring, and they tied the boat securely fore and aft.

• • • • •

By the time Anne's train pulled out of Euston station, Marnie's plans for the coming days were in place. She would stay on *Rumpole* that night after her meeting, or whatever it was to be, with Ray Curtis and drive up to Ralph's cottage in Murton on Friday morning. On Monday she would collect Anne from Leighton Buzzard, and they would return to Knightly St John for a day or two to get their projects underway, before Marnie went briefly to London to see Malcolm Grant. She would discuss his redecoration scheme and compare notes on the Tim Edmonds affair. With any luck, life might return to normal, and they could look forward to spring. Marnie was pleased with her plans. They were as neat as one of Anne's lists.

• • • • •

Thursday 12 January – evening

Crossing the busy roads outside the tube station that evening, Marnie had no difficulty in spotting the Mondeo estate car in the side street. She climbed in and found herself sitting beside a man with a pleasant face, a friendly smile and a warm handshake.

"It's nice of you to see me, Mr Curtis."

"First of all, call me Ray. Only my bank manager calls me *Mr Curtis* … makes me feel nervous. Second, it's a pleasure. And I mean that. Philip said it would be."

"Well, I'm still grateful. Anything I can find out about Tim Edmonds might help me understand what's going on. I feel completely in the dark. The police don't tell me anything … the press and media don't give any news except repeating what they've already said."

"That's how it works, isn't it? We only get half the story … or less. No one tells the public what really goes on." He laughed. "I'm sounding like a taxi driver! Probably because we're sitting in the car."

"Would you like us to go somewhere … for a drink, perhaps?"

"We could do."

"I know quite a good wine bar not far from here."

Ray shook his head. "Not what I had in mind."

"Okay. You choose. I'm easy. I'm just glad to have a chance to talk with someone who knew Tim Edmonds."

"Oh, I didn't know him."

Marnie felt her cheeks tingle. "I thought you'd done work at his house ... a building contract ... Philip said ..."

"Sure. But I couldn't say I *knew* him ... not really. I met him a few times, but only to talk about the job. I mainly dealt with the site agent."

"But ... you can give me ... information about him?"

"Personally, no. But, as they say, I know a man who can ..." He started the engine. "We just have to go for a little ride. Won't take long. Just sit back and relax."

"Well ... I don't know ... I thought ..."

"It's all right, Marnie. Trust me. You're in for a surprise ..."

• • • • •

Anne had only been home five minutes when her mother called her to the phone. It was Ralph. He sounded worried.

"I've been trying to get Marnie on the mobile, but it seems to be switched off. I've left a message on the office phone, and I thought I'd just try this number for luck. I'm rather surprised to get you there, Anne. Why aren't you with Marnie?"

Anne hesitated before replying. Why did Ralph not know about Marnie's meeting? Why had she not told him? "Did Marnie speak to you this afternoon?"

"No. She left a message at the porter's lodge to say she'd see me at the weekend and would ring back later to finalise things. She hasn't rung yet. That's why I'm phoning."

"And it's okay for the weekend?"

"Of course. But where is she now?"

"Er ... she had a meeting."

"It's after seven, Anne. Isn't that late for a meeting?"

"An evening meeting."

Ralph's turn to hesitate. "Okay ... do you know where?"

"Not exactly ..."

"Anne, is something the matter? I was only phoning to confirm weekend arrangements, and I'm picking up strange signals. Has something happened?"

All sorts of questions were racing through Anne's mind. Why had Marnie not explained about the meeting that evening? She could have mentioned to the porter that she would be out and not contactable. Why had she not even told Anne any of the details? Where was she exactly? "Ralph, I expect Marnie just left a simple message with the porter to save explanations."

"Naturally. So can you tell me about this meeting?"

"She was going to see a clerk of works who'd done a job for Tim Edmonds. She wanted to see if she could get any information that might clarify things."

"Where were they meeting?"

"Somewhere in Fulham, near a tube station. He was going to meet Marnie in his car. That's all I know. That's all Marnie knows."

• • • • •

As they drove through the evening traffic, Ray Curtis said little at first, negotiating the lights and making a succession of right-hand turns that required his full concentration. Marnie was wondering if this meeting had been a good idea.

"Ray, surprises aren't something I'm lacking these days. I think I'd like you to tell me where we're going."

"It's not far."

"That's a start, I suppose. But I have to say, this is making me a little nervous."

"*Nervous?*" He sounded surprised. "Oh no ... don't be nervous. It's just a bit, well, tricky ... and it might not even work out. I can't promise. It's just something that came up."

"That's meant to reassure me, is it? Can you just tell me where we're going? Are we going to look at something? Or meet someone?"

They turned into a residential side street in a fashionable quarter. Ray drove slowly along until he found a gap in the parked cars. He reversed into the space. Marnie looked out. It was too dark to see much, even with the street lights, but it looked like a normal upmarket road with big houses set back from the pavement. There was an air of quiet, discreet wealth.

"This is it," said Ray. "Leave all the talking to me."

He stayed where he was and switched off the engine and the headlights. Marnie looked out again. The street was deserted. There was no movement in the shadows. Only faint traces of light could be seen from the windows of the houses that were heavily curtained against the winter evening. Not a soul stirred. "Talking?" she said quietly.

Ray's voice was equally quiet. "Yeah. Better say nothing. Just sit tight."

Marnie thought *I could really do without all this.* She was about to speak when a torch lit up the inside of the car. It took all her self-control not to jump out of the seat. She swallowed hard, wondering what was going to happen next. Her pulse was racing.

Beside her, Ray was a model of calm. He wound down the window and looked up. "Hallo, Chris, how's it going?" The light went out.

Marnie's eyes were beginning to focus again after the brightness of the torch. In the half-darkness she could just make out that the man with the torch was in uniform. Police.

"Evening, Ray. What brings you here?"

"We just need to look in on the lads for a minute. Won't take long."

"We?"

Ray waved a hand vaguely in Marnie's direction. "I've got a colleague with me tonight." He made no further effort to introduce her, and Marnie stayed quietly in the background.

"Job nearly done?" said the policeman.

"Not far off. How's business?"

"Very quiet ... as usual. You're the only excitement so far."

"Lucky you. Shall we go on, then?"

"You know the way."

"See you." Ray started the engine and manoeuvred the car out of its slot. He began advancing slowly along the road. Glancing back, Marnie had the impression that the policeman was talking into his lapel radio.

"What was all that about?" said Marnie. She felt completely bewildered.

"All will be revealed any minute now. Relax. I told you it'd be a surprise."

"You can say that again."

Ray turned onto the drive of a house that looked imposing against the skyline, but which seemed to be empty. No lights could be seen either inside or outside. As they rolled forward, the drive sloped down steeply. In the headlights Marnie saw a garage door opening in front of them. Still no lights came on, and they entered the garage in total darkness. By now, Marnie was feeling distinctly ill at ease. Beside her, Ray muttered quietly, "Here we are." And as he spoke the garage was flooded with light, so bright that for some seconds Marnie lost her vision and squinted against the glare.

"What the hell's this?" she blurted.

"This," said Ray, "is a secret. You're going somewhere that most people don't know exists." He smiled across at her, pleased with his private knowledge.

"You mean like a spy base or something?" She felt absurd speaking like that, but could not imagine anything else. It seemed like a scene from a sixties spy movie, and she half expected Michael Caine or Sean Connery to leap out in front of the car.

Ray frowned. "No ... nothing like that. This is someone's house."

"Whose? Is this ... where Tim Edmonds lived? Is this where you were doing the building work?"

Ray shook his head. "Much more secret than just an MP's house." He turned and pushed open the car door. "Come on. Time for the visit." Before getting out, he swivelled round and looked Marnie in the eye. "By the way ... this is something you won't be able to tell anyone about. Don't forget."

"Who lives here, Ray?"

He put a finger to his lips, turned and got out. Marnie followed him from the garage into a narrow corridor. Stopping outside a door at the end, he turned to her again.

Marnie spoke first. Quietly. "I know ... I keep quiet and let you do all the talking."

"Oh, no ... you have to ask the questions. I don't know what you want exactly."

"I'm not sure I do. I'm not even sure why I'm here ..."

Ray smiled. "You'll see."

• • • • •

Anne tried to collect her thoughts, trying hard not to panic. There was probably a simple explanation to all this. Marnie had gone to see a man she did not know, and they were going off together somewhere of which she was ignorant. That made two of them. She had no way of contacting Marnie or getting her any kind of help. She had no phone numbers. If she phoned the police, she could give them no information about what was happening ... or why she was worrying. *Oh God!*

There was a tap on the door, and her mother came in with a mug of cocoa. "I thought you were working. Are you all right?"

"Oh yes. Fine. Thanks for the cocoa."

"Are you sure you're fine?" Jackie asked. "You look as if you're sitting staring in front of you."

"That's because I am ... I mean because I'm thinking about something."

"What's up, love?" Anne fidgeted in her chair. "You're worrying about something. You can't fool me. What is it?"

"I've lost track of Marnie."

"*Lost track?* That sounds a bit extreme. What do you mean.? I thought she'd gone out for the evening. She's in London, not the Gobi Desert."

"Mum ... I don't know how to ... It's difficult to talk about it ... I don't want to worry you ..."

Jackie sat on the corner of Anne's bed. "You are getting me worried now. Why should you be concerned about Marnie?" Anne frowned. "You are, aren't you?"

Anne bit her lip. "It's all this Tim Edmonds business ... Marnie's trying to get to the bottom of it. She's gone to meet a man ..."

Jackie thought back to the previous summer when Marnie had tried to find out about another mysterious death. It had almost got her killed. Not a thought that she wanted to share with her daughter. "And you're worried because you don't know where she is."

Anne nodded. "We always have a system so that we can keep in touch. We set it up after ... you know, last year ... This time she's gone off without letting me know how to reach her."

"Why would she do that?"

"I suppose because the man she's gone to meet is a friend of Philip."

"There you are, then. It's bound to be all right, if Philip knows him. He wouldn't send her to see someone dodgy, would he?"

"No. I suppose not. Of course not." Anne picked up the cocoa and looked into it like a gypsy staring into a crystal ball.

Jackie stood up. In the doorway she looked back at Anne. "You could always give Philip a ring. It's not late."

"I don't have his number."

"Why not ask Directory Enquiries? He lives in London, doesn't he?"

"I don't know."

"Worth a try."

Anne put down the mug. "Mum, you're a genius!"

"Everyone's heard of Directory Enquiries, my love."

"No. The night message at Everett Parker. After working hours, they have a night message with a contact number."

"Do people need an emergency number for an architect?" Jackie asked, puzzled.

"It's in case there's trouble at one of their sites ... vandals, a break-in. We have an out-of-hours number in case someone needs us. I bet that's where Marnie got the idea." She ran downstairs and rang Everett Parker Associates.

"*... office hours are from eight thirty am to six pm, but if your call is urgent, please try our emergency number ...*" Anne wrote quickly and redialled.

"Philip Everett."

Anne sighed. "Oh ... thank goodness!"

"Who is that?"

"It's Anne Price, Marnie's friend. I'm so relieved to get through."

"BT's not that bad, is it? What can I do for you, Anne?"

"I wanted to contact Marnie. She's gone to see Mr Curtis."

"Tonight?"

"She was meeting him outside Fulham Broadway tube station."

"Right."

"With all that's happened lately, I was getting worried that I didn't know where she'd gone. Then I remembered that he was a friend of yours, and I thought you'd be able to tell me where he lives … just to set my mind at rest."

"Well, Anne, actually … I've no idea, to tell you the truth."

"But he is a friend of yours?"

"Not an actual friend … as such. I just met him recently at a site meeting. He seemed a decent sort. He's a good clerk of works, I know that."

"I see."

"No need to sound so worried. I'm sure everything'll be fine."

After hanging up, Anne sat lost in her thoughts. Jackie eyed her daughter across the living room, wondering if the situation was as bad as Anne seemed to imagine. Suddenly Anne reached for the phone again.

"Ralph? It's me again." She gave him an account of her call to Philip and asked his advice.

"Might be worth trying the mobile. Perhaps she had it switched off for some reason."

"I think I'll have to. She did say we should only use it in an emergency."

"If you like, I'll keep trying it. I'm going to be working late tonight … proofreading the book. I'll ring her every half hour … call you if there's any news."

"Okay. I'll take a phone up to my bedroom. Ring at any time."

There was nothing else to be done. Anne tried thinking what Marnie would do in the circumstances, but even Marnie could not magic a solution out of thin air. Patience. Whoever said it was a virtue had obviously never had to try it. What *would* Marnie do? Anne thought hard. Yes. Marnie would prepare for the unexpected. She would take action rather than sit around worrying. But what action? Anne was not even aware of her mother being in the room, and she jumped when Jackie spoke.

"Are you sure you're not just worrying about nothing, Anne? Marnie's grown up. She knows what she's doing. I'm sure she'll be okay."

"I suppose so, mum. It's just that last year …"

"I know. Look, why not try the mobile again. You never know …"

"We try to avoid using it … in case it can be traced …"

"*Traced?* Who by? No one's going to listen to your calls. Why should they?"

"Marnie thinks it tells people where you are, so she likes to restrict it."

Jackie was unable to fathom this. It was worlds away from her kind of life and experience. To her, the world was what it seemed. Adverts on TV gave a biased view; she knew that. But on the whole she believed that large companies made and sold products without seeking political power. Mobile phones were like any other machine … you used them to tell people you were on your way home or wanted something at the supermarket. Politicians were basically trying to make people's lives better. The police were there to protect citizens from criminals. Life was straightforward, without hidden layers. Honest people would always be protected if they told the truth. Crime did not pay. Justice prevailed.

"So you don't ever use the mobile?"

"Hardly ever," said Anne. "I did use it today, though. Just once."

"And it wasn't the end of the world, was it? You used it to phone Ralph?"

Anne tried to remember. "No ... I just used it to phone the office. Oh, and then to ring Malcolm Grant. He's an MP that Marnie knows."

"An MP? Well that would be all right, wouldn't it?"

• • • • •

Ray Curtis knocked twice and pushed open the door, walking into the room ahead of Marnie. This was not what she expected. It was the size of an average living room, but there the similarity ended. The room was occupied by three men in blue shirtsleeves and black ties. Two of them were seated at a long desk facing a bank of electronic equipment, including four television monitors. It reminded her of the gallery where the production team sat in a TV studio. The screens showed views outside the house, plus the road where they had parked. The images were clear, but each was bathed in a cool green light.

The third man, who looked older than the others by about ten years, was sitting at a normal desk in the middle of the room. He could have been any office worker in any company in the country, except that he was cleaning a pistol. On the wall opposite the monitors was a row of grey metal cupboards with one of the doors slightly open. Marnie's eyes strayed towards it, and she saw a rank of guns, rifles or machine guns she could not tell. Casually, the man at the central desk leaned over and pushed the cupboard door shut as he stood up. In the same movement he dropped the pistol into a drawer.

"Hallo, Ray. You're working late."

"It's your guvnor, he's a slave driver ... wants everything doing yesterday, if not sooner."

"Ah, well, we have been having some bother. Can't have any mistakes here, not in the electrics."

While they were speaking, the other men glanced round at Marnie. She had the usual impression that they were looking her up and down. Ray did not refer to her or attempt to introduce her.

"Okay," he said. "I'll pop up and take a look. The contractor swears it was operative when he finished on Tuesday."

"Today's Friday," said the man with the pistol. "The work can't be out of guarantee yet."

"Give me five minutes." Ray crossed the room and opened the door at the opposite side.

Marnie was uncertain about what to do. Should she follow or stay? Why did Ray not speak to her? She was about to open her mouth when one of the men at the long desk turned towards her. "So ... you're Marnie."

"Er ... yes ... I was waiting to be introduced."

"You already have been."

"You knew I was coming." She did not need to make the statement into a question. The policeman nodded slowly, staring at her. It had happened to Marnie before that she seemed to observe herself as if from outside her situation. This time, she was inwardly wincing that she was sounding like the dialogue in an old gangster movie. Mr Big – probably in the form of Sidney Greenstreet – would surely appear at any minute. She resolved at all costs not to speak in clichés.

"What is this place exactly?" Failed again. "I've no idea where I am." And again.

"What did Ray tell you?"

"Nothing much. He said it was someone's house."

"There you are, then."

Marnie was feeling increasingly irritated, bordering on aggressive. Probably not a wise move in a secret room with three policemen and a cupboard full of weapons. She pulled a chair from the desk and sat down. In as even a voice as she could manage, she said, "Look, we can play word games all evening. The alternative is, you tell me why I'm here and perhaps also where I am. Then we might make some sort of progress."

The answer came from the man sitting across from her at the desk. His tone was calm. "You're here because you asked to be here. You want information. You think we have it. Tell us what you want, and we'll see if we can give you it."

"I'm trying to find out what I can about Tim Edmonds. You know why."

"Why? You tell us."

"You know I found him in the canal. Since then, rightly or wrongly, I've felt myself under suspicion. I'm convinced he was murdered. I wasn't sure at first, but I am now."

"Why are you so sure?"

"For the same reason that you are."

"The case has nothing to do with us. The Met's handling it."

"Yes it does. You know all about it. You're part of the … what d'you call it … the Parliamentary and Diplomatic Branch … or something like that."

"And why do you think we're treating it as murder?"

"Because of the evidence of the tramp … your witness."

The policeman looked appraisingly at Marnie. "Non-witness. Useless."

She went on. "If there were two people there when Tim Edmonds went into the water and died, that other person must have been involved. It can't have been an accident, surely."

"The other person could've been you, Marnie."

"No. You know that's impossible. Dodge told you I came along afterwards. Anyway, the idea that I might've been involved is ridiculous. I had no reason to want to harm Tim Edmonds. I didn't even know the man, and I doubt I would've been able to overpower him if I'd tried."

"You knew Malcolm Grant."

"No. I know him *now*. I didn't know him then." The implication of the policeman's remark suddenly struck Marnie. "Malcolm was at home waiting for Edmonds to visit him. You know that."

"Because you produced a note."

"Yes. From Tim Edmonds. I saw it with my own eyes. It had his signature. At least I think it was his. It's evidence that can be checked by experts."

"It proves he sent a note. It doesn't prove Grant was at home."

Marnie's patience was wearing thin. "Oh, come off it! I know why you're interested in Malcolm and me. You don't suspect us … you think that one or other of us will lead you to whoever did it."

"Do you think you know who did it, Marnie?"

"No." She sighed. "I've got no idea. Not the foggiest. That's why I want to find out more about Tim Edmonds." In the silence that followed, Marnie rubbed her hand across her forehead in a weary gesture. She gazed around the room. All three men were looking at her, though the two at the console glanced at the screens every few seconds. In a quiet voice she said, "Are you going to tell me where this is?"

"It's the house of a VIP."

"So it's not a base of some sort." The policeman shook his head slowly. Marnie felt dejected and subdued. She had wasted her time coming here. The police had set this up to find out what she knew. Again. "Well ... he must be a very important VIP to have you lot in his basement with all this." She made a gesture towards the monitoring equipment.

"*Her* basement ... not *his*."

"A woman? Oh ..." Marnie wanted to show that she could work things out for herself, wanted to reject the game being played of keeping her in ignorance so that she, a woman, felt at a disadvantage compared with these men and their macho armoury. Her mind was racing. What woman would receive this kind of security? She had no idea anyone had armed police in the house, presumably day and night, to guard her. It could not be the Queen, not here. Then who? An idea began to form. "Not ... could it be ... Princess Di?"

The policeman across the desk smiled. A smug I-know-something-you-don't-know smile. The two others smiled at her, pityingly. *Damn!* She hated this. Why did they always play games with her? Marnie was no militant feminist, she just wanted to have the opportunity to get on with her life on an equal footing with everyone else, but there were times when she wished she had the power to strike back at the attitude of ... Ah ... power ... power that even men like these would respect ... She sat back in the chair, ready for one more throw of the dice. She had nothing to lose. "I see," she began, "so it's the Iron Lady, is it?"

The smile faltered, only for half a second, but Marnie knew she had hit the target. It was a small triumph. The other two turned to study the monitors. One made notes on a pad while his colleague adjusted the equipment. Marnie looked at her watch.

"Even now she's no longer the PM she gets this treatment? How long will this go on?" The policeman shrugged and said nothing. "Have you been running this sort of operation since she left office?" Marnie persisted.

"I've worked for her since she was in office ... known her for years."

"That's a lot of taxpayers' money. I'm amazed she approved ... with her attitude to public finance. No cuts here, then ..."

"She's worth it. She's got more balls than the rest of them put together."

"Presumably she's not here at the moment?"

"If she was, you wouldn't be."

"But you guard the house day and night in case of intruders. Even now."

"Of course."

Marnie thought about the strange world of politics and power. How people could have that much ambition, she could not understand. The awesome responsibility, the public rows, the backstabbing, the life conducted in an atmosphere of hostility and confrontation. Every action interpreted by the press, every statement analysed in the media. The perks were there, of course, the red-carpet treatment, the privileges, the accolades when a vote was won in the House, the adrenalin surge on winning an election. But there was the downside. The fall from grace, the treachery from your own colleagues, the slide into the backwater of anonymity. All privileges withdrawn. All the dreams an illusion. Despite the trappings, everybody knew you had failed, been passed over. A bitter taste in the mouth. A bitter pill to swallow. A suicide pill, taken three times a day.

"Do you ever get to see her at all?" Marnie was reduced to making small talk, wondering how much longer Ray would be inspecting whatever electrical fault had brought him here. If it was not all just a set-up.

The policeman relaxed in his chair. "Sure. We get to see a lot of MPs, ministers, officials. Especially her. She's not as aloof as people might think."

"I can't imagine her looking in to see you're all right down here." Marnie smiled to herself at the idea of the Iron Lady popping down in dressing gown and hair curlers with mugs of steaming cocoa before turning in.

"You'd be surprised."

"A woman's touch," Marnie mused.

"Lady," said the policeman firmly. "She's a lady, not a woman. I mean, a real lady. At all times, day and night. You never forget it."

"So she can cut public services to the bone, throw millions out of their jobs as part of a vendetta against the unions, but it's all right because she wears suits and carries a handbag?"

"It's not easy to break the mould without people getting hurt. She's like Churchill. A real leader."

"And a lady," Marnie added. It was meant to sound mocking, but the policeman took it the other way.

"That's right. And it's true what you heard about her not needing sleep. Just like Churchill. Three or four hours a night, that's all he needed. She's just the same. Amazing. I've known her come down to security late at night after a big do. She'd stand there with a glass in her hand and chat. Next morning, she's on the early news on the radio, sparring with those smart-Alec interviewers, bright as a button. You wouldn't believe it. Nobody knows half the story."

"Really?" said Marnie. The policeman nodded conspiratorially. "I always thought she was a bit of a prude ..."

A guffaw came from the men at the console. "You're joking!"

"But I understood she hated scandal or excess ... upholder of Victorian values and all that ..."

"That doesn't mean she can't enjoy a drink with her friends."

"Yes, but look what happened to Tim Edmonds."

The policeman narrowed his eyes and leaned forward in his chair. "What do you mean?"

"I don't mean how he died. I mean ... losing his job in the government because of the divorce scandal. He wasn't the only one, either. Loads of them got the push if they strayed from the straight and narrow."

"She had standards, that was the point. She admired people who had standards, too. The trouble is, most of them couldn't keep up with her. Didn't have the ..." He hesitated.

"Balls?" Marnie suggested helpfully.

"Stamina."

"Oh ... right."

"Some of them she had a lot of time for. She thought the sun shone out of

Major's ..." He hesitated again. Marnie decided not to try to be helpful this time. "... Eyes."

"I'm glad to hear it."

"And your bloke, too. She had a lot of time for him ..."

"*My bloke?*" Marnie tried to imagine Ralph and the Prime Minister sharing a decanter of single malt on a sofa in number ten.

"Grant. She thought he was all right. We saw him quite a bit at one time. Mind you, she wasn't pleased when he helped Edmonds out after that divorce business."

"She confided like that in you ... about one of her own MPs?"

"Didn't need to. It was obvious. Decidedly cooler for a while. What saved him was that he acted out of loyalty, as she saw it. She forgave him, but never wanted anything to do with Edmonds again. He'd blown it."

"Did she like him before that?"

"Not as much as Grant. I think she suspected Edmonds was the sort of bloke to ... you know. Very sure of himself, especially with women."

"Would that be ... lady's intuition?" Marnie suggested.

"If you like."

"Come on, Pete!" One of the men at the console called across, turning in his chair. "You know she had a twinkle in her eye for Edmonds. Him and that Grant ... they were always round there at one time. Everyone knew they'd both be ministers in the next reshuffle. She didn't go for the 'old boy' line, but she thought those two were gentlemen, and that mattered. Even when they'd had a few – and they could knock it back, those two – they were always gentlemen as far as she was concerned. Edmonds got in because of Grant, but I'm sure she liked him. A lady's man, he was."

"An Iron Lady's man?" Marnie offered.

"No. Not like that. She was never like that. But she liked her admirers round her."

"Are you saying that Tim Edmonds used his looks ... his *charm*, to curry favour?"

"Don't *you?*" said the policeman opposite her, bluntly.

"I'm not a court favourite," said Marnie.

The policeman laughed. "It was a bit like that. What did she used to call them? ... *the gentlemen of the libation*. That was it. She had nicknames for quite a few people ... but that's another story."

• • • • •

There was only light traffic as Ray drove Marnie back the way they had come.

"Where can I take you?"

"Oh, any tube station will do. I don't want to take you out of your way."

"Okay."

"Ray? How did you fix all that? I don't get it. Did you and Philip plan this evening?"

"Not at all. Phil knew that I'd come across Tim Edmonds and said you were trying to find out about him. He thought we might just have a chat. At first I didn't see the point. But then I got a call from the site agent about the electrics going on the blink and I remembered the police talking about Edmonds after he was found dead. Grant's name cropped up too. So I thought this was a chance that was too good to miss."

"Just a chance ... a coincidence ..."

"Sure ... cub's honour." They drove on in silence. "So was it any use, Marnie?"

"Good question."

"Did you learn anything?"

"After talking to the police ... do you ever?"

"Oh ... I was trying to be helpful."

"Sorry, Ray. I didn't mean it like that. I just need to think about it. Whatever else it was, it was certainly one of the strangest experiences of my life."

"And you won't go talking about it to anyone."

"No. I'll be as silent as the ... well, you know."

Ray dropped her at the nearest tube station. Arriving back at Warwick Avenue, she realised for the first time that evening that she was hungry, and walked round to the late supermarket. A ready-mixed pasta salad and a melon were all she wanted apart from a glass of wine. She stopped off at a call-box to ring Ralph.

"Marnie, where have you *been?*"

She was surprised at the anxiety in his voice. "To see a friend of Philip's, that's all."

"Anne was so worried about you. She rang me to ask what to do."

"She knew where I was going ... ah, no, she didn't ... for a good reason ... neither did I. I'll ring her directly."

"I think you should. How did it go, your meeting?"

"Well, it was really rather ... extraordinary. I'll tell you about it when I see you."

"And you're okay? You sound okay."

"Yes, I am. I'm fine. I think things are becoming clearer. I can see what the police have been doing. It makes more sense now." She looked over her shoulder, aware that she was standing in the street, at an open call-box, discussing the most controversial murder enquiry in the country.

"But are you any nearer to understanding what actually happened?"

"Well, that's another matter, really. I think I can see – *my God! What was that?*"

Marnie peered round the side of the call-box, frantically trying to make sense of what she had seen. A sudden flash had lit up the area, followed by a deep booming that rocked the ground.

"Marnie? Marnie? What's happened? What is it? Speak to me!"

She could hear Ralph's voice from the receiver. She answered him breathlessly. "I don't know. It was like a fireworks display ... must have been an explosion. *Dear God!*"

"What is it? Marnie, you must get away from there. At once. Don't hang around. Get a cab ... anything ... get to the station. Come to Oxford. I'll pick you up. Go now!"

"Right."

"You mean that? You'll leave straight away?"

"Sure. See you!" She put the phone down and added "... as soon as I can." There was something she had to do. It took her a minute to reach the pool of Little Venice, where heads were appearing from boats, and people were coming out on deck. Across on the other side of the bridge she could see flames reflecting off the water under the bridge over the arm leading to

Paddington Basin. The arm where until that morning she had been moored. She jogged in the direction of the bridge by the bank where the waterbuses tied up, the bridge that would take her back towards the mooring. The night air was blasted by the sound of fire engine sirens wailing. Seconds later she saw an ambulance screaming over the bridge. Cars had stopped by the roadside, doors left open, their passengers leaning over the railings trying to get a view of the blaze. All traffic had stopped. Marnie kept running, turning down the road under the elevated motorway, trying to make sense of what she had seen.

Ahead, two fire engines were lined up at the side of the road, their orange lights flashing. As she drew nearer, the air became heavy with the smell of burning, a strong odour like oil and rubber that irritated her throat and brought tears to her eyes. She pulled the scarf round her mouth and jogged on. Hoses lay across the pavement and disappeared through the door in the towpath wall. Under arc lights, helmeted figures wearing bulky uniforms were milling backwards and forwards, and although no one paid attention to her approach, Marnie knew she would not be able to push past them to see the fire. Without slackening speed, she crossed the road and skirted the fire engines and the ambulance that had pulled in behind them, reaching the pavement again twenty metres further along where the drive led back to the wooden canal gates.

Marnie reached in her shoulder bag, first taking out a handkerchief to wipe her eyes, then finding the BW key that she always carried. With all attention diverted by the blaze, nobody noticed her opening one of the gates. Once inside, Marnie stood in the shadows and surveyed the scene. It was her worst fears. A nightmare. A boat was blazing, flames and smoke pouring from the windows. Teams of firefighters were aiming hoses through smashed windows into the cabins. Marnie shuddered at the realisation that the burning boat was tied up at the mooring that until that afternoon had been the temporary home for *Rumpole*. In the beams of light from the fire engines, she could see the name of the stricken boat clearly. It was *Magician*.

Marnie leaned back against the gate and drew breath, immediately regretting it as the acrid air choked her and she began to cough. Wiping her eyes and pulling up the scarf, she pressed ahead on instinct, desperate to find out about Jonathan and Michelle. When she was still several metres from the boat a figure stepped forward and blocked her way. Marnie tried to pass, but it was impossible. The firefighter raised the visor on the bright yellow helmet and, to her surprise, Marnie found herself looking into the eyes of a young woman.

"Get back!" she shouted. "You shouldn't be here! Leave the area now!"

All Marnie could say was "My boat ..."

"That's your boat?" the firefighter cried out against the roar of the fire. "Is anyone on board?"

Marnie shook her head. It was too complicated to explain. At this distance it was obvious that anyone on that boat was not going to survive.

"Are you sure there's no one on the boat?" The firefighter was shouting in Marnie's face.

With an effort of will Marnie pulled herself together. "Jonathan and Michelle."

"Right. Now please get away. There's nothing you can do. Give your name and address to the officer at the fire engine. Go now!"

Marnie nodded and began to turn. Suddenly she stopped and grabbed the arm of the young woman, pointing over her shoulder. She shouted. "In the hatch at the bows ... be careful. There may be spare gas bottles. Big ones. Thirteen kilos. I don't know for sure, but watch out."

"Right."

"I'm going."

"Okay."

Marnie moved away, holding the scarf to her mouth, as the firefighter turned back to the blaze. She saw her speaking urgently with other members of her team, and they moved purposefully towards the still-burning hulk. Marnie steadied herself against the wall to consider her options and backed into a pile of timber. She turned to find the tarpaulin that covered the MG. The plan took shape in her mind in two seconds. She heaved back the heavy material and stacked it on top of the timbers, gathered together the blanket and sheet that lay across the car and dumped them in the passenger seat. Pulling the BW key from her bag, she ran to the gates and dragged them open. The engine fired at the second press on the button, and Marnie eased slowly out into the street, stopping only long enough to close the gates behind her. Without looking back, she accelerated tentatively away, the engine still jerky and cold.

She was lucky to find empty parking spaces round by the moorings, and was able to park the car close to one of the gates giving access onto the towpath. In record time, she changed into her flying gear on the boat while the kettle boiled. Minutes after arriving, she threw some clothes into her overnight bag, wrapped two hot-water bottles in towels and locked *Rumpole* securely. First stop, the call-box by the tube station.

"Ralph, it's me."

"Are you on your way? Are you on the train?"

"No. Slight change of plan. Listen. I've got the car. I couldn't leave it there. Too dangerous. I'll meet you at the cottage."

"*Dangerous*? You've been back to the boat?"

"Yes. I'll explain later. Ralph, I'm fine – okay? No injuries, nothing. But it's terrible what's happened. The boat on our mooring has caught fire. It's horrible."

"Anyone hurt?"

"I don't know. Look, I've got to get away. Expect me any time. See you."

Marnie pointed the little car north and headed for the M40. Just before leaving north London for the motorway, she pulled into the side of the road feeling breathless, needing to calm her nerves for the journey. A few people were passing on the pavement and paused to look at the unusual car and its unusual driver. Marnie paid no attention, her thoughts on the blazing boat and its young owners. She rested her forehead against the steering wheel and breathed slowly and deeply, fighting to keep images of destruction out of her head.

Against all her efforts, she heard a dreamy, contented voice. "You could solve all the problems in the whole world like this ... Tea, coffee, a pint, a spliff ... anything'd do."

Not quite all the problems, Michelle, she thought, pushing the gear lever into first and pulling away from the kerb.

Part 21

Friday 13 January – morning

Marnie came into the kitchen while Ralph was laying the breakfast table. The change in atmosphere since her last visit to the cottage had struck her as soon as she awoke. She had arrived very late and shivering to find Ralph waiting up with a hot toddy. They had collapsed into bed in each other's arms, and Marnie had immediately fallen into an exhausted, unrefreshing sleep. Her first thought that morning had been of Jonathan and Michelle, and she had come as close as she could to praying that they had been somewhere else when *Magician* exploded. Before taking her shower she had phoned Anne to let her know she was unharmed. Ralph raised a finger and nodded at the radio as she walked in.

"*... are still unsure of the cause of the fire that destroyed a narrowboat in Little Venice, in central London, late yesterday evening. Three firefighters, two men and one woman, were injured when a fuel tank exploded as they fought the blaze. All three were taken to St Mary's Hospital, Paddington, where their condition was described as comfortable. Deputy Chief Fire Officer Martin Blake has appealed for any witnesses to come forward. The police are particularly anxious to interview a woman who spoke to a firefighter at the scene. She is described as in her twenties or thirties, wearing a long dark coat and fur hat ... The Home Secretary will today make a statement in the Commons about the state of the country's prisons ...*"

Ralph switched off the radio. "No prizes for guessing who that was. Did you get through to Bruere?"

"No. I left a message. He's not expected in until later this morning. Nor is Sergeant Wallace." Marnie yawned. "Did they say anything about people being on the boat? Anyone injured ... or anything?"

"Not that I heard. You came in just as they mentioned the fire department. You caught the rest."

"Nobody could've survived that, Ralph. It was an inferno. I hope to God they weren't on board."

"Did they live on the boat?"

"Yes. They didn't have much ..." Marnie's voice failed her. She sat down. Ralph knelt and put an arm round her shoulder. He could hear her breathing slowly and deeply, trying to keep control. She cleared her throat. "What do I do now?"

Ralph stood up decisively. "You have something to eat, and we work things out."

As they ate breakfast, Ralph respected Marnie's silence, leaving her to think matters over quietly. Like her, he had lived alone long enough to know the need for privacy. He was also unsure what he could say to alleviate her worries. After a while, Marnie looked up and smiled bleakly. "Sorry. I'm not good company this morning ... lost in my thoughts."

"It's hardly surprising, Marnie, after what happened last night ... after all you've been through these past weeks. You could do with a break from it all."

"I could do with finding out what happened."

"Last night, you mean?"

"That … and the whole Tim Edmonds affair." She looked drawn and weary.

Ralph stirred his coffee absent-mindedly. "Actually, Marnie … last night, when you rang just before the explosion … or whatever it was … you said you thought you understood what was going on … or something like that. Do you remember?"

Marnie frowned. "When I phoned you … yes. But I keep thinking I've got something worked out … then it all changes."

"Can you remember what it was this time?"

Marnie stared at her plate for a few seconds. "I got this idea … I may be totally wrong, of course … but I had an impression … from what somebody said …" She shook her head.

"Go on," said Ralph. "What was it?"

"Well … I realised that the police don't in fact suspect me or Malcolm. They're keeping us on a string … I'm not sure how to put this … it's as if they're just watching us, using us to see if we might lead them to whoever murdered Tim Edmonds."

"You're definitely convinced it was murder, then?"

"Oh yes, I think so. If Dodge, the tramp, was right, I don't see how it could've been anything else. There were two people there when he died. Can you think of any other possibility?"

"Has Dodge told the police what he saw?"

"They interviewed him at the time. He told us they didn't believe him, or they couldn't use his evidence in court. They probably have a point about that."

"And they haven't spoken to him since he first gave his account of what happened?"

"They've put him out of the reckoning. Anyway, I suppose they might still think he's dead. He was the one reported drowned in Limehouse Cut at Christmas. Even if they know he's alive, they regard him as of no use."

"And he's gone back to where he lived? I wonder if that was such a good idea."

Marnie nodded. "Probably the last place anyone would expect to find him. It's the same reasoning as me using the MG … nobody would expect me to be in the most conspicuous car on the road. Great minds think alike, as the saying goes …"

Ralph got up to fetch toast from the grill. "I can see why you think the police are hoping you and Grant might give them a lead, but frankly I think they're being over-optimistic."

"Desperate, more like. Unless … I suppose …"

"What?"

"Well, perhaps Malcolm might have some idea who could've met Tim Edmonds in the park that evening while he was waiting for him. As his friend, there's a fair chance he'd have a better clue than anyone else."

"Has he given any hint that he might know something?"

"No, not really."

"But you're convinced it had to be someone that Edmonds knew. It couldn't have been a stranger who fell into conversation with him … asked for a light … asked directions … an attempted mugging that went wrong?"

"I would've said all of those were possible if it hadn't been for Dodge. He said they were chatting in a friendly way, and were even drinking out of a bottle."

Ralph looked sceptical. "Are you serious about that, Marnie? I mean, can you really imagine Tim Edmonds standing around in the cold and dark, drinking out of a bottle on the towpath? It just can't be right. I can see why the police thought Dodge was dreaming it up."

"At the risk of looking a fool, Ralph, I believe what he said. I don't think he had any reason to lie."

"But was he sober? Did he really see anything? It's not much to build a case on ... not for a murder investigation."

"I know." Marnie sighed. "I just thought that Dodge was telling the truth. No one'll believe him because he's a tramp and a wino. End of case. But it's not the end of the story. He's the only evidence there is, the nearest to a witness you could possibly have."

"We're just going round and round the mulberry bush," said Ralph.

"And getting nowhere," said Marnie. "It's all so frustrating." She nibbled a piece of toast without enthusiasm. "Can't your hindsight theory come up with anything?"

"Now I know you're really desperate."

"I'm serious. Can't you use your brainpower to help? You go round the world telling governments what to do ... telling them where they're going wrong ... Can't you tell me where I'm going wrong?"

"It's really just a system of analysis, Marnie. My career is built on theories. That's what I do."

He sounded so despondent that Marnie reached for his hand. "I'm sorry. I didn't mean to denigrate you. I really was just wondering if you could find a way to resolve things ... if you could spot the clue or whatever that would make everything come clear ... your key whatsit ..."

"My Key Significant Factor, the KSF, yes. Well, it's true that there is usually a vital fact, or set of facts, at the heart of any issue. That's fairly obvious to anyone. The trouble is you need to know all the facts to be able to build them into a conceptual model. In economics you can usually do this because in hindsight you can see all the forces at work. But in this case ..."

"There's got be something," said Marnie. "It's getting me down, just sitting around unable to do anything about it, wondering all the time what's going to happen next."

Ralph looked at Marnie sitting at the table, breakfast largely untouched in front of her. Her sense of frustration was so strong, he could almost feel it across the room. "I know what you need, Marnie. Come on. We're going out. Let's go for a walk ... blow away the cobwebs. You could use some fresh air."

$$\bullet \quad \bullet \quad \bullet \quad \bullet \quad \bullet$$

The walk took Marnie and Ralph under pale grey skies across fields and through small woodlands, away from the canal. Ralph chose the route so as not to have reminders of boats and the disasters that can happen to them. The countryside was flat and uninspiring compared with the gently rolling landscape around Knightly St John, but the air was bracing and they both felt better for being outdoors. They said little at first, wrapped in their scarves and in their own thoughts, until they came to a stile at the edge of a spinney. Ralph climbed over first and turned to offer his hand to Marnie. Unaccustomed to being helped, she had not noticed the outstretched hand until she had already touched the ground. They smiled at each other.

"Don't tell me," said Ralph. "I'm not very politically correct, am I? Practically Neanderthal."

"You are that rare and increasingly vanishing breed … a gentleman."

Ralph bowed. "Thank you, kind lady. But seriously, is it … irksome, the way I behave?"

"Of course not. It all depends on how it's meant." She took Ralph's arm and they walked on through the thin trees, crunching frosted leaves under their shoes.

"How can you tell how it's meant?" he asked.

"Oh, a woman can always tell."

"For example."

"All right … to take an extreme case … if George Stubbs offered his hand, it would be accompanied by a leer, even if you couldn't see it. You'd know what he was thinking … slavver, slavver, slobber, slobber. He'd call you *my dear*, and you'd feel as if you were wearing a crinoline and bonnet, with long frilly drawers down to your ankles. That's how he'd see you."

"Good God," said Ralph. "You could sense he'd have all that on his mind?"

"Oh absolutely, especially the frilly drawers!" They laughed out loud in the silent wood. Nearby a squirrel broke cover and ran bouncing along the ground before sprinting up a tree and away to the top branches.

"I suppose, as a woman, you have to have all sorts of defence mechanisms," said Ralph.

"Instinctive," said Marnie. "We're programmed at birth."

"To be wary of men?"

"Some men, not all. Remember, we're also programmed to like men. That's how the system works. At least for most of us."

"Thank goodness for that. And do you have a theoretical model for sorting out the ones who are okay?"

"It's an instinct, I told you."

"And how reliable is it, this instinct?"

"Ah … now that's a good question. Many a girl has been mistaken in her judgment."

"*Men were deceivers ever?*" Ralph quoted.

"Yes. But again, not all men."

"We're not all like George Stubbs."

"In a way, you are, Ralph. You're totally transparent, but basically harmless. The same applies to both of you, but you're at opposite ends of the spectrum. It's all a question of whether the attentions are welcome."

"That's very reassuring. I'm relieved to hear it. At least, I think am. What about someone like Malcolm Grant? Where does he fit in the scheme of things?"

"Malcolm Grant … mm … Well, he's a gentleman – old-fashioned term, but you know what I mean – he doesn't come over as a predator, that's for sure."

"I suppose it's small details," said Ralph, "patterns of speech and behaviour, that give you clues as to whether you can trust someone or not."

"Yes, I suppose so. Tone of voice, gestures, mannerisms, the way someone looks at you ... They're all indicators." Marnie suddenly stopped and turned to face Ralph. "Actually, there was something I was going to ask you. I've just remembered what it was. You know when someone is given a peerage or a knighthood ... do you know how it works?"

"In what way?"

"How do they get to know about it in advance?"

They resumed walking while Ralph pondered the question. "It's strange you should ask that, Marnie. Until a week ago, I'd never thought about it. I expect someone contacts you from some government department and you take it from there."

"How long in advance?"

"Well, that's the point. Normally, I gather, it's several weeks before the announcements are made. Of course it varies as the officials in the Cabinet Office make contact with all the people being offered an honour ... there are several hundred every time."

"So you'd expect a fair amount of notice?"

"Normally, yes. Why are you asking this, by the way?"

"Anne and I had tea – at the Ritz, no less – with Anthony James and Priscilla Barnes two days ago."

"Oh yes, he got a knighthood. New Year's Honours. I saw it in the press."

"I didn't," said Marnie, grimacing, "and it was the waiter who told us. Otherwise I wouldn't have known to congratulate him. Slightly embarrassing, but he took it well. Anyway, apparently he'd been told weeks before Christmas."

"I think that's the normal procedure," said Ralph.

"I have a feeling it wasn't the procedure followed in the case of Malcolm Grant's peerage," said Marnie.

"That's very interesting. Why do you think that?"

"When I was in his office, it was obvious he'd made no preparations to move from the Commons to the Lords. You'd think it had come as a last-minute afterthought. Does that surprise you?"

"No, not at all. That's what I was going to tell you. On my trip to Japan, one of the officials in the British delegation to the conference was a Grade Five in the Cabinet Office – that's quite senior – and he remarked on Grant's peerage when he saw it in *The Times*."

"He was surprised Malcolm got it?"

"Not really. Anyone can get offered an honour. These people don't surprise easily. You only have to think of some of the characters who get knighthoods ... No, what surprised him was that he'd been involved with the list before leaving for the Far East, and he couldn't remember Grant being included at all."

• • • • •

It was a couple in much better spirits who returned to River Cottage that morning. Ralph went straight to the kitchen while Marnie tackled the phone. She tapped out the numbers for the office and interrogated the answerphone. She heard the beep for the first message. It was timed for the previous afternoon.

"Marnie, it's Malcolm. Just to thank you for the message via your ... er, colleague, the young lady. I look forward to hearing from you. 'Bye now."

Young lady, Marnie thought with an inner smile. Yes. The machine beeped a second time. It was Malcolm Grant again, but the tone of voice had changed markedly.

"Malcolm again, Marnie. I'm terribly shocked about the fire on the boat in Little Venice. Awful business. Did you know the couple who were killed? I'm so sorry. Keep in touch and take care."

Marnie slumped back in the chair, her head swimming ... *the couple who were killed* ... She put a hand to her forehead, feeling faint and dizzy. Ralph put his head round the door.

"Marnie, do you want coffee or shall I make us something to – What's happened?" He rushed across the room as Marnie put the phone down. She could only think of Jonathan and Michelle, with their dreamy attitude to life ... gentle hippies. She was choked, and felt tears streaming down her face, soundless and numbed as she saw the young couple sitting happily together that day on *Rumpole*, sipping their tea. They were so contented with so little. Marnie could not believe things could go on getting worse like this. When would it all end?

A dreadful thought hit her like a hammer blow. Could it have been Anne's use of the mobile that had led someone to their mooring? Could that innocent act have brought them to a horrible end in that blazing inferno of flames and black smoke? She was aware that Ralph was near her, that he was saying something. She tried to focus, to concentrate, but he stayed out of range. All her mind was taken up with the awful tragedy. It seemed to trigger again all the grief she had felt the previous summer when Toni Petrie had been murdered. Marnie felt like the Angel of Death, and was overwhelmed by the feeling that she was going to pass out. It was the smell of the brandy that began to bring her back to her surroundings. Ralph was holding a glass in front of her. She saw her hands shaking as she tried to grasp it. Ralph held it to her lips while she sipped the warming liquid. She coughed, and Ralph put the glass on the phone table to hold her in his arms.

"Marnie, Marnie," he said softly in her ear. "Just hold me quietly. I'm here. Don't worry. I'm here for you." He rocked her gently back and forth like a baby, holding her firmly but carefully. She held on, swallowing hard, trying to get her feelings under control. They both jumped as the phone rang beside them. Ralph automatically picked it up.

"Ralph Lombard."

"Ralph, it's Anne." Her voice sounded jarringly cheerful. "Are you all right? You sound a bit ... rushed."

"No. It's ... er, a bit difficult at the moment ..."

"Oh, sorry, I'll ring later. I only wanted to say how pleased I was with the good news. I'll call back this afternoon. 'Bye ..."

"No, no ... Anne ... don't go. What good news?" Marnie raised her head to look at Ralph, her face wet with tears.

"About Jonathan and Michelle ... from the boat that was burnt out."

"Tell me."

"It was just on the news. Apparently they'd gone to stay with Michelle's parents for a few days."

"You're sure about this?"

"I've just heard Jonathan talking about it on the radio."

"Just a minute ..." Ralph spoke to Marnie. "They're safe. They weren't on the boat at all."

Marnie swayed in her seat as if the shock of good news was as great a shock as the bad news had been. "There's no doubt?" she stammered.

Ralph shook his head. "None whatever." Marnie sagged forward, head in hands. Ralph spoke into the receiver again. "Sorry about this, Anne. We'd just heard the opposite. I'm so glad you phoned."

"Me too. Look, I'll ring back later about arrangements ... when you've had time to catch your breath."

"Thanks."

Marnie wiped a hand over her face. "Strike me pink ..."

"I second that," said Ralph. "Whatever it means." He picked up the brandy and drank it in one gulp. "Would you like some more?"

"No. I'm fine."

Ralph pulled a tissue from his back pocket, and Marnie dabbed it over her wet cheeks. She blew her nose and smiled a bleary smile. "Did Anne say what had caused the fire?"

"No ... just that they were off the boat when it happened."

"I feel as if I've been put through a wringer."

"If you don't mind me saying so ..."

"Don't bother ... I know. But I don't care. You'll just have to suffer the sight of me."

"My pleasure." He gave her another tissue.

"If they were okay, why did Malcolm leave that message? You'd think he wanted to shock me like that ..."

"It is rather strange."

"I had the most awful thought ... Do you think Anne's call to Malcolm could've been traced to the mooring?"

"I'm not sure how these things work. Why do you ask?"

"Could it just have been a coincidence that the day after Anne rings Malcolm, the boat on that mooring gets blown up? The mooring where we'd been staying ..."

"I don't know ... I suppose it has to be a possibility. But we'd better not say so to Anne."

"If I know Anne," said Marnie, "she's already worked that out for herself."

• • • • •

While Ralph worked in his study, Marnie spent much of the afternoon on the phone arranging meetings, fixing delivery times with contractors, confirming details with clients and generally bringing life back to normal. She spoke to Anne and agreed to pick her up on Monday morning at the bus station in Milton Keynes.

When Chief Inspector Bruere finally got through in response to Marnie's message, he sounded irritable, the result of having made repeated attempts to phone her while the line was engaged. Feeling cheered that Jonathan and Michelle were safe, Marnie ignored Bruere's tone.

"I just wanted to let you know that I was the person who spoke to the firefighter by the boat."

"Right."

"You don't sound surprised."

"Where you're concerned, Mrs Walker? What were you doing there?"

"Just checking that Jonathan and Michelle were all right. I've been using that mooring and I'd met them."

"And the car you drove away?"

"*My* car."

"You can prove that?"

"It's here if anyone wants to inspect it. It's the old MG I told you about … easy to identify."

"Okay. I suppose I ought to thank you for coming forward."

"Don't mention it."

He hung up. Marnie pulled a face at the phone.

The last name on her list was Malcolm Grant. Before dialling his number, she keyed in 1-4-1 to prevent Ralph's number being traced by the 1-4-7-1 system.

"Ah, Marnie, good to hear from you. You've caught me just before I leave for the weekend. Perfect timing."

"I'm not holding you up?"

"Not at all. How are things with you?"

"A lot better than they were after I got your last message."

Malcolm sounded unsure of her meaning. "My last message … I'm not sure I follow …"

"You said you were sorry about the young couple being killed in the fire on the boat."

"Well yes, of course. It was dreadful."

"But they weren't killed, Malcolm. They weren't even there. They'd gone on a visit."

"Are you sure?" His tone seemed genuinely incredulous.

"It's been on the news."

"Good lord … I've been in a meeting all afternoon … I had no idea …"

"What made you think they had been killed, Malcolm?"

"I heard it on the news myself this morning. I'm sure of it. But you say they're safe? That's astonishing … I mean, it's *wonderful* news. Were they friends of yours? I mean … *are* they friends of yours?"

"In a way, yes. At least, I know them."

"Well, I'm very sorry if I caused you any distress, Marnie. I assure you I only left the message after hearing the news on the radio."

"Right."

"Were you wanting to fix a time to get together?"

"Oh yes. Have you got your diary handy?"

They agreed to meet on Wednesday afternoon.

• • • • •

That evening after dinner in the conservatory by candlelight, Marnie and Ralph sat close together on the sofa in the drawing room, a log fire crackling in the inglenook, with coffee and brandy. This time it was definitely non-medicinal. They had shut out the winter night, and the weekend was before them. Both were determined that they would relax as far as was possible and gather their strength ready for whatever lay ahead. In the background a Vivaldi concerto was playing softly. It was a perfect atmosphere and a perfect evening.

Despite themselves they found it impossible to settle down to anything but the matters that were uppermost in their minds. They calmly and quietly talked over the Tim Edmonds affair, Marnie hoping Ralph might spot the key factor that would lead them to an understanding of exactly what had happened. She told him about the strange visit to the home of the Iron Lady. She described the meeting with Dodge. All the events were clear in their minds, and Ralph was coming to agree with Marnie about the police using her and Malcolm Grant to try to find a way to the killer. One thing was evident to them both: they were not in possession of the facts, at least not enough of the facts to be able to point to a definite solution.

"Do you realise you laughed this morning, Marnie? You haven't done that for a while."

"Yes, I know. It was the reference to the frilly drawers ... Fancy you remembering that ... You have an immoral memory."

"And you sound like something out of Noël Coward," said Ralph. "Have some more brandy."

"I told you so ... utterly transparent ... just like George Stubbs ... You see? Men are all the same. One-track minds."

"Nice to know George and I have so much in common," said Ralph.

"Oh, that doesn't mean it's not welcome."

"Now you're smiling. That must be progress."

Marnie turned to kiss Ralph. They tasted of brandy. "I may be wrong, and it wouldn't be the first time in all this sorry business, but I have a feeling that things are going to get sorted out. Don't ask me why ... I just feel that way."

"Yes," said Ralph. "Brandy has that effect on me sometimes, too." Marnie threatened violence and Ralph got up to put a log on the fire. Crouching in the inglenook he asked, "Would you like me to go with you when you see Malcolm Grant on Wednesday? I actually have a meeting in London that day. I could easily arrange things to be flexible."

"I suppose it would help if we put our heads together. On the other hand, it might look like a deputation. And we are just supposed to be talking about his interior design."

"Well, you could call me on the mobile if you wanted me to join you. I won't be far away. It's an external examiners' meeting at UCL."

"Okay. Let's see how it turns out."

Ralph put a log on top of the fire and poked the other logs to set it in place. He spoke over his shoulder, "But don't let me muscle in if you want to talk it over just the two of you. It's no problem. I detect a slight reticence on your part."

"Of course not. It could be helpful to have you there ... It's just that ..."

"What?"

"People who associate with me have a habit of getting their fingers burnt."

Part 22

Monday 16 January

From time to time on that Monday morning, Marnie found her thoughts drifting back to the weekend. Waiting on the phone to be put through to a client, hearing the recorded music intended to placate the impatient, she would hear the sounds from Ralph's hi-fi system. She would see the logs smouldering in the late evening, relive the walks across the still countryside, taste the wine. It had been perfect, almost perfect, had it not been for the mystery and menace hanging over them. Then the client would come on the line and she would be back to her busy world. In her professional life there were at least some certainties.

Marnie and Anne went through their action lists, applied themselves to their usual routine. Dolly came in and went out at times that coincided with the opening of milk bottles. The day passed in a blur of phoning, organising, designing, liaising with suppliers, planning. Marnie fixed a date for the radiators to be delivered and calculated that the central heating would be working in cottage number two in about two weeks. Anne celebrated by making coffee and heating up the last two mince pies from the freezer. And by drawing up a new list.

Marnie rang Days of Yore, the furniture removers who had her furniture in store, and arranged delivery times with Frank Day. His personal involvement in the previous summer's murder was a reminder of the less cosy world outside, and he seemed subdued these days when he spoke to her. With that exception, she was happy to plan moving into the cottage. On the notepad Marnie doodled in the margins of her list, a chimney with smoke curling out, the grandfather clock that Ralph had given her at Christmas. She thought of her furniture. What was fine in a smart London flat would be less suitable in an eighteenth-century cottage. She talked with Anne about new pieces they might buy. They discussed colour schemes, fabrics, carpets.

In the late afternoon, as Anne was gathering together the letters to be posted and the list for the shop, Randall Hughes phoned. He would be calling by to see the new vicar and wanted to look in at Glebe Farm. They left the time of his visit flexible and promised that the kettle would be on as he came through the door. Anne set off up the field on her usual afternoon trek, armed with the shopping bag, a scarf pulled up round her face. Despite the cutting edge to the air, she was happy to be back to normal, shrugging off the cold, stepping out on the hard rutted track.

Coming out of the shop she met Ronny walking back from the school bus. Gallantly he offered to carry the shopping and walk down with her to Glebe Farm. She accepted his company, but told him she was still strong enough to manage a loaf of bread, some vegetables and a box of Mr Stubbs's best free range eggs. They chatted about this and that. Anne told him of their plan to move into cottage number two; he told her about his university options.

Halfway down the field track, Ronny suddenly stopped and turned to her. "D'you remember when I set off that jumping cracker and you jumped out of your skin – straight into my arms?" He was beaming.

Anne did her best to flash him the heavy eyelids. It almost worked. She tried her deepest voice. "Not the kind of thing you're likely to forget in a hurry," she admitted, indulging him.

• • • • •

Anne leaned forward and sniffed the seats, her nose twitching like a rabbit's. "I think I can smell smoke on this leather, Marnie."

"That's hardly surprising. The car was only a few metres from the fire." Marnie dropped the MG's dustcover on the bonnet and leaned into the cockpit to sniff. "I think you're right. You wouldn't believe how dense it was. I could hardly breathe. The smell of it ..." She shook her head. "It'll probably be a while before it goes. That's one advantage of an open car, I suppose."

She retrieved the MG's dustcover and began draping it over the front of the car. Anne took up her position on the opposite side, and together they spread it out until the whole car was wrapped up against the elements. There were no doors on this barn, which was scarcely bigger than a double garage.

Marnie began fastening the corners to the chassis to keep the cover from blowing away. "I remember once, not long after Simon and I were married, a bottle of perfume got dropped in his car ... he had a VW Beetle that he'd restored himself ... looked like new ... it was his pride and joy. Anyway, the perfume spilled out and the car absolutely reeked of it. Simon said his beloved car smelled like a Bessarabian joyhouse." She laughed at the memory.

"A what?" said Anne.

"That's what he said. He was not best pleased I can tell you. In fact his humour wasn't improved by my calling the car *the love bug* ..." Marnie laughed again.

"Whose fault was it that the perfume got spilled?" said Anne.

"Oh, it was Simon's fault ... oh yes. I would've been more contrite otherwise. I'd been using the car and left my bag in it. He'd put the bag on the back seat and the bottle fell out. When he pushed the driver's seat back for his long legs, he ran over it ... it cracked under one of the runners. The smell stayed in the car for months. When he came to sell it, he had to have the whole thing valeted and steam cleaned."

Dusk was coming down as they walked through the spinney. Marnie sensed that Anne had something on her mind and she waited, certain that it would come out. She was right.

"Marnie?"

"What is it?"

"I know I shouldn't ask, but ... did you and Simon have rows?"

"No, not really ... oh, the odd disagreement like in any marriage, but nothing serious. The perfume incident was in our honeymoon period, if that's what you're thinking. No, the problems went deeper than that. Things were going well in my job and not so well in his. It didn't worry me that I was earning more, but it bothered him a lot. After a while it undermined the whole relationship."

"Is it very different being with Ralph?"

"Of course. Everything's different. He's established in his work and I am in my mine. We're not in competition, and the differences make it interesting. That's a simplified view, but it does help us get along." She glanced sideways at Anne. "Is this anything to do with Ronny by any chance?"

"Well, he was telling me about applying to go to university and planning a gap year."

"So you're comparing your life with his."

"It was more the other way round really. He said he thought it was odd for me to have my gap year now before I do A Levels."

"But he doesn't know about your circumstances and how you worked out what you wanted to do."

"No."

"Did you tell him that?"

"I said I needed to broaden my experience and the chance came along now ... so I took it."

"Fairly forcibly," said Marnie, "as I recall." She laughed and put an arm round Anne's shoulder. "You were very persuasive."

"I get the impression that Ronny thinks things should be done in a certain way. Do you know what I mean?"

"You think he's conventional?"

"In a way," said Anne. "I suppose most people are ... that's what makes conventional. It's just that I've got used to the way you do things."

"I don't think of myself as particularly unconventional," said Marnie.

"No, I understand that, but you always think things out for yourself. You don't do something because everybody else does it that way. Ralph's the same. You both have interesting lives and you make things happen."

"Quite a few things seem to happen to us, whether we like it or not," said Marnie ruefully.

"Yes ... but maybe that's because of the sort of people you are."

"I'm the sort of people who finds bodies floating in the canal?"

"Oh, you know what I mean. You run your own business ... Ralph has his theories ... conceptual models or whatever ..."

"Yes, I suppose we do have an independent outlook." Marnie stepped up onto the stern deck of *Sally Ann* and opened the doors. The air in the cabin was warm and welcoming. They went through to the galley, where Marnie lit the oil lamps and Anne drew the curtains. Waiting for the lamp globes to warm up, Marnie looked around her. "It is good to be home again. *Rumpole*'s a nice boat, but it isn't like being on *Sally*. It'll be strange moving into cottage number two in a couple of weeks."

"Exciting," said Anne. "Ralph's cottage is beautiful."

"Very," Marnie agreed. She lightly touched the lamp globes and turned the wicks up a fraction. The increased light reflected in the brass curtain rods and rings.

"Did you have a nice time?" Anne turned to fill the kettle.

"Really relaxing ... just ate, drank and went for walks. I felt much better at the end of the weekend than I did when I arrived."

"I suppose you talked about the Tim Edmonds affair?"

"It's hard to get it out of our minds. It's always there. At least I think I have a better idea of what's going on now. And I think Ralph agrees with me."

"It's a pity his theories can't help you work it all out." Anne lit the gas under the kettle, and Marnie unscrewed the lid of the pasta jar.

"That's what I said. I asked Ralph if his theories could be applied in this case and we talked it over."

"Did he come up with anything?"

"No startling revelations." Marnie washed tomatoes in the sink and rolled them in a tea towel to dry. She began assembling ingredients on the galley workbench: garlic, mushrooms, shallots, oregano, sage.

"Why do you think you've got things clearer, then?" said Anne laying the table.

"Do you fancy garlic bread with this or shall I do a green salad?"

"I'm easy. Either would be fine by me."

"Salad, I think. Can you put one of those part-baked baguettes in the oven?"

Anne rummaged in the cupboard under the sink. "There's a half-full bottle of wine with a vacuum stopper down here."

"Only half?" Marnie laughed. "Is it that Spanish red? Great. Sorry, you asked me a question. I got distracted."

"About getting things clearer ..."

"Mm. Some things, perhaps." Marnie turned the lamp wicks up higher.

"But you're no clearer about who actually did it?"

"No. That's still unclear. And it's like Ralph's hindsight theory. It only works out if you have all the facts, and we certainly don't have everything we need."

"Perhaps you've gone as far as you can ... perhaps you've just got to let the police sort it all out."

"But they might be using Malcolm and me. And I'm not sure that's going to get them anywhere. I don't see how it can. Why don't we talk about it over supper? I suddenly feel hungry ... and I could sure do with a glass of that wine ..."

• • • • •

Marnie poured the last drop of red wine into her glass. Anne used her last piece of bread to mop sauce from the plate.

"I love that French dressing, Marnie".

"Yes, we haven't got much balsamic vinegar left. Molly doesn't keep it at the village shop. We'll have to call in at the Food Centre. For dessert we've got yoghurts, I think, and there's some of that cheese we ought to use up, and those apples. They're Cox's. I'll have one of them. Take your pick. I'll make coffee."

Anne cleared space on the table. "So that house where Mr Carter took you ... was it really hers? Her actual home?"

"The very same. Or rather, that's what they led me to believe."

"But why did he take you there? This hasn't got anything to do with Mrs Thatcher, has it?"

"No. Nothing at all. At least, not directly."

"Then why?" Anne opened the fridge and took out a yoghurt.

"The officers on duty said they knew Malcolm and Tim Edmonds. They'd seen them with her over a number of years. Malcolm was certainly a fan of hers ... he makes that very obvious." She grimaced.

"And Tim Edmonds too, presumably?"

"I'm not so sure. He seems to have been a hanger-on, coat-tailing on Malcolm. I think Malcolm took him along as a sort of protégé."

"Like me?" Anne grinned at Marnie.

"Not quite. I don't think you have the same ambition ... to take over everything. That's politics."

"Are you sure about that, Marnie? About the ambition?" An impish smile.

"Come to think of it ..." Marnie grinned back. She filled the coffee pot and brought it to the table. "But seriously, it was Malcolm who led the way. He always did. And when Tim was in disgrace after the divorce scandal, it was Malcolm who stood by him."

"Through thick and thin."

"Yes. Of course, that was under the new regime after Major had come in. Malcolm wasn't such a favourite then ... too right wing. Even so, he was still tipped for a government post."

"Why didn't he get one sooner, under Mrs T, if he was such a favourite of hers?"

"That's what I asked Ralph. He said Malcolm didn't have enough experience at that time. By the time he was ready, she was out of office. Tough luck, really. Bad timing."

"But things weren't quite so bad for Tim Edmonds?"

"No. He'd restored his reputation through hard work, doing things that nobody else wanted to do ... all those unwinnable by-elections and so on. In fact it looked for a short time as if they both might get government posts together."

"Why didn't they?" said Anne.

"First there was the leadership crisis. And then ... then Tim Edmonds got murdered. And that was that."

"And Mr Grant goes off to the Lords." They fell silent. Anne spooned her yoghurt. Marnie sliced an apple.

The cabin was warm and snug against the cold winter night outside. The two oil lamps glowed silently and without odour, casting a soft light on the Liberty curtains in gentle shades of red, blue and cream, held in place by their brass fittings. There was a shine on the varnished tongue-and-groove pine that lined the walls. A safe and secure place in a world that was not what it seemed.

"It's still all very confusing, isn't it?" said Anne. "I mean, we don't know much for certain, do we?"

"We know a fair bit. Look." Marnie reached over and pulled a notepad from the bookcase. "We know Tim Edmonds made an appointment to see Malcolm before Christmas. I saw the note. It was signed, and the signature is apparently authentic." Marnie made a brief note. "Second, we know Malcolm was expecting Edmonds to keep the appointment. Indisputable fact. When he failed to turn up, Malcolm left a message on his answerphone." Another note.

"And that message led the police to Mr Grant," said Anne.

"Yes. It was an unlucky coincidence for him. If he hadn't tried to ring Tim Edmonds he would probably have been left in peace."

"Except he would've given his evidence anyway when the police started making inquiries."

"Yes. I suppose so. That doesn't alter the fact that we know for certain why Tim Edmonds was on the towpath that evening and where he was going." Marnie looked at her notes. "Third point. I found the body soon after the murder. Dodge confirmed the timing and was an eyewitness to there being two men on the towpath shortly before I turned up on *Sally*." She scribbled quickly. "It must've been a murder. The police questioned Malcolm and me, treating us as suspects, appearing to be uncertain if it was a murder or not. But they knew from Dodge what had happened, even if they couldn't use his testimony. They never had any doubt about what happened. All the time they were using us to see if we might lead them to the killer."

"How could you do that?"

"I don't know. Perhaps they thought we might uncover something ... or remember something ... some other contact ... some link that might prove to be significant."

"Like your business card ..."

"Exactly. They were wrong about that, but it could've been anything."

Anne put her hands to her face. She spoke softly and slowly, "Like the bombings."

"One bombing," said Marnie. "We only know it was a bomb that blew up my car. *Magician* could've been a gas explosion." She had tried not to dwell on the possibility that someone had deliberately blown up the boat in Little Venice. The docking area at Glebe Farm where *Sally Ann* was kept was too remote and lonely for that thought to be comfortable.

"But what about the bombing of your car? That couldn't have just been a coincidence ... could it?"

• • • • •

By an unspoken agreement, they decided that Anne would sleep on the camp bed in the saloon on *Sally Ann* that night. While Anne pulled her sleeping bag from its case, Marnie folded the table, trying hard to keep images of burning narrowboats out of her mind. They extended the camp bed and put the pillow in place.

"Marnie? We didn't get very far with your list, did we?"

"I thought I'd written down everything we knew ... all the facts that were certain."

"Three facts," said Anne. She sat down cross-legged on the camp bed.

"Not enough to make Ralph's hindsight theory come to life, you mean ..." Marnie slid down and sat on the floor, her back against one of the galley units.

Anne said, "Does Ralph's theory mean you have to have all of the facts and you can only use facts?"

"What do you mean?"

"Well ... there are other things, aren't there? There aren't just facts."

"Things like what?"

Anne shrugged. "Reasons for doing things ... things people believe ... things they like ... things they don't like ... Don't they count?"

"I hadn't thought about it like that," said Marnie. "I just supposed you had to have facts, like a scientific experiment. Ralph's always said economics is a sort of science."

"Yes, but he did say you could put all the economists end-to-end and they'd fail to reach a conclusion, or something like that." In her mind she saw economists lying beside the road all the way from Land's End to John O'Groats and she smiled. "So it can't just be about facts, can it? Or can it?"

"I see what you mean. But what else do we have to go on?"

"I don't know." said Anne. "I'm just trying to grab anything and everything that might help. I want to get this sorted. I want to be able to go back to my own room in the loft and not have to worry if there's somebody out there wanting to ..." She shivered. At that moment Marnie would have done anything to keep Anne out of it.

"Yes. Yes, I know. But what else do we have?"

"What about Dodge?" said Anne unconvincingly.

"Yes. I was thinking about him. Can we really just take some of his evidence and throw out the rest? What would Ralph think of that? Shouldn't we follow up everything he told us?"

"The police didn't. They didn't take anything on board ... not properly."

"No, but then they deal in facts. Maybe you've got a point, Anne. The trouble is, what he told us was so far-fetched that nobody would believe a word of it. I think he was sozzled and imagined he saw people behaving like other winos ... like himself. Perhaps he was confusing something he'd seen another time."

"And what if he wasn't?"

"I don't know. I wish Ralph was here to talk it over with us."

"You wish Ralph was here full stop."

Marnie smiled. "D'you know what Ralph told me?" She laughed. "This is girl talk ... we're like schoolgirls in the dorm in one of those old stories ... *The Fifth Form at Saint Bede's* ... Ralph said he felt inferior to me."

"Inferior? How?"

"He said I had a quick mind, flair and I thought fast on my feet ... it made me feel like action woman!" They laughed together.

"But that's true," said Anne.

"Even if it is, it doesn't make him inferior. Actually, I don't like that idea. I don't like him putting himself down. Ralph's an intellectual with a brilliant mind. I'm not. Look at all the things he does."

"I think he's great," said Anne. "You're just different characters, that's all. And I know he's brilliant, but theories haven't helped us solve the big problem."

"No. Have we even found a KSF?"

"Dunno. Could Dodge be that? Can it be a person? I thought it had to be an event or a happening."

"Our meeting with him was an event. Our conversation happened. It certainly made me see things differently ... more clearly."

"Then perhaps you've got to believe what he said. Perhaps you've got to accept it as a KSF. I bet that's what Ralph would say."

Marnie looked down at the floor. "You know, Anne, I sometimes think you're the one who sees things clearly. Tell me something. Do you believe what Dodge told us?"

"Mm ... it's difficult, isn't it?"

"You mean about him seeing Tim Edmonds and another man drinking?"

"Yeah ... but more than that ..."

"Go on."

"Well, something's been bothering me all along." Anne frowned. "How could that person – the killer – get out if the towpath gates were all locked?"

"He must've climbed over."

Anne shook her head firmly. "No way. It doesn't work. The gates are too high. I've seen them."

Marnie sighed. "So ... we have to discount Dodge as a witness, just like the police. It was crazy to think we could do what they failed to do."

"No it's not," said Anne, as firmly as before. "We've got to go along with Dodge. I saw him ... I believed him. I think he's all we've got."

"But you just cast doubts on his whole story."

"I know, but I think we've got to accept what he said and move on from there ... even if it does seem strange. What else can we do?"

Marnie tried to think this through. She tried to imagine the scene that dark evening when Tim Edmonds met an unknown person by the canal under the blow-up bridge. She tried to imagine him having drunk so much that he fell into a stupor and toppled into the water. There he was, waiting for her to come along and find him. She saw his face, pale and cold, his lips blue and slightly open, the water in his mouth, his eyes closed. It was horrible. Then she saw Dodge watching from the other bank in the darkness, half hidden by trees and bushes. What did he see? What did he think he saw? He certainly saw her ... and heard her on the phone calling for backup. He saw *Sally Ann* clearly enough to know that she was not *Rumpole*. Yes. His evidence was accurate.

"You're right, Anne."

"Mm?" Anne must have been lost in her own thoughts. Marnie's voice jerked her back to their conversation.

"Who gives you a drink?"

Anne blinked. "What?"

"Just follow it through. Who gives you a drink?"

"A barman?"

"No. I mean socially."

"I'm not sure I get you."

Marnie imitated the tramp's voice. "*You're a real mate, love* ... Well, would we have accepted a drink from the tramp?" Anne pulled a face. Marnie went on. "What if he'd offered us a swig from his bottle?" Anne gasped, clutched her throat and pretended to throw up. "Quite. So ... who gives you a drink?"

"A friend? Someone who's like you?"

"Exactly. Whoever gave Tim Edmonds a drink on the towpath must've been known to him, if we can believe Dodge."

"Which we do?"

"Yes. The police believed him too, or gave him the benefit of the doubt. They were convinced Tim Edmonds knew the man he met, knew his killer. If he knew that person, chances are that Malcolm Grant also knew him."

"And because he had your business card, you might've known him."

"Yes. We weren't suspects ... we were bait."

Part 23

Tuesday 17 January

Anne was in charge of the office and she loved it. That Tuesday morning Marnie had spent twenty minutes on the phone to Beth before dashing off to a site meeting at one of Willards' restaurants further north up the Grand Union Canal. Not quite dashing. It was the first time she had used the MG for a business meeting. It was the first time she had gone to a meeting of any sort armed with a hot-water bottle. They had warmed up the car as usual with fan heaters, and Marnie had sat in the office with her leather flying jacket and helmet slung over the back of the chair like a Spitfire pilot waiting to scramble. Now Anne was left to keep things under control and spent a happy hour or two bringing the month's accounts up to date, drafting replies to correspondence for Marnie to check and, best of all, studying Marnie's designs for the pubs and restaurants that were their biggest contract. She was delighted to see that some of her own ideas had been incorporated into the schemes, and made notes of some refinements that she thought were worth trying out to talk over with Marnie at their project review meeting later that afternoon.

The arrival of Dolly beside the desk told Anne it was time to make coffee for herself and pour a well-earned saucer of milk for a cat who had spent most of the morning curled up under a radiator. The sound of tyres rolling over hard ground outside made them both prick up their ears. Anne glanced through the window to see an ancient VW Beetle pulling up in the yard. Randall Hughes got out, wearing a dark grey coat over his long black cassock. He saw Anne at the window, smiled and raised a hand. True to Marnie's promise, the kettle was already heating up as he came through the door.

"It's only Dolly and me, I'm afraid. Marnie's had to go to a meeting."

"And you probably have jobs to see to," said Randall, hesitating by the door.

"I've just put the kettle on for coffee. Can you stay?"

"If you're sure I'm not intruding …" He squatted down to stroke Dolly's head.

"Have a seat. Give me two minutes." She turned to the kitchen end of the office while Randall lowered his tall frame into Marnie's chair, abandoned by Dolly who homed in on her saucer of milk, quietly purring. "Marnie will be sorry to have missed you. We have a lot of catching up to do after Christmas and … well, you know …"

"I can imagine. You always seem very busy. But you still make the best coffee in this parish."

"New vicar better at communion wine, is she?" Anne said, grinning over her shoulder.

Randall laughed. "Am I so obvious? Don't let on!"

"Is she settling into the village?"

"Yes. She hopes to come down to meet you both later in the week. Will you be around?"

Anne poured water into the cafetière. "I'm not sure, actually. We have to go to London tomorrow. I don't know how long we'll be staying." She loaded the tray. "Perhaps Marnie can give her a ring, fix a time so she doesn't come down here only to find we're away."

"Good idea."

Anne picked up the tray, concentrating on keeping it balanced. She had taken three steps into the office when the phone began ringing. She stopped, working out whether to go forward or back to the sink.

"Shall I pick it up?" said Randall.

"Please. I'll just put these down."

As Randall went to reach across the desk, the answerphone cut in. He waited. After Marnie's brief message, there was a sound like an intake of breath followed by a sniff. Anne remained where she stood, still holding the tray.

"It's me," said a gruff voice. "You there?" Randall looked surprised. This did not sound like the sort of person who engaged an interior designer.

"That's Dodge," said Anne in a stage whisper.

"Dodge?" said Randall.

"Anybody there? Sod it!"

"Randall, press the 'hands free' button, would you? I don't want to miss him. It could be important." She stepped forward, careful not to drop the tray.

Anne called out. "Dodge? Is that you?"

"Yeah. Who's that? You the posh bird?"

"No. It's Anne ... her friend."

There was a pause. The voice was doubtful, suspicious. "I don't know no Anne."

Randall was baffled by the conversation and looked enquiringly at Anne. "Yes you do ... we met the other day on the canal."

Another pause. More suspicion. "I don't know no Anne," Dodge repeated.

Anne felt helpless, desperate not to lose the call. "Yes you do ... you remember ... er ..."

"You ain't the posh bird ... posh bird with the lovely arse ..."

Randall's brows knitted together. Anne had a sudden flash of inspiration. "No. I'm ... er ... skinny bint, no tits."

The effect on Dodge was recognition. "Oh yeah ... right ..."

The effect on Randall was more dramatic. His mouth gaped open and he sat bolt upright in the chair. Anne tried not to laugh and only just managed to level the tray as the coffee pot began sliding across it. Randall collected his wits. His mouth closed with a snap. He coughed.

"Someone there?" said Dodge.

"No, Dodge, it's just me. Marnie's out. I can take a message for her."

The voice was full of doubt again. "I dunno ..."

"Yes. You know me. You can tell me what it is. Please don't hang up. What is it?"

"The police've been back ..."

"Right. I'm sure they won't hurt you, Dodge." Anne quietly lowered the tray onto Marnie's desk.

"It ain't the police I'm worried about ... it's the bloke, 'e's been back too. 'E was lookin' over 'ere. I think 'e saw me."

"Are you sure?"

"Nah. Dunno."

"Did he say anything ... call out to you or anything?"

"Messin' about with a stick ... couldn't make it out. He were up to somethin'."

"What was he doing exactly?"

"I couldn't see proper. It were dark."

"Dark? When was this?"

"Last night ... late."

"Any idea what time?"

"I dunno. It'd been dark a long time. I seen 'im before. It were 'im."

"What did he look like?"

"Too dark to see. 'Ad an 'at on ... dark clothes. Dropped a stick in the water. Took 'im a long time to get it out."

"What was he like ... young or old? Tall ... short? Fat ... thin? Can you think of anything I can tell Marnie when she gets back?"

A pause. "'E was ... like a fit man."

"Okay. Did you see what kind of stick it was?"

"Dunno ... maybe like a walkin' stick."

Anne shook her head. "What did he do with it? I don't quite understand about the stick in the water."

"I *told* yer." Dodge was becoming impatient. "'E kept ... grabbin' at it ... like it was slippery and 'e couldn't get 'old of it. That's all I know."

"Okay, Dodge. I'll tell Marnie. And thank you very much."

"Right. I don't want no trouble." There was a click and he was gone.

Anne stood silently pondering for a few seconds, chewing her lip, certain that there were many more questions she should have asked. She became aware of Randall again.

"Obviously not a client of yours," he said quietly.

"Believe it or not, that was our witness."

"*Witness?*"

Anne nodded. "He may have been there when the MP was murdered."

"So he was definitely murdered?"

"We think so. He's a tramp. He's quite nice, really, even if his language is a bit ..."

"Yes."

"I'm sorry if I sounded rather crude. It was the only way to remind him who I was. I hope you weren't shocked."

Randall smiled. "No. Well, not really. Believe it or not, I'm regarded as being on the liberal wing of the clergy."

"I thought you weren't supposed to be political."

"No. I mean, we're meant to be the broad-minded ones ... taking things in our stride however, to use your word, 'crude' they might be."

"You should try being a woman," said Anne with feeling.

Part 24

Wednesday 18 January

It was easy, even in the darkness before dawn, to push *Rumpole* out of her mooring, steer into mid-channel and point her nose towards the black hole of Maida Hill tunnel. The street lights on both sides of the canal gave enough background illumination to make their task simple, and Anne had walked slowly back along the towpath to join Marnie on the stern deck as the bows swung out and they pulled away from the bank. Standing together, they both yawned in unison, the yawns turning into suppressed laughter.

Marnie pulled the collar of her ski-suit up around her neck, musing that she seemed to be spending more time in fancy dress these days than in normal clothes. The breath clouded in front of her face, and she felt its warmth reflecting back onto her chin as she guided the boat into the tunnel.

Anne leaned forward and turned on the headlamp, yawning again from cold and tiredness. Croissants were warming in the oven, with a further batch standing by in case they met Dodge. *It's hideously early ... how do we get into these larks?* she thought, dreaming of her warm bed. It was all too clear. The previous day at Glebe Farm, she had told Marnie about the call from Dodge as soon as she returned from her meeting. Because he had spoken on the answerphone, they could listen again to the conversation and Marnie had replayed it three or four times, listening intently. Without hesitating she had persuaded Randall to take them to Milton Keynes to catch the first available train to London. Marnie seemed obsessed with the idea that they had to be on the spot to find the solution to the mystery of the death of Tim Edmonds.

The whistling of the kettle brought Anne back to her surroundings, and she gratefully went below to prepare breakfast. Attending to her mundane tasks, she wondered if Marnie was becoming excessively dominated by the mystery, driving herself to the limit to try to resolve it. Her worries were confirmed when Marnie called down asking Anne to pour a shot of cognac into her coffee.

Back on deck, Anne held out the mug. "Are you okay, Marnie?"

"I'm fine."

"Are you sure?"

Marnie smiled through the steam. "You think I'm going loopy because I ask for a drop of brandy?"

"You don't usually drink alcohol at breakfast time."

"Actually, I'm thinking of having it on cornflakes in future. It'll make a pleasant change. You can order some of that marmalade with whiskey in too, if you like."

"I'm serious, Marnie."

"I'm not. So don't worry. I just felt cold inside, that's all." She pulled a glove off to pick up a croissant and dunk it in her drink. "Mm ... a big improvement with Courvoisier!"

Anne smiled at her. "To tell you the truth, I was worrying that you might be getting a bit obsessive about things ..."

"And it was driving me to drink? Of course. Logical conclusion. No, actually, what's worrying me is Dodge."

"You think he may have imagined what he saw?"

"No. The more I think about it, the more I believe every word he said. Really. No, I'm worried about why he phoned us. It was a miracle he phoned at all."

"I thought he just wanted to be helpful. You'd been nice to him, and he wanted to pay you back."

"Maybe. But I think he was motivated by fear. And I think he was right."

• • • • •

They motored slowly past the boats moored in the basin of Lisson Grove, through the short tunnel under the tube line, to emerge into Regent's Park. In the light borrowed from the street lamps some distance away outside the park, they could see ducks sleeping, heads tucked under wings, on landscaped grassy banks sloping down to the path. Within a few minutes they saw the outline of the blow-up bridge looming ahead of them. Marnie reduced the engine speed to let *Rumpole* drift gently up towards the bridge, easing her into the side to come to a halt a few metres before the steel columns.

"I think we've got to assume the man was searching the water roughly where I found the body," said Marnie. She spoke in little more than a whisper.

"I know it sounds a silly thing to say," Anne began, "but you don't think it could just have been a man who'd dropped a walking stick into the canal and was trying to get it out?"

"I don't."

"He could've been having difficulties grabbing it because he had a bad back … or something … if it was a walking stick."

"Humour me, Anne. I know it was more than that. It can't just have been a coincidence."

"Okay." They looked down at the grey water in the darkness, Anne at a loss to know what would happen next.

"Won't be a sec," said Marnie, disappearing below.

Anne heard a door open somewhere in the cabin, followed by sounds of rummaging. A minute later, Marnie reappeared holding a child's fishing net. "I knew we had one of these. Right, where do we start?"

"Good question," said Anne.

Marnie switched off the engine, hopped onto the towpath and walked a few paces. "I think it was about here." She dipped the net into the water and reached down till she touched bottom. "I think there's nothing for it but to drag up and down until I find something."

"What about using the magnet?"

"I don't know that it'll be metal. Let's see how we get on with this." She walked slowly along the edge of the towpath, scraping the net through what felt like a thin layer of soil on the canal bed, while Anne watched her. After a few moments, the girl went below and came back holding a pair of trainers. She stepped down to join Marnie.

"Try these. I think you've got to have a system. Why not mark the bank in sections and use *Rumpole* as a boundary?"

Marnie agreed to let Anne try out her idea. They first pulled the boat forward to mark out the approximate area of the search, then tied her up at each end, using the gangplank at the stern to hold her away from the bank, and the short pole wedged up at the bow. This gave them a sweep of the length of the boat and a channel of nearly two metres width. Anne placed the trainers about two metres apart on the bank at the end nearest to the bridge, and Marnie began systematically trailing the net slowly up and down between the shoes.

"I like your system, Anne. It at least makes me feel I haven't covered the same area twice, or missed part of it."

"I'll do the next section, if you like, while you have your coffee ... and brandy."

Marnie smiled sweetly at Anne in the half light. "One day, Anne, you'll make a really interesting mother-in-law." Anne stuck out her tongue.

Very soon afterwards, Marnie stopped dragging.

"Got something?" said Anne. She unhooked the torch from beside the control panel and shone it down at the surface.

"Yes. I can definitely feel something down there." She fiddled with the net handle, trying to get some purchase on the object. "The trouble is, now that I've located it, it isn't easy getting a hold." She tried twisting the handle in an attempt to scoop up her find.

"Can you feel how big it is? Is it heavy? Why not try dragging it towards the bank?"

"That's an idea." Marnie held the handle in both hands and began scraping the net towards her. "It's moving. I don't think it's all that heavy. It seems solid, though. God knows how I'm going to get it out. It'll be like one of those fairground crane things where you keep dropping whatever you're trying to pick up."

"What about a bucket?" Anne ran back into the boat and brought out the plastic bucket from under the sink. She tied a light rope to the handle and kneeled down to tilt it on its side in the water until it filled up. It sank, and she dragged it close to the bank, angling it with the rope to face the net. Marnie kept scraping her prize along the bottom.

"I'll never believe it if we find it first time," said Marnie, concentrating hard.

"Have you any idea what it is you're looking for?" said Anne.

"Not really. But I think I will know when we find it." She scraped firmly with the net. "That definitely moved. I think we're there. Try lifting the bucket ... very carefully. I don't want it to fall out."

Anne took up the strain on the rope and pulled inch by inch against the weight of the water. Soon the bucket broke clear of the canal, and she hoisted it onto the bank. Marnie began rolling up her sleeve, muttering, "This'll be pleasant, plunging my arm into icy water in mid-January, but I daren't risk tipping it back into the canal."

"Be careful, Marnie. Whatever it is might be sharp."

Marnie knelt on the path and winced as she felt around in the bucket, up to her elbow in freezing muddy water. "God! This is cold. I must be mad – don't agree with me!"

"Never said a word."

"Ah ... what's this?" She gripped her catch carefully and lifted it out. Anne shone the torch onto a small object covered in slime, almost the size of a paperback book. Marnie swished it around in the water to rinse off the mud. "Oh ..." She swished it again and held it up to the light.

"What is it?" said Anne.

"I think it's a hip-flask."

"Is it what you expected ... now that you've found it?"

"Mm ..."

"You sound disappointed."

"Well ... it's not much of a murder weapon, is it?"

• • • • •

There had been an atmosphere of anti-climax on *Rumpole* for the rest of the morning and all through lunch. Marnie had examined the hip-flask through the transparent bag, but there were no marks to identify the owner. They had spent almost another hour fruitlessly searching the rest of the area they had marked out on the canal until finally, as the sky was lightening, they had turned the boat back to Little Venice under a dull grey dawn. They had seen nothing of Dodge and had had no thought of disturbing his rest on the other side of the canal in the shelter of the tall bridge under his pile of blankets and tarpaulins. Thoughts of the way he lived only added to the gloom of that icy morning as *Rumpole* headed for home.

Back at the mooring they had planned their day, Anne sitting opposite Marnie at the galley table, notepad open, ready for anything.

"What do you reckon about the hip flask, then?" Anne asked.

Marnie hesitated. "I'm not sure."

"Aren't you going to take it to the police?"

"In a way, I suppose I should. But ..."

"But what?"

"Well ... they would've found it if it had been there all the time, surely."

"You think they dragged the canal?"

"That's what I don't know. Perhaps they didn't. He had a head wound and was drowned. So would they drag the canal? Is that their normal procedure?"

"You should still let them have it, Marnie."

"And probably make myself look a fool, as usual. I mean ... what does it prove? It's a hip flask covered in mud. I want to think about it before I decide." She sighed. "Let's hope this isn't all a waste of time ..." Her disappointment was sliding into despondency.

"You've still got your meeting with Mr Grant. You had to come for that, so it won't all be wasted."

"No, I suppose not, but I've dragged you down here for nothing."

"That's all right. I'm part of the team. But you won't be wanting me at the meeting, I expect ..."

Marnie shrugged. "I want to try out my ideas about the police using us as decoys, and I don't think I could do that if we weren't alone. Malcolm's not likely to speak frankly if someone else is there, particularly someone he doesn't know."

"Right. No probs," Anne said brightly.

Marnie reached across the table and touched her friend's hand. "No probs," she mimicked, smiling. "So, what would you like to do? You can have the afternoon off ... do something interesting."

Anne thought for a moment. "Well ... I could spend most of the time queuing for the exhibition at the Tate in the cold ... Oh, I know ... I could go to the sales. I've got some Christmas present money to spend."

"Good idea. I feel quite envious."

"When's your meeting?"

"Half three."

"And what's our fallback position? What do I do if ... for any reason ..."

"There won't be any trouble."

"No, but I'm not going through all that worry again, like the time you went off with Mr Carter and I had no idea where you were."

"Call the Fire Brigade," said Marnie flippantly.

"I mean it, Marnie."

"Nothing's going to happen."

"But you know what a worryguts I am. We always have a –"

"I know, okay. I give in. You're right, of course. I expect I'll be at Malcolm's flat till about five o'clock. If you don't get a call from me by half past five, ring Ralph and get him to come and meet me there. That'll be my excuse to leave. And if Ralph rings first, you can suggest he goes to Malcolm's for five. Okay?"

Anne nodded and made notes. She looked much happier.

• • • • •

Marnie paid the taxi driver and walked up the steps of the house where Malcolm Grant's flat occupied the first floor. In her bag she carried the hip-flask, still muddy and wet, in its polythene bag. When the buzzer sounded she pushed open the door and walked up the stairs to be received by Malcolm in the doorway, holding a phone. He welcomed her in as his conversation came to an end.

"It's been like that all day. I'm sorry to greet you in the middle of a phone call. Most uncivilised." He kissed Marnie on the cheek. "Let me take your coat. My goodness it feels cold. You must be frozen. Come and warm up."

"I've come at a busy time. Are you sure it's convenient?"

"Of course it is. I've been looking forward to seeing you, Marnie, and I'm dying to see what you've prepared for the flat. I find the whole thing very interesting."

"To tell you the truth, Malcolm, I always feel nervous at this point ... just before showing a client my proposals. Even after years of doing this sort of thing, it still gives me butterflies."

"I can quite understand that. It must be like talking in the chamber of the Commons. You think it would only be the maiden speech that makes you nervous. Believe me, for some of us, it never leaves you."

"I saw a clip of you speaking on television a while ago. You looked very calm and composed to me."

"All a façade. Inside, I was trembling. It's as tough as going into action. In the army, at least you're doing what you're trained to do. You've got backup ... support ... you're part of a team. Standing up there in the House facing the other side, you're on your own. Benches or trenches, it's all adrenalin. You need have no worries, Marnie. I know that you'll produce something splendid."

"We'll see."

"Of course. You're among friends. Well, a friend. Nothing to worry about. But first things first. Make yourself at home. How about tea? I have some of that Darjeeling you like ... with lemon?"

• • • • •

Kensington High Street looked as if a plague of locusts had hit it, and Oxford Street was not much better. The January sales had started just before Christmas, and Anne was half expecting to find Easter eggs and bunnies creeping onto the shelves depleted of stock after more than two weeks of scavenging by London's shopaholics. She began working her way up from Selfridges to Hennes via the flagship Marks and Spencer and John Lewis, calling in on smaller boutiques along the way.

Just as she was beginning to think she had missed the boat and could only see clothes that she would not touch with a barge pole – amazing how her thoughts were dominated by canal images these days – she came across a whole rail of dresses that were her size in one of the big stores. She tried on two or three. They had designer labels and would normally have been well out of her range, but the 'Final reductions' tags had brought them down to what she could afford. Just. They were long and in deep colours, burgundy, purple, russet and olive green, ideal for going to meetings.

She looked in the full-length mirrors in the changing cubicle, turning from side to side, and could see at once why they were still on sale. Only a girl built like a stick insect stood a chance of slipping into these creations. She walked out of the changing rooms to get a better view on the shop floor. Standing at a distance from the mirror, she made up her mind. Beside her, another girl was trying on a jacket. She had what the retail trade would call a fuller figure, and glanced at Anne from the corner of her eye. Turning sideways, Anne noticed her.

"I hope you're not going to say 'does my bum look big in this?'" the girl said quietly.

Anne smiled, thinking of how Dodge had described her. She changed into her own clothes, took the dress to the till and paid. The other girl was there in front of her, buying the jacket.

"It really suited you," she said. "The last time I could've worn anything like that, I was about twelve."

"Being skinny has advantages sometimes," Anne said. "But not often."

When it was her turn to pay, the sales lady said, "You're lucky. You have the kind of figure that most girls would die for, like a model. The dress looks great on you."

"I just wanted something nice and simple for meetings at work."

The sales lady folded the dress and slipped it into a bag. "I'd say it was restrained and elegant. It suits you. But that girl was right. You have the kind of figure that would look good wearing a sack."

Anne was happy as she left the store, thinking how lucky she was to have her life ... if only they could get the murder business sorted out and back to normal, everything would be perfect.

• • • • •

Marnie had laid the cuttings and sketches out on the floor of the drawing room, and she knelt beside Malcolm as she explained her proposals. For almost an hour they discussed her plans in detail, occasionally standing up to walk from room to room while she related the wall colour to the curtain samples, picking up how they fitted in with the carpets, soft furnishings and fitments. Malcolm asked intelligent questions. *Will the existing curtains fit in with that wallpaper? What about the hall ... should we change that to match the wall colour in the drawing room or the dining room? Have you assumed that the dining room will be mainly used in the evening? The hall carpet is starting to wear – what colour should I get to replace it?*

Eventually, they sat back on the sofa, Malcolm mulling over the whole scheme, Marnie feeling that she had done justice to her ideas and to the flat. It was time for Malcolm to give his verdict.

"Frankly, Marnie, I'm impressed on two counts."

"Only two?"

"Two very important counts. First, I think your design is a knockout."

"Thank you."

"You can't have had any doubt about that. It's brilliant. I wish I'd known you years ago." He hesitated before going on, looking down at the sketches. Almost inaudibly he said, "For all sorts of reasons." He smiled inwardly. "But secondly, and most importantly ... I don't need to spend the million that you threatened when you came before. No need to spend a fortune."

"No. When the basic structure is as good as this, really fine, the main thing is to let its own strengths come out. I've just chosen to understate, to bring out the quality of the flat itself, its proportions, its detailed features and fittings. Look at these windows and doors ... they're beautiful. There'd be no point in swamping them with excessive patterns that would compete and overpower them."

"I admire what you do, Marnie. And you make it seem so easy. I'd never have thought of all this, but you make it appear obvious what has to be done."

"It just took a little time and thought, and getting to know the flat and its situation."

"But you've been bold, where most people would have been cautious."

"Being bold has got me into scrapes in the past ... but not in my work. What did you expect me to produce, magnolia walls and brilliant white window frames?" She laughed.

"Exactly. But you didn't do that. Look at all this. Beats me how you worked it out."

"I tried to provide what would suit your life. The original architects would probably have chosen very muted colours – that's what was around at the time. But looking at the way the light falls in through those windows, I wanted to use richer, warmer colours to brighten the room. I wanted it to be lively ... still elegant, but more stimulating and uplifting. The new curtains in here will add to the effect. And I thought the dining room could take more bold colours. It's mainly an evening room – for dinner parties, candlelight, cut glass and silver. Why not be bold?"

"Sounds just right, Marnie. And may I be bold? Perhaps I might tempt you some time to come to dinner here? I'd like you to meet some of my other friends. I'm sure you'd find some of my colleagues more pleasant and better company than you might expect ... Perhaps, when all that other business is behind us?"

"That would be nice. Thank you."

Malcolm leaned over and touched her hand. "We've been through a lot together, you and I."

"We certainly have ..."

·   ·   ·   ·   ·

Walking to the tube station, carrying her new dress in a bag bearing the designer name and logo, Anne glanced in the shop windows with only a modicum of interest. She had spent almost all her Christmas present money, and did not want to spot something else that might bring a twinge of regret to her afternoon outing. She had to wait to cross the road and looked vaguely in a shop window as the traffic flowed past. She noticed her reflection and found herself wondering about the strange world of fashion, a world in which she was to some extent involved. On one level, she saw it all as superficial nonsense. But she liked to think that in her work and Marnie's they were bringing colour and pleasure into people's lives. In her reflection in the shop window she saw a smart young woman in fashionable clothes, her long skirt, blouson jacket, apricot scarf and beret.

Feeling the need to cut herself down to size, in case she was too carried away with her own image, she remembered how Dodge had described her... *skinny bint, no tits* ... The memory brought a half smile to her face. In that moment, glancing down, she saw another face looking up at her. It was not a reflection. On the pavement, against the shop window sat a beggar with a handwritten sign, "Homeless and hungry – Please help me" and a hat lying next to it. Anne swallowed, her smile disappearing.

She was immediately overcome by guilt at her good fortune and reached into her bag to find a coin. She quickly walked over to the beggar and dropped the coin into the hat. With a sense of shock she saw that the face looking up at her was a girl's. The beggar was about the same age as Anne. The pedestrian light on the crossing changed to green and Anne turned to go on her way. In her mind she saw again the boy tramp at Randall's hostel. She felt like throwing her designer bag and its designer logo into the gutter. She wanted to go back and talk to the beggar girl. But she knew she could not live her life for her and she had no wish to patronise her.

Anne tried to work out why she had reacted so strongly. Was it that the beggar had seen her apparently smiling in self-contentment at her reflection in the window? A complacent young trendy with designer clothes! Was it Randall's hostel? Was it Dodge? Or was it the fact that it was almost a matter of luck that she was not in the same position herself? She rarely forgot that she had set off to run away from home two years before when her father was made redundant. Anne had looked at the beggar girl and seen herself.

In the tube station was a sign urging travellers not to give money to vagrants, "many of whom operate in organised groups." The management suggested that donations be sent to recognised charities who cared for the needy. What about the needy who stare you in the face, Anne thought. Was that girl part of a group? Would she pack up at five o'clock, at the end of her shift, and go home to some latter-day Fagin? Perhaps she lived in a hostel like Randall's. Anne hoped so. And what about Dodge? Where did he get money? Why did he live on a pallet under the blow-up bridge? It was crazy. There had to be a better way to live than that. In her mind she saw Dodge lurching towards her, but she was not frightened of him. She could smell his beery breath, hear his gravelly voice … *you're a real mate, love …*

• • • • •

"Assuming I can afford all this," Malcolm gestured at the plans that were still spread over the carpet, "when would you be able to make a start? Presumably you could find a decorator and someone to make up the curtains?"

"Yes. I know some reliable people with fair prices. I'd have to get quotes from them, and timing would depend on how much work they have on, of course. But I think we could make a start within, say, two or three weeks. Four at the most."

"Soon as that? Very good. It'll be nice to have something to look forward to for a change." The phone rang and Malcolm muttered, "Here we go again." He excused himself to take the call in the kitchen.

Marnie stretched her legs, pleased with the way the meeting had gone. If only all her clients were like Malcolm, she thought. It was good to be appreciated. He had a quick grasp of what she was proposing and showed trust in her judgment. She was looking forward to getting the job done.

She stood up and walked around the room. They had been sitting or kneeling for the past half hour. Idly, she glanced at the sideboard, with its cluster of bottles of various spirits – *bottlescape*, she remembered, like Churchill's painting. She liked that word. At one end of the sideboard there were several photographs in frames, some of them silver. The Christmas present in its smart wrapping was no longer in sight.

Malcolm came back into the room. "Sorry about that, Marnie. Actually, we've had fewer interruptions than I'd expected. There's going to be another call, though, in a short while, I'm afraid."

"Then I'd better go and leave you in peace. You can mull over the scheme and let me know what you think. Take your time. There's no rush."

"Oh no. There's no need for you to rush off, either. It'll just be one of the Government Whips in the Lords wanting to talk about what committees I'm to serve on, that sort of thing. No quick decisions needed. The Lords goes at a more sedate pace than the Commons."

Marnie recalled Malcolm's expression: … *put out to grass* … She sat down again. "If you're sure …"

"Of course. I don't want to push you out into the cold any sooner than is necessary … unless you have urgent matters to attend to …"

"I can't stay long," Marnie said, "but there was just something I wanted to ask you. I wondered if you'd heard anything new about the police inquiry."

"They haven't contacted me for a while," said Malcolm. "Have they been in touch with you?"

"No, they haven't. But I've been thinking about the case a great deal, and I have an idea – it's just a theory."

"Go on, Marnie. I'm intrigued."

"Well, I don't think the police really regard us as suspects at all. I think they've been using us to see if we'd lead them to the person who did it, or at least give them some clues."

"Really?" Malcolm turned the idea over in his mind. "You could have a point there."

"I think it makes sense. You knew him better than anyone else, so you'd know all the people likely to associate with him."

"That's certainly true. But you didn't know him at all, Marnie."

"We both know that, but remember he had my business card in his wallet. One of my colleagues had given it to him, but they only had my word for that. Both of us stood a chance of knowing the murderer and we could either of us have given the police a lead on his identity."

Malcolm nodded thoughtfully. "That all adds up, but it presupposes that Tim definitely was murdered." He stood up and went to look out of the window.

"Personally I'm in no doubt about that," said Marnie.

"No. It's just that the whole business is fraught with doubts and uncertainties. That's why I intervened to get Cornforth to put that question to the Home Secretary."

"So that was your doing."

"Yes. I thought it might've helped to kick the police up the backside. I just want to get the whole matter settled and laid to rest ... like Tim. All I want is for him to be able to rest in peace."

• • • • •

Leaving the tube station at Warwick Avenue, Anne looked at her watch. Half four. She wondered how Marnie was getting on in her meeting, convinced that Malcolm Grant would like the design. It was a beautiful flat, judging by the Polaroids that Marnie had taken. Anne wished she could be there to see it. Ahead of her, two men were taking furniture from a van into a house, and she had to stop while they crossed the pavement carrying a bulky sofa. In her thoughts she was still pondering the design for Malcolm Grant when there was a sudden loud bang right beside her. She gasped in shock and jumped back. A third man looked round the back of the van, his face showing concern.

"Sorry, love, did I give you a fright?"

"Oh ... er ... yes, a bit."

"The shutter came down faster than I expected. It gave me quite a turn as well. Are you all right?"

"I'm fine. I was just ... miles away. Silly really ..."

"I'm ever so sorry." He looked as if he meant it.

"That's okay. No probs." She smiled and continued on her way feeling more than a little foolish. It was a reminder that the bomb that had destroyed Marnie's Rover had exploded on the opposite side of the street from where she was walking. Anne reflected that reacting to loud bangs had started to become a habit. She had felt the same when Ronny had let off his jumping cracker. Making a mental note to try to be less nervous, she quickened her pace and crossed the road towards the towpath gate.

Back aboard *Rumpole*, she switched on two fan heaters to warm the boat up quickly, hung the new dress in the cupboard and changed into her jeans. Automatically she put the kettle on and checked the mobile for messages that might have been left while she was in the underground. Nothing from Marnie, Ralph or anybody else. *Be patient,* she thought.

To pass the time, she picked up the file of photographs that Marnie had left on the galley table and began studying Malcolm Grant's flat. Marnie had told her that some of the antiques, including the Chippendale sideboard, had been in the Grant family since new. Anne found it hard to believe that one of his ancestors had probably actually talked to the great craftsman at the time of ordering it. It was another world, far away from anything she had ever known. She wondered if Grant was what people sometimes called a 'grandee', whatever that was.

In the photograph the sideboard shone with generations of polishing and care. At one end was a brass table lamp with a gold satin shade. A cliché perhaps, but it looked good. In the middle stood a collection of bottles, and Anne recognised the shape of one of the brandies, Marnie's favourite cognac. At the other end was a group of photographs. And there, at the front, was the sad Christmas present, waiting for Tim Edmonds who never came for it ... who never would come.

Anne wondered what the package contained. It looked too small to be a book, more the size of the hip-flask or perhaps a boxed set of CDs. It could even be some of those tapes of talking books that Marnie sometimes played in the car on long journeys as a change from music. She looked at her watch again. Forty minutes before she should start making phone calls. If she had been in the office she would have found jobs to do. Here there was nothing for it but to wait patiently. She sat sipping coffee and let her mind wander.

The shopping expedition had been good. She was looking forward to showing Marnie the dress, but she was sad about the beggar girl. Her thoughts turned to Dodge again ... *you're a real mate, love* ... It probably did not matter that Marnie had given him that whisky. One drop more would do no particular harm. He lived for drink. Poor old soul. ... *I know when I see people drinkin' booze out of a bottle* ... Suddenly, Anne sat bolt upright in the chair, her cheeks tingling ... *drinkin' booze out of a bottle* ... Or a hip-flask. Her mind was racing, flooding with impressions and images all at once crowding in on her, making her dizzy. She shook her head to try to clear it, blinking and breathless.

She picked up the photograph of the sideboard and stared at the present in its shiny gold wrapping. What if Malcolm Grant had met Tim Edmonds on his way to the flat? They might have walked along together. In the cold, Grant might have offered him a drink from a hip-flask. Men sometimes did that sort of thing. She had often seen it in television costume dramas, when they were out hunting with their dogs ... men of that class, what were they called? ... the gentry. They might have stopped before the bridge where there was a lamp. They could see what they were doing. *Not much of a murder weapon, is it?* ... Marnie had said. But what if it had something with a drug in it? That would be possible. Perhaps it would make him drowsy and fall in the water.

Anne knew these were just rambling thoughts, but it seemed to make sense. If some sort of drug could knock him out, perhaps it would not be traced in a body that had filled with water. It could look as if he had simply passed out from too much alcohol and then drowned. Was this all stupid? Anne was frowning, desperately trying to make sense of it all. Where did it lead? She grasped at anything that might help sort out the muddle. What else was there?

There was the car bomb that had nearly killed Marnie. If it had not been for Malcolm Grant, she would have been in the car when it exploded. He had saved her life. No doubt about that. And the fire that had destroyed *Magician*? No. That must have been an accident. No doubt about that either. So back to the car bomb. Her mind wandered hopelessly trying to drag in anything that might help. Explosions. Like the shutter banging down on the van just now. Like Ronny's firework. No. He had done that deliberately to make her ... An idea formed. It was clear and obvious.

What if Malcolm Grant had planted the bomb? What if it never was intended to kill Marnie, just persuade her that Grant was on her side, that he was as innocent of the murder as she was? Where did this all lead? She was wracked with doubts and indecision, convinced that she was raving, but there seemed to be no other way out. She looked again at the photograph. Everything led to Malcolm Grant.

• • • • •

"There's something else I want to talk to you about, Malcolm, something I want to show you ..." The phone rang again, interrupting Marnie before she could produce the hip-flask.

"I'm awfully sorry about this."

Malcolm went out to the kitchen while Marnie contained herself in patience. She got up and wandered around the room again, drawn inevitably to the sideboard. The photographs seemed to be mainly of people in uniform, and she tried to spot Malcolm as a young man. There were group shots, mainly in formal military dress, and the odd individual photo posed in various locations. At the back of the collection was an engraved pewter tankard. She leaned forward to read the copperplate inscription, which was not easy with the light reflecting from the surface, and could just make out the name Grant and ... *youngest colonel in the Falklands* ... It seemed to be a gift from the officers and men of his regiment. It must have been his last action as a soldier, the year before he entered politics. No wonder the Iron Lady took a liking to him, one of the heroes of her war in the South Atlantic. Judging by some of the photographs, Malcolm seemed to have been in the Commandos.

Marnie recognised several faces in other parts of the collection, and was not surprised to see the former Prime Minister herself in more than one. Here, a formal posed group during a visit to his constituency, the MP proudly standing beside his leader; there, a group shot perhaps from the party conference, with ministers and the PM plus acolytes, one of them Malcolm and just behind him ... Tim Edmonds, looking out as if from Malcolm's shadow. She recognised him from newspaper articles and from another photograph of the two MPs together, Tim Edmonds again standing slightly behind his friend, as if in his protection. Despite their smiles, strain showed in Tim's handsome features, and Marnie guessed that this came from the time of his fall from favour when Malcolm was his only friend. A good friend to have in time of trouble.

• • • • •

Anne was feeling anxious, but determined to keep a cool head. She made up her mind to ring Ralph at once and left *Rumpole* to make the call. She did not want to use the mobile while still on the boat, just in case. In case of what, she was unsure, but she was would take no chances.

Two streets away from the canal, she switched on the mobile and pressed the button to bring up the memory system with its list of phone numbers. It was blank. *Impossible.* She stared at the mobile, cursing under her breath. *Not impossible.* This was the new phone, and Marnie had not yet built up its list of numbers. *Damn!* What could she do? *Think quickly, Anne.* The address book was back in the office. Not much help there. How could she contact Ralph? She set off jogging towards the tube station and found the phone box.

"Directory Enquiries, what name please?"

"It's All Saints College, Oxford. Porters' Lodge, please."

As the electronic voice read out the number, Anne keyed it into the mobile's memory. She checked her cash – a few notes, but very few coins – and made a short call to Oxford.

"All Saints, good afternoon."

"Hallo, I'd like to speak to Professor Lombard's office, please."

"Professor Lombard doesn't have an office here as such. He's not in today. Would you like to leave a message for him?"

"I have to contact him at his meeting and I don't have a number."

"I'm sorry, miss, I can't help you."

"Does he have a mobile?"

"Oh no, miss." He made it sound as if that would be the end of western civilisation.

After hanging up, Anne chewed her thumbnail in frustration. What was she to do? What college was Ralph visiting? UCL ... She had seen University College. It was enormous. Somewhere in that pile of buildings Ralph was sitting calmly talking about examinations, while she was out here fuming and fretting. Another call to directory enquiries. Another number.

"Economics department, good afternoon."

"Good afternoon, can I speak to Professor Lombard, please? It's urgent and he's expecting me to call."

"We don't have a Professor Lombard in this department, I'm afraid. This is University College."

"Yes. He's from Oxford. He's at an examiners' meeting."

"Ah, yes. The external examiners meet in Senate House."

"Oh ... I don't suppose you have a number?" Anne was close to despair. It must have shown in her voice.

"I can transfer you, if you'd like to hold on."

"Brilliant! I mean, thank you. Yes, please." Anne had one more coin left and wished she'd asked for the extension number in case she ran out of money before she was connected.

A new voice at the end of the line. "Were you wanting Professor Lombard?"

"Yes, please."

"He's in a meeting at the moment."

"Yes, I know, but he wanted me to call him. It is urgent."

"I see ..."

Anne was close to exploding and felt like threatening this calm woman with violent bodily harm. "I'd be very grateful if you could ask him to come to the phone ..."

"Actually, the meeting room is at the other end of the building."

Anne wanted to scream: *Then start running, you moron!* She said, "Would it be possible to get a message to him?"

"I can't promise, but I'll see what I can do. Would you like to hold on or can I ask him to ring you back?"

"Thank you. Can you ask him to ring Anne Price on this number." She gave the mobile number and rang off. This was awful. She felt like screaming and stamping her foot in anger and frustration. It was dreadful having to depend on other people like this. And then, suddenly and without warning everything became clear. She would not depend on other people. She would follow Marnie's example, what Marnie used to call the Royal Marines School of Management ... seize the high ground. Quickly she delved into her bag and pulled out her notebook. In it she found Malcolm Grant's address.

• • • • •

Malcolm came back into the room as Marnie was looking at his army photographs. He stood next to her at the sideboard, staring at his life laid out on its shiny surface.

"So you were in the Commandos?"

"Royal Marines, yes. Fourteen years."

"You must have joined straight from university."

"That's right. Even at university I was on a military studentship."

"Do you think it was a good preparation for the world of politics?"

Malcolm reflected. "I suppose so, though that isn't why I joined the army. It taught me to be self-reliant and disciplined, taught me about leadership."

"What about the Lords? How do you feel about that?"

Malcolm turned away and went back to his chair. "The Lords?" His tone had cooled. "It's quite an honour, really."

Marnie sat down. "Ralph was talking about the Lords with Michael Blissett when I was in the Commons once. I thought it was a kind of promotion. They said it was the end of a political career to go to the Lords. Is that how you see it?"

"Frankly, Marnie, I never had a burning ambition to get to the top. I just wanted to serve and do my bit ... a hangover from my time in the army, perhaps."

"Yes. I suppose your military career must have shaped your whole attitude to things. I hadn't realised you'd been a soldier until the day my car was blown up."

"Really?" The tone was casual. "What do you mean? I'm not sure I follow you."

"The way you reacted after the explosion. It was very impressive. In fact, one of the people in the pub referred to you as 'the soldier'. Curious. Up till then I'd not thought about it. But I saw at once what he meant."

Malcolm smiled lightly and shrugged. "Old training, you see."

"Yes. You were decisive when everyone else was afraid." She smiled.

"Going out there with no backup, no team, no support at all. You seemed to act with no thought of fear for yourself."

"You were pretty cool, too, as I remember, Marnie. I was likewise impressed. Who knows what might have happened? Not many people would've done that."

"No. My friend Anne would've been scared."

"Anne? … she's very young, isn't she?"

"Of course. You know, the other day a boy let off a firework beside her. The result was that she jumped straight into his arms."

"Understandable," said Malcolm. "Probably nice for him."

"That's what I thought. A very predictable reaction for a girl, perhaps, to jump into the arms of another person, particularly a man, or a boy in that case, when confronted with that kind of danger. Wouldn't you agree?"

"Well, yes. I'm not sure what you're getting at, Marnie."

"I was just thinking of how most people would react to a bomb going off. It takes a lot of confidence to be able to go out into the unknown after an explosion. After all, we've all heard about secondary devices."

Marnie heard the clock tick five times before Malcolm stood up. "I think I'll put on some coffee," he said.

As soon as he had left the room, she went over to the sideboard. It had a drawer fitted with two neat brass handles. She pulled them, and the drawer slid open with a smooth action. Inside she saw a box of cigars, a cigar cutter and the sad Christmas present, still in its wrapping. She noticed that it was about the same size as the hip-flask in her bag. She noticed one other object in the drawer. Lying on the box of cigars was a revolver.

• • • • •

Anne looked out of the window of the bus and saw Regent's Park go by. She looked at her watch … repeatedly. She looked at the mobile, praying for Ralph to ring, desperately needing backup. To her surprise, it rang while she was looking at it. She jabbed hurriedly at the button.

"Ralph?"

"Hallo. Is that Anne Price?" It was the calm woman from UCL, the one she wanted to strangle with her bare hands.

"Nice of you to phone back," said Anne, gritting her teeth.

"I'm afraid I've not been able to speak to Professor Lombard. He's just left."

"He's gone back to Oxford?"

"No. I understand he's catching a train to Bristol."

"*Bristol?*"

"Yes. He's speaking at a seminar there tomorrow morning. He's gone to stay overnight."

"Thank you for trying. Very kind of you."

"No trouble at all. Good-bye."

What do I do now? Anne thought. She was determined never again in her entire life, no matter what the circumstances, even to herself, even in her wildest moments, to say how perfect everything was in her life. Not ever again.

• • • • •

When Malcolm came back with the coffee, Marnie was just sitting down. She began smoothing out her dress, giving the impression that she had shifted in her seat and was making herself comfortable again.

"Do you feel like a biscuit to go with this?" Malcolm asked. "I think I was given some chocolate Bath Olivers at Christmas. They're very good, you know. What d'you say?"

"Sounds tempting."

"Let me just think. Where did I put them? Won't be a minute." He left the room looking pensive.

As soon as he went out, Marnie delved in her shoulder bag and took out the flask in its plastic bag. She went over to the sideboard and placed the flask on the silver tray where the Christmas present had stood. She was back in her armchair by the time Malcolm returned. He set about pouring coffee into Spode cups, offering cream from an exquisite Georgian silver jug, with cubes of demerara sugar in a matching silver sugar bowl complete with tongs. The Bath Olivers lay on a Spode plate, and Malcolm passed them to Marnie. It was all very civilised.

"Is it very different working under this Prime Minister compared with Mrs T?" Marnie asked casually, making conversation.

Malcolm snorted. "Chalk and cheese," he muttered.

"He comes over as quite a nice bloke ..." Marnie ventured.

"As my lot go, you mean?" Malcolm's smile was rueful. He shook his head. "Nothing like Maggie. You can't compare them, Marnie. Maggie was a real trouper." As he spoke, Malcolm had a dreamy, faraway look in his eyes. She had seen others with that look when talking about the Iron Lady, and she wondered what led people to want to follow her. It must have been a sense of strong leadership, she supposed.

"It must have been hard for you to see Tim Edmonds on the opposite side in the Prime Minister's leadership contest," Marnie suggested.

Malcolm's expression changed at once. "Of course I should've known Tim would opt for where his own interests would be served." Marnie was surprised at the bitterness in Malcolm's voice.

"But don't you think he genuinely held the same views as Mr Major? Wasn't it just a matter of principle, like all your usual arguments in politics?"

"You can't be too naive about these things, Marnie. He may well have held the same views, but he was determined to exploit the situation for his own ambitions. He'd decided that he still had some, you see ... ambitions, that is ...and in the end he didn't mind who got pushed aside so that he could get back on track."

"I see ..."

"I wonder if you do see, Marnie. I wonder if you really can understand."

"Well ... I remember someone telling me that every MP believes he or she can one day get to the top, be Prime Minister."

"That sounds like your friend Lombard, or someone of that ilk."

"I think it probably was, actually. Was he right?"

"Oh, academics are usually right." Malcolm made a dismissive gesture. "But then they would be, wouldn't they? They're the ones who write the books. Let me tell you, Marnie, it's always easier to judge other people than actually do the job."

"But you don't think Tim Edmonds believed he could get to be Prime Minister?"

"Not any more, but he thought he was in with a chance of high office. That's why he ingratiated himself with the PM and everybody in sight who had influence."

"You make him sound pretty ruthless."

"*Ruthless,*" Malcolm repeated. "Do you know what was the unkindest cut of all? It was Tim telling me that I was going to be kicked up to the Lords. Tim of all people."

"When did he do that? I thought you hadn't seen him."

"He'd already hinted at it. He said it was best for all concerned. The PM's lot wanted as many as possible of his opponents to be weakened or weeded out. I was considered expendable. With my backwoods constituency I wasn't going to be able to marshal a big defence, and I could make way for a more sound man. They needed all the allies they could get."

"One of us?" said Marnie.

"*One of us*, that's right. That's what Maggie used to say. I always was *one of us* in her day. And I had a future in her day. I just got left behind when she got the chop. So bloody stupid, ditching Maggie ... so bloody unfair. She was good for another victory, no matter what the wets said. People like a leader, someone with ideas they can understand. Do you know Tim actually thought I wouldn't mind going to the Lords."

"Why did he think that?"

Malcolm ignored her question. "It got me wondering that it was his idea. Well, I told him he had another think coming."

"When did you do that?"

"When he sent that note. I rang him straight away ... told him I was going to fight every inch. That made him panic. He saw himself caught up in a big row. It would never do, just after Major had held on to his post. It would be a serious failure if he couldn't handle even a simple job like telling a friend he had to go to the Lords."

"Perhaps he thought you'd be better off in the Lords than stuck permanently on the backbenches."

"It was betrayal, Marnie, however you try to dress it up. That's what Tim tried to do. No. He betrayed me like they'd betrayed Maggie. We shared the same fate."

"I don't see why he'd want to betray you, Malcolm. You were friends. What would be the point?"

"It wasn't personal. It was a job he was given to do ... tidy me out of the way without a fuss. Who better to do that than his best friend? That was the price of his advancement. And I'd be paying the bill."

"That's why he was coming here ... to talk about it ... at your invitation ..."

"Yes. It would count against him, you see. I knew the PM would be worried about stirring everything up again. This loose cannon could cause a lot of trouble just at that moment. I knew he'd come like a shot ... I said we had to discuss it man to man."

"But you never did see him in the end ... Or did you?"

"What? Oh, er, no ... of course not."

"So you never had time to put things right between you." Marnie was stalling. *Where was Ralph?* She had a quick glance at her watch.

"No. We never put things right," said Malcolm.

· · · · ·

Anne had never been in this part of London before. She asked the way from another passenger getting off the bus at her stop, and set off in the right direction, walking quickly in time with the thoughts that were racing through her brain. She pulled the mobile out of her bag and pressed the buttons for directory enquiries. They gave her the number for Bristol University. She stopped walking and asked the switchboard operator for the Economics department.

Another calm voice. An answering machine. "The departmental office is now closed and will re-open tomorrow morning at nine o'clock."

Anne's shoulders slumped. She switched the phone off with a sigh, desperately needing backup. What could she do? Who could help her? The answer was simple: no one. She was on her own. Or was she? What if ...? The idea began to form. Yes. It might be worth a try. She made one more quick call before setting off again at a fast pace.

A minute later she arrived at the end of Malcolm's street. It was a quiet backwater, and she knew the canal was only a short distance away. As she walked, she wondered if the local residents could obtain keys to the British Waterways gates controlling the towpath. She reached Malcolm's number and slowed down so that she could see the names on the door bells. Grant was on the first floor.

There was no one else in the street. Anne turned back and slowly approached the house, casually mounting the steps, like a cat coming home patiently waiting for someone to let her in. She put her hand on the door and pushed. It was locked, of course. Almost at once there was a sound of movement inside the house, and Anne wondered for a second if she had accidentally touched a bell. She jumped back down the steps and moved away, pretending to be just passing by. Hearing the door open, she looked round hoping that Marnie would be coming out. A woman emerged with a small dog tucked under her arm. A Jack Russell terrier. She bent down to put the dog on the pavement, leaving the door to swing shut on an automatic mechanism. Talking cheerfully to her dog, the woman set off without a glance in Anne's direction.

Without hesitating for a second, Anne skipped across the pavement, took the steps in one leap and had her hand on the door before it could click shut. She waited. The woman continued on her way, now deep in conversation with the Jack Russell. Anne leaned against the door, and it opened silently. She slipped inside and let it close behind her.

· · · · ·

The conversation was going slowly, Malcolm seeming to relive the last hours of Tim Edmonds's life, Marnie playing for time, wanting Ralph to arrive on the scene. Past experience told her that he would not be there.

"So you did know what you were going to talk about with Tim Edmonds. I thought you said you didn't."

Malcolm seemed to have given up on his story. "No. I knew all right. I was going to tell Tim that I would not be giving up my seat. I told him I'd fight for it."

"Was that when you spoke on the phone?" said Marnie.

"On the phone?" Malcolm looked puzzled. "Oh, yes, on the phone, yes, that's right."

"When you arranged for him to come here."

"Do you know, Marnie, he described me as a man with a brilliant future behind him ... one of his blessed one-liners. That was the last straw ... reducing me to a soundbite! Just like Blair or Mandelson. He made me think I was just lobby fodder ... or cannon fodder ..." His voice tailed away.

"But you'd get over it in time, Malcolm. You could have a new career in the Lords, be part of the government."

"No guarantees."

"It wouldn't stop you remaining friends and being ... drinking companions," said Marnie. "... *gentlemen of the libation* ..."

Malcolm ran a hand across his forehead. "I don't know about you, Marnie, but I could do with something a bit stronger than this. Fancy something to go with your coffee?" He stood up and crossed to the sideboard where the bottles of drink were standing. Marnie glanced quickly down at her watch, and was almost caught in the act as Malcolm spun round. "What did you say ... *gentlemen of the libation*? How peculiar ... that's what Maggie used to call Tim and me ... it was her nickname for us ... How on *earth* did you know that?"

"I'm not sure ... I ..."

"You couldn't possibly ..." He shook his head in confusion, putting both hands on the sideboard.

"I suppose I must've ..."

"Nobody knew that name. I can't think how you could ..." He stopped in mid-sentence, looking down at the sideboard. "*What the hell!*" He reached out a hand towards the hip-flask, clearly visible in its bag. "Where on earth did this come from?" He turned to look at Marnie with fury in his expression, fury mixed with fear and amazement. He pulled open the drawer and looked in, gripping the sideboard as if he was going to faint. Thoughts of the revolver brought Marnie to the edge of her seat. At that moment, from the hall came the unmistakable sound of a mobile phone ringing. Malcolm looked up and went out to check, shutting the drawer as he left. Marnie stood up and stepped forward, straining to hear what was happening outside.

Malcolm found the hallway empty, but still the phone was ringing. He opened the front door as the ringing stopped and was surprised to see a girl standing there, a thin girl in jeans wearing a beret, holding a mobile phone to her ear.

In the drawing room, Marnie could hear an all too familiar voice, though she could not make out what it was saying. *Oh no, please, dear God,* Marnie thought, *please not Anne, not here.*

Anne smiled tentatively at Malcolm while talking into the phone. "Oh ... Professor Lombard?" she was saying. "Professor Ralph Lombard? Hallo, this is Anne. I'm at the home of Mr Malcolm Grant ... yes, the Member of Parliament, though I think he may be Lord Grant now ..." While listening to the caller, Anne mouthed *Sorry* at Malcolm and walked into the hall.

Bemused, Malcolm led her to the drawing room, where Marnie was standing waiting for them. Anne seemed to be winding up her conversation with a promise to phone back as soon as it was convenient.

"My cue to go, I think, Malcolm," said Marnie. "I'm sorry about this interruption, but I have to be getting along now. Meetings, meetings .. you know how it is. We'll resume our talk later perhaps." She kissed Malcolm on the cheek and turned Anne towards the door, grabbing her coat as she passed.

Behind her Malcolm was speaking, obviously still confused as if caught off guard. "Yes, perhaps. But I'm not sure there is much more to be said." He was looking towards the sideboard as Marnie and Anne reached the door.

"I know the way, no need to show us out." Marnie had Anne in the hall with the door closing behind them in seconds. They set off down the stairs, two steps at a time.

They had gone before Malcolm had had time to take stock of the situation. He stared at the sideboard, resting both hands on its polished surface. Slowly he pulled himself together and reached down to open the drawer.

● ● ● ● ●

Marnie opened the front door in the downstairs hall and almost pushed Anne through it. While Anne was intent on asking questions, Marnie all but frog-marched her along the pavement in the direction of the main road, looking out for a taxi.

"Where did you spring from?"

"I had his address in my notebook, so I just took off. I got this idea about what might've happened and I couldn't bear to wait any longer."

"You nearly gave me heart failure, turning up like that. It could've been dangerous."

"I thought it was dangerous for you," said Anne, breathless with rushing.

Marnie shook her head. "Well, all I can say is thank goodness Ralph rang just then and knew where we were … it stopped Malcolm doing anything … made him think twice."

"What makes you think it was Ralph on the phone?" said Anne.

"I heard you talking to him, quite distinctly. You said Ralph's name."

Anne's turn to shake her head. "It was my brother … I got Richard to ring me from home. I was just pretending. I knew Mr Grant wouldn't harm us if he thought Ralph was on the line. The police would believe Ralph."

"What made you think Malcolm might harm us?"

"I told you I had this idea about what happened that night. I got scared. I thought I shouldn't take any chances … just in case. Then, when I saw your face, I knew I'd done the right thing."

Marnie hailed a taxi on the opposite side of the road. It paused, waiting for a gap in the traffic to turn. "You are truly amazing, do you know that?" She adjusted the bag on her shoulder.

"Are you okay, Marnie? You look rather pale."

"I'm fine … just a touch of headache. That meeting was a bit of a strain." She adjusted the bag again. "These past weeks have been a strain."

"Can I help you with that?" Anne asked. "Let me carry it."

"No, it's okay." Marnie looked at Anne, aware that a dull pain was growing behind her eyes. "It's surprising how heavy a revolver is. I've never had one in my bag before. I didn't realise they were so big."

Anne gaped at her. "*Revolver?*" The taxi began its U-turn to meet them.

"Malcolm's. I took it from the sideboard."

"That's brilliant, Marnie."

"Not if we're stopped and searched by our friends, the police, it isn't. Technically, I've just stolen a firearm from an MP. In a my-word-against-his session, I wouldn't like to put money on which of us would be believed." She opened the taxi door and slumped onto the seat. Before Marnie could speak, Anne called out an address. Marnie heard it, nodded and closed her eyes.

Part 25

Thursday 19 January

Anne sat on a stool in Mrs Jolly's kitchen, as usual holding a mug of coffee in both hands, her thin features making her look like an orphan or a refugee.

"It's really nice of you to do this, Mrs Jolly."

"The least I could do to help, my dear. Now, let's see about breakfast. One thing's for sure ... Marnie won't be wanting anything. That was no ordinary headache yesterday. Did you realise she was going down with a migraine?"

"No. She's not had one since I've known her. She just looked so drawn and pale suddenly. I thought here was the best place to come."

"You were quite right."

"I should've thought of her sister's, but it's a long way from here, and I didn't have the address."

"Don't worry. It's perfectly fine. You did the right thing. Now we have to decide what to do next."

"I've just left a message for Ralph to ring on the mobile. He's at a seminar in Bristol today. I've rung the Economics department, and they've promised to get an urgent message to him."

"Good. He certainly gets around."

"Never stops." Anne looked at her watch. "I suppose we ought to contact the police. I wanted to yesterday, but Marnie wasn't up to it."

"And she isn't yet, either. I think we've got to give her time to recover before bringing the police in. She couldn't help them in her present state."

"How long will it take? I don't know much about migraines."

"You're lucky. I hope you'll never know about them. My friend Vera's a martyr to them. They can last from twenty-four to thirty-six hours. Horrible. I'm not letting the police anywhere near Marnie until she's absolutely out of the woods. She wouldn't be much good to them anyway."

"Right. You don't think Malcolm Grant will try and do anything?"

"I've no idea, Anne. At least he can't reach us here. Our first concern is to get Marnie better. That's all we can do for now." Mrs Jolly looked up, cocking her head on one side. "Can you hear something?"

Anne got up. "It's the mobile." She brought it in from her bag and pressed a button. "Hallo? ... No, I'm afraid she's not available at the moment. Who's calling, please? ... Oh, Inspector Bruere, no ... I can't disturb her just now ... No, it's not possible ..."

Mrs Jolly reached out towards Anne, who passed her the phone. "Hallo? My name is Mrs Jolly. What can I do for you? ... Really? Well, inspector, I'm afraid you're not in any position to insist. Mrs Walker is ill. She is in bed with a migraine. You can ring back later ... much later." She pointed at the mobile. "How do you turn this thing off, Anne?"

• • • • •

Around twelve noon Mrs Jolly went up to see if Marnie was well enough to eat, leaving Anne sitting at the kitchen table attempting the crossword in that morning's edition of *The Times*. The mobile rang. Anne was half smiling when she reached for the phone, expecting it to be Ralph returning her call. She was sure this would be him. She was wrong.

"Good afternoon." The voice stressed the word *afternoon*. "This is Chief Inspector Bruere. I'd like to speak to Mrs Walker."

"I'm sorry, she's not available at the moment. She's unwell and can't come to the phone."

"I think she'll speak to me if you tell her who it is."

He thinks I'm stalling, Anne thought. "But she really is unwell. She's in bed with a migraine."

"Who is this?" The voice was cold and intimidating.

"I'm Marnie's colleague, her assistant, Anne Price." Anne had never felt so much the vulnerability of her sixteen years.

Bruere spoke even more slowly, even more quietly. "Then I think you'd better assist her by telling her I want to talk to her. And I want to talk to her now. In person. I have to see her."

Anne felt her hand shaking. She stood up and walked out of the kitchen, meeting Mrs Jolly at the foot of the stairs. The old lady signalled that Marnie was improving, with a smile and a thumbs-up. The arrival of reinforcements made Anne more confident. "Mr Bruere, is it really urgent?"

"You obviously haven't heard the news."

"I'll go and see what state she's in and I'll ring you back in a minute or two. Is that all right?" To her surprise, Bruere agreed, gave his number and made her promise to phone back within five minutes. His tone made her believe there would be consequences if she failed.

"Are you all right, Anne?" said Mrs Jolly.

"That was the police ... Inspector Bruere again ... *Chief* Inspector Bruere. He wants to talk to Marnie ... *now*. He sounds very tough."

"Well, he'd better not try being tough on us."

Anne grimaced. "I said I'd see if Marnie was able to talk to him. He wants to see her."

"She's awake, more or less, but still groggy. I think you'd better ask her if she feels up to it."

Anne went up and tapped gently on the door. The curtains were drawn, and Anne walked quietly over to the bed. "Hallo," she whispered.

"Hi." Marnie's voice was weary, but had a hint of a smile at the edges.

"How are you feeling? Silly question?"

"Coming round, I think. Have you come to cheer me up?"

A twinge of guilt. "Not exactly. I have a message for you."

"From Ralph?"

"No. From Chief Inspector Bruere."

Marnie closed her eyes. "That makes my day. Whatever day it is."

"He wants to see you. I've tried to put him off. He doesn't know where we are."

Marnie sighed. "No. But he'll find out sooner or later. We'd better get it over with."

Anne made the call.

· · · · ·

With the visit from the police imminent, Mrs Jolly went upstairs to change, leaving Anne drinking a cup of tea in the silence of the kitchen. The radio was switched off to keep the house as quiet as possible for Marnie's sake.

You obviously haven't heard the news. That was what he said. The phrase turned itself over in her mind. What could it mean? Anne pondered for a while, but could make no sense of Bruere's enigmatic statement. ... *haven't heard the news* ... One way to find out. Anne decisively gulped down her tea and scribbled a note for Mrs Jolly. Seconds later she closed the front door quietly behind her and set off down the street towards the news-stand by the tube station.

As she approached, she saw him slipping a new notice into his *Evening Standard* billboard. She presented a coin when he straightened up.

"Sorry, love. You're too early. It's not here yet."

"Okay. I'll come back." She turned to leave and walked a few steps before turning round to call out.

"How soon will they arrive, do you think?"

The newsman shrugged. "Anybody's guess ... give it another ten minutes?"

She hardly noticed his reply because at that moment she caught sight of the headline on the billboard.

DEATH IN LITTLE VENICE

• • • • •

Turning the corner across the road from the canal, Anne saw a man and a woman walking up to Mrs Jolly's front door. She reached the house as Mrs Jolly was letting them in and hoped the old lady would not be too intimidated by the detectives. Chief Inspector Bruere had brought a woman colleague whom he introduced as DS McLeish. The four of them stood close together in Mrs Jolly's small entrance hall.

"Now, Mr Bruere," Mrs Jolly began, "you are a visitor in my house, and I know you have a job to do. I have to tell you that Marnie is just recovering from a migraine. You may talk to her for five minutes. If you stay any longer I will make a formal complaint to your superiors. Do you understand?"

"Mrs Jolly, we are –"

"I am a personal friend of the Commissioner. In fact, his mother is my bridge partner. Have I made myself clear?" Bruere rolled his eyes, nodded and said nothing. Mrs Jolly looked pointedly at her watch and led the way upstairs. "I don't want you opening the curtains. You can leave the door ajar to let some light into the room."

Bruere suspected that Mrs Jolly had other motives. "For our talk we shall need privacy."

"You shall have it." She showed the detectives into the bedroom and went back downstairs to where Anne was waiting.

Anne was wide-eyed. "Gosh, Mrs Jolly," she whispered. "How long have you known the Commissioner?"

The old lady gave it some thought. "Oh, I think it must be all of ... two minutes."

• • • • •

Bruere approached the bed in semi-darkness and pulled up a stool from the dressing table, leaving his partner to stand near the door.

"How are you feeling, Mrs Walker?"

"Been better."

"You've had a migraine, I understand. Do you often get them?"

"Not had one for a long time." Her voice was faint. "Started as a headache and just got worse. I wasn't quick enough to stop it."

"How long have you been here?"

"Since yesterday afternoon."

"Did you know that Malcolm Grant was dead?"

Marnie jumped, winced and closed her eyes as a shooting pain pierced her skull. She put a hand to her forehead. Bruere watched and waited. There was a long silence broken only by the sound of Marnie's laboured breathing. Gradually she settled down and half-opened her eyes as if checking that Bruere was still there. She swallowed. When she spoke her voice was dry and unsteady.

"Did Malcolm ... did he take the ... poison?"

"*Poison?*" Bruere spoke so loudly that Marnie raised a weak hand to silence him. "Did you say poison, Mrs Walker?"

"Mm ... yes."

"What poison?" Marnie shook her head gently. "I said ... what poison?"

"I heard you."

"Then I think you'd better explain. Take your time. We've got all day." From the doorway came the muffled sound of a cough. Bruere half turned his head before looking again at Marnie.

"We found a hip-flask in the canal ... the spot where I found the body. I think it might have contained poison or some drug."

"And why did you not contact the police at once, Mrs Walker?"

"I was going down ... brain wasn't connected."

"You do realise it's a serious offence to withhold evidence from the police?"

"I know, but I was in no fit state and it may have had nothing to do ..."

"We should be the ones to judge that."

Marnie began breathing more quickly. She seemed agitated. "I assumed that you must have done a thorough job as professionals and that it might have got into the canal after the murder." Bruere followed her line of reasoning and even in the gloom with her eyes closed, Marnie could sense his annoyance. "So did he take the poison?"

"No. He collapsed while out jogging on the towpath in Little Venice. He seems to have had a heart attack or some kind of seizure. By the time they managed to pull him out of the water, it was too late to save him."

From outside the room came the sound of someone slowly climbing the stairs. Another faint cough from the doorway. Bruere stood up.

"We shall be wanting a full statement from you, Mrs Walker. I'll be back."

• • • • •

Ralph had phoned Anne in response to her message and arranged to come straight back to London after giving his paper at the seminar. His arrival early that afternoon coincided with Marnie taking her first sips of water.

"I don't know what I'm going to do with you," he said, holding her lightly. "As soon as my back is turned ..."

"At least I didn't get murdered this time."

"We must be thankful for small mercies, I suppose. Your record is definitely improving." He shook his head, suddenly serious. "You know, I blame myself for what happened to you."

"What do you mean?"

"If I hadn't agreed to speak at that seminar ..."

"But I would've told you to go anyway."

Ralph looked miserable. "I never seem to be there when you need –"

"Hey, stop that. Don't get all guilt-ridden."

"I tried to ring you from Bristol. It was all such a rush going from my UCL meeting to catch the train. Then, when I did ring, all I got was a voice telling me I couldn't get through to your mobile for some silly reason."

Marnie smiled. "Technology was never your strong point." She kissed him gently. "Come on. It's all right."

Ralph smiled back. "I'm the one who's supposed to be comforting you."

"You're useless."

"Thank you."

Marnie told Ralph the story of her visit on Wednesday to Malcolm's flat and her theory about what happened to Tim Edmonds. He listened to her narrative in silence, nodding occasionally, shaking his head in astonishment when Marnie told him of Anne's arrival and her pretended phone conversation with him. She ended with Bruere's visit.

"Yes," said Ralph. "I heard about Grant's death on the news. Extraordinary business. The newspapers are going to town, as you can imagine. Two MPs dead in the same canal within a few weeks of each other ... closest friends ... It's certainly taken some of the pressure off the problems facing the government for the time being."

"Lying here, I've been thinking about your hindsight theory."

"A lot of help that was ... but then it wasn't meant as a way of solving crime."

"No. But it was all so clear in the end ... the KSF."

"The peerage business."

"Yes. Or rather the sense of betrayal. It was all too much for Malcolm to take from his closest friend, the man he'd stood by in the worst crisis of his life."

"Hardly surprising," said Ralph. "And quite disgraceful. I know it sounds dreadful, but I don't really blame him for wanting revenge. If I'm honest, I think my sympathies are with Grant."

"I know what you mean, but murdering someone ... that's another matter. I don't believe in the death penalty, and that murder was planned in cold blood."

"I wonder how he felt afterwards, after he'd actually done it."

"That's easy," said Marnie. "He was grief-stricken."

"You really believe that?"

"Yes. I got to know Malcolm over these past weeks. Those were real tears I saw in the church that evening. I'm convinced of that."

"Well, it was the loss of his dearest friend, I suppose, even if he'd been the one to kill him."

"Oh it was more than that, Ralph ... much more. It was the loss of everything ... his friend, his career ... all his political ambitions ..."

"Yes. Powerful motives."

"But there was more to it than that, I'm sure of it. For Malcolm the worst thing would be to lose his good name. His loyalty to his friend, the respect of the other MPs, the high regard of his regiment, his reputation as a war hero … all that would be forgotten if he was found out. An officer and a gentleman … he'd just go down as a murderer. All his life he'd been the good guy. He'd thrown it all away in a fit of pride."

"How ironic … the murderer deserves more sympathy than the victim. Despite all that, you're going to tell Bruere what happened?"

"Yes."

"I suppose you must. You don't have any choice."

• • • • •

By late afternoon the patient was making a steady recovery. Anne had walked along to the tube station with Ralph and brought back a newspaper. There was a three-page spread about the life and times of the two MPs, going over all the ground that had been covered at the time of Tim Edmonds's death, and adding the final chapter of Malcolm Grant's demise from a heart attack. Anne took the paper up to Marnie with a plate of crackers and a glass of mineral water. She found Marnie on the phone to Beth, reassuring her sister that she was fine.

Marnie had washed, brushed her hair and changed into a nightdress provided by Mrs Jolly. It was white, made of thick cotton in a Victorian style buttoned to the neck, and Marnie looked like a character from a Jane Austen novel. She was sitting up in bed attempting her first cracker when Bruere arrived, in the early evening, again accompanied by DS McLeish.

"Are you feeling better, Mrs Walker?"

"More human than last time you came."

"You appear to be making a remarkable recovery." Marnie did not reply, but took a sip of water. "Tell me about the poison, Mrs Walker."

Marnie explained about finding the hip-flask in the canal, the testimony of Dodge, her theory about Tim Edmonds being poisoned or at least drugged as a way of getting him into the water to drown.

"You seriously believe Mr Edmonds would stand around in the cold and dark of a winter's evening on the towpath having a friendly drink when he was supposed to be visiting a friend nearby who would presumably have something to drink in his warm and comfortable flat?"

"Based on an eye witness's statement, yes. There's nothing incongruous about two friends walking along together, stopping for a moment to have a nip from a flask."

"And this *friend* would be Malcolm Grant, no doubt."

"Who else could it be?"

"Who else, indeed? You have evidence to prove this?"

"Malcolm made it clear by his reaction on seeing the hip-flask."

"I was talking about evidence, not about intuition or feelings. I think you should be very careful about making unfounded accusations, Mrs Walker."

"Dodge saw what happened. If you handle him carefully, I think he could identify Malcolm. He's more reliable than you seem to think."

Bruere shook his head. "A good brief would make mincemeat of him in court. He'd be worse than useless. You can forget about him. It leaves your case a bit thin, I'm afraid."

"But if you put everything together, it all fits."

"Try me."

"The car bomb."

"What about it?"

"Malcolm had been a soldier, a commando. He knew all about explosives. He used it as a diversionary tactic to make me think he was an ally. He knew it was safe to go out after the explosion. I think he just wanted to check his handiwork."

"You seriously think he would've risked killing innocent passers-by just to make you think he was a friend?"

"What if he had an accomplice, some loyal friend from his army days ... someone who wouldn't ask any questions ... able to set it off when no one was passing?"

"Don't you think that's rather James Bond, cloak-and-dagger stuff, Mrs Walker? There was no evidence to link Mr Grant with the bombing."

"What about the fire on *Magician*?"

"A leaking gas pipe. Forensic have established it beyond any doubt. The flame of the pilot light in the water heater was enough to set it off. Wrong again, Mrs Walker."

"You don't think that was a strange coincidence after everything else?"

"Coincidences do happen."

"There was a special car disguised as a taxi that he sent me home in once. What was that about?"

"So? Hiring a taxi isn't a crime, and there are plenty of hire firms about. Did you get its licence number?"

"Of course I didn't. Only the police think like that."

"The police like evidence and hard facts. So do courts of law. You yourself found the note from Edmonds to Grant, Mrs Walker. Are you saying that was a set-up?"

"No."

"But you thought it corroborated Mr Grant's story."

"Until I realised it proved nothing. He told me he'd phoned Tim Edmonds after getting the note. He met him on the towpath, and they walked together. It's clear that they stopped for a drink under a lamp by the bridge. Malcolm knew the towpath would be deserted because it was closed after sunset. As a resident he had a key to the gate. He suggested a quick snifter to keep out the cold until they got back to the flat."

"You can't prove any of this or produce any evidence that would stand up in court."

"In Malcolm's flat I found a gun, a revolver."

"Oh yes? Did he threaten you with it?"

"No. He didn't get a chance to. I took it to stop it being used."

"Really? Where is it?"

"In my bag, wherever that is."

"You admit taking a firearm without the owner's consent?"

"Yes. I was worried stiff what might happen. Anne was there. All I wanted was to get her away in safety."

"Did you know if he had a permit for it?"

Marnie sighed in exasperation. "I didn't ask him. I just got scared and took it."

Bruere wagged a finger. "Oh, Mrs Walker ... And what about the hip-flask? Will we find that in your bag as well? We've found no trace of any such object in the flat."

"I left it behind in my rush to get away with Anne and the gun."

"You left behind a flask that you suspected might contain poison? That was your only evidence, Mrs Walker, and you left it behind ..."

"I was in a rush – I wanted to get Anne to safety. I just grabbed the revolver and ran."

"So you have no actual proof of anything at all."

• • • • •

Ralph stayed for supper at Mrs Jolly's invitation. She prepared a light meal, and Marnie felt well enough to come downstairs. She looked pale and tired, but was no longer in pain. Inevitably the conversation was dominated by Malcolm Grant and Tim Edmonds, two ghosts not yet laid to rest, at least not as far as Marnie was concerned. By the time they reached the dessert course, a traditional rice pudding sprinkled with nutmeg, they were convinced that Bruere was right. Marnie was equally convinced that she was right, too. Everything she had experienced told her that Malcolm Grant had killed Tim Edmonds out of a sense of betrayal. She also recognised that she had no proof that would convince a court. They turned their attention to loose ends.

"It's curious that Malcolm left that message on the answerphone," said Marnie. "It led the police straight to him."

"They were bound to question him anyway," said Ralph.

"Was it a sort of decoy?" Anne asked.

Ralph nodded. "I suspect he left the message because it gave a time for him being at home that the police could check. It would place him there at about the time Tim Edmonds was murdered. He hadn't counted on someone coming along on a boat when you did, Marnie. Without your arrival on the scene, the message was as good as an alibi. And he hadn't expected there to be a witness across the canal who had seen the two men together. No one ever thinks of tramps."

"The answerphone message was a kind of bluff, wasn't it?" Marnie said. "If he was guilty, he'd hardly link himself with the victim. That's what he wanted the police to think."

"What about the car bomb?" Anne asked. "Was that a decoy too?"

"We'll never know definitely, but there isn't much doubt in my mind. I'm sure he didn't want to kill me, though."

"My goodness," said Mrs Jolly. "I've never had conversations like this at my dinner table before. What a horrible business this has been. I for one am heartily glad it's all over."

"Me too," said Anne.

"This kind of thing can poison your life unless you're very careful." Mrs Jolly stood up. "Just leave these things on the table. Let's have coffee in the sitting room."

Part 26

Friday 20 January

Marnie and Roger Broadbent stood on the steps of the police station, hunched up against the cold.

"I can't believe I just did that," said Marnie.

"You didn't have any choice. You told the police what happened. That's all you could do."

"But I wanted to make them believe me."

"Look at it from their point of view, Marnie. They have to convince the Crown Prosecution Service that there's a case. You yourself said Grant didn't actually confess to anything."

"Not in so many words."

"Unspoken evidence is no evidence, Marnie. Certainly not a confession."

"But what about the poison? Bruere admitted that Malcolm had taken something, some sort of drug. They found it in his bloodstream. I know he took it and just went jogging till it took effect and he collapsed. I know it."

"With nothing else to go on, it's not enough."

Marnie sighed. "That Bruere made me so ... I don't know."

"Be careful, Marnie. You admitted leaving a hip-flask possibly containing some sort of poison with Grant. They then find some strange substance in his bloodstream at the autopsy. They could link you with that and make things tricky for you."

"But –"

"Added to the fact that you also admitted to taking his revolver. My advice to you as your solicitor, and as a close friend, is to leave things alone. Put it down, Marnie."

"But I know Malcolm killed Tim Edmonds. For the sake of his family, I think they need to know that. And what does Bruere say? *The man was a hero, Mrs Walker ... a war hero in the Falklands.*" She sighed. "The man was a hero! This is a cover-up, Roger."

Roger stared at the traffic rumbling past. "That may or may not be so, but there's nothing you can do about it. You've got the chance to get your life back to normal, Marnie. Isn't that what you want?"

"Of course."

"Then take it. You can't bring them back. Time to put things down."

"I just wish I had proof so that I could set the record straight."

"It's over, Marnie. Let them rest in their graves."

· · · · ·

Mrs Jolly had lit a fire in her sitting room, and it took little effort to persuade Marnie to have a sandwich when she returned from the police station. Marnie told Mrs Jolly and Anne about the interview and about what Roger had said.

The old lady was concerned for Marnie's health. "I'm going to speak to you like an aunt, my dear."

Marnie smiled. "You used to think I was a water gypsy. Now suddenly I've become your niece."

"By adoption."

"Fine by me."

"What Roger said was right, and you know it really. Power and politics are a long way removed from the life you wanted for yourself – and for Anne. Time to let go. You've had enough of that kind of stress to last a lifetime."

"You can say that again," said Anne.

· · · · ·

Mrs Jolly took it as a sure sign that Marnie's recovery still had some way to go when she agreed to have a lie-down that afternoon. They left her for an hour or two while Anne helped in the kitchen preparing vegetables for supper. For her it was a blissful return to normal life, and she hummed as she cut parsnips into chunks for roasting and peeled off the outer leaves of Brussels sprouts.

Eventually, as dusk began to fall, Anne crept quietly up the stairs and peeped in at the bedroom door. Marnie sat up and smiled at her friend, reaching over to turn on the bedside lamp. It cast a warm glow over the room. Marnie still looked tired.

Anne went across and sat on the bed. "You okay?"

"Yeah. I've been thinking."

"I can guess what about."

"Yes. Now that it's all over, it's hard to get it in perspective. Malcolm did a terrible thing, but he'll be remembered as a hero and nobody wants to see it any other way. Doesn't that strike you as weird, Anne?"

"I suppose so. But I'll tell you what I think ... betraying a friend like that, betraying your best friend, the way Tim Edmonds did, that was a terrible thing, too."

"I suppose so. Betrayal, murder ... the whole affair just keeps going round and round in my head. It makes me feel dizzy."

"I don't want you going down with another migraine, Marnie."

"Blimey, it's two aunts now!"

"I mean it. I was quite worried about you. Just when we thought you were really well again."

"I know. So what would you like to do?"

"Easy. Get our life back. Move into cottage number two. Move on."

"Me too. Let other people fight their own battles."

"Do you mean that?"

"Yes, I do."

"Good."

"Let's go back to Knightly St John tomorrow," said Marnie.

"Great. I can hardly wait."

"We can meet the new vicar and have tea! Village life doesn't get much more normal than that." They laughed.

Outside, they heard Mrs Jolly call up the stairs. The mobile was ringing, and she offered to bring it up. Anne took it from her in the doorway. Mrs Jolly said sternly, "If it's that Inspector Bruere, pass the phone to me." It was Beth. Anne took the phone over to Marnie, and Mrs Jolly went back to her cooking.

"It's all over, Beth. I've given my statement. The case is closed. At least I think it is."

"That's great. I've been reading about it in the press. They've had a field day. Two tragic accidents ... You've probably seen it."

"Yes. Sad business. So tell me about you."

"Oh, things here are much the same as usual. People coming to dinner. We're in for a pulsating evening. One of Paul's colleagues. I never understand a word he says ... lives on his own little cloud ... a low-temperature physicist ... no small talk."

"You'll have to break the ice," said Marnie.

Beth snorted. "You're obviously on the mend. Your jokes are as bad as ever."

Marnie yawned. "What else is new?"

"Nothing really. I'll tell you something, though. You won't believe it, but I can't get used to the garage not having your MG in it. We still leave our car on the drive ..."

Marnie blinked drowsily in Anne's direction as Beth was speaking. She closed her eyes and lay slowly back against the pillow, the phone slipping away from her ear. Anne leaned forward and took the mobile from Marnie's hand. She could hear Beth's voice chatting on, as she bent down and kissed Marnie on the forehead. She turned out the light and tiptoed silently out of the room.

Postscript

It was late morning when Marnie and Anne reached Glebe Farm, the taxi from the station dropping them in the courtyard outside the office barn. Anne went off to check the heating on *Sally Ann* as Dolly came in and rubbed her side against Marnie's leg. Everything looked pleasantly normal, including the pile of letters on the floor. Marnie dumped them on her desk, spotting one envelope bearing the embossed scarlet crest of the House of Lords. She slit it open and tipped out the contents. There was a newspaper cutting showing Malcolm Grant ushering Tim Edmonds into a car. Tim Edmonds looked haunted and grey. Malcolm's concern for his friend was obvious. With the picture was a betting slip. It read:

Marnie

Why? Loyalty is everything. Try not to judge me too harshly. There was only one honourable way out. I know you understand.

Yours now and for ever, Malcolm.

Marnie studied the picture for some time and read the note over again. She stood deep in thought and then, slowly and decisively, turned to drop the photograph and the betting slip into the bin.

Also by Leo McNeir, the exciting prequel to
Death in Little Venice:

Getaway with Murder

Marnie Walker is an interior designer with a passion for boats, in particular her sister's boat Sally Ann, which she borrowed the previous summer for an extended trip on the Grand Union Canal. While on her travels, Marnie had discovered a derelict farmhouse in a Northamptonshire village.

Now, wishing to set up her own company, she finds herself buying the farm to restore it as an investment and a base, aided and abetted by her sister Beth and her friend, Anne with an 'e'. But she does not reckon with the tensions underlying the peace and tranquility of her new home. All is going well until Marnie finds herself embroiled in not one unsolved murder but two, separated by almost 350 years.

The old feuds of the Civil War period seem to be fermenting again in a village becoming torn apart by factions. It is only a matter of time before something sinister emerges to shatter the calm of the countryside, and Marnie herself is dragged into the ancient conflict with terrifying results.

Available from your supplier or, in case of difficulty, direct from the publisher:

Enigma Publishing
PO Box 1901
Wicken
MK19 6DN

or visit our web site at: www.enigma-publishing.com